The Ellie Haskell Mysteries from Dorothy Cannell

THE THIN WOMAN
DOWN THE GARDEN PATH
THE WIDOW'S CLUB
MUM'S THE WORD
FEMMES FATAL
HOW TO MURDER YOUR MOTHER-IN-LAW
HOW TO MURDER THE MAN OF YOUR DREAMS
THE SPRING CLEANING MURDERS
THE TROUBLE WITH HARRIET
BRIDESMAIDS REVISITED
THE IMPORTANCE OF BEING ERNESTINE
WITHERING HEIGHTS
GOODBYE, MS CHIPS
SHE SHOOTS TO CONQUER

SEA GLASS SUMMER

SEA GLASS SUMMER

Dorothy Cannell

This first world edition published 2012
in Great Britain and in the USA by
SEVERN HOUSE PUBLISHERS LTD of
9–15 High Street, Sutton, Surrey, England, SM1 1DF.
Trade paperback edition first published
in Great Britain and in the USA 2013 by
SEVERN HOUSE PUBLISHERS LTD

British Library Cataloguing in Publication Data

Cannell, Dorothy.
  Sea glass summer.
  1. Maine--Fiction. 2. Love stories.
  I. Title
  813.5'4-dc23

ISBN-13: 978-0-7278-8183-0 (cased)
ISBN-13: 978-1-84751-441-7 (trade paper)

All Severn House titles are printed on acid-free paper.

Severn House Publishers support The Forest Stewardship Council [FSC],
the leading international forest certification organisation. All our titles that
are printed on Greenpeace-approved FSC-certified paper carry the FSC logo.

Typeset by Palimpsest Book Production Ltd.,
Falkirk, Stirlingshire, Scotland.
Printed and bound in Great Britain by
MPG Books Ltd., Bodmin, Cornwall.

For Jordan Thomas, who inspired me to write about a boy with a heart of gold who is also the world's best potato peeler.

Acknowledgments

Thanks to my friend Lesley Perry for introducing me to village life.

One

Look to the ocean for an eternal constant, forever new. Such was
Sarah Draycott's thought as she stood one May morning gazing
out of French windows at a lawn that sloped down to a flight of
wooden steps. She could not see them from this distance, but just
knowing they were there, her steps, leading down to the beach,
brought a surge of proprietary delight. It was hard to believe this
was not a childhood vacation, of the sort that included a bucket
and spade. As of today she was a resident of Sea Glass. She had all
the time in the world to spend selecting flat stones to send skipping over the waves, or clambering among the rocks searching for
sea glass. For surely any wholehearted inhabitant of a village with
that name must start a collection.

Those French windows brought welcome light into the kitchen.
Sarah filled the red enamel kettle she had brought with her from
Chicago, set it on the front burner of the stove and ignited the
gas flame. Her first domestic act in her very own house. The
zippered cable knit sweater she wore was also red. A color that
suited her dark hair and hazel eyes. Cheerful clothes for cheerful
doings. It sounded like a slogan from the nineteen fifties, when
the home was a woman's queendom, and the washing machine
her prince consort. Her mouth curved into a smile. Despite hair
left rumpled from that morning's sketchy combing, she was feeling
very queenly right now.

Surveying the empty kitchen she saw not its current drabness,
but the unfulfilled promise. It was a long if rather narrow room,
with just enough space at the end with the French doors for a
small table and chairs. Next week, maybe before, she would get
started painting the cabinets a crisp glossy white and the walls a
custard yellow. As to what was to be done about the vinyl flooring
. . . she would have to think about that. A lot of work lay ahead,
but it would be fun and, if she were sensible, well within her
handy-woman scope. It was a small house; the real estate agent
had stressed that fact before showing it to her.

'Just sufficient for a couple with perhaps one child,' she'd said, 'but perfect for a single woman. Unless, of course, you like to do a lot of entertaining, host big parties; that sort of thing works better with an open-floor plan.'

Unlikely to be an issue. Other than the agent, who, though pleasant, couldn't as yet be considered a friend, Sarah didn't know anyone locally to invite to a party big or small. As for out-of-state visitors, they weren't likely to arrive all at once.

That conversation had taken place just six weeks ago. In early April she had flown to Maine to attend a college friend's wedding in Portland and rented a car for a couple of extra days, exploring. Her meandering had brought her to Sea Glass. At thirty-four, she had never previously considered the possibility of leaving Illinois. Now it was as though this seaside village, with its bronze statue of a local hero in the center of the tree-shaded common and the surrounding pink, yellow and green cottages, had been awaiting her arrival. It was offering her the chance to start over. She'd spotted the real estate office nestled between Plover's Grocery and Mary Anne's Flower Shop and headed for its door.

A couple of hours later, when the realtor drew up alongside the little white brick cottage with the friendly-sized windows, green tiled roof and two storybook chimneys, Sarah had known with equal certainty it had likewise been waiting for her to show up. Her brother Tim, four years her senior, would have warned against getting ahead of herself. He believed she'd made that mistake when marrying Harris Colefax. Tim had always had her back, but she didn't believe that past mistakes should stop her from ever trusting her instincts again. Within taking a couple of steps toward the front door with its time-tarnished brass dolphin knocker, she'd made up her mind to buy this house. She'd also decided she would finally get the dog she had always wanted. It came to her that Bramble Cottage liked the idea of a dog almost as much as it welcomed the prospect of her moving in.

'Some people don't like the idea of a corner house,' the agent had said with painstaking frankness while producing a key, 'but you do have this screening of firs and shrubbery on both sides. And there's a half acre to the rear, with access to the beach, more than making up for this handkerchief up front. As I warned you, the interior isn't spacious, just the two bedrooms, unless you count the storage area under the eaves. It does have a window so maybe it could work at a pinch as a home office. Wood floors throughout, except the kitchen and bathroom, and the one thing the seller did before putting the place on the market was have them refinished. Down the road you could add on a master suite above the garage. Always a good investment for resale.'

'That's a thought, but I want to put down roots.'

During her seven-year marriage to Harris, home had been a high-rise condo on Lake Shore Drive in Chicago. After the divorce eighteen months ago she'd moved into an apartment in Evanston. Neither had been her ideal. She and Tim had grown up in a house with all the charm of one built in the nineteen forties. For Harris it had been different. A glass-sided aerie was his natural habitat, his childhood and adolescence having been spent in the penthouse where his widowed mother still lived in contented proximity to theaters and museums. He hadn't foisted his wishes on Sarah, merely pointed out the pros of not having to deal with maintenance, and the freedom to come and go as they wished. She had put up no resistance when he'd taken her to see an industrialized loft space they would be crazy not to buy. Wildly in love, she'd have lived with him in a tent on a swamp if that was what he wanted.

Sarah rummaged in the cardboard box she had brought into the kitchen and hefted onto the butcher block counter. Producing a jar of instant coffee, a cup and a spoon, she smiled. Her first caffeine fix since setting off from New Hampshire at dawn, having spent the night with her Aunt Beth. She would have preferred a freshly-ground brew, better yet a double shot cappuccino, but this would do. In the box were a couple of pastries thanks to the kindness of Aunt Beth, but she was too excited to feel hungry. She was home. Bramble Cottage! Just think of it! Her cozy little house had its very own name and it stood at the entrance to one of the loveliest-named roads in the world: Wild Rose Way.

She took a deep, reviving sip before picking up her cell phone to let her parents know she had arrived. Barney Draycott answered at the first ring.

'Hey, Dad!'

'Made it there?' He spoke in his usual leisurely way. She could see him as clearly as if he were in the room, a square-jawed, stockily-built man, with a thick thatch of graying brown hair.

'Ten minutes ago. I'm savoring the moment.'

'Proud of you, honey. It was time to make a new start.'

'Thanks, Dad. Picture me celebrating with a cup of instant before the movers arrive. That should be in a couple of hours' time.'

'Be sure and make time to eat something; have to keep up your strength for the unpacking.'

Sarah laughed. 'Is Mom telling you to say that? She's the one who'd know.'

'Some daughter you are! Think I'm incapable of basic common sense advice? Your mother's out grocery shopping.'

'You always did let her have all the fun.' Sarah sipped at her coffee. Striking out on her own adventure had nudged her parents into fulfilling their own dream of moving to Florida. 'Any nibbles on the house?'

'A woman came through yesterday and she's coming back this afternoon with her husband.'

'Better start packing.'

'Honey, we've been here forty years. A lot of thought will have to go into downsizing. You know your mother. Getting her to part with anything from a chipped coffee cup to Tim's old bedroom furniture will take professional mediation.'

Sarah laughed. 'Don't be mean. She was the one who gave me those two leather recliners. You didn't look any too pleased at parting with them.'

'Craftiness on my part. If I'd seemed gung-ho to get rid of them she'd have decided they were only fit for the attic and I'd have been the one hauling them up there. Think of my back, honey, and enjoy them.'

'Thanks, Dad. For everything. I don't know how I'd have gotten through the past few years without all the emotional support from you and Mom, but it's time for you both to think sunscreen and margaritas by the pool. Tim, Kristen and the girls will be down to visit every chance they get and you can seriously count on my showing up when winter sets in.'

'Fat chance!' Barney laughed. 'You'll be too busy skiing. Anyone would think you were born on the slopes.'

'I'll tear myself away. And remember the road runs both ways. I can't wait for you to come here and visit. I think you and Mom will see why I fell in love with Sea Glass.'

'We'll be there once you've settled in. Before I let you go, how was your overnight with Aunt Beth?'

'Welcoming, in her own special way.'

'Still got that white sofa she won't allow even herself to sit on?'

'It'll go a virgin to the grave.' Sarah set down her empty coffee cup. 'She told me I looked anemic without blush and thought I'd looked better with longer hair. The last time I saw her she told me I ought to cut it. She did admire the Coach purse Kristen and Tim gave me for Christmas but said my shoes and raincoat didn't live up to it. Top of my to-do list is to send her a thank you card. You, along with all our friends and relatives, will be hearing about it if I don't.'

'You're right. A phone call wouldn't sufficiently meet my sister's standard of etiquette.' He chuckled. 'Same old Beth.'

'But it's hard not to halfway like her. I always feel I should suggest taking her out clubbing.'

'Softie! Now off with you. Can't keep the movers hanging about on the front step with their arms full of furniture.'

'Bye, Dad. Love to Mom.'

Sarah clicked off the phone and slipped it in the pocket of her dark blue jeans. There was nothing she could do inside until the movers arrived, but even if there had been she would still not have wanted to waste a moment getting down to the beach.

Opening the French doors she went out onto a flagstone patio containing a number of abandoned plant holders displaying only dried leaves on dead twigs, likely remnants of last year's annuals. There was a path of the same stone leading from the patio. Ignoring the saturated clouds and quivering chill that signaled impending rain, she followed the path's looping progression down the sloping lawn that was bordered on either side by hedges tall enough to provide only a minimal glimpse of the house next door. It was owned, the real estate agent had told her, by a couple from England. Sarah liked that the hedges weren't fiercely clipped. What looked to be elderly fruit trees stood ankle-deep in daffodils, surrounded by outcroppings of granite. It was a garden that seemed to have been allowed a personal say in how it wanted to dress for the various seasons, which somehow made the previous tenant seem suddenly very much present.

According to the ever-knowledgeable realtor she had been a woman named Nan Fielding, who had moved to Sea Glass from New Hampshire ten years previously, after retiring from teaching high school English. Single, inclined to be reclusive and, as was apparent from the tired interior of the house, not one to make above minimum demands on her landlord. He had put the house on the market after her death in late March.

Reaching the wooden steps, Sarah stood with arms at her side, taking in the rocky beach, inhaling the tang of seaweed, absorbing the murmur of the foam-streaked water. Walking alongside its edge was a woman with a small child hopping and skipping a few paces behind her, both wearing zippered jackets. Sarah was pierced by one of those moments of regret, less frequent now, but still painful. She breathed out, letting the damp breeze carry the emotion out to the gently shifting waves with their backdrop of lavender-brown hills.

After two years of marriage she and Harris had started trying for a baby. Six months later, when she failed to become pregnant, she'd gone back to her gynecologist and the round of tests had begun. Another year passed, during which she'd increasingly felt she was going it alone, with Harris off on the sidelines. When she was told in vitro was the next option he refused to consider it, saying he'd come to think having a child wasn't such a great idea. Why disrupt the lifestyle they'd come to enjoy? Three months later he'd phoned her from his office to say he'd made dinner reservations for them at their favorite restaurant. When he ordered champagne she felt a thrill of excitement. He was going to tell her he'd changed his mind. Happiness turned quickly to numbed confusion. He wanted a divorce. He'd fallen in love with Lisa Bentley. She was pregnant and he hoped Sarah would be civilized about the whole thing. Civilized! That part she did grasp. It was why he'd chosen to break the news at a restaurant where the maître d' looked as though he would clutch his chest and gasp for air if a patron burped. No chance of Sarah making a public scene. Or so Harris thought. She had tossed her glass of champagne in his face and walked out. The maître d' had approached her in the foyer with regal tread, to say it would be his privilege to summon a cab for her. Lisa Bentley had been her best friend from high school on, the maid of honor at her wedding, her confidante through all the fertility clinic disappointments.

The woman and child down on the beach disappeared from view. The sky was now so low it had become one with the ocean, but Sarah's spirits lifted as she went down to the beach. She had come to Sea Glass to make a new life for herself and she wasn't going to waste a moment of her first day dwelling on what was over and done. Single women today adopted children all the time – in the case of a friend of hers a little girl from Ethiopia. There were half a dozen red and yellow downturned kayaks along with a dory in front of the sea wall. Sarah had done quite a bit of river kayaking and loved it. She would have to get one. And maybe, in the future, a sailboat. She paused to look at some driftwood before crossing the pebbles, interspaced with the rugged groupings of rock, to stand at the water's edge. The wind-whipped waves came foaming up within inches of her feet. Bending, she gathered up a handful of suitably flat stones and one by one sent them skimming across the water. Her highest number of skips was seven. Tim, the grand champion, had once achieved twelve. But against that, she smiled; she had left him trailing in most of their kayak races.

There were no boats out in the bay, but Sarah's mind filled with the image of an eighteenth-century vessel with billowing sails arriving from Boston with the families who were the original settlers of Sea Glass. On her initial visit she had paid a visit to the historical society museum, two doors down from the realty office, and eagerly soaked up the information provided by the volunteer on duty. Among the settlers was a woman named Martha Cully who had remarked shortly before landing that it was a good omen that the sea was as smooth as glass, hence the naming of the village. She and her husband had been forced to leave Cornwall, England when his smuggling activities threatened to catch up with him. Throughout the coming generations the menfolk had all been seafarers, of the reformed, respectable sort, with the exception of Nathaniel Cully, born 1837, died 1925. Sarah had a fluke memory for dates. It was this man's life-sized bronze statue mounted on a six-foot granite pedestal that took pride of place in the center of the common. His father and brothers had been whalers, adding nicely to the family coffers. The Sea Glass Historical Society was the proud possessor of their remarkably fine collection of scrim-shaws, bequeathed by Nathaniel's granddaughter and only descendent, Emily Cully, born 1908, died 2001. The family home, a grim red Victorian across from the common, had been left to a distant cousin of hers in New York. He had subsequently been killed in a plane crash, along with his wife, younger son and daughter-in-law. And the house now stood empty, abandoned to neglect by the remaining son. Only the essential maintenance funded by a provision in the will had prevented the grounds from becoming a wilderness. The volunteer had looked very severe when relaying this fact. No wonder the place was developing a reputation of being haunted. She had brightened when getting back to Nathaniel Cully, speaking as if he were an old friend, recently deceased. The *dear man* had suffered from sea sickness from childhood on; an embarrassing affliction, given his family background. He had found his true calling as the local doctor, delivering babies and taking care of everyone's ills, from croup to broken bones and final hours for nearly fifty years, never letting the worst weather keep him from getting to his patients in his horse and buggy. If that wasn't doable he had walked. Always beloved, he had sealed his place in the hearts of the community at the age of seventy-four. The volunteer had done a great job bringing the narrative to its climax. The statue didn't exaggerate Nathaniel's height, she had proclaimed proudly. He was the proverbial giant of a man and robust well into old age. On an April evening, when no one else appeared on the beach to help, he plowed the family rowboat out to rescue a group of six young people who had decided to go sailing, all lacking sufficient experience to deal with a sudden squall. He had brought them safely to shore despite his seasickness.

Sarah had been captivated by the story; it was there in her mind as she looked out at the scurrying waves – the indomitable old man and the chastened, foolhardy young people crawling out of the boat onto the safety of the beach. She incorporated into the vivid image several gulls crying hoarsely overhead, as some were doing now. Such disgruntled-sounding birds. But for them she'd had the beach to herself. Now two women with dogs, a black and a yellow Labrador, were walking her way. And coming from the other direction was an elderly man with a Cavalier King Charles spaniel. All three people waved on drawing closer and she cheerfully returned the greetings, then watched with pleasure as the Labs bounded, splashing into the water. It was a delight to watch such unbridled joy. The urge for a dog of her own strengthened, but she would have to do the responsible thing and wait until she was organized.

Sarah walked on to her left, detouring around the rocks, all the while searching the ground for a sparkle of color that could be sea glass. She soon found it was easy to be tricked by a pebble, especially a green one, polished to a wet gleam by a higher tide. She rounded the point. Above her now were the backyards of mansion-sized houses built in the era of large families and readily available servants. Her eyes were drawn to the red brick Victorian built by Nathaniel Cully's father. Glimpsed through the shadowing trees, she decided the volunteer at the museum had been right, it did look haunted. A shiver slid down her spine and the thought slipped into place – it was fear standing at first one window then the next. Waiting. Counting down the minutes to some unavoidable crossing of the threshold. Whatever was stirring in that house was roused by the tumult of the present, not the past.

What idiocy! Did she now think all houses spoke to her? Sarah had forgotten for the moment about sea glass, but when her foot slipped on the uneven surface and she looked down, there it was – quite a large piece of opaque aqua, obviously from the base of a bottle. Picking it up, she traced a finger around it. How many months . . . years of being tumbled against sand and stone must it have taken for all sharp edges to be buffed away? Here was her good luck omen, the start of her collection. She was so happy she could have danced back to Bramble Cottage through the now-sprinkling rain.

A glance at her watch told her she should hurry. There was always the possibility the movers would arrive early. Picturing them as her father had described – out front with their arms filled with furniture – she entered the house the way she had left it, by the kitchen's French doors. After placing the piece of sea glass on the window sill above the sink, she crossed the foyer to look out the front door. The scattered drops of a few moments ago had turned into a blowing curtain of rain with a filmy lining of fog, but there would have been no hiding a small car let alone a massive moving truck. She withdrew inside and felt the house settle comfortably around her.

If quick, she could go through the house and reassess her mental image of furniture placement so there would be no dithering when giving instructions to the movers. The foyer's peeling wall-paper with its little pink flowers on silvery-blue stripes looked the more tired in contrast to the refurbished wood floor. She liked the dark stain chosen by the seller, perhaps under the guidance of someone with an updated outlook. 'Espresso' best described it. On her left was the good-sized living room, to her right a much smaller one. What would she call it? The den, she decided; the study sounded a little too eagerly important. The two rooms were entered through rounded archways, indicative of the nineteen thirties when the house had been built. One of its charming features, as pointed out by the agent, despite both rooms being painted uninspired beige. Each room had a fireplace, surrounded by built-in bookcases. Those shelves looked as though they wouldn't feel happy until lined with Tolstoy, Hawthorn, Dickens and other classics force fed in school; the sort of reading more in line with a woman of Nan Fielding's generation. What sort of person had she been? Renters aren't in general encouraged to leave their imprint. She went between the two rooms, summing them up. The dining end of the living room was designated as such by a dated nineteen seventies chandelier. It, like the kitchen, had French doors to the outside. She had only the two brown leather recliners donated by her parents to put in the den.

Back in the hall she picked up her purse that she had set down on the bottom stair and the raincoat she had tossed over the banister post and took them with her upstairs. The door to the bathroom at the top stood open. It was surprisingly spacious with a charming claw-foot tub, but the tile floor, along with the vanity and fixtures, would need replacing.

Sarah took a quick peek into the narrow space at the far left of the hallway. She'd decided it would work as her home office, as the agent had suggested, if she took the doors off the closet. There was no point in checking out the bedroom next to it because she had nothing yet to put in there. She'd need to purchase a bed and a dresser before any guests came to stay. She was particularly eager for her nieces, Julia and Lauren, ages thirteen and ten, to visit. They were great kids. The next bedroom was not much larger than the proposed guest one. More outdated wallpaper. Other people might consider it inadequate as a master. No en suite or walk-in closet. Sarah didn't mind the lack of either. Ninety-nine percent of the time she wouldn't be waiting her turn for the bathroom, and she had donated anything she was unlikely to wear again to Goodwill before leaving. On the positive side, the newly-refurbished wood floor would perfectly offset her white bed linen and filmy curtains; their lace edging would take up the cottage appeal of a sweetly-sloping ceiling.

Time to stow her raincoat and purse on the shelf in the closet and get moving. They were now half an hour later than promised.

The rain was coming down hard against the windows, which probably accounted for it. Sarah was ready for another cup of coffee. The doorbell rang as she stepped back into the hallway, sending her quickly downstairs.

The two men she welcomed inside, although well into their fifties and damp around the head and shoulders, exuded a hearty efficiency. They apologized for the delay, caused by a detour resulting from road work. They took a brisk tour of the house, said they had the layout logged, and thought they could be done in two to three hours. Sarah had hoped this would be the case. Given that her apartment in Evanston had been a one bedroom she didn't have a lot of furniture, nor a large accumulation of accessories. If it hadn't been for the washer and dryer she could have rented a van and towed her car, although the drawback to that would have been not having anyone to help her unload. She offered coffee and was pleasantly refused. They had their Thermoses.

The olive-green armoire came in first, to be positioned against the living-room wall facing the fireplace. It was followed by the sofa and two armchairs – stripped of their slipcovers for the move. Feeling like a traffic cop, Sarah beckoned them on. Forty minutes later her natural pine harvest table and dark bentwood chairs were in place. The brown leather recliners went into the den. All boxes not designated for upstairs would go in there too. Sarah had assumed she'd have to set up her queen-sized bed with its iron headboard, but a peek round the door showed it waiting to be readied for the night. Last in were the washer and dryer. Again the men went above and beyond in getting them hooked up for her in the mud room.

She headed upstairs to get cash from her wallet to give them each a generous tip, then stood waving goodbye from the front step as they climbed aboard the truck. They had been there just over three hours. The house was already to beginning to look like home. A few weeks and lots of paint would pay maximum dividends. Her former mother-in-law had given her a hand-blown glass vase that she was now ready to put back out on the half-moon foyer table. Iris Colefax was a lovely woman. Sarah missed their relationship.

She was finally hungry and had just finished a hasty meal of tomato soup and a grilled cheese sandwich when she heard a cat meowing plaintively somewhere outside. As she was peering through the rain-streaked panes of the French doors, the bell rang.

'Who can that be?' She stood, momentarily flummoxed, before making for the front door. She opened it to see a sturdily-built older woman wearing a sensible coat along with bright orange Crocks standing on the steps. Her plump face was a maze of fine wrinkles, but her bobbed dark hair was only sparingly threaded with gray, and her posture was upright, making the stick in her right hand look like a prop. Tucked under her left arm was a plastic-wrapped loaf of something.

'I'm Nellie Armitage from across the road,' she announced cheerfully. 'Your official nosy neighbor. They don't just exist in books, you know.' Sarah knew those who would have kept a stranger on the step, but she hadn't been brought up that way.

'Hi, I'm Sarah Draycott. Please come in,' she encouraged.

'Just for a moment.' The woman entered nippily, confirming Sarah's thought that the stick was mainly for show. 'I hear you're from Chicago!' The dark eyes twinkled. 'Word gets around on winged feet here. I've brought you a loaf of banana bread.' She poked at the Saran-wrapped oblong.

'Oh, that is nice.'

The round face broke into a beaming smile. 'It's been in the freezer for months if not years. I'm not much of a sweet eater. Just a blatant excuse to get my foot in the door. But you look too nice a girl to hoodwink with trumped-up offerings.'

'Thank you.' Sarah took the bread and set it on the table by the staircase. 'I'm sure I'll enjoy it.'

Coat and cane deposited in the foyer, Nellie Armitage followed Sarah into the living room. 'My, you've already got your furniture in place. Looks right comfy.'

The room did look inviting, even with the sofa and chairs lacking their slipcovers. A fire would have made a nice contrast against the rain streaming down the windows. Sarah hadn't yet decided between gas logs and wood burning. She wished she could have offered sherry, although she doubted alcohol was ever needed to bump up her visitor's obvious zest for life. Nellie closed her eyes and inhaled deeply.

'Good aura. No restless spirits here, so far as I can tell.'

'That's nice to know,' said Sarah; she'd just as soon not see Nan Fielding floating down the stairs. 'Are you a medium?'

'Can't make that boast,' Nellie replied with beaming honesty, 'but I do attend the spiritualist church out by Dobbs Mill. Wouldn't call myself devout, though. Take anything too serious and it stops being fun. That's the way I look at it.'

Sarah bit back a smile. Her Aunt Beth would not think speaking of religion as a recreational activity amusing. 'How about a cup of coffee?' she suggested when her guest was seated on the sofa.

'Just had one. You sit yourself down; I'll guess your feet need resting after a busy morning.'

Very hospitable, thought Sarah. Increasingly amused, she settled herself in one of the armchairs.

'Glad to have you in the neighborhood.'

'I'm really looking forward to living here.'

'Mind if I call you Sarah?'

'I'd like that.'

'How old do you think I am?' Nellie fired the question as if sure of a winner.

This was tricky. Sarah had learned from her grandparents and their friends that the older people got the more eager they were to admit to their true ages, even to the point of boasting of the number of years under their belts. Best to go with the honest answer.

'Seventy-five?'

'Ninety,' Nellie shot back smugly. Sarah tried and failed to smother a laugh. Given the bubbling echo from the sofa no offence was taken. Her visitor was fully aware of her entertainment value.

'Well, you certainly don't look it.'

'I was the youngest of seven, the only one left now. Never married and can't say it worried me any.' She went on to talk about Reggie, her devoted great-nephew living only a few miles away in Ferry Landing with his nice wife Mandy and nine-year-old son, Brian. 'Reggie will be coming to collect me at five. Always spend Friday nights with him and the family. Now tell me about you. Did your job bring you up here?' Nellie leaned forward as if hanging on the answer. Sarah could see the irrepressible little girl peering from those sparkling brown eyes, awaiting further revelations.

'No, I'm lucky in having work I can do anywhere. Being single I don't have any ties. I design patterns for knitting magazines.'

'What a fun-sounding job!' Sarah could read the unspoken question in the revealing eyes. Did it pay well? The answer would have been *very nicely.* 'But aren't you rather young not to want to be out in the hustle and bustle?'

'I'm thirty-four.'

'You don't look close to that, and such a pretty girl. My mother would have described you as bonnie.'

'Thank you.'

Nellie looked around the room. 'Would you believe I haven't been in this house since Nan Fielding moved in? She was a teacher. Taught high school English, did you know that?'

'Yes, the realtor told me. What was she like?'

'Kept to her lonesome. Didn't let the conversation go beyond the weather and an occasional mention of her garden if I saw her outside.'

Sarah considered this from Nan Fielding's vantage point. She could reasonably have sized Nellie up as the sort who, once having got a foot in the door, would be constantly showing up when least wanted and increasingly hard to budge.

The brown eyes met hers with a knowing twinkle. 'I can guess what you're thinking, but Nan was just the same with everyone else – kept them all at a distance. I sure will enjoy having you for a neighbor.' Nellie nodded decisively. 'A good number of people on this road are summer people, only here from June through September. Oh, sometimes they begin trickling back in May, but not this year. It's been too cold and wet.'

'Does it seem a little flat when they go?'

Nellie gave the question its due deliberation. 'I miss the children. My great-nephew's boy Brian always enjoys the excitement they bring. This is a great place for family vacations. The parents like being able to let the older ones go off and enjoy themselves in the good old-fashioned way without constantly worrying something dreadful could happen to them. There's so little crime here, you see. Most people round here don't bother locking their doors. The only person I ever knew to have an alarm ringy dingy put in was Nan Fielding.'

'There's not one here now. I'd have noticed.'

'Taken out. I saw the van pull in and spoke to the driver. Said the real estate agency didn't think it was a good selling feature.' Nellie preened, then sobered. 'You have to ask yourself what happened in Nan's life before coming here to make her feel in need of home protection.'

Sarah looked doubtful. She had some curiosity about the former tenant but it wasn't overwhelming. 'Can we assume something bad happened? The majority of people I know have them.'

'That's Chicago.'

'Gangsterville.' Sarah laughed. 'Where did Nan come from?'

'Boston. Can't tell you more than that.' Clearly this was disappointing. Nellie's interpretation of only staying for a moment was an unusual one, but Sarah couldn't get annoyed – she was old and very likely lonely. And it did feel good to just sit.

'So you don't get many break-ins around here?'

'They're a rarity and I never heard of one turning violent. The last I heard of anyone letting himself in where he'd no business going uninvited was Willie Watkins. He's a sad drunk and you can't blame his daughter, who's past her own prime and has a leaky roof and bad knees to worry about, for kicking him out when he gets to singing all night. Not that he has a bad voice,' Nellie conceded in the manner of giving the devil his due. 'And it was winter – this past January, so you can't rightly blame the old cockroach for getting under cover.'

'No, I suppose not.' Sarah pictured the red nose, stubbly-gray chin and knitted gloves with most of the fingers gone. 'Did he wake the householders up?'

'Two things you have to know about Willie: he's a coward and canny as a fox, even when swaying like a tree in the wind. What he did was hole up in the cellar of the Cully Mansion. Everyone called it that; its name used to be Fair Winds. It's been empty since old Emily Cully died way back at the start of this century. She was the granddaughter of a man whose statue is on the common.'

'I've seen it.' Sarah instantly felt more alert. She found the Cullys far more interesting than poor Nan Fielding.

'I like to kid myself the reason I never married was because no living man could compare to Nathaniel Cully . . . caring for the sick, rescuing those sailors.'

'Did you know his granddaughter?'

'Not as a friend. Emily didn't have friends. Too conscious of her family's status dating back to the first settlers. Proud as a peacock that an ancestress of hers named the village. Her one true pal was her parrot. Luckily it died before she did. That bird had the foulest mouth I've ever heard. But Emily didn't shut herself off as complete as Nan Fielding did. When the mood suited she'd entertain by way of what she called her soirees. Dried up tidbits, served on plates with spider web cracks. Once or twice I got included as part of a group. Emily had polio as a child; left her embittered. Have to feel sorry for her, but wouldn't think her housekeeper had the treat of a lifetime working for her.'

'What did you think of the house?' Sarah was remembering her reaction that morning on glimpsing it through the overgrown garden.

'Couldn't turn for bumping into Victorian bric-a-brac. Items Willie Watkins could have turned to account if he'd got to them. All I ever saw of the place – with the exception of the powder room with its red flock wallpaper, thick with dust – was the living room; shadowy as a cave. Contained her bed at one end, a great four-poster with tapestry hangings. That room was where she spent all her time, boasting that she had never been in the kitchen for fifty years, let alone up to the second or third floors. And in all likelihood she'd never been down in that cellar in her life, not with her being crippled like she was. So no need for Willie Watkins to fear bumping into her ghost when settling in for what turned out to be a three-week stay.'

'Was his daughter worried about him?'

'Well, he wasn't what you'd call missing,' Nellie explained reasonably. 'He was seen around in the daytime, showing up at the soup kitchen and going after soft touches for money. I expect the poor woman was glad of a break.'

'How was his hiding place discovered?'

'A policeman followed him back one night, with the result that he's been installed ever since at Pleasant Meadows, a nursing home between Sea Glass and Ferry Landing.'

'No charges issued against him?'

'Waste of time and money to keep him in jail. Wasn't like he could have stolen anything. The door at the top of the cellar stairs was locked; doubt anyone has a clue where the key went. Of course, the police notified the current owners of the house – that would be Gerard Cully and his wife, Elizabeth – and she did come down to look the place over, the first Sea Glass had the privilege of seeing her. That was the last of it so far as Willie's brush with the law.'

Sarah was glad the man had got off lightly. 'I heard Emily Cully left the house to a distant cousin.' Fully alert now, she was eager to learn more than she had from the volunteer at the museum.

'He also came in for all the contents, excluding the scrimshaws; those went to the historical society. That cousin was Gerard Cully's father and, you may also have heard, he didn't outlast her long. Don't know that she'd ever met him, but blood counted with Emily.'

'From the way you describe the place it sounds like an albatross. I wonder why the son hasn't sold it.'

'That's rich people for you,' said Nellie smugly, 'won't let go of a half-eaten sandwich.' She shifted as if about to get up, and then hovered indecisively. 'This has been very nice, Sarah, but now it has to be getting on time for me to be going. Reggie, my great-nephew, will be along soon to pick me up.'

Sarah looked at her watch. 'It's four thirty.'

'Time enough then to fill you in a bit more on the Cully family.' Nellie sank comfortably back into position.

'I'm interested.' Sarah thought impishly that she'd soon know enough to become a volunteer at the historical society museum.

'It's this way.' Nellie's face clouded for the first time during her visit. 'The cousin that inherited had two sons – Gerard and his younger brother Max. There'd been a falling out between Max and his parents because he'd married a girl named Clare Andrews from Ferry Landing and they didn't think her good enough to fit in with their grand friends. You can never get through to snobs. Clare was a great girl, lovely inside and out, the only child of a decent, hardworking, loving couple. Grew up just a few houses down from where Reggie and his family live. Seems Max came out here the summer before his last year of college. Curious about the family roots. Had to have been shortly before Emily Cully died. Whether he got to see her or not I don't know. By that time who he was probably wouldn't have registered anyway; she'd been failing mentally as well as physically for a good long time come the end.'

'And that's when he met Clare?'

'At the July Lobster Fest here in Sea Glass. Must have been interested in learning about the family history. Seems to me, if I remember the timing right, Emily would've been past seeing him by then, but I do recall her saying at one of those gatherings of hers that she'd exchanged letters with one of the cousin's boys. Love at first sight is how her father, Frank, described Clare and Max to Reggie. Seems Max had already been accepted at one of

the big law schools – could have been Harvard. But his parents
told him he could bark financial help from them till he bust after
he refused to back down from marrying Clare. So what does he
do but go to work for the Ferry Landing Bank. According to
Reggie, they thought highly of him there and he might likely
have moved up fast.' Nellie sighed like a gusty wind. 'Good to
think those two young people knew true happiness in their short
time together; the crowning joy had to have been the birth of
their son. Named him Oliver after Clare's mother.'

'Olivia?'

'Olive. Give praise to the Almighty she and her husband Frank
had their grandson to live for after the plane crash took their
daughter and son-in-law. Heard about that?'

'Yes, but not about the little boy.' Nellie's telling made him
touchingly, almost painfully, real.

'Reggie's son and Oliver are best pals. See why I take the story
so much to heart? Poor little guy wasn't much more than a toddler
when it happened. One of those stupid little planes. Clare and
Max were flying back from Mexico, having left the child with
Olive and Frank, when it happened. Bitter as it sounds, seeing as
the senior Cullys got killed as well, I lay the tragedy square at their
door. They'd arranged the trip, supposed to be an attempt at
reconciliation, but more likely a try at breaking them up is what
I think.' Rain no longer pattered against the windows. Momentarily
silence lay upon the room.

'Any others on that flight?'

'Only the pilot. Shame about him, of course. It'll be seven years
now. And Olive Andrews' dead as well; been a while for her too.
I'd have to ask Reggie just how long it's been since she passed.
What I do have clear is that Gerard Cully and that wife of his
haven't bothered one lick about Oliver. Not so much as a short
visit when she came in about the Willie Watkins business. That's
my grudge against the two of them. Frank's carried on marvelous
with the boy, who takes after him in looks something remarkable
– sandy hair and freckles, sturdy build. What's going to happen to
him now is the question.'

'Why?'

'Sounds like Frank will very soon have to go into a nursing
home. Probably Pleasant Meadows, seeing as it's closest. He's been
battling Parkinson's and is sadly now getting beyond the care of

the nurse, who's been living-in for the past couple of years. Looks to be a mighty good woman, does Twyla. Met her a few times when she's come to fetch Oliver home from playing with Brian.'

'Maybe Frank Andrews will give her guardianship.' Sarah got to her feet, as Nellie was doing.

'That's what I've been hoping. She and Oliver have got mighty close since she came. Of course there's always nasty-minded people that wouldn't see it working because of her . . .' Nellie cut herself off upon looking at her watch. 'Have to be going; Reggie'll be on his way. What a grand afternoon this has been, Sarah! Must do it again at my place, two doors down across the road. Got that?' She was already scooting for the foyer, where she grabbed up her stick and would have been out the door without her raincoat if Sarah hadn't grabbed it off the banister knob and helped her into it.

She was halfway down the path with Sarah close behind her when she turned back. 'Blame my age for talking your ear off.'

'I enjoyed every minute. And you were anything but nosy.'

'Think not? I found out everything I wanted to know.'

'Which was?'

'That you're a very nice young woman.' Nellie was off again before Sarah got the words 'thank you' out of her mouth. So far the stick hadn't touched the ground.

Even though the rain had ceased, the sky remained heavy, creating a swarthy cast of shadow suggestive of a later evening hour, and making it unthinkable to turn back before seeing the old lady safely across the road. Nellie was on the sidewalk, about to step into the road, when a pickup truck came around the corner from Salt Marsh Road. And Sarah had just got hold of her arm and drawn her back when it slid to a halt in front of them. A man got out, a thin, balding man in his late thirties to early forties, his mouth lifting in a crinkling smile.

'What you up to, Aunt Nellie?'

'Reggie.' His great aunt needlessly identified him to Sarah. Having made the introductions, she rather grandly allowed herself to be helped aboard. The vehicle moved cautiously off to turn into the driveway of a house two down on the opposite side of the road, reverse, and go back the way it had come.

Sarah was returning to the house when she heard a faint meowing. She stood listening, waiting for a repeat; there had been something desperate in the sound. She wasn't sure where it came from, only that it was close. There it came again from her right and close to the picket fence. It took her a couple of moments of searching under the shrubbery before she spotted the bedraggled tabby. Was it the one she'd heard just before Nellie arrived?

'It's OK, sweetie,' she murmured, afraid it would flee before she could pick it up, but it allowed her to do so. Fear apparently giving way to need. She continued to whisper soothingly. 'It's going to be all right. No need to be scared.' The ears that had been drawn back relaxed.

She would take it inside and try to get it to lap a small amount of lukewarm chicken noodle soup. She had read somewhere that you shouldn't allow a starving animal to eat too much too soon. And if this poor little creature were a stray it would fit that category. So far it hadn't so much as flinched, causing her to hope she could start moving without startling it into wriggling an escape. Softly, smoothly . . . she hadn't thought about having a cat as well as a dog. Now that possibility was in her arms. But not for many seconds longer.

The roar of an approaching vehicle sent the cat clawing up onto her shoulder, and then it was gone. Sarah did not see where it went. She did not look. She had eyes only for the car driven at breakneck speed down the steep incline of Ridge Farm Rise. It wasn't going to cross Wild Rose Way. Her house was on the corner, and the car was swerving toward it. She stood frozen, paralyzed into resignation. The realtor had said some people didn't like a corner house. Another thought unreeled in slow motion. How ironic that this day, with all its promise of a new beginning, might be her last.

Two

But for the soft spattering of rain on the long, narrow windows, the early nineteenth-century house on Ridge Farm Rise was steeped in silence. It might have been not only empty but unoccupied by human presence for a very long time. A house at rest. A house so deeply asleep even dreams of days gone by did not intrude. Mid-afternoon masquerading as night.

Seventy-eight-year-old Gwen stood at the foot of the stairs. To the right was a long-case round-faced black Pennsylvania Dutch clock with faded detailing of once brightly colored birds and flowers. She was a slim, silver-haired woman of five foot seven, wearing a violet jersey knit dress that heightened the blue of her eyes. Elegant even in flat black shoes, she had the bone structure and clarity of skin that allowed it to be said she was still a very pretty woman and must once have been lovely. Gwen would have responded that it was her sister Rowena, two years her senior, who had been the beauty.

Hearing nothing, she returned to a room lined with floor-to-ceiling walnut bookshelves. She did not regret that the first two weeks of May had rarely, and then only briefly, seen a clear sky. Sunlight these days seemed to strike too harshly, shedding its cruel spotlight on inescapable reality. Rain was kinder. It blurred not only the windows but the endless present. It had been a particularly difficult day up until half an hour ago, when she'd followed him upstairs to his room and settled him into bed.

During the rare moments of fragile respite from her worst anxiety, Gwen strove to open her heart to the gift of the ordinary. A cup of Earl Grey tea with her two-year-old brindled bull mastiff Jumbo stretched out by the fireplace. The opportunity to pick up the beloved, much-read copy of *Barchester Towers* conveniently to hand on the small pie-crust table. From the beginning she had recognized the necessity of doing everything possible to shore up her physical and mental resources.

So much depended on his moods. They veered from apathy to anger. There were times when he seemed fully cognizant of what was going on around him, sharply so, bringing out the paranoia at its worst. Gwen endeavored to meet well-meaning advice from people with all the answers with an appreciative response. She should be patient; one had to be. It was true that Pleasant Meadows, just eight miles away in Ferry Landing, had an excellent reputation, and for many in her position it would be the right choice. Sometime in the future it would come to that – a nursing home. But not now, not when he still drew comfort and some happiness from being in known surroundings and her presence.

The cause of his agitation today had sprung from overhearing her telling Madge Baldwin on the phone that morning that she needed to renew her driver's license, but wasn't sure if the place would be open on a Saturday. There had been a distressing scene a few months back when she'd found Charles in the driver's seat trying to get the car out of the garage. On that occasion it had taken an exhausting ten minutes to get the car keys away from him. Since then she had kept them hidden. Mercifully, he had said nothing more about driving until coming upon her, on the phone with Madge Baldwin.

This neighbor had called Gwen, hoping she could borrow her car for the day while her own was being worked on. Hearing him behind her, Gwen had quickly acquiesced, saying her own plans were always flexible. She'd hung up, sensing the impending tirade. *Why should she get her license renewed? Why not him? She was keeping him a prisoner. It was a plot. She was wicked.* The rage she could handle. He had never threatened her physically. It was when he had started to cry that the anguish came close to being unbearable.

Gwen continued to hover within a couple of feet of the doorway. No sound but the dulcet patter of the rain. No blundering footsteps overhead, no slamming of doors, no agonizingly agitated voice to send her hurrying up the stairs.

Jumbo, having woken from a nap, crossed the room to nudge companionably up against her. Gwen bent to stroke his broad head. What a comfort he was to her. No well-intentioned advice from this quarter; his offering was twenty-four hours of unstinting devotion. More than any other living being he kept her going these days. But had her love for him become a selfish indulgence? How unfair to him was the situation? What had once been twice daily walks of forty-five minutes to an hour had dwindled to one at best. Even those were slow-paced and of short duration. It was impossible for her to take Jumbo out on her own anymore, which was what the dog would have preferred. He had begun avoiding the man who had once been his friend. The fenced back garden, while fairly large, could not provide anything approaching sufficient exercise for a young and powerful dog.

Gwen also missed the outings for her own sake. Never good at sports as a girl or young woman, she had relished lengthy walks in all but the most frigid weather. Another nudge from Jumbo brought her back to her senses. Sleep had hopefully granted temporary oblivion to the other inhabitant of the house. The duration was uncertain but whether counted in minutes or hours it must not be wasted in straining to hear sounds of renewed activity. The dimly-lighted book room offered the sort of ambience that would have welcomed Paul Revere to relax after his long ride. The dusky green velvet sofa that matched the drapes invited her to sit, but Gwen read the look in Jumbo's eyes. Not the moment for either of them to dawdle, was his kindly if not unbiased opinion.

For the past couple of hours he had been inhaling the enticing aroma of split pea soup creeping up from the stockpot on the stove. Patient he might be, but the awareness of a ham bone in his immediate future was becoming salivatingly acute. There was no prancing as he followed Gwen down the hall into the comfortably-sized kitchen with its glazed brick floor, dark blue cabinets and cream appliances. Prancing was as alien to Jumbo's nature as it would have been to a country gentleman grounded in Greek and Latin and supremely content with his wainscoted library with its well-worn leather chair, elderly slippers and after-dinner glass of port. Excepting, of course, for extensive walks across hill and dale or along a rugged shoreline . . . Never unrestrained ebullience from Jumbo. But at that moment, a decided lift to the tail.

'First things first, my dear.' Gwen opened the door from the mud room into the garden for him then went to stir the richly thick soup before removing the bone to the farmhouse sink for rinsing under cold water. This done she placed it on a paper towel, all the time alert to a break in the silence. None came. She had to get past this edginess. That it had been a particularly bad day suggested the respite might be as much as a couple of hours. A block of time in which to either rest or get something accomplished. Again she checked the soup, replaced the lid, and readmitted Jumbo to the kitchen.

'Good boy! Here's your reward.' He took the bone as softly from her hand as if his mouth was made from the same velvet as the book room's sofa and drapes, and she watched him transport it sedately to his rug in front of the woodstove. Such a gentle giant, the bull mastiff, although she admitted people might be misled when given a display of those stalactite teeth. They were at work in earnest now and the heavy crunching scattered into the stillness, relaxing the tension of the void. The rain still slid down the windows, but now in trickles of silent tears. The wind had worn itself out an hour ago like a sleep-deprived child.

French bread and cheese would go well with the soup. There was also fruit in the bowl on the butcher block island. Gwen kept meals simple these days. Counted among her blessings was that Plover's Grocery Store on Main Street continued to deliver, as it had done for more than half a century. All she had to do was make her list, pick up the phone, and await Mr Plover's kindly voice in her ear. A chip off the old block was Gerry Plover, like father and grandfather before him. A Mainer through and through. In the view of many in these parts there were few higher compliments. Though not among the original settlers, the Plovers went back a long way in Sea Glass.

Turning off the gas burner under the soup, Gwen glanced up at the wall clock. Three o'clock. Madge Baldwin had said she would have the car back by two. She opened the refrigerator to stare at the Camembert and white Cheddar on the plastic-wrapped cheeseboard, as if expecting them to rearrange themselves on the platter.

Could Madge have returned the car while she was upstairs dealing with getting him into bed and settled down? But surely Madge wouldn't have done so without handing back the keys, as had been agreed? Suddenly the silence that had seemed a gift throbbed with dreadful possibility. Barely aware of the dull pain in her chest, Gwen opened the door to the garage. White walls. Concrete floor. No car. Pressing a hand on the kitchen countertop to steady herself, she felt her breathing slowly ease.

Knowing she would not regain her equilibrium without checking that he was indeed safely in his bed, she went slowly up the stairs, holding onto the rail – something she rarely did – and opened the door to the room with its hunter green walls and colonial four-poster bed. The small glow from the brass bedside lamp revealed the pale profile below the gray hair. She yearned to move closer, to smooth that hair, once so golden, to press a kiss upon the exposed cheek. But she would not risk waking him. Retreating back into the hallway, she stood motionless, hands clasped, praying out of ingrained response, but without conviction.

At the foot of the stairs she found Jumbo waiting for her. He never followed her into that bedroom these days. 'Come, my dear.' She returned him to the kitchen to be reunited with his bone and

went back into the book room. All was well. Quiet time. What to do with it? In the aftermath of fear came fatigue, verging on exhaustion, but she doubted she could settle to doze. Was this finally the moment to write the letter submitting her resignation as chair of the garden club? She could not keep putting it off. She'd missed too many meetings in the past six months. It wasn't fair to continue abdicating her responsibilities to Madge, who had enough of her own as Treasurer along with being the primary organizer of event planning.

Resigning as secretary of the historical society had been a wrench, though not as sad as informing the Sea Glass Choral Ensemble that she could no longer continue as their regular pianist. She played well, even without her abilities approaching a sublime gift. That had not mattered to her. She had never yearned to be among the chosen few. Gardens, more than music, had always been her source of inspiration, joy and solace.

Gwen sat down at the secretary desk and reached for the box of stationery. Keep it short and simple. Her sister Rowena had considered sentimentality vulgar. She laid a piece of monogrammed cream vellum on the leather-bound blotter and picked up the fountain pen that had been her parents' gift on her sixteenth birthday. At the thought of her mother and father, long gone now she was back in the garden she had first loved. The one behin the colonial brick house in Concord, Massachusetts, so treasur a part of her childhood and adolescence. A garden ever wait with balmy breath for summer. Honeysuckle and privet hed daisy and buttercup sprinkled lawns, the sound of the brook be the back gate murmuring its secrets to the weeping willow piccolo sweetness of birdsong . . . and family.

Images bright as poster paint schoolroom pictures emerge father providing rides in a wheelbarrow when she and h were small. Rowena, the older by four years, with her ex and vivid coloring. Her pretty, golden-haired mother we rock garden, looking round from kneeling position t them. The old gardener leaning on his spade as he st up at the big apple tree in full white and pink b proclaiming it to be a sight for sore eyes. Those en days, echoing back the laughter. And always and for drenched scent of roses.

Clearest of all, talking with her mother in t

afternoon in the week before she and Charles Norris were to be married under an arbor on the far lawn. Was she remembering or dreaming? That other Gwen was eighteen, Charles twenty-seven. She had known him her entire life, had woven secret dreams from adolescence onward of his declaring his love, never seriously believing, up until six months before, that he would ever see her in a romantic light. Not when there was vibrant, beautiful and stylish Rowena to overshadow her. Charles' parents and theirs were close friends, had been from before their own marriages. Her father could not have been happier about the engagement. But that afternoon her mother, who had always seemed to think the world of Charles, gently voiced her concern that Gwen was too young.

'Life, my darling,' she had said, 'hasn't yet laid a finger on you. I regret not speaking out before. I should have done so when you told me Charles had proposed and you'd accepted him, but I hated the idea of doing anything to diminish that lovely glow.'

Gwen heard her in shocked disbelief. 'You've been talking to Great-Aunt Harriet. She made a crack about going from the schoolroom to the altar.'

'She's outspoken, but not someone to influence me.'

'I can't believe this is how you've been feeling. Does Daddy agree with you?'

'No, dearest, he unequivocally believes that the two of you are perfect for each other.'

'And Rowena? Has her enthusiasm been a pretense?'

'She loves you.'

Gwen was too distressed to reflect on the lack of answer in this response, but she was to play it over in her mind countless times in the years ahead. Now she set aside the pen, got up wearily from the desk and settled herself in her fireside chair, only vaguely aware of Jumbo's return.

'It's not too late,' her mother had continued gently. 'Why not give yourself a little more time? What the girl thinks is right for her may not be what the woman wants or needs. I know you love him. How could you not? He's good-looking, personable, ambitious, and he's been part of our lives for a long time.'

'Sounds like faint praise,' replied Gwen resentfully.

Her mother did not answer that. Their blue eyes, so very alike, met. 'I know you love him, but has there been one moment of breathless, heart-stopping rapture?'

This was startling. Her serene mother with her pearls and pastel clothing choices talking of rapture! It lifted the cloud, making ridiculous what had been not only unsettling but hurtful.

Gwen said patiently that of course there had been such moments. Many of them. And it was true. There had been the thrilling one when Charles had placed the sapphire and diamond ring on her finger, the heady delight of being showered with envious congratulations, the fairy-tale vision of her reflection in the bridal shop mirror. Ivory silk, heirloom lace veil and orange blossom. Of course she loved Charles. Deeply. She could not ask for more from life than to be his wife. That would never change.

A week later she had glided in a glow of happiness, hand on her father's arm, to join her bridegroom under the arbor. A violin was playing *Jesu, Joy of Man's Desiring*. The pure, sweet accompaniment of song came from the birds. *From this day forward . . . forsaking all others . . . till death do us part . . .* She had made that vow as a girl imagining herself in the starring role of a play. Time, that ruthless archivist of all things young and foolish, would make that clear to her eight years later in another garden – the one behind the house in Boston that Charles had inherited from his grandmother shortly after their marriage.

It was in that Eden with its gnarled pear trees and goldfish pond that her mother's fears were realized. At twenty-six Gwen was the mother of a beloved seven-year-old son, who from the age of three had gravitated to the piano. Happy? Yes, she was happy. Who but an ingrate would not have been? Admittedly Charles traveled increasingly with his job. The necessity of conducting audits all over the country was the lot of a successful CPA. But he was a fond and considerate husband, insisting that they hire a full-time housekeeper so that Gwen would not have to fend for herself during his absences. One concern was his occasional irritation with Sonny for groundless reasons. She had hoped for another child, had expected to quickly become pregnant again after having Sonny so soon. It hadn't happened. And she had come to think that was perhaps for the best, that Charles wasn't cut out for a bigger family. His was of a reserved nature. Gwen had been surprised a week beforehand when he had drawn her to him and told her that where she had once been pretty she was now beautiful. It had been a prelude to presenting her with a diamond necklace. This from the man who usually told her to buy herself whatever she wanted at

Christmas or for her birthday because he had no imagination when it came to gifts.

It was around eleven on a Saturday morning in June. The idyllic sort of June she remembered from that childhood garden, when her perfectly painted, rose-scented world existed under cloudless blue skies. For the first time in nearly a month Charles was home for the weekend. There was also an added treat in store. Her parents and Rowena, newly returned from a three-month vacation in New Zealand, were arriving in time for dinner and to spend the night. Gwen was kneeling by the rockery, hoping to get in another half hour of weeding before it was time to go and get ready for lunch. Charles would not appreciate her appearing at the dining room table in her old, faded blue cotton dress. Footsteps approached. She looked up, shading her eyes with her hand, to see a dark-haired man coming down the flagstone path towards her. Charles was so fair. She would sometimes laughingly tell him that her ideal man had always been tall, blond and handsome. Despite his characteristic reserve they did have their teasing interchanges. The unknown man stopped a few feet from her. Not as tall as Charles, nor as good-looking. As their eyes met it seemed important to make note of that distinction. He smiled at her, and the air was instantly charged with something she did not recognize.

'Hello.' His voice was deep. In keeping with eyes of so dark a brown they could have been black. 'So you're Gwen. Rowena insisted you and your husband wouldn't object to springing me on you as a surprise, in addition to an earlier-than-expected arrival. I'm not convinced your mother thought it a good idea.'

She came slowly to her feet, very much aware of her grubby hands, knowing she should say something welcoming . . . warm, light-hearted words. The fast beating of her heart prevented them.

'Rowena sent me out here to introduce myself. I'm her fiancé, John Garwood.'

'Oh, how lovely! What happy news!' The world steadied. The heady feeling of shimmering anticipation was explained. Subconsciously she had hoped for this revelation. Suspected . . . guessed. That had to be it. Over the years she had longed for Rowena to finally find love. Instead, her admired, restless sister drifted from one fleeting affair to the next. It had begun to seem as though she didn't want more than that, but along had come this man with the intent, dark gaze. Typical of Rowena to spring a surprise. It would have appealed to her mischievous side to send him out alone to break the news of their engagement, and John Garwood would love her for those flashes of insouciance. Love her with a fierce tenderness. His was a face capable of intense passion and . . . aching longing to have that desire fully returned. Gwen froze. What thoughts! Charles would be shocked. She could equally imagine Rowena's wry amusement. Hadn't she once laughingly exclaimed, 'Darling Gwen, for a married woman you do remain something of a repressed Victorian virgin.' She had resented her sister's comment at the time, but now Rowena had been blindingly proved true. Gwen had never in the giddiest moments of girlhood delight experienced such thoughts about Charles – even when in his arms.

'I've been looking forward to meeting you,' John Garwood said without inflection, as though he was thinking of something else. And yet . . . there was that smile warming his mouth. It was, she thought, a wonderful mouth, neither thin nor full-lipped. A lover's mouth. *Oh, God,* she begged, *I have to stop this or I'll end up like some nineteenth-century vicar's spinster writing obscene anonymous letters to respectable members of the parish.*

'I'm so happy for you both. You're very blessed to be marrying my sister and I'm sure she feels herself equally fortunate,' she heard herself say.

'Thank you.' He held the hand she extended for the briefest moment. Did he release it so quickly because he sensed the impact his touch had upon her, every nerve-ending exposed? She could feel her color rise. That he did see. The awareness was in his eyes. She hoped he blamed her confusion of feeling on embarrassment. 'Now your hand is grimy too.' She added in a rush, 'I should wear gloves when gardening, Charles is always telling me so, but I love the feel of the earth. It's so quietly alive.'

'Tranquility.' He stood looking down at his spread hands. She expected him to produce a handkerchief and wipe them off, then offer it to her, but he continued to stand motionless for several moments longer.

'It's what I look for in a garden,' she said, praying the sensation of being swept into a whirlpool would subside. 'Yes,' he said, upon raising those eyes to hers again. Quizzical now, above the strong nose and gently curving mouth. 'Green-shaded loveliness; Rowena told me I would find it here. Shall we be getting back to the house?'

She was afraid he would offer her his arm on the walk up the path. But he maintained sufficient space between them so that they did not once brush against each other, and he addressed his words ahead of them. Their eyes did not meet again. He was a civil engineer, had been working in New Zealand when he met Rowena in Auckland at the home of a mutual acquaintance. That had been two months ago, and they had returned to the States together when his contract ended the previous week.

Moments later they were in the room Charles had named the library, even though its shelves were filled with his personal memorabilia rather than books. Gwen embraced her sister, wishing her a lifetime of happiness, and admiring her truly exquisite engagement ring; the stunningly simple setting, the diamond like a great drop of rain water. Rowena's sultry lashed eyes went from Gwen to John Garwood as if seeking the answer to a question, one that shut out everyone else in the room. Something passed over her face and was gone, leaving her lovely mouth curving into a thoughtful smile. There was nothing Gwen could read in her future brother-in-law's face. It was closed to her. She recognized out of some feminine instinct that he wanted it so. He knew . . . He was a man to know that he had aroused in her a physical and emotional response that was terribly, wickedly wrong. How could he not regard her as tawdry? A disloyal sister and a shame to her husband. Humiliation flamed as she turned to her parents, not thinking clearly. She only vaguely noticed the look of strain beneath her mother's smile and that her father seemed to have aged.

Coming downstairs after making herself presentable, Gwen had a moment alone with her mother in the hall. Taking her hand, she asked, 'Are you and Daddy all right? You are happy about the engagement?'

'Very much so. John seems an extremely nice man. And by now Rowena should know what she wants.'

'And there's nothing else wrong?' The question was automatic. Gwen wished Charles would allow Sonny to join the family in the dining room, rather than eating in the kitchen with Mrs Broom the housekeeper. She had stressed that it was a special occasion, and her parents never wanted to miss a moment with their grandson, but he had remained adamant. Sonny could be included for afternoon tea, when it was to be hoped he wouldn't spill something or drop a plate.

'I've been a little concerned about your father.'

'Why, Mom?'

'My dear, I expect I'm worrying unnecessarily. It's just that he hasn't seemed himself recently, but maybe that shouldn't come as a surprise. I used to wonder if he'd have a difficult time entering retirement. He's always had so much energy and he's only fifty-five. Some friends warned me that their husbands went through a mild depression at first. Probably all he needs is an energetic vacation, somewhere rugged where I can't wear high heels and will be forced to eat yak.'

'The Himalayas?' Tears blurred Gwen's eyes. She yearned to confide, to press her face against that forever shoulder. 'Darling Mom, you continue to be such an inspiration.'

'I shall keep a diary about my selfless heroism and make a great deal of money publishing it. And your father will call me a shameless hussy.'

Gwen hesitated. 'That isn't the problem? I mean . . . Dad isn't worried about finances? Something gone wrong with your investments? Because if that's the case you know Charles and I will do anything we can to help.'

'Bless you, dearest, but no, nothing like that. Can you imagine your circumspect father gambling wildly on the stock exchange? We're talking about the man who wages an inner battle every time he's asked to buy a raffle ticket.'

Her mother's dulcet laughter drifted with them into the dining room, its long, oval walnut table set with Royal Worcester china, Georgian silver and crystal worthy of the bottle of excellent vintage champagne Charles held ready to uncork. Against a backdrop of watered silk walls and draperies, lunch began with vichyssoise, prepared and served by the irreplaceable Mrs Broom. Understandably Gwen's father stared at his bowl in perplexity after his first spoonful. In his world view soup was meant to be served hot. And if he said little during the course of the meal and had to be asked twice to pass the salt and pepper, that was also not surprising given the flow of conversation around him. He had always enjoyed sitting back and listening.

The voices rose and fell, fueled by an energy that seemed on the surface as light and effervescent as the champagne that continued to flow. But beneath the bubbling merriment, the laugher, quips and repartee of a celebratory occasion, lay something more troubling.

Initially Gwen assumed that this palpable undercurrent emanated only from within herself as she strove to speak neither too little nor too often to John Garwood.

But as the meal progressed through poached salmon, saffron rice and green salad to the finale of a crème caramel dessert, even her self-absorption could not prevent her noticing that Charles was too determinedly the perfect host, that Rowena's witticisms seemed a little fevered, that even her mother appeared overly eager to 'make the party go.' In the midst of this artificially elevated atmosphere her father's silences loomed, not as a rock against which to lean as in days gone by, but one that was slipping beneath the waters stirred by turbulence, presaging a storm that would reduce all their lives to wreckage.

What dark nonsense! Claptrap! That would have been Great-Aunt Harriet's word. But Gwen could not shake the belief that John Garwood (must not yet allow herself to think of him only by his first name) remained the one person in the room who had himself completely in hand. For the barest moment she allowed herself to look directly across the table at him. He was speaking to her father, waiting attentively for a response, and there was such a look of gentleness on his strong, dark face that she was overwhelmed by a wave of tenderness such as she had never experienced except for her child. Never, ever for Charles. To be physically attracted to a man other than her husband was bad enough, but to feel herself falling in love with this twice forbidden stranger was intolerable, corrupt.

To delude herself that he was not unknown . . . that in some incredible way his face, his voice were as belovedly familiar as waking to the morning sun, was weakness. The thought raced through her mind like a rat in a maze: *I must never see him again.* Such was her panic that the impossibility of such a resolve did not strike her. She would dedicate herself to being the perfect wife, offer to travel with Charles on some of his work trips. Equally important was that Rowena should never guess her sister's inward betrayal; nothing must be allowed to further dishonor that bond. Out of the past came a memory. Rowena touching her cheek and saying lightly, 'Sweet Gwen! The world is your very own private garden, so naturally you should get to pick the prize blooms.' Words to boost the self-confidence of the less visible younger sister, readily laughed aside. Untrue then and unquestionably so now. Gwen did not figure in John Garwood's thoughts beyond a willingness to welcome her as a sister-in-law. She had to, *must*, believe that to be the case with every ounce of strength she had. This infantile sense of their being destined to come together for each to be whole was a one-sided fantasy. The best scenario would be if Rowena and her bridegroom returned to live permanently in New Zealand.

The rest of the day passed at an agonizingly slow pace. Coffee in the living room. Sonny coming in afterwards to join them, circling his grandparents, eager to tell them a story about Mrs Broom's cat getting lost for a day and a half and being found shut up in the attic. The rest of those present were reduced to moving shadows on a faded screen, because only by shutting her mind could Gwen get through the hours until nightfall. Pressing on her was the need to talk to Rowena about the wedding, ask what was planned, demonstrate interest and enthusiasm while hoping against hope that she wouldn't be asked to be a bridesmaid. But on her first attempt her sister did not remain still long enough to say more than it was all up in the air. Much depended on how soon John would have to start his next job, likely not to be in Australia this time, but one never knew. His company had a way of changing its mind; he was a pawn really, not a knight or a king.

Half an hour later, Gwen tried again. 'Tell me at least, will it be a church wedding?'

Rowena took a moment to turn her head. 'Are those tears in your eyes? Such a sentimental little darling! Didn't I always try to discourage you from reading Dickens? He's so incorrigibly weepy. No, I think John and I will skip the church. Can't you just hear Great-Aunt Harriet pounding on the floor with her stick while proclaiming on the unsuitability of my gliding down the aisle in white? And I suppose it would be a trifle unseemly. No,' squeeze of the hand, 'you wouldn't think that way. Unlike me, you never did have unkind thoughts. Sorry, must away. Mom's beckoning. She really shouldn't worry so much about Dad. Look at him laughing now with Sonny. You and I will get together in the next few weeks and talk trousseau to your heart's delight. For now why don't you go and pound out something bridal on the piano? Perhaps that holy-minded thing you and Charles had at your wedding? Handel, wasn't it? I'm sure John would love to hear you play. He can be frightfully high-brow himself. It adds to his inescapable appeal.'

The last thing Gwen wanted was to make herself the centerpiece
of the afternoon but Charles, having overheard the suggestion,
urged her to play. When she said she'd just as soon not, he'd
whispered irritably that the piano wasn't there taking up half the
room on the basis of its ornamental value. She didn't want John
Garwood thinking she considered herself a brilliant pianist, and
was relieved when Sonny came to join her on the bench, but
Charles ordered him back to the sofa. Her heart sank. And yet,
that afternoon the piano was waiting for her as it had never done
before. She sat, eyes closed, hands feeling for the keys, as if they
were fingers known only to her, longing for her touch, responsive
to her every half-formed thought, taking her to a place deep
inside the music. Not Handel, the choice for her wedding. Chopin,
transitioning into Mendelssohn, then Mozart. Their music, theirs
alone. All else, all others, left behind. For he, John Garwood, was
there with her. She knew with absolute certainty that he had
followed her into this momentary heaven. She could feel his heart
beating in tune with her own.

Then a disturbance, dragging her upward to the surface: something
heavy falling, the sound echoing until it became a pounding like
fists on a door. And somewhere a dog was barking distantly. Still
she could not get her eyes to open. She was fuzzily aware of having
slumped forward, pushing the piano bench backward; also that the
commotion had been caused by Sonny having elbowed a vase, and
in the process of trying to straighten it, had knocked over the table
on which it stood. She had to go to him, tell him that it didn't
matter, that she loved him . . . would always . . . Suddenly, startlingly,
she was awake. That living room of nearly fifty years ago, and those
gathered within it, gone. She was seated back in the book room on
Ridge Farm Rise, her neck stiff and cramped from being tilted at
an awkward angle. Someone was banging on the door with increasing
urgency.

'Who, what . . . ?' She ran the short distance to the hall, Jumbo
moving aside to allow her clearage. Her hands fumbled with the
front door knob as panic squeezed her heart with a tight fist.

'Gwen . . . Gwen!' an outdoor voice called.

Moments passing . . . passing . . . and then the face of Madge
Baldwin staring wild-eyed at her from the doorstep. 'Oh, I thought
you'd never come. I've been banging for five minutes. It's Charles.'

'Tell me!' The words clawed their way up her throat.

'He's taken the car. When I drove it into the garage he came out through the mud room. He asked for the keys and when I said no, he grabbed them from me and there was nothing I could do to stop him. Please don't look like that! Maybe it will be all right – he got the engine started without any problem. I know it would have been better if he hadn't, that would have bought time, but he wasn't weaving as he went down the road. At least the rain has stopped. Let's think positive, Gwen.'

'The police.'

'You think you should phone them?'

'I have to think. I don't want him frightened, but I can't stand by and wait for him to cause an accident. Listen! There's a car coming. Oh, please, God, let it be him!' While Madge remained rooted to the step, Gwen hurried distractedly down the path to stand peering up and down the road. A car that was not hers drew up alongside the curb. The driver's-side window slid down and a man's head appeared.

'Problem? Struck me you look panicky?' It was a rumbling English voice, somehow the more reassuring because it was bluntly matter of fact. 'Need help?'

Gwen drew her first full breath since waking up. 'It's my son,' she said steadily. 'Charles Norris. He shouldn't be driving and he's taken the car.' And then she heard herself add with the irrelevance of such moments: 'He was named after his father. To family and friends he's always been Sonny.'

Three

Nine-year-old Oliver Cully woke at 5 a.m., two hours earlier than usual on Saturday morning to a pale, clear sky. The sun was already up, but who cared about seeing the sun today? He knew it was wrong to think that way when God had put it in the sky, but his heart had hardened towards the Almighty over the past few days and he had already gone off Him some since Grandpa got sick. Oliver usually got up at seven. On school days this allowed him plenty of time to be ready for the bus that arrived at 8.15 a.m. On ordinary, happy weekends he wasn't about to waste precious minutes lying in bed. Even so, five would normally have been a bit too early for a Saturday. But today was to be anything but ordinary.

This morning was the last he'd spend in this house with Grandpa, the person he loved best in this world. Two people he'd never met were coming to take him to live with them. He knew of them as Uncle Gerard and Aunt Elizabeth. Grandpa had always referred to them that way, although not often because all he really knew of them was that Gerard had been Oliver's father's older brother and that he and Elizabeth lived in New York City.

The furniture in Oliver's bedroom was old, but his bed was painted red and the side tables, dresser and chest a dark blue. It had been that way since he was six. Grandpa had let him pick the colors and the curtains and comforter with cowboys on them. They had done the painting together. And Grandpa had let him use the big brush half the time. On top of the chest were several photos of Oliver's Mom and Dad, one with them holding him as a baby and another when he was two and holding his teddy bear. Oliver still took it under the covers at night. He never fell asleep without saying goodnight to Mom and Dad's smiling faces. But, Grandpa explained, they would be right there anyway while he slept. Those photos and Teddy were now in one of the cases he would take with him that morning.

Oliver dangled a leg before climbing disconsolately out of bed. How could you be expected to like people who'd never bothered about you ever before, apart from very occasionally sending a letter? Hah! He'd overheard Twyla saying to Grandpa when one came last year that it sounded so much like those mass mailings she was surprised it didn't start out: 'Dear Distant Friends.' Twyla had lived with them for nearly two years now. She was Grandpa's nurse. Why couldn't he stay with her? He loved Twyla. Not as much as Grandpa, of course, but a lot. Those other two were only taking him to their place because Grandpa had to go into a nursing home. It was called Pleasant Meadows, which sounded to Oliver a silly name, because how could there be anything pleasant about it? People went to nursing homes to wait to die. He was glad he'd given God a piece of his mind last night.

There was only one small, good thing about the future. Those two strangers wouldn't be taking him miles and miles away to New York immediately; that wouldn't happen until the fall. For now he would only be dragged as far as Sea Glass, which as Twyla kept saying was only down the road. He would be able to go and see Grandpa often before the big move. That's if Gerard and Elizabeth would drive him to Pleasant Meadows, Oliver thought darkly. He would never even think of them as Aunt and Uncle, unless they asked him not to call them that and he could have his secret revenge. After Grandpa wrote to them last week to explain the situation, Gerard had telephoned to say that he and Elizabeth had decided to spend the summer in Sea Glass at an old house that had been in the Cully family for a long time. Something about a break-in and feeling they should be there to prevent others from getting the same idea.

Stupid, when they'd be leaving again at the end of summer; that's what Oliver's best friend Brian Armitage had said. And stupid for Gerard and Elizabeth to come for him before summer vacation started, which wouldn't be for almost four more weeks. Even though Grandpa needed to go into the nursing home before then, Oliver could have stayed on at home with Twyla until school was out. Why were they so keen to take him right now? Brian said he had overheard his parents, Mandy and Reggie Armitage, talking and they thought the only reason could be that Gerard and Elizabeth wanted to immediately get their hands on the social security benefit checks Oliver received once a month because he was an orphan. That would make them very greedy because they were already very rich. Oliver thought Mr and Mrs Armitage were pretty darn smart.

He wasn't sure how he knew Gerard and Elizabeth had lots of money; it was just one of those things he'd grown up knowing. His parents had only had the money Dad earned working at the Ferry Landing Bank. Brian said rich people always wanted to grab at every last penny even if they risked breaking their necks to get at it. That piece of wisdom hadn't come from his parents but from his Aunt Nellie. She was actually his great-great-aunt and ninety years old. Brian was sure she would one day get into the Guinness Book of World Records for living longer than anyone had ever done. He was very proud of her because she still had her whole mind, even if none of her teeth. He also liked her because she said a lot of interesting things. 'Actually' was currently Oliver's most frequently tossed-in word; the previous one had been 'positively.'

Grandpa said words were something to hold in your hands like rainbow-colored drops of rain. One he and Oliver used to like to say together was 'ventriloquism.' Just on its own, because it tried so hard to catch on your tongue. Twyla liked words too. That was one of the things that made it seem like she'd always been meant to be with them. 'They're like people,' was her take on words. 'Choose carefully what ones you want to make your friends.'

Oliver trudged to the bathroom in the manner of a French aristocrat approaching the guillotine. He and Grandpa had watched a black and white film called *A Tale of Two Cities*. It had been very sad, but in a good sort of way because the hero had been very brave while waiting for his head to be sliced off, saying it was the best thing he'd ever done; only he said it in a poem sort of way that Grandpa already knew by heart. Oliver, brushing his teeth with his head bowed over the basin, was far from nobly resigned to believing that going to live with Gerard and Elizabeth was the best thing. But the thought flickered pathetically that there was still a reason to be a hero, because to act miserable would worry Grandpa.

'OK,' he told his round-cheeked, sandy-haired reflection in the mirror haughtily, 'I already know that, but if they decide they don't like me and say I'll have to live with Twyla, or even Brian's parents, I don't think Grandpa would mind a bit. He's only sending me to them because Gerard was Dad's brother and he thinks it's the right thing to do. How can I get out of living with them without behaving in a way that would upset Grandpa?' That would take consultation with Brian, who had already expressed a wish to blast Gerard and Elizabeth to Mars or Venus, whichever was the farthest away. What Brian wasn't as keen on was visiting the Cully Mansion because it looked real creepy from the outside. His Aunt Nellie, who lived quite close to it, had made him take a look and he was sure he'd seen a ghost glide past one of the top windows.

Returning to his bedroom, Oliver slowly got himself dressed in his almost new jeans and the green cotton sweater Twyla had given him for Christmas. On any other morning he would have dragged on his clothes so he could race down to breakfast.

Grandpa believed that getting ready for the day included sitting down to a proper breakfast at the kitchen table. He said breakfast was the most important meal of the day. Bacon or sausage and eggs, juice and toast or English muffins with strawberry or raspberry jam.

Never grape jelly. Oliver thought grape jelly was yuck. Grandpa said Oliver's mother hadn't liked it either, so Granny Olive had stopped making it. She had died a couple of years after his parents were killed in that plane crash. He only remembered that he'd loved her and felt safe when she held him. The narrow two-story house in Ferry Landing could have been a sad, empty place. But Grandpa hadn't let that happen when Granny Olive died. He hadn't let it happen even after getting the diagnosis from his doctor that explained what Grandpa called the 'trembles.'

He had continued to manage fairly well for a while, and Oliver had done his best to help out. Grandpa had told him he was the best potato peeler ever, and that was saying something because Granny Olive had been something to see with a paring knife. Twyla believed boys should know how to cook and not go thinking it was a girl's job. It had been a great day when Twyla arrived. She'd said straight off that she didn't mind a bit doing the cleaning and cooking the meals as well as being Grandpa's nurse. Twyla was black. Oliver had never met a black person before. She said if people wanted to call her African American that was OK too; it made not a speck of difference to her. It was what was in people's hearts that counted. 'Don't you go letting anyone decide who you are,' she'd told Oliver when he'd let on about being bullied by two boys at school. 'Seems to me, lamb baby, those children don't know the Golden Rule.'

Oliver went to church with Twyla now that Grandpa couldn't take him. It wasn't the same sort of church she'd gone to in Virginia, she told Oliver, but going to St Michael's was just dandy with her. If God made the rounds every Sunday, she could go somewhere else for a change and be secure in His being there in one of the pews, not minding the slightest who had on their Sunday best and who didn't. Oliver thought now, God sure hasn't been sitting next to me. Then he felt disloyal to Twyla, like he didn't believe her. And he did; at least he thought he did.

His spirits sank even lower as he stripped the sheets and pillow cases from his bed so Twyla wouldn't have to do it. He wondered if she would make blueberry pancakes or waffles for breakfast because they were among his very best favorites. He was sure he wouldn't feel like eating anything, but he would have to try, to please her and Grandpa. Sometimes Grandpa wasn't able to get out of bed and onto the StairMaster to join them at the kitchen table for breakfast, even with Twyla's help. But as often as he could he managed to be there in his wheelchair. Grandpa had claimed to be very excited when the StairMaster was installed, saying it was going to be so much fun whizzing up and down on it and that he was going to charge Oliver a quarter a ride. Actually it went very slowly, but Twyla made a joke about wishing there was room for one on the other side so they could have races.

Oliver knew Grandpa would get down for breakfast that morning if he possibly could. It hurt to hear him trying to say the blessing clearly and to see how badly his hands shook as he tried to get the food into his mouth and sip a drink through a straw without Twyla helping him. Grandpa's *trembles* were really called Parkinson's. Twyla said Parkinson's wasn't something children got and one day there would be a cure, but Oliver didn't care about what might happen *one day*.

All those prayers every night before falling asleep that Grandpa would get well; instead he'd only got worse. Hah! Twyla said the pastor at the church she'd gone to in Virginia had talked very loud to God. Not in an impolite way, but because praising the Lord made him jump up and down and shout out for joy fit to take off the roof. Or did he do it, Oliver wondered as he tied his sneakers, to make sure God would hear him over all the thousands, millions of people around the world trying to get his attention all at the same time? And then there were those bands of angels up in heaven adding to the noise. Oliver always pictured rock bands, with guitars and drums in addition to the harps and big, big singing voices. But maybe not rappers. Somehow Oliver just couldn't imagine God sitting on clouds listening to rap. It had to be OK for Twyla's pastor to get excited when praying, but Oliver knew the rules for children were often different from the ones for adults. He prayed quietly so there was no chance of his sounding rude. But maybe he had still gone wrong somehow and that was why God hadn't answered. Surely getting rid of Grandpa's Parkinson's should be a snap compared to making the entire world in less than a week.

Grandpa must have known for a long time now that he would have to go into a nursing home. It was obvious he needed more than Twyla could single-handedly provide. There had been that frightening time when he had gotten out of bed while she was on the phone and his legs had locked in the hallway as he tried to get to the bathroom. He'd fallen before she could get to him.

'Impatient old fool!' Grandpa had said quite clearly from the floor. Twyla had phoned for assistance, and two nice medics had arrived to get Grandpa back to bed. One of them gave Oliver a sucker. Grandpa had said with a wink: 'I'm the sucker.' Oliver had tried to smile back to show he thought it a good joke, but it had hit him like a punch in the face that one day in the future – perhaps very soon – the vehicle that pulled into the driveway would be an ambulance and Grandpa would be taken out to it on a stretcher never to return.

'It's a cruel thing being forced to depend for your every, most personal need, on others,' Twyla had said to Oliver with her arm around him after the medics left. 'But your grandpa, he's a man of faith. He knows the good Lord will watch over you both like he's always done. I sure understand you not putting much store by that right this minute,' Twyla always seemed to know what he was thinking, 'but you will some day. For now just take a hold of every living moment that you and that good man are together in this house.'

From that day onward the words 'nursing home' had hovered, mostly silently, even over the happiest times. At the end of school yesterday Oliver's teacher had asked if he would be in class on Monday, and he'd told her that someone, he couldn't bring himself to say his aunt or uncle, would drive him in.

He wondered as he looked toward the full-length mirror if they would take one look at him and decide he was fat. The bullies he told Twyla about had called him 'Fatty,' among other names. Afterwards he'd tried to be honest, but had never been sure of the answer. The blue-green eyes looking back at him would display optimism one moment and pessimism the next. His cheeks were definitely round. Pudgy. There was no escaping that truth. Twyla said his face was fine, better than fine, and that there was nothing wrong with the rest of him either. He was big boned – that's all there was to it. What was so great about being a stick anyhow? 'You go right on doing like your grandpa tells you. Eating three good meals a day and when it comes to snacks make them healthy. I've yet to see you filling up on junk or not getting enough exercise. So you come right here, Mr Handsome, and give me a hug.' Oliver had never known Twyla to tell a lie, but then she loved him, and people who love you always see the best. Gerard and Elizabeth didn't love him.

The mirror had belonged to his mother, Clare. And after today she was going to seem very far away, not close by the way Grandpa always talked. Gerard and Elizabeth couldn't have loved Mom if they'd never bothered about him until now, when they'd got stuck and couldn't wiggle out. Gerard had phoned last night to say they were at the Cully Mansion. Brian was right; the name did sound spooky. They would come to collect Oliver at nine in the morning. Grandpa said it didn't have to be that early, but the time wasn't changed. Probably, thought Oliver nastily, picking him up for Those Two would be like going to the dentist: best to get it over quickly so they didn't have to keep thinking about it.

Brian had offered the information that his Aunt Nellie, who at ninety had to know pretty much everything, thought Gerard and Elizabeth were a disgrace to the Cully name. If it were up to her the old lady that used to live there would come back to haunt them. This, Brian had added solemnly, explained the shadow he'd seen at the window that he was sure was a ghost. Oliver had thought it would be super great if Gerard and Elizabeth were driven screaming all the way back to New York, but was scared the old lady spook would be so much on Oliver's side that she wouldn't leave him alone, even in the bathroom. And, as Twyla had agreed with him, a boy of nine liked his privacy. There was no doubt about it: God had let him down real bad.

The conversation with Brian had taken place in the playground during recess and, after a quick look around, Oliver had lowered his voice. 'If it weren't for letting Grandpa and Twyla down, I'd become an atheist.'

'Seriously, Ol? How do you spell it?'

'Don't know.'

'Then that's out. You can't be something that you can't spell.'

Secretly relieved, Oliver said that in that case maybe he'd become a Mason. He didn't know what a Mason was, except that its members had a secret handshake, which sounded satisfactorily sinister.

'Good.' Brian had brightened. 'My Dad's one of those!'

Oliver now noticed that the two suitcases Twyla had helped him pack weren't on the bench under the window. She must have taken them down after he fell asleep, not wanting him to see them first thing when he woke up. This was really happening. He looked at the empty space on the top of the chest of drawers where the photos had been. That's how he felt – empty. He shut his eyes tight. If only Mom and Dad could show up right now. He wouldn't be scared of their ghosts – or if he could just hear their voices telling him what to do. And suddenly he did, not out loud, but in his heart.

'We love you so much, Oliver. And you're not fat.'

He answered in a whisper even though he was alone, because this was such a private conversation, 'I love you guys, too. Say hi to Grandma Olive and my other grandparents.' He always thought it polite to mention Dad's parents even though they'd never seen him because they hadn't wanted to. It wasn't Grandpa who'd told him that. Again, it was something Oliver seemed to have always known.

Tears filled his eyes but he brushed them away and went out to the hallway, then down into the living room. Empty. He couldn't hear Twyla moving about in her bedroom or Grandpa's either. He'd told them last night he might go for a bike ride if he got up real early. A blue Chevy was coming down the road as he went out the front door. It stopped at the bottom of the drive and Mr Hodgkins who lived down the road stuck his head out the car window. He worked nights at the airport and was just coming home, Oliver knew.

'How you doing, young man?'

'OK, Mr Hodgkins.'

'I guess this is the day then?'

'Right.'

'We'll miss you and your grandpa. 'I'll be down to see him at Pleasant Meadows, and don't you be a stranger. You let us know when you're coming in, and Mary' – Mary was Mr Hodgkins' wife – 'will bake those brownies you and Brian like so much.'

'Thanks.' When the car drove off Oliver got his bike out of the shed and pedaled around the corner. He slowed for a goodbye look at the Armitage's house. As he was about to ride on, the front door opened and Brian came out, his dark hair sticking up from not being brushed. He was wearing a Boston Red Sox sweatshirt that he must have dragged on in a hurry, because it looked like it had been bought when he was six. His glasses were higher on one side than the other.

'I've been watching for you,' he said as he came down the step.

'Hey, dude.' Oliver leaned on his handlebars.

'Dad said last night he'd bet his next meal you'd go for a ride round this morning. He said that's what he'd do in your place. We've got Aunt Nellie staying over. She couldn't believe you're going to your aunt and uncle.'

'Let's not talk about them.'

'Right.' Brian collected his bike from the side of the house and pedaled alongside Oliver around the next corner onto the stretch of road that went past the grade school. 'Aunt Nellie said she was just talking to a new neighbor about you yesterday, like how you and me are friends and all that.'

'Why would her neighbor care?' Oliver hunched a shoulder.

'Probably didn't. Aunt Nellie thinks you and your grandpa and Twyla are great and she doesn't like . . . those two people. Sorry – forgot.'

Oliver rode faster. He wasn't mad with Brian. He wanted to go so fast that the thought of Gerard and Elizabeth couldn't catch up with him. He wasn't just sad, he was scared – scared worse than he would have been going alone into a big dark cave. Before Grandpa got sick the future had always been friendly. Even afterward, up until the last week, it had seemed sort of fuzzy. They passed Bigg's Furniture Store and Kayak Rentals and then drew to a standstill at the cemetery entrance. At the front were the older gravestones, some of them dating back a hundred and fifty years. Mom and Dad were farther back, close to the path. Grandpa had chosen that place because it was shaded in summer by a giant oak tree.

'Want to go in?'

'Came with Twyla yesterday. We brought yellow roses that she got at The Flower Box. Mom carried those on their wedding day.'

'It's not like you're really going today. You'll be in school on Monday. Maybe Twyla will take you to see your grandpa at Pleasant Meadows when we get out of class.' In contrast to yesterday's crying bout, Brian seemed determined to look on the bright side.

Oliver gripped his handlebars tighter. 'If they don't make me go straight back with them.'

Having listened to Aunt Nellie and his parents talking last night Brian had decided they sounded as bad as the aunt and uncle in *Harry Potter*, but again he made a big effort to sound hopeful. 'Guess what?'

'What?'

'Mom and Dad said they'll take me over to Aunt Nellie's as often as I like when school's out, and we can hang out there, and p'raps they'll let me come out to the Cully Mansion. I think it'd be cool if we saw old Emily's ghost, but maybe,' his voice perked up, 'they won't think having her there so great. And they'll decide to clear out and go back to New York.'

'I thought of that, but it's stupid. They'd take me with them and then I'd never see Grandpa or Twyla.'

'Not if they've decided they don't like you. Remember we talked about you making sure they don't.' The words hung in the air.

'Right.' Oliver was staring off into the distance at the big oak.

'Worth a try, don't you think? You could do it by pretending to be nice, or at least reasonable.'

'How?'

'Tell them you're really into sports. They'll get sick of you real quick if they have to spend half their time running you to baseball or swimming. And if that doesn't do it you can say you want to take piano lessons.'

'Actually, I would like to learn. Thanks, bro.'

'And if that doesn't work something else'll happen. Aunt Nellie says it always does if you trust your spirit guides. She goes to that church at Dobbs Mill. Dad says it's no nuttier than any other church.'

Oliver was no longer listening. His ears had choked up along with the rest of him. It was time to turn back. After parting from Brian, he rode slowly up his own drive, returned the bike to the shed and went back into the house, through the still-empty living room up the stairs. Back in his bedroom, he lay down on the bed to think. He didn't get far. Within a moment his eyes closed and he dozed, waking with a start half an hour later. Jumping up he hurried down the hallway.

From the top of the stairs he could now see Grandpa in the wheelchair wearing his plaid bathrobe, with his gray hair combed flat to his head. If he couldn't get dressed in real clothes, it was all the more important that his hair didn't stick up the way it always wanted to do. Twyla was sitting across from him on the sofa. Her dark hair was speckled with silver and buzz cut so it sculpted to her head. Brian's mother, Mandy Armitage, had said she didn't know any other woman who could wear her hair that short and look great. It required a perfectly shaped head. If she tried it, she'd joked, she'd have looked like a light bulb. Twyla was tall and rangy. She didn't look cozy, but she was. From above Oliver saw her get up and cross to the wheelchair to lean down and kiss Grandpa's cheek. He'd been a big man once, filling out his plaid flannel shirts, but he'd shrunk.

'It's going to all work out just fine, Frank.' Twyla had a voice like warm molasses. 'It's a good place, Pleasant Meadows, and I'll be over to see you most days.'

'You're . . . one in a . . . million; my Olive would have . . . thought same.' The words came out as if squeezed exhaustingly through a straw. 'But isn't . . . me . . . worried about.'

'I know. I know. It's that dear boy. Nothing would make me more joyful than taking guardianship of him.'

'That's what we'd want, Oliver and me both, but Gerard is his next of kin,' Grandpa kept going, 'and gave me to understand he'd go to court to get him if I'd other plans. Don't understand what's brought this on.'

'Has me pondering too, Frank. Trouble is he's in the bird seat. Not only am I no relation to Oliver, I'm sixty-six, and while I'm fit as a flea right this minute a judge could hold my age against me. Maybe rightly so. Should something happen to me, Oliver could be at the mercy of the State. Least with them there's two. And whatever's done and gone, they're family, and people can change if they want to good and hard enough.'

'Could . . . be they've . . . held back for . . . fear,' Grandpa had to wait to get out the rest, '. . . that I've talked against . . . them.'

'Maybe. They don't know you.'

Oliver had been brought up not to listen in on other people's conversation. But he couldn't move. He leaned against the top banister, gripping the knob in his hands. He could see his suitcases by the front door. Grandpa had told him that Granny Olive hadn't been into decorating schemes. They'd bought what they could afford and not given it much more thought. But Oliver loved everything about that room from the tweedy brown sofa and armchairs with their orange and green Afghans to the fall landscape picture above the pot-bellied stove. Most of all he loved the photos on the bookcase. Especially the ones of his parents, different from those that had been on his chest of drawers, but with the same smiling faces. Mom, so pretty with her curly red hair and the same blue-green eyes as his own. Dad, dark and handsome. Best of all, they looked kind. Oliver squeezed his eyes shut. He had to remember that room exactly as it had always been.

'Let's pray the aunt and uncle will do right by your boy,' said Twyla in a soft, crooning voice as she continued to stand by the wheelchair with her hand on Grandpa's shoulder. 'Can't help but grow to love him. Born with a heart of gold was Oliver. So they told you way back that they weren't geared to children, but life changes people. Could be that with the Lord's grace they'll come to see him as a gift.'

'He's been my blessing. Couldn't have gotten over losing Clare and . . . and Max . . . came to love him like a son . . . then Olive . . . without him. Had Clare later in life than most couples back then. Grandpa's voice had strengthened, evened out. It happened that way sometimes, making him sound almost like his old self. 'We wanted children right off the bat . . . didn't happen and then we got to adopt her. Best thing . . . best daughter. Oliver cut from same cloth. Never believe that business about blood being thicker than water, Twyla.'

And yet in the present situation it had to be. The day ahead had to be faced. Silence, one that stretched like a fitted sheet on a bed. Oliver knew the grown-ups were deep in thought. He had always known that his mother was adopted. It had made her seem even more special. Out of all the families wanting a baby, God had chosen Grandpa and Granny Olive to be her parents. He was glad now that he'd decided not to become an atheist; it could have been a close thing if he'd known how to spell it. Not that atheists couldn't be really nice people – Brian's dad was great. Oliver just wasn't brave enough to go it alone.

'Oliver surely is dear to me as if he was my own.' Twyla broke the silence. 'Some days I feel like I'm about to spill over with love just looking at his face. So you take heart, Frank; I'll see every bit as much of him as his aunt and uncle will let happen.' She paused. 'I wonder if they'll tell him about the house.'

'Been thinking about that myself. Somehow don't think so; best maybe if he doesn't find out. No . . . need to load up on young shoulders.'

Were they talking about the Cully Mansion being haunted?

They could have heard that rumor from Brian's parents, passed on to them by Grantie Nellie, as Brian called her. But now Grandpa was talking about his parents' wills.

'Made 'em before . . . going on that trip. Told us they'd left guardianship to Olive and me. Could've been Gerard took offence to that.'

'Maybe, but surely in light of the estrangement . . .'

Grandpa and Twyla looked up and saw Oliver standing at the top of the stairs. He started down feeling at once very young and quite old. 'I am going to try to like them.' He didn't stretch his smile too big, because then they wouldn't have believed it. 'P'raps they'll bring me to see you real often Grandpa, and let Twyla come and stay at the house. Maybe even Brian too.'

'That's my boy,' said Grandpa.

Oliver ran to kneel down beside the wheelchair and lay his face against the knee beneath the plaid dressing gown. He didn't have to see Twyla's face to know that she was also trying not to cry. He felt the trembling hand upon his sandy hair.

'Remember what you said, Grandpa, about Mom and Dad and Granny Olive never being far away because heaven isn't some place miles up in the sky, but so near we can touch it? Well, then, you being in the nursing home and me in Sea Glass is going to work out just fine. Probably you'll get so sick of seeing me come through the door you'll hide under the blankets.'

'Won't.' A weak echo of Grandpa's old chuckle. 'Be getting my squirt gun out from under the pillow.'

'If anyone's not nice to you at the nursing home I'll give them one in the eye with it.'

'Heard place is better than a spa. Get your own monogr . . .'

'Monogrammed?'

Grandpa nodded. 'Toothbrush.' He was tiring quickly.

'Breakfast.' Twyla whisked through the archway into the kitchen. 'Blueberry pancakes or waffles?'

'Mind if I go and help?' Oliver said, not only because of the closing eyes, but to make it sound more like an ordinary day.

'Love you, boy.'

Twyla was standing with her back to the sink with her head bent, but she looked up the instant Oliver came into the kitchen and held out her arms. They closed around him. He was glad she was tall and bony. She was like a tree, strong and sheltering. 'You did good in there, lamb baby,' she whispered. 'Came back to me that saying about when things get tough . . .'

'I know,' Oliver whispered back, 'the tough get going.'

'What I prefer to say,' she stroked his hair, 'is the tough keep growing.'

'I'll remember.' His voice cracked, but the smile he gave her was real.

She responded in true Twyla fashion. 'Not that neither of us are likely to grow a hair's breadth if we don't get to that breakfast.'

Out came the frying pan, mixing bowl and whisk. Oliver got the bacon, butter and eggs, remembered the blueberries and returned to the refrigerator for them. While Twyla cooked he laid the table.

'I'll wheel in Grandpa,' he said when she was almost ready to dish up. A moment later he came back alone. 'He's asleep.'

Her amber-brown eyes met his. 'Is it important to you that I wake him?'

He returned that look unflinchingly. 'I want him to sleep. Actually I hope he stays that way till after they come for me. We just said goodbye, didn't we?'

'You did, lamb baby, you and that dear man both. Shall I get him upstairs now, while you eat your breakfast?'

'Yes.' Oliver knew she understood why he turned away to pick up his plate and take it to the stove.

The blueberry pancakes smelled wonderful, but he knew, as he lifted one with the spatula, that after today it would be a long time, if ever, before he wanted to eat them again. The bacon he just couldn't face – he left it in the pan. He could hear the sound of the wheelchair being pushed across the living room and then the murmur of Twyla's voice as she got Grandpa onto the StairMaster. He wished he had a dog to stroke. Grandpa had promised to get him one just before the Parkinson's came on. A cat would be nice too. Brian said cats were better than dogs. They'd had one of their friendly arguments about it. Oliver knew what he was doing. He was stuffing up his head with thoughts so he wouldn't break down.

He got the pancake down with the help of a glass of water, then he slowly washed and dried his dishes, put them away in the cupboard and wiped off the table. The kitchen clock said almost eight o'clock. He almost wished now that the time would go faster. The book he had been reading was in his suitcase, but he doubted he could have taken in one word out of three. A comforting thought came: he would go and sit in Grandpa's chair, the one that used to be his before the wheelchair. It was just like the one Oliver always sat in. But they'd never switched. Grandpa had said that the Anderson men were creatures of habit. Oliver Anderson Cully . . . it was a good name. He had barely sat down when he felt his eyes closing. It had already been a long day and Twyla said sleep was nature's medicine. He wasn't sure that he was really asleep; his thoughts continued to float like clouds whose shapes he kept trying to figure out. And suddenly he heard Twyla coming downstairs. It usually took her an hour to get Grandpa to the bathroom and then into bed, but it couldn't have been that long this time.

'Almost nine, lamb baby.' Before he could answer the doorbell rang and she crossed the room to open up.

They were here. Gerald and Elizabeth were stepping inside. Oliver had pictured them in his mind so often during the past few days as a pair of eagles swooping in to grab their prey, so it was a surprise to see two ordinary people. Gerard did have a beaky nose and flat black hair and Elizabeth's lipstick looked sort of smeary, like she'd put it on without looking. She had lots of untidy hair, sort of blond with dark roots. That was a surprise; somehow he'd thought she'd have it done every day. It didn't look like she ever combed it. This might have made him more hopeful about her, because it made her seem more real, if her smile hadn't looked as though she'd been practicing it for days. Maybe she was scared? But why should she be? He was a kid. And Twyla wouldn't have scared anyone. She had introduced herself pleasantly.

Elizabeth looked nervously around as if expecting someone else to leap out at her. 'Hello, Oliver. We've been counting the days till we could come for you. Isn't that right, Gerard?' That sounded rehearsed.

'Going to have lots of good times.' Gerard wasn't good at faking enthusiasm; his dull stare made it clear he wanted to open the door and run back out.

'Hi,' Oliver mumbled, frozen in place.

Gerard stood, arms pressed to his sides. If he'd been anyone else Oliver would have felt sorry for Elizabeth. Her face was all flushed. She extended a hand to Twyla. No nail polish; that was a surprise.

'You must have been a lifesaver during this difficult time. I always think nurses are wonderful. You have to be cut out for it . . . I just wouldn't have it in me. Anyway, we want to thank you for all you've done for poor Mr Andrews.' She looked at Gerard, who nodded. She continued in a shaky sort of voice while staring at the picture of a red barn over the fireplace. 'I do hope we're on time. You're probably anxious to get going on what comes next for you . . . Nurse.'

'No rush. We're all ready for you. Would you like to sit down?' Twyla beckoned them forward, a gesture they ignored; they stayed right where they were, close to the door. Twyla's smile was her usual nice one. 'Frank won't be leaving until this afternoon. He's asked me to stay on here, till he decides what to do about the house.'

'What a good idea; I'm so sorry I can't remember your name from the letter he wrote us.'

'Washburn. But please, make it Twyla.'

'Thank you.' Elizabeth took a step forward as if released by the press of a button. 'Gerard and I,' tugging on his arm, 'fully understand that Mr Andrews wants you and Oliver to see each other while he's readjusting. If only we weren't faced with settling into this monstrosity of a house. It's in such a state we don't know where to begin. That's what has us both so nervy. This should all be about our finally doing right by Oliver.' His stare deflected her glance.

'If it would be easier if I could come to you.' Twyla put her hand on Oliver's shoulder.

Elizabeth fiddled with her watch strap, her eyes uncertain. 'At the moment it's so depressing.' She tucked her hand through her husband's arm, bringing it up in line with hers. 'Such a change from our light-filled condo in New York, but we'll work on making it homelike, won't we, Ger?'

'Should only take a century or two.' Gerard's dark hair was the only resemblance Oliver could see to the photos of his father. But Dad hadn't been going thin on top. Gerard's smile was also thin. 'Where is the old guy?' He now sealed his fate with Oliver. 'Thought he'd be parked at the ready to run us through the mill.' Oliver made no allowances for this poor attempt at a joke being the result of nerves.

He looked his uncle up and down out of narrowed eyes and

was rewarded with a gift he couldn't wait to tell Brian about so they could laugh their heads off. To think he hadn't noticed till now. 'Your fly's undone,' he said with relish.

'Oops!' Gerard went a bright red, looked down and dragged at his zipper, which didn't budge until the third desperate tug.

'I thought it only kind to tell you,' said Oliver with every appearance of owlish sincerity, and then saw that Twyla was looking worriedly at Elizabeth.

'You don't look good, better sit down.' She helped the other woman into a chair and pressed a hand to the back of her neck. 'Keep your head down for a few moments while I get you some brandy.' She was gone and back within seconds with a filled glass.

'I'm so sorry, what a fool to make of myself!' Elizabeth laughed shakily after taking a few sips. 'The room just started to spin!'

Gerard took the chair beside hers and reached for her hand. Suddenly he looked almost human and his voice carried its own tremor. 'We've both worked ourselves up into a state about today. No idea what to say, or how to say it; felt sure we'd come off sounding like Victorian melodrama villains and haven't we just!' He had been talking into the space between Twyla and Oliver, but as if by a great force of will he now looked his nephew in the eyes. 'Facing you is the hardest thing I've ever had to do. I've chosen not to see you all these years because doing so was bound to remind me what a lousy brother I was. But for me he might still be alive.' He reached for the glass his wife had set down and drained what brandy remained.

'You couldn't have talked your parents out of arranging that fatal trip.' Elizabeth tightened her grip on his hand. 'And I should have encouraged you to be a presence in Oliver's life before now. All we can hope is that in time he'll come to forgive us.' Her appealing look again went unmet.

Gerard talked to the glass he was still holding. 'Always the coward's way out – that's my life story. Can't even stand up to myself.'

'And I'm selfish, always have been. Me first, last and always, but everyone can change, can't they, if the wake-up call is loud enough? And that's you for us, Oliver.' The smile illuminated Elizabeth's face, making her look – to Oliver's astonishment – warmly attractive.

'Right,' he said. His eyes made clear he hadn't been taken in. 'Are we leaving?'

'Don't you want to say goodbye to your grandfather before we take off?' Gerard remained seated. The blank look had filtered back into his eyes. Was he wishing himself somewhere else, or was he drawn against his will back into the past and his brother Max? Who cared what he was thinking?

'We already said goodbye.' Oliver stared straight ahead. 'And it's not like I won't be seeing him often at the nursing home. Twyla will take me.'

'Sure will,' she squeezed his hand, 'if Mr and Mrs Cully are OK with that.'

'Absolutely! What could be better than the three of us working together for the very best outcome all around? Gerard and I don't deserve your kindness, and believe me, we're appreciative . . . and humbled.' There was no denying the gratitude in Elizabeth's voice as she stood up, or Twyla's relief.

'Agreed.' Gerard, also back on his feet, was again smoothing back his thinning hair. Oliver hoped it would all fall out. He hoped Elizabeth's smile would split her face open. He hoped they weren't going to turn out to be reasonably decent people, making it wrong to hate them.

'I suppose we shouldn't prolong this.' Elizabeth reached for Twyla's hand. Gerard was picking up the suitcases.

The next few minutes passed in a blur. Oliver's life in the dear old house was over. He was now in the back seat of a car that smelt richly leathery; Gerard was driving.

'Watch out for that woman on the bicycle!' Elizabeth warned. The woman was Brian's mother, Mandy Armitage; she was waving because she had gotten a glimpse of Oliver. He laid his face against the window and wished he could fall back asleep, but Elizabeth turned around and wouldn't stop talking in a nobly cheerful rush. Bet she felt her halo growing.

'You are wanted and will be loved, although you might not think it from my cooking; I've never had to do much of it, we've always tended to eat out. You don't have to call us aunt and uncle, Oliver. I can understand that might be difficult, at least at first. Elizabeth and Gerard will be just fine.'

'Thank you.' And then just for something to say, he added, 'There's an Elizabeth in my class, but she's always called Bess.'

'Well, don't ever call me that! It's a trashy abbreviation. People named "Bess" live in trailer parks.' A cog had slipped in Elizabeth's mechanism, necessitating hitting restart. 'Sorry, it's hard kicking the snob habit.'

Oliver pulled a face at her now-turned head. 'Grandpa told me that there was a queen of England, not the one now, but hundreds of years ago, named Elizabeth, and she was called Good Queen Bess. He's got a book on her. And I wouldn't have thought she lived in a trailer park. Of course, I don't suppose they had them then.'

'I never got into English history.' Gerard spoke into the sudden silence. 'Far too bloody. Give me the old American story.'

'Wasn't killing off the Native Americans bloody?'

'I'm talking,' Gerard raised his voice as a car with the radio going full blast past them, 'about all those monarchs chopping people's heads off at the drop of a hat.'

'Well, there is that,' agreed Oliver in what he hoped was an annoyingly amiable voice. 'At first I couldn't understand why she was called Good Queen Bess because she sent almost every friend she ever had to the block. But, like it said in Grandpa's book, in those days chopping off your head was letting you die nicely. If they were really mad they had you hanged, drawn and quartered while you were still alive. Of course, everybody has to be alive to be hanged, but you know what I mean. And after thinking about things for a while I decided a queen has to do what a queen has to do. I wonder how far blood spurts when you're beheaded.'

'For a boy who grew up in the sort of house that has a picture of a red barn on the wall, you can paint a very nasty picture.' Elizabeth pressed a hand to her forehead.

'Oh, I'm sorry. But it's all so interesting. Do you know parents used to have their children watch the executions?' He really, truly would work on his promise tomorrow, but after the way she had talked to Twyla she deserved to feel sick. 'Just like it was a picnic with a packed lunch and drinks. A shame there wouldn't be a van with a man selling ice cream, but you can't have everything.'

'Now, Oliver,' Gerard attempted the role of reasonable adult, 'how about sitting back and relaxing?'

'I like to talk. All the time. Don't you ever wish you could travel back in time in one of those machines? It would be so much fun to sit there on the grass soaking it all in. Well, not the blood, but all the excitement.' Would they turn and take him back home? Was that what he'd really been hoping for? He had made himself sound wicked. Suddenly he was fighting back tears. One slid down his cheek. 'OK, I'm going to sleep now,' he mumbled.

Neither Gerard nor Elizabeth spoke for at least ten minutes, and then he heard her say, 'Oliver?' in a questioning voice.

He breathed more deeply.

Then came: 'In case you're interested, that fainting turn in there was for real. I thought this is our punishment; I'm going to die in this fusty room with its banal picture of a red barn, but given the future maybe I don't mind so much.'

'Don't be a fool, Liz.'

'Can you tell me that's not one seriously disturbed child?'

'He was getting at us, Elizabeth. He can't be overjoyed at all this upheaval. And come to remember Max was into history if you include genealogy. If he hadn't been so into seeking out his roots he wouldn't have come to this godforsaken place and met that girl.'

'He needs a psychiatrist. And you know what I think?'

'What?'

'He's only going to get worse over the next nine years.'

Oliver very nearly shot up in his seat. What startled him more than the words was the chilling optimism in Elizabeth's voice. It pressed him backwards into rigidity.

'Meanwhile I have to look at the kid day after day, knowing that I'm the one who . . .'

'Shut up.' There was something in the whisper that forced Oliver's eyes shut and locked him in place. 'The situation's bad enough without you falling completely to pieces and leaving me to dig us out of this mess on my own.'

Until that moment Oliver had been both scared and angry. Now there was only room for fear.

Four

Sarah was an early riser, a morning person. Even so, she didn't wake as early as Oliver Cully had done that Saturday morning. It was only a little after six when she emerged from a muddled dream which featured Nellie Armitage climbing a tree to rescue one of the furniture movers, while a cat watched from the bushes.

Surprisingly there was no nightmarish quality to the semi-transparent images, no revisiting of a car hurtling toward her at annihilating speed, no volcanic eruption of headlight glare disintegrating into doomed blindness. No heart pounding terror to jolt her upright.

As the scene faded into drowsy consciousness, she was vaguely aware of lying in a constricted position, knees drawn up, elbows pinned to her side and lacking in covering. She opened her eyes to fuzzy unfamiliarity. Not surprising given yesterday's move to Bramble Cottage. She must have fallen asleep on the sofa. Then uncertainty filtered in. The feel of the fabric under her was soft velvet, not the linen of her slip covers; also the soft glow from a mulberry-shaded lamp wasn't right. Elbowing up into a sitting position she realized with a jolt that the whole room was wrong.

The pewter-stemmed lamp stood on a secretary desk along with a cluster of small silver-framed photos and a fountain pen lying across a sheet of writing paper on a leather edged pad. Sarah had never owned a fountain pen, didn't know anyone who did and only recognized it as such because the cap lay beside it exposing the nib.

The room's ambience could have been culled from a period novel; of the sort her ex-husband, Harris, would have termed 'junk food for the mind.' By his standards Jane Eyre was a bodice ripper. Forget his opinions. Sarah knew where she was now: in a house on Ridge Farm Rise. It belonged to Sonny Norris and his mother Gwen. Sonny was the driver of the car that crashed through her fence. She had driven them back here last evening, and ended up spending the night. Wrapping herself in the blanket that had fallen off the sofa while she slept, she looked toward the doorway into the foyer. Were Sonny and Gwen still asleep, or lying wakeful in their upstairs bedrooms? Was either one reliving the nightmarish events of the night before?

Sarah shivered at the memory of seeing death coming for her, surprised she had slept at all. The car had been a silver gray Cadillac. It had taken a moment for her to absorb the silence that had followed its coming to a stop, indicating the engine had stalled or been cut off. Then something had clicked on inside her, and she had darted forward to get at the driver's-side door. What if it were locked? Thank God it wasn't. Wrenching it open, she had willed her heart to slow its thudding. Thankfully there was still sufficient light to reveal the driver, the lone occupant, slumped against the steering wheel. A gray-haired, gray-faced man with eyes eerily wide open in an empty stare. She was sure he was dead; he looked dead. Then a muscle twitched in his cheek and he blinked, the vacuity supplanted by bewilderment.

'Where am I?' A thin voice that sounded to Sarah to be directed not at her but into some clouded void. He was in shock, poor man.

'It's OK,' she'd soothed, 'you're safe. Anything hurt?'

He didn't answer. Just stared, those eyes drained of color like the rest of him.

'Let me help you out of the car.' There was no resistance when she reached in to draw him back against the seat. He must be eighty or more, she thought, no longer fit to drive. A heart condition, high blood pressure or something of the sort could explain his losing control of the car, and he wasn't wearing a seat belt. Why hadn't someone stopped him from taking the car? No time to be judgmental. She remembered the resistance put up by her maternal grandfather, when faced with a family intervention to persuade him to give up driving. 'I'll take you inside to my house.'

'No! No!' The man's voice rose to a shout.

'Then we won't do that. You'll tell me where you live and I'll get you home.' She was trying to turn him sideways, without success; she'd have to lift his legs. It didn't occur to her that perhaps she ought not to move him. All she could think of was getting him out of the chill night air. The blank look was back, and he was unable to offer any cooperation. She straightened up and looked around, hoping to see someone coming to their assistance, but the road was empty. It was a Friday evening, a night people tended to go out or be entertaining in their homes. In addition, Nellie Armitage had said several of the houses were seasonal ones, not yet opened for the summer.

Sarah hesitated. It would only take moments for her to run next door in hope of help, but ought she to risk abandoning the driver even for that short time? What if he panicked? Her attention was jarred back to him when he shouted out angrily, his voice so distorted she couldn't make out the words.

Anger wasn't the right word. Rage now blazed at her from eyes previously lacking any emotion. The transformation was startling, but maybe that was how shock worked. Something told her not to attempt to lean toward this man, let alone touch his shoulder.

'What are you trying to tell me?' she asked gently.

'I want,' his glare approached frenzy, 'I want my mother.'

'Sure you do,' she placated. Had he hit his head? Here she was wasting time, when she should have gotten her cell and phoned for an ambulance immediately. She'd race inside now and get it, but before she could move on this intent he started to cry, the slow, devastating tears of a terrified child.

'Where did she go? Find her, make her come.'

'I will.'

'I want her now.'

'I'll find her.'

The right approach; he was moving, first groping a veined hand toward the car door. Once found, it provided him with sufficient traction to extend his left leg, which dangled limply before making contact with the ground. Slowly the rest of him followed. Sarah had backed off from the urge to assist, but stood ready to provide support. When he straightened up, swaying slightly, he revealed a height only slightly above average, although the drooped shoulders might subtract an inch or two. Out in the open his eyes gained blueness that contrasted with the pallid face and general grayness of his appearance, hair, sweater and slacks. She took this as a hopeful sign. He stood looking around, but giving no indication of interest in the missing section of picket fence or the rear of the jutting Cadillac.

'I know why she's not here,' he said in a male timbre that startled Sarah. 'She won't leave the dog. Do you know,' he turned towards her confidingly and in doing so, shed several years, 'she loves that dog more than me. I want her to get rid of it. You can understand that, can't you?'

No jacket, only that sweater, and it was getting colder, but he looked better physically. If she could manage to get him to tell her where he lived she could drive him home. 'Do you mean your wife?' There couldn't be a mother.

'She's dead. Sometimes I can't remember her name. That frightens me. Do you think it should?' He asked it in a mildly puzzled way, as if inquiring why it had rained so much lately.

'No, there are lots of things I can't remember.'

The perplexity faded; he seemed finally to bring Sarah's face into focus, staring at her as if a tiny flame of happiness had been lighted behind those increasingly blue eyes. 'You're Rowena. I liked it when you came to visit.' He was touching her shoulder when the sound of an approaching vehicle reached them. They both turned to see an SUV skirt the rear of the Cadillac and stop just short of the driveway. A man was getting out of the driver's side, his concerned voice carrying clearly.

'How are things?'

'I'm fine,' Sarah raised her voice against the breeze, 'but I can't assess beyond myself.' She wasn't going to shout out that her companion was still badly confused. He added nothing; his eyes had emptied again.

The driver of the SUV was now opening the front passenger-side door. She watched the newcomer assisting someone in getting out. A woman. Judging from the glimpse of silver hair she had to be elderly, or at the least not young. Relief at the arrival of support was tamped down by continued concern over the car crash victim's behavior.

Sarah guided him across the lawn to the driveway which the arrivals now approached. The man was tall, ruggedly built with a thatch of white hair, and wore a lightweight jacket open to reveal a thick knit navy sweater. The woman was slim, fairly tall with an upright carriage and a suggestion of quiet elegance, perhaps partially supplied by the pearl earrings and single strand around her neck. She was coatless. The strain on her face was evident as they drew nearer, although Sarah sensed control over panic. Was this the wife, whom she'd been told was dead?

The four met at the foot of the driveway, the woman dividing her gaze between Sarah and the man who had now taken hold of her hand in a surprisingly strong grip. 'Look,' he was drawing her forward, triumph in his voice, 'it's Rowena.' Resentment filtered in, tightening his profile. 'You said she lived . . . somewhere else.'

The silver-haired woman put her arms around him as he released Sarah's hand and shambled up to her. 'No, Sonny. This isn't Rowena, although I understand why you would think so; the dark hair and similar height. Now why don't you go and talk for a minute to this nice man who so kindly brought me to find you, and then we can go home.'

'I don't want . . .'

The other man cooperated promptly, a smile warming his

fresh-complexioned face. Up close Sarah assessed his age to be in the early- to mid-fifties. The hand he extended to Sonny looked as if it was regularly put to manual use. He had a British accent.

'Good to meet you, Mr Norris. I'm Sid Jennson from next door.'

'Are you?'

Sarah had been informed by the realtor that an English couple owned the neighboring house. Mr Jennson gave her a kind look before turning his attention back to Sonny Norris. 'The wife's gone for the weekend, visiting our daughter, so you'll be doing me a favor giving me a bit of a chat. How about we go take a look at your car and see what it'll take to get it chugging?'

'It wasn't my fault.'

'I'm sure. Nasty hill that one, had problems with it myself. I understand you were a piano teacher. Always wanted to take lessons as a kid; think I'm too old to give it a try?' The response was a mumble, but lacking in hostility.

The silver-haired woman waited until the two men moved away before turning her blue eyes to Sarah. 'Rowena is my sister. She lives in Cyprus. I'm so terribly sorry for what you've been put through; such a scare for you, the shock of the car coming at your house must have been dreadful. I hope at the very least you were indoors.'

'I wasn't, which was for the best,' Sarah added quickly, 'because I was able to get to him at once. It was a relief to find he didn't appear badly hurt. But do you think you should come inside and phone your doctor to take a look at him?'

'I think I'll wait on that, seeing he appears physically OK.' The woman hesitated and Sarah noted worriedly her damp pallor, the beading around her upper lip.

'Even so, do come in and sit down for a moment,' she urged.

'That is kind, but best to get Sonny home as quickly as possible. Now what about you? Do you wish to notify the police? There is the damage to the fence, which of course I will pay for, but I will understand completely if you wish to file a report.'

'Please don't worry.' Sarah felt incredibly sorry for her. 'I wouldn't do that to you or your husband. The entire fence needs repainting, so replacing the part that's gone will be nothing.'

'I do appreciate your forbearance. Even so, you must allow me to insist on taking care of the expense.' Another hesitation. 'My dear, Sonny isn't my husband. He's my son. Early onset Alzheimer's. My father had it, although we didn't know the name for it in those days.'

It was hard for Sarah to get the words out; there were none that would be adequate. Mr Norris had pleaded for his mother and that part had not been nonsense. 'What a tragedy for you both.'

'We manage, with the obvious exception of today. Do forgive me, I realize I haven't got round to exchanging names.'

'Sarah Draycott.' She wished she were wearing her raincoat so she could have taken it off and placed it around the other woman's shoulders.

'Gwen . . .' The beading of perspiration had increased and now she swayed. Sarah had an arm around her when Sid Jennson came back with Sonny Norris. He had driven the Cadillac into his driveway.

'I don't think you should drive it home,' he told Gwen. 'If it's all right with you I'll check it out, see if there's been any damage. In the meantime I'll run you and your son home.'

'Maybe I could do that,' Sarah offered. An exchange of eye contact told her this new neighbor understood the sense this made. She would be able to offer assistance, if necessary, that a man could not, such as helping Gwen Norris into bed – surely the best place for her right now. At that moment she appeared in more need of a doctor than her son.

Leaving Sid Jennson to provide the supportive arm, Sarah hurried indoors to gather up her purse and cell phone, along with a throw blanket, and then out through the kitchen door to the garage to back out her car. The ride to the house on Ridge Farm Rise took only a couple of minutes with Sonny Norris sitting silently in the back. Even with a knitted blanket around her shoulders, Gwen looked ill, had trouble unbuckling her seat belt and needed Sarah's support from the driveway to the front door. Sonny preceded them, leaving it open behind him, to become a shadowed figure mounting a silhouette of a staircase. A large, brindled dog emerged silently to survey them from the foyer.

The house was a dark red, New England, two-story, but Sarah took in nothing of its surroundings. Her mind was entirely occupied with getting Gwen inside and off her feet. They entered the room lined with bookcases to the left of the front door, followed by the dog, and again Sarah observed little beyond the available seating. The now visibly trembling Gwen grasped the arm of the sofa and sank onto it with Sarah's help, murmuring that she was reacting like an old woman and would only need a moment before going upstairs to check on her son. Her hand moved to stroke the dog now lying beside her feet.

'Jumbo . . . my gentle giant, ever faithful, utterly devoted.' It was not clear whether she was speaking to him or Sarah.

'I like dogs – I'm hoping for one of my own. Can I get you anything? A cup of tea?'

'Nothing, thank you. I'll be right as rain if I just stay still until this silly dizziness passes. You should be getting back home, my dear.' The blue eyes strained to focus. 'I know that house has been empty so you can only just have moved in, to be confronted so soon by all this disturbance.'

'Don't give that a thought. You and your son are what matter. Is there anyone I can call? Your doctor or someone to spend the night with you, so you can get a decent rest?'

'What a thoughtful young woman you are, but I'm already feeling better.'

It was clear to Sarah that this was overly optimistic. When Gwen attempted to stand she had to grab for Sarah's hand to steady herself. As if sensing impending movement the dog had risen before his owner did and now stood off to the side. Sarah knew at that moment she would have to spend the night, but this could be voiced later. The immediate necessity was getting the other woman upstairs and into bed, and this was accomplished with only token protest. Sarah turned her back while Gwen undressed and slipped on a nightgown. Head resting on two plump pillows, Gwen smiled in weary gratitude as Sarah tucked the bed covers around her.

'Why don't you have an hour's sleep? Then I'll come back and see if you would like something to eat and drink.'

'There's soup on the stove,' the voice was increasingly faint, 'and salad and such in the refrigerator.'

'Meanwhile, shall I check in on your son?'

'Bedroom to the left, but he won't answer your knock unless he chooses. Probably sleeping after . . . everything. Don't think he'll try to leave again, but worry I may not wake if . . .'

'Don't, I'll be here till morning, camping on your sofa. Any sound will rouse me. I've always been a light sleeper.' No answer.

The worn-out mother had slipped into a temporarily merciful reprieve. Leaning closer, Sarah was relieved by the even breathing and a return of better color to the face and mouth.

As it happened there was no need to check on Charles Norris: as she closed the door behind her he came out of his room, merely responding to her greeting with a mildly puzzled look.

'Your mother's sleeping,' she told him.

'She does that.' He went down the stairs ahead of her and the dog that had been waiting at the bottom moved away without haste, but with a sideways look that suggested avoidance. When Sarah descended, he returned to stand alongside her, staring upward, placidly allowing her to stroke his great head. Then he climbed the steps, one silent paw at a time until turning in the direction of the bedroom she had just left.

Across from the bookcase-lined room, to the right of the front door, was another room of equal size, decorated in a similarly muted color scheme with a congenial grouping of chairs around the fireplace. Other pieces provided a tasteful blend of graceful antiquity and function. It was in here that Charles Norris had disappeared. Sarah stood at the entrance looking at him with an overwhelming compassion that she couldn't remember experiencing for anyone since her world had crashed in upon her. His mother . . . his poor, poor mother! How could she take the daily pain of watching him suffer what should have been – if it had to be either – her lot? He was seated at a bench before a grand piano, shoulders slack, gray hair straggled untidily from the wind, his hands drifting soundlessly the length of the keys, eyes staring straight ahead into some fathomless void.

'Would you play me something?' Sarah asked gently.

'Can't.' No turn of the head, his voice seeming to echo from a darkness within. 'The music's gone. The doctor tried to trick me it would come back if I took my medicine. They all do it. Treat me like I'm a child. Mother had a woman in to watch me, but got rid of her . . . stealing my things. They all do it.'

'That's bad.' A painful squeeze at the base of Sarah's throat. 'What if you closed your eyes and imagined you were playing for your Aunt Rowena? Remember,' she hesitated, took a step into the room, 'you said I reminded you of her. Maybe she was sending you a memory, to let you know she wishes she could hear you play again.'

'I liked her. She called me a young Mozart. My father never thought I was any good. Now Mother only cares about that dog. It's so alone in here.' He tapped his head. 'Sometimes,' he finally turned, blue eyes – so like his mother's – meeting Sarah's hazel ones, 'sometimes I think I'm losing my mind. Do you think I could be?' The question was the more harrowing because it was so reasonably, almost conversationally spoken.

'No. I think you're just tired and that can make anyone feel down.' A psychiatrist might not consider this to be the correct response, but it felt right to Sarah to offer a soothing reply to someone old and confused. The tragedy was that Sonny Norris wasn't old, he was middle-aged – a time of life which for many promised many vigorous, productive years ahead. She thought of her parents, eagerly anticipating a move to Florida.

Sarah was turning on the gas under the stainless soup pot when the first halting sounds of melody drifted her way. In the time it took to remove a glass bowl of green salad from the refrigerator and set it on the counter the notes were gaining in confidence. She knew very little about classical music, had brushed it aside from teenage years on in favor of rock and some folk, but she did recognize Beethoven's *Fur Elise*. A given for anyone who had sat (however bored) through a basic high school music class. The word exquisite hadn't come to her then. It did so now as she stood absolutely still, absorbing not only the aching loveliness of the sound but also the poignancy of Sonny Norris finding, within his long term memory, a sanctuary. He was now shifting tranquilly into *Moonlight Sonata*. Could his mother hear him from behind her closed bedroom door? Sarah's hope was that she was still asleep and the gift of her son's return to something of his former self would seep into her dreams.

The rest of the evening had passed quickly. When the music ceased half an hour later, Sarah asked Charles if he was ready to eat. He came without protest to the kitchen, where he consumed without interest and in silence a few spoonfuls of soup and poked fitfully at the salad. Pushing back his chair, he retreated upstairs. The dog then came into the kitchen and headed toward the door at the back of a mud room. Having let him out into the fenced area beyond, she spotted a container of dog food on a shelf. Below it were two bowls: one filled with water, the other empty. Possibly he didn't get fed at this hour, so perhaps she should wait and ask

Gwen. Once he was back inside and had allowed her to pat him, she went up to check on Gwen to find her still asleep, not so much as a stirring between the opening and closing of the door.

Sarah decided to feed the dog . . . Jumbo . . . if she remembered his name correctly. Following her into the mud room, he munched on the food she put in his bowl. When it was empty he gave her an appreciative look from those surprisingly gentle eyes for an animal with so powerful a build and such ominous jaws.

'No one could say you have a weak chin,' Sarah told him. He sat, tail wagging appreciatively, and disarmed her by holding up a paw. She knelt to shake it. 'Good to know you. Nice boy. I think I could get to like you very much. And I thought I could only relate to small, fluffy dogs.' Might she reconsider limiting her choice when getting one of her own? Perhaps not – she wanted one that would snuggle on the sofa with her, but when it came to loyal devotion to his owner Jumbo could be second to none. He returned to his post outside Gwen's bedroom door, and Sarah, suddenly hungry, ladled a bowl of soup for herself. It was as delicious as its aroma had promised. She had a second helping along with some of the salad of mixed greens and citrus dressing she had removed from the fridge. A glance at the kitchen clock showed it to be getting on for nine. She did the dishes, wiped the table and counter top, and made a couple of further trips to look in on 'her patient' with the same results as before. To rouse her with the offer of a meal didn't make sense. Following her final check at ten thirty Sarah took a blanket from a linen closet – the same blanket that was to slide off the sofa during the early hours of the morning, causing her to wake feeling chilled.

She was still sitting, with sunlight gilding the beautifully polished desk and tables, thinking what a contented feel there was to this house despite the distressing situation under its roof, when she heard footsteps on the stairs. She got to her feet and went into the foyer. Gwen was coming down the last few steps, wearing a sapphire-blue velour robe with a matching satin sash, the perfect complement to the forget-me-not eyes and silver hair. Looking at her, Sarah thought she must have been lovely as a young woman – still was, for that matter. A complexion to die for at any age. And she did look better for a night's sleep.

'You stayed.' The smile illuminated her, as if from a light turned on within. 'I must have known you did, for I slept the night through, something I haven't done in a while. How extraordinarily kind of you, especially under the circumstances. And, I'm ashamed to confess, I've forgotten your name.'

'It's Sarah Draycott.'

'Sarah . . . a lovely name, it suits you. Did you manage to get any rest yourself?'

'Plenty. I was perfectly comfortable on your sofa.' Sarah should have been eager to leave, to get back to Bramble Cottage and all that needed to be done that day, but she found herself in no hurry. Instead she wanted the chance to get to know this woman a little better and, if possible, to reach out and be of some small help. An idea had already come to her. She could offer to take Jumbo for a daily walk. It would be good preparation for when she got a dog of her own. 'I helped myself to a blanket from your linen closet. That was after enjoying a wonderful meal; I hope you don't mind my making myself that much at home.'

'My dear, I would feel terrible if you hadn't done so.'

'I'd love the recipe for your split pea soup.'

'An old standby; I'll get it to you.'

'Your son didn't eat much.'

'He doesn't. Lack of appetite, no interest in food. Goes with the condition. Wonderful that you could get him to the table.' Gwen bent to stroke Jumbo, who had now padded down to join her in the foyer, then let him out into the fenced yard. She smiled at Sarah. 'Would you like coffee before you leave?'

'I'd love a cup.'

The kitchen looked even more friendly in the morning light. Gwen moved lightly between the cupboards and refrigerator. 'I thought I heard Sonny playing Beethoven in the evening, but I must have been dreaming; it's so long since he's touched the piano.'

'I found him there. He talked for a little and when I was getting the meal ready I heard him begin that first piece. So beautiful.'

'Then, my dear, I am even further in your debt. Music was his passion from the time he could crawl to the piano bench. His dream was to be a great concert pianist, but by the end of his first year at Julliard he knew that wasn't in the cards. There's such a huge gap between the exceptionally gifted and the sublime. Accepting that realization took time.'

'That must have been hard.' Sarah felt her eyes sting. A brilliant career might have compensated in part for what he was enduring now.

'Sonny's given name is Charles. He was named after his father, a tradition going back three or four generations. My husband didn't want him to be Charlie. We assumed he'd shift to Charles as he got older, but he refused.' Gwen opened the door for Jumbo, and then filled the coffee cups. 'His wife, Beatrice, joked about their wedding, claiming he mumbled: "I, Charles Edward Norris," as if afraid someone would jump up and accuse him of using an alias. She was a lovely person, with a great sense of humor. She taught business at Fieldhurst, a small, private university in Rhode Island, where Sonny headed the music department. What inspired him most was working with promising children, recommended by their grade school music teachers. No children for him and Beatrice, something never discussed with me; sadly she died from breast cancer five years ago. And shortly afterwards Sonny moved in with me. It worked well for both of us. He was ready to retire from the university and concentrate on tutoring. The first indication of his decline was when he began forgetting appointments with students.'

'How terribly sad for you both.' The heartfelt words sounded flimsy to Sarah's own ears.

Gwen lightly touched her shoulder. 'I'm glad we've met. I only wish it could have been under different circumstances. Let's sit down and enjoy our coffee. Sonny and I have both known a great deal of happiness, separately and together. And there will still be joy ahead; finding it is rather like searching for pieces of sea glass washed up onto the beach. Just when you're about to stop looking, it's there to be picked up – something small and beautiful. Perhaps that sounds fanciful.'

Sarah looked across the kitchen table at her. 'What you just said was rather wonderful, Mrs Norris.'

'Thank you, my dear, but I should have mentioned that my name isn't Norris. Sonny's father and I divorced. A year later I married my late husband, John Garwood.'

Five

After days of rain the sky was as blue as Gwen's eyes, and the garden bathed in sunshine. She welcomed its comforting warmth as she knelt, dressed in an old pair of slacks and sweater, weeding a perennial flowerbed in the front yard. The chill that had penetrated her body on discovering that Sonny had taken the car had still been there when she had woken that morning. It had ebbed during the hour she had spent talking with Sarah Draycott over coffee and croissants, but had seeped back when that nice young woman left. Reality had to be faced. Last evening could have been so much worse, but it served as a warning that more must be done to protect Sonny from himself. Sarah had been so generous, making light of what had happened, and even offering to return in the coming week and take Jumbo for a walk. Gwen had gratefully accepted for the dog's sake and her own. She very much wanted to spend more time with Sarah, without forcing a friendship.

Gwen set the trowel down and straightened up, to look toward the rustic bench where Sonny sat, holding a newspaper, but looking over it with that unfocused gaze. Sometimes he appeared to read, but how much he absorbed she didn't know. He had always been keenly interested in politics and what was happening on the world scene. Now that was lost, along with so much else, including, until last night, any willingness to sit down at the piano. He had not mentioned Sarah this morning. A burst of yellow, like concentrated sunshine, from the forsythia bush behind the bench, along with the deep pink of the azaleas, emphasized his depleted appearance. He had grown from a sensitive boy into a serious man, but one with a dry sense of humor, which included an ability to laugh at his own foibles. A trait developed, perhaps, as a defense against his father's ever-ready criticism of any blunder or ineptitude.

As she walked toward him, the memory returned vividly of the afternoon when Rowena's engagement to John was announced – she at the piano – and the scene that had dragged her up from her music. Sonny knocking over the lamp and his father's enraged reaction. Anger out of all proportion to the incident. The more shocking because such a display had never previously occurred when company, even family, was present. And rarely in private. Charles had, in general, vented with the cutting barb, or by icy withdrawal. Caught up in all the emotions John had evoked in her since their meeting in the garden, Gwen hadn't dwelt on the reason for her husband's loss of control. She had hurried Sonny from the room to the kitchen to console him. The kitchen because Mrs

Broom was there to produce a cookie and glass of chocolate milk. Sonny had loved Mrs Broom. And she, in turn, had been devoted to him.

Gwen sat down beside her son on the bench. He glanced at her without speaking, but she saw his expression lift. Sometimes their closest communication came without talking. This was such a beckoning time of year. A good part of her love for gardens was the sounds. Some enlivening, some dreamily soporific, as with the bee now buzzing among the azaleas. The family two doors down on her side kept hives, selling the honey at the village market. So many cottage industries in Maine. There were few houses on Ridge Farm Rise. Hers, the original farmhouse, sat a good distance back from the road. She could only see half of the Baldwin's house, across the road, from where she sat.

Poor Madge. Gwen had phoned her, after doing the breakfast dishes, to briefly fill her in on the outcome of Sonny's taking the car. She had stressed that Madge must not blame herself for his having taken it. On ending the call, she had remained uncertain that she had put the matter to rest. Madge was a nice woman, warmly generous and a tireless volunteer for good causes, perhaps taking on too much. Gwen sensed she was also the type of person who thrives on drama.

Beyond the houses was a wildflower meadow that in summer resembled a Monet; it was fringed by woodland through which ran a walking path that ended at Halcyon Street, on the edge of Sea Glass's shopping and business area, above the common. It was getting warmer; the weather forecast had predicted highs in the mid-seventies. It was good to sit idle, bathed in warmth, hearing the small waterfall to her left splashing musically down a rocky incline to disappear under a culvert and reappear as a brook on the other side of the road. So peaceful, but she couldn't allow her mind to drift. She had to think how best to locate an in-home carer, one with a personality acceptable to Sonny.

A few months previously she had hired a woman from an agency. She had been told, by several people, that she was the best in the area. Sonny had resented her from the start; she had fidgeted over his every move, talking at him rather than to him. When ordered, rather than cajoled, to take his medication, he had responded with belligerence. The agency had sent someone else. That hadn't worked out any better. He had subsequently lumped both women together, never mentioning there had been two, talking about *that* woman you brought here. Gwen wondered now if her mistake had been having the help during the day time, her idea being that this freed up time for her to take care of what needed to be done, including getting Jumbo out for his walks. Also it had enabled her to take afternoon naps, in compensation for broken nights' sleep. This time she would seek a person willing to do the night shift. On Monday, she would place an ad in the local weekly paper.

She felt better having that sorted out in her mind. There was something about a garden at this time of year, on the verge of summer, which was visibly hopeful. The leaves on the trees still had that look of tender awakening. The lawn was a lush green, still too wet for mowing. The Hardwicks, the family with the hives, had a teenage son who did the mowing for her. He was a delightful boy and completely reliable. He would come over as soon as the time was right. Sonny had been so good with that age group, with all the children he tutored. He turned to her now. 'Where is Mrs Broom?' It was one of those questions that came out of the blue.

Gwen hesitated; she always attempted to gage what truth he could accept. 'She died, dear, but after a full life, and she and I continued to keep in touch throughout the years. The last time I heard from her she had become a great-grandmother.'

It took several moments for him to answer. So often his mind wandered off in another direction, from one sentence to the next. Not this time. 'I loved Mrs Broom.'

'We all did. She was a wonderful woman, and perhaps the best friend I ever had.'

'She didn't like the way Dad treated me.'

'Didn't she?' Gwen reached for his hand. 'Oh, Sonny, your father was fond of you; he just had difficulty expressing affection.'

'He thought I was too like you. Why didn't you leave him sooner?' It was a man's question, voiced with concerned interest.

'I convinced myself I was the one to blame.' She kissed his cheek. 'How do you feel about our taking Jumbo for a walk?'

'I'll stay.'

That, of course, wouldn't work. Time to go back inside. She had just recovered the trowel from the flower bed, when a car – her car – turned into the driveway. It drew to a stop in front of the garage. She hadn't given the Cadillac a thought since the Englishman,

Sid Jennson, had offered to assess its drivability. Now here he was getting out of the driver's side.

'Checked out just fine,' he said as she came up to him.

'Thank you so very much, you've been more than kind.' She smiled back at him. She had never met him before yesterday, which made his coming to her aid the more appreciated. That was Sea Glass for you. Someone always seemed to turn up in a crisis to lend a helping hand. It more than made up for the fact that nothing remained a secret for more than ten minutes. Sonny was ambling toward them. The contrast between the two men was stark, especially so considering they were probably around the same age. Mr Jennson, upright, vigorous and healthily complexioned, his thick hair gleaming silver in the morning sunlight. Sonny slump-shouldered and way too thin.

'Want me to drive it into the garage?'

'That's all right, I'll do it.'

'Righty-ho.' He handed over the keys. 'By the way, I've fixed that fence. Had some of the same picket in the garage, left over from fencing in an area for the dog. The wife would have conniptions if it got loose and anything happened to it. I don't think anyone will notice the repair. I did it early enough this morning; doubt any neighbors saw the damage.'

'What kindness. Such a weight off my mind.'

Sonny had reached them, and Gwen worried that he would turn belligerent, even accuse Mr Jennson of stealing the car, but that didn't prove to be the case.

'I know you,' he said. 'You're a friend of hers, the one who looks like my Aunt Rowena.'

'I think I heard that. I have an aunt, she lives in England. Miss her a lot, I do.' Mr Jennson drew a hand through the thick silver hair. 'Enjoy talking about her when I can get someone to listen. How'd you like me to come back with my car, so we could go for a drive and then maybe over to my house for a chat? You'd be doing me a favor, with the wife gone visiting our daughter, I'd be more than glad of the company.' He was now looking at Gwen.

'What do you think, Sonny, of Mr Jennson's invitation?' she asked.

'Make it Sid.'

'I'll go.'

'It's only a short walk to your house, Sid.' Gwen's face was alight with gratitude. 'So if it's all right with you, there's no need to fetch your car.'

'Suits me. How about you, Sonny?'

'Fine.'

'Then let's say,' the friend-in-need said to Gwen, 'we'll be back when your son's had enough of me, hopefully not for a couple of hours at least. If you've a fancy to get out for a bit yourself, you could leave the door unlocked. We could come in and wait for you if necessary.'

'Thank you, I'll do that.' This was such a gift; she could feel tears welling up, but managed to hold back until he had disappeared from view. No second thoughts about allowing Sonny to go off with a virtual stranger. Nellie Armitage, whom she had known for years, spoke highly of him and his wife. They lived across the road from her on Wild Rose Way. Nellie eventually got round to talking about everyone. And if anyone knew the ins and outs of human nature it was Nellie. Gwen had gotten acquainted with her through the garden club. She was not a member, attending only sporadically for, she admitted frankly, the social aspect. Which, Gwen thought with a smile, that blended with the tears that had slipped down her face, meant keeping a finger in the pie. Nellie took a similar interest in the dinner theater, the historical society, and the Sea Glass Lobster Fest Committee, to name but a few. She was also a staunch advocate for the food pantry and soup kitchen.

Jumbo greeted Gwen in the hall. She wiped away the tears and told him they were going for a walk, at which he woofed enthusiastically and fetched his leash from the mud room. She would like to get him out for an hour. If Sonny could not settle with Sid Jennson and asked . . . demanded to be returned almost immediately, that would mean quite a wait for her return. But it would be unfair to Jumbo to waste this opportunity. She attached his leash and left a note, stating when she would return, taped to the front door.

Jimmy Hardwick, who mowed her lawn, was skate boarding on his black-topped driveway. She returned his smiling greeting – such a lovely boy – and with Jumbo trotting to heel reached the meadow which spread out on both sides of the road. Its softly stirring grasses were already sprinkled with buttercups. She proceeded along the woodland path. When they had gone a little deeper, she would let Jumbo off the leash so he could enjoy a good ramble. He always came immediately when called, otherwise she would not have risked it. The trees grew very close together in places, the tops of the pines a dark olive, making other leaves appear lime green in comparison. It extended for a couple of miles. Not a place to get lost in, especially at night. Signs were posted at regular intervals, instructing walkers to keep to the path. The proximity to the woods contributed to Gwen's inability to get a good night's sleep. She always dead-bolted the front and back doors before going to bed. But there was no way, without her being on hand, to stop Sonny from getting out of the house if he was determined to do so. She had convinced herself that this was unlikely; it had taken increasing persuasion to get him to leave the house. This had made his willingness to go with Sid Jennson seem little short of a miracle. But, after yesterday, she could allow no mistakes when it came to ensuring he did not get away from the house on his own.

On reaching a wooden bench set back from the path she released Jumbo and sat down, feeling winded. She hadn't been getting enough exercise. The dog hesitated, sniffed the air, padded forward into the start of a run, then came back to lie down at her feet. No amount of encouragement resulted in his taking off. He shouldn't feel this way, she thought, he's young. It's not right that he feels chained to my side; I want him to enjoy life, to romp and play. He needs a child, or at least someone young, to teach him how to have fun. Have I turned into a selfish, irresponsible old woman? Am I also keeping Sonny with me for my sake more than his own? She had been through this many times, always reaching the same answer. Placing him in a nursing home, while he still had periods of awareness, would be agonizing for him. In addition to placing the ad for a carer in the weekly paper, she would phone Mr Plover. He would gladly pin a *Help Wanted* notice for her on the grocery store's bulletin board.

Gwen stood up, re-clamped Jumbo's leash, and walked on for a half mile before turning back. She was relieved to find the note still taped to the door. Removing it, she went inside and saw by the Pennsylvania Dutch clock that it was almost noon. Sonny had not demanded to be brought home yet. With Jumbo reunited with his ham bone, she heated a bowl of split pea soup in the micro-wave, placed an apple, a wedge of white Cheddar, a slice of buttered French bread on a plate, and settled at the table. Sometimes when eating lunch alone she'd bring in a book, enjoying the companionship that reading had always brought. There can be no truer friend, she remembered her father saying when she was about six years old, than a book that speaks to your heart. Today she needed to just sit, feeling the old house wrap itself around her.

She had just finished what was always her last cup of coffee for the day when the doorbell rang. The obvious expectation was Sonny and Sid Jennson, but she was wrong. It was Nellie Armitage standing on the step. As usual she carried the stick that seemed to be more of a fashion statement than a necessity. She was wearing the inevitable orange Crocs.

'Hello, Nellie. What a pleasant surprise. Do come in.' Gwen ushered her into the book room, with Jumbo following a few steps behind.

'Sure this isn't a bad time, Gwen?'

'Not at all, I have the house to myself for a moment.'

'Your son's not home?'

'No.' Gwen did not expand on this. The mention of Sonny had increased her nebulous anxiety about Nellie's visit.

'I only intend staying a few moments, so don't worry yourself about offering me coffee.' Nellie planted herself well back on the sofa. 'My, this is comfortable.' She laid the stick alongside her. 'It's about your son that I'm here.'

'I see.' Gwen sat in one of the fireside arm chairs, her expression giving nothing away. Jumbo settled on the floor beside her. This had to be about the car accident.

'Interfering you could call it, and I'm first to admit I'm known for sticking my nose into other people's business. But in sensitive situations I do turn to my spirit guides for wisdom on whether, or not, to stay out of things.' Nellie squinted a glance at Gwen, assessing whether she bought this.

'Some might call them your conscience. In any event, you felt you should come and talk to me. What about my son?'

'You'll have guessed it. I heard about him crashing the car through that fence.' The usually twinkling brown eyes met Gwen's soberly. 'Got the story straight from the horse's mouth.'

Gwen felt a stab of disappointment. She had thought Sarah Draycott would say as little about the incident as possible. Of course, being determinedly fair, that wasn't realistic. What could Sarah be expected to say in answer to questions?

'Well, you know how she is,' Nellie continued frankly. 'Madge

Baldwin couldn't keep it to her lonesome if she found a white egg in a carton of brown ones. I'd no sooner walked in the door from spending the night at my great nephew Reggie's house in Ferry Landing, than – darn it – there went the phone. Madge! Pouring out the story like she'd cut an artery. All about her being to blame for your son taking the car. How she should have got it back sooner, so you wouldn't have been taking a nap when she returned it.'

'Not Sarah. Gwen relaxed against the back of her chair. 'It wasn't Madge's fault; I told her so when I phoned this morning.'

'In one ear and out of the other, obviously. I had a cousin of Madge's sort, more than happy to take the blame in any drama going if it put her center stage. Very good at springing tears and getting lots of clucking sympathy. But I'm not here to tell tales and make you feel worse, Gwen. Madge mentioned, at the end of her wail, that you once tried bringing in a carer for your son. And it didn't work out.'

'There were two. Sonny reacted negatively to both.'

'And why not, if they weren't his sort?' The brown eyes were suddenly very kind. 'His feelings count. He still has an identity; that's what gets forgot by some people.'

Gwen was deeply touched. For all her talk of spirit guides, Nellie was not a frivolous woman. 'That was the problem,' she agreed, 'both women were pleasant – one of them very kind – but they treated Sonny as a standard case, a diagnosis. No effort to get to know him as a person.'

'So here's my reason for coming. I know someone I believe could be just the one to step into the breach. She's a trained nurse, and even more importantly has been a wonderful support, above and beyond what could be expected, to her most recent patient, an elderly man struck down with Parkinson's. He's just gone into the nursing home. She'll be visiting him daily as they've become dear friends, but there are reasons why I think she might like to be in Sea Glass.'

'Nellie, how very kind of you to put yourself out like this.' Gwen's eyes misted as hope flowered inside her.

'Not at all.' The mischievous gleam was back. 'If I don't do what the spirit guides tell me, they go hide my stick.'

'Tell me more about this woman.'

'Her name's Twyla Washburn. Widowed lady, mid to late sixties. A year or so after her husband died she took up as a traveling nurse – way to see places she'd never been before. Upshot is, when she did a stint in Maine she liked it up here, decided to stay on for a while, doing in-home care. For the past two years or so she's been taking care of this nice man I've been talking about. His going into Pleasant Meadows couldn't be put off any longer.'

'These debilitating diseases steal so much.'

'Cruel, that's what they are. His name is Frank Andrews, grand-father of young Oliver Cully. Perhaps,' Nellie gave Gwen an enquiring look, 'you know his story?'

'Oh, yes . . . the plane crash, such a terrible tragedy. I remember vividly reading about it in the paper; I'd met Clare Andrews once when she was about twelve or thirteen.'

'You did?'

Gwen nodded. 'She had come with her school class to a perfor-mance of the Sea Glass Choral Society, for which I was playing the piano. A couple of days later she phoned and asked if she could come and see me. She arrived on her bike, having ridden over from Ferry Landing. She wanted to know if I'd give her piano lessons, or knew of someone else who might do so. Such a pretty, sweet-faced girl. She told me she'd been saving her allowance for over a year and that she already played a little by ear. I had her sit down and show me what she could do. I was impressed. There was no doubt she had a natural ability.'

'Well, that's something I hadn't heard.' Nellie shook her head as if acknowledging a shortcoming.

'The problem was practicing between lessons. Clare had been using a neighbor's piano, but that person had moved and she said she couldn't ask her parents to buy her one. She knew they'd find a way, but it would require too many sacrifices on their part.' Gwen sighed. 'When I read about her death I wished I could take back that time with her, have offered to let her practice here after school or on weekends. But tell me, how is her son?'

'Now there I could go on all day. Oliver's a great kid, as loveable as they come. Could eat him with a spoon, I could. Him and my great nephew's son Brian are best friends. Live just around the corner from each other.'

'What happens to Oliver now?'

'His uncle – his father's brother – and his wife, that he's never met before, have taken him to live with them at the old Cully Mansion. Come fall he'll be going back with them to New York.

Which brings us right back to Twyla Washburn. She and Oliver have grown very close. She and Frank would have liked her to have guardianship of him, but the aunt and uncle nixed that. Anyway, you'll see what I'm getting at. Twyla wants to see as much of Oliver as possible while he's in Sea Glass. Helping you out with your son would mean she'd be real close by if he needed her quick for a hug and some perking up. Now, I'm not saying she'd be running out the door every minute, but . . .'

'I understand.' Gwen heard a car pulling onto the driveway. 'Nellie, she sounds like a wonderful person. I can't tell you how much I appreciate you coming to tell me about her. Have you mentioned our situation to her, so she'll know who I am if I phone?'

'All taken care of,' answered Nellie smugly. She must have heard the car too, for she was getting to her feet. Though she was going on ninety, her hearing always appeared to be as acute as an eight-year-old's. 'Already given her a call. Did so after thinking on what Madge had to say. Wouldn't have been right to raise your hopes for nothing. Left it with Twyla that she'd come over here Monday morning around ten, unless she heard different from you. Now I'll skedaddle and let you get on with the rest of your day.' She took a couple of steps, remembered the stick, retrieved it and headed for the door. 'No need to turn me into a saint, Gwen, for a simple act of neighborliness. I've always liked you. You're what my mother would've called a real lady.'

The comfort of Nellie's visit, along with the prospect of meeting Twyla Washburn on Monday, stayed with Gwen for the rest of the day. When she asked Sonny if he had enjoyed his time with Sid Jennson he had nodded. Half an hour later he mentioned a cat.

'It was outside that man's house when we got there and he took it in.'

'That was kind.'

'Gray. I like cats.'

'I know you do, dear.'

'Beatrice did too. We always had cats. She found Fur Ball out in the rain.'

It was the first time in a long while since he'd mentioned his wife. Gwen kissed his cheek, her heart full. She had loved Beatrice. Sonny wandered away upstairs to his room, and Jumbo emerged looking hopefully up at her. She produced a biscuit and set about preparing a pot roast for dinner in the way Mrs Broom had taught her years ago, dusting it with flour and salt and pepper and searing it in a little vegetable oil on top of the stove before adding a cup of red wine and bouquet garnish; then covering and placing it in a 325-degree oven for three hours. She had known little about cooking when she married. Spending time with Mrs Broom in the large, comfortable kitchen of the house in Boston had awakened her interest. She'd seen what enjoyment the other woman found in putting a meal together, especially when producing Sonny's favorites. Mrs Broom had welcomed him to sit chatting and watching while she worked. Passing him a bowl of batter to beat, asking if he'd be kind enough to brush milk on top of the apple pie and sprinkle it with sugar before it went in to bake. Gwen had felt like a child herself, learning along with Sonny, rolling out her own scraps of pastry and proudly producing cinnamon sticks. In times of stress she had increasingly gravitated to the kitchen, to be soothed by Mrs Broom's solid presence and soft-voiced instructions. She was always kindly encouraging.

'You're a rare one for getting the hang of it, Mrs Norris. Now let me show you how to fold the sugar into the egg whites for the meringues . . . that's the way of it. You taking that over gives me time to put on a pot of coffee. It's about that time, isn't it? Like I say, a weary cook is a bad cook. Have to take a break once in a while or you'll end up putting mint in the brownies instead of the peas, although maybe that wouldn't be such a catastrophe – mint can give chocolate a nice little kick. Never be afraid to try something different, Mrs Norris. That's how you get to be your own woman in the kitchen: you don't let even a tried and true recipe think it's boss. Put your foot down.'

Dear, dependable, ever-supportive Mrs Broom. While readying the vegetables, carrots, onions and potatoes, to be added to the pot roast half way through its cooking, Gwen wondered if it would be helpful to Sonny if she were to find a kitten for him. He had brought the elderly Fur Ball with him when he moved in, but when she died a year later he had said he wasn't ready for another. She could not imagine Jumbo giving a cat, let alone a kitten, a hostile reception and perhaps having his own animal to love would reduce Sonny's antagonism towards the dog. The problem was his unpredictability. Best to wait and see if he, having had the thought triggered, expressed a desire for a cat.

That unpredictability was evidenced the next morning when they were having breakfast. His asking what day it was did not diverge from the norm. That was one of his first questions every day, but when she told him it was Sunday, he surprised, amazed her by saying he wanted to go – must go – to church. He and Beatrice had been Episcopalian, albeit sporadic attendees. He had attended St Anne's a few times after moving to Sea Glass. Gwen had accompanied him on those occasions, but could not remember the times of its services, so now looked these up in the telephone directory. 8 a.m. and 10.30 a.m. There was just time to make the later service if they hurried, which Sonny surprisingly did. He came back downstairs in a gray suit that she could not remember seeing him wear before. His collar was askew and his tie awkwardly knotted, bunching up midway on his neck. She refrained from making adjustments. He had done so well. It was his self-assurance that mattered, not what anyone else might think.

He made no mention of the accident on the short drive. St Anne's was the white church with the simple spire on the common. It had been built in the nineteen twenties as the First Baptist Church. But when a fund-raising movement in the eighties had enabled its congregation to build a larger facility, the Episcopalians had moved in. Their own church had burned down. Knowing the service must already have started, Gwen, having little hope of finding a space in the narrow lane reserved for church parking behind the common, left the car outside the grim red-brick Victorian that was the Cully Mansion. Always considerate, she made sure not an inch protruded onto its driveway. Additionally, she had sensed – from her conversation with Nellie – that the uncle and aunt, who had taken young Oliver to live with them, might be a testy couple.

She and Sonny entered the church to find, as she had anticipated, the service well in progress. A voice to the right of the altar announced: 'The first reading from the Book of Isaiah.' Her intention was to lurk at the back until the moment came when they could, as inconspicuously as possible, find room in a pew. Foiled! As she was endeavoring to shut the door without an alerting bang behind her, a balding, middle-aged man approached them. Beckoning them forward, he marshaled them up the right side aisle, until they reached a midway half-empty pew. Having bowed them in, Gwen first, then Sonny, he retreated. Just as they sat the

organ swelled forth and they had to stand back up, rather like
Jack-in-the boxes. This didn't appear to bother Sonny; his face was
rapt. He might be pleased with what he heard, or waiting intently
for a false note, it didn't matter. He was where he needed to be
at this moment.

Smiling, she glanced left at the profiles of the only two other
people in the pew. An African-American woman with closely
cropped gray hair, and a sturdy, sandy-haired boy of perhaps ten.
Both joined in the psalm now being sung. The thought crossed
Gwen's mind: *Joyful voices raised unto the Lord.* Both had perfect
pitch. Sonny now looked their way and nodded. When all sat for
the next reading, the fingers of both his hands played out some
piece he was hearing internally, on his trousered knees. Then came
the Gospel read from the pulpit by a tall, thin, scholarly-looking
man in a cassock and white surplice, whom Gwen assumed to be
the priest; but on making his descent, he retired to a side chair.
Whereupon, a woman garbed much the same rose from the seat
beside him and crossed in front of the altar, with its green and gold
embroidered cloth, to stand on the chancel steps. Then this must
be – Gwen glanced down at the service pamphlet she had found
on the pew – the Reverend Marjorie Ansteys. How times had
changed since this church was built. The stark simplicity of its white
walls, clear glass windows, and strictly serviceable pews gave such
an impression of seventeenth-century Puritanism that the elaborate
altar cloth and gleaming brass candlesticks already seemed incon-
gruous. Had this been four hundred years ago the woman would
have been stoned before being dragged to the stake. But how
worthily had we advanced? Gwen wondered. We still had our
prejudices, based on fear and ignorance. Racial and religious hatreds,
condemnation of the undeserving poor, avoidance of the mentally
ill, as if all were potentially violent. Mercifully, there were multitudes
of truly decent people. She wondered how the African-American
woman felt amongst the sea of Caucasian faces. The boy held her
hand as he leaned against her.

The Reverend Ansteys, rosy-faced and red-haired, looked as
though laughter would bubble forth from her mouth as readily as a
sermon. She had embarked in a musical voice on an anecdote about
a man on a train.

'We'll call him Mr Smith. He found himself sitting opposite a
former college acquaintance; we'll call him Mr Jones. They began

to talk, reminiscing about old times, and all the while Mr Smith was noticing the shabby clothes, the hair in need of a barber, the down-at-the-heel shoes, the demoralized expression and voice of a man who had been a brilliant student twenty years before with a successful career on the horizon. Mr Jones explained that he had lost his job when the bank he had worked for had failed, and had now been unemployed and out of work for over two years. He was on his way to an interview, but his hopes were dampened by knowing he didn't look his best. Mr Smith had left home with very little cash in his wallet and on impulse,' Reverend Ansteys paused, 'he removed his gold cufflinks and handed them to Mr Jones, telling him to pawn or sell them.'

At that moment Gwen's thoughts turned inward. She was back in the bedroom she had shared with Charles in the house in Boston. She could see him vividly behind her closed lids. He was standing with his back to her, looking into the mirror as he removed his cufflinks. She had just come out of the bathroom after putting on her white lawn nightdress. It was about eleven on the night following the announcement of Rowena's engagement to John Garwood. The day she had thought would never end, and was now willing tomorrow to come so it too would be over. Her sister and fiancé were to leave with her parents after lunch. If only they'd change their minds and decide go as soon as they finished breakfast.

'It won't work.' Charles dropped the cufflinks on the dressing table, continuing to stare into the mirror, his voice so harsh it startled her.

'What won't?'

'This ludicrous engagement of Rowena's.'

'Why ever not?' Feeling the room shift, Gwen had sat down on the bed. Had he guessed? Was Charles about to accuse her of making a fool of herself in John's presence? Was he suggesting that, for all he cared, she was at liberty to spin out her juvenile fantasies to her heart's content?

'Because, my dear Gwen, the man's not her type. Too much the strong, silent type.'

'He was conversational. He talked to my father a lot.' But that wasn't true, she immediately thought. He had listened attentively, drawn the older man out of the shell within which he had, so unaccustomedly, retreated.

'Oh, for God's sake, Gwen!' Charles finally turned from the

mirror, removed his tie and flung it onto a chair. 'That's not what I'm talking about. The fellow's never going to pour out his passion in blank verse, annihilate himself on her behalf. And nothing less from a man would ever satisfy your sister. She's a carnivore. A beautiful beast of prey.'

'That's a dreadful thing to say.' Gwen had been shocked out of her self-absorption.

'But accurate. Rowena was never cut out to be a wife. She's a born mistress. Mark my words, my sweet, she'll be bored with this fool in a month and toss away his carcass.'

'Charles,' she was stunned, 'why are you reacting this way? Why so heated? I always thought you were fond of her. I used to think, before you and I discovered our feelings for each other, that it was Rowena you loved or had at least captured your interest.'

He laughed, and the sound was even harsher than his voice. 'I had too much sense to be reeled in and she knew it. I wonder if the betrothed, as we'll call him for the moment, will creep into her room when we turn off the lights in here. But why waste time thinking about their antics when you are looking so delectable in that prim Victorian shift thing.'

Charles had subsequently made love to her with a fervor amounting to ferocity, and she had striven to respond, until his hands and mouth hurt her too much. She doubted he noticed. He had never used her in this ruthless, impersonal way before, but she was too numbed to seek out the reason, beyond his having been irritable all day, his anger exploding when Sonny broke the lamp. She lay wakeful long after Charles fell asleep, feeling spent, empty and praying that she would not see much of Rowena and John in the coming weeks. The next day bruises were visible on her breasts and the insides of her thighs. Thankfully, her parents and the engaged couple did decide to leave immediately after breakfast.

As it turned out, she did not see any of the four until a month later when John arrived alone, late on a Saturday evening, to break the news that her father had died. Sonny was asleep, Charles in California for the weekend, and Mrs Broom at her own home. There had been only one shoulder to weep on.

Gwen drew her thoughts back to the present; she had missed the outcome of the two men meeting on the train. Reverend Ansteys was ending her homily and people were reaching into pockets and purses, suggesting it was nearing time for the collection. Gwen felt

Sonny clasp her hand. The African-American woman's warm brown eyes took in the faces of mother and son, their linked hands. Something passed between her and Gwen, something constant and enduring that brings the gift of peace in small moments freed to rejoice. The organ poured forth once more, the congregation rose for the next hymn and Sonny joined forth full force. The sandy-haired boy looked at him, raised a thumb, and smiled from an endearingly round face, damp with tears.

Six

After church that morning, Twyla took Oliver to Matey's, a gray-shingled diner on the corner of Herring Bone Lane, behind the common. There was a pirate with an eye patch on the sign above the door, which was cool. Oliver and Brian liked playing pirates and saying – *Aaargh! There's treasure aboard that one, me hearties!* Brian's pirate name was Captain B. Curdle and Oliver's was Walker Plank. Grandpa had come up with the names when they were six and made them each a wooden cutlass. They'd both practiced leering in the mirror until, in Brian's opinion, they'd both got it down real good. Those happy times all seemed part of a far, distant past. Now looming was not a vessel loaded with booty, but a return to the Cully Mansion.

When he had stepped inside the shadowy hall with Gerard and Elizabeth and heard the heavy door close behind them, he'd been overcome with the dread that he'd become their prisoner and that all the promises of allowing him contact with Twyla were lies. It seemed he'd been wrong about that because no protests had been raised over his leaving with her this morning. And last night had to have been a dream . . . a nightmare – when he thought he opened his eyes in the middle of the night to see Gerard standing at the side of the bed, hands outstretched toward him. How could it have been real? Gerard had said nothing, done nothing when Oliver gasped his name, only stared at him with blind eyes before turning and gliding out into the hall. Oliver hoped his thoughts didn't show on his face. The lady minister's sermon had inspired him to try and be a better person, which meant in this case casting aside suspicion. Grandpa said that human nature, being what it was, this noble intent didn't last more than five minutes, so best to make the most of them. A lot of good could be done in five minutes.

Oliver had wanted to go and see Grandpa right after church, but Twyla had explained that the staff at Pleasant Meadows would be doing the rounds with lunch about now, so they might as well have something to eat themselves before heading out there. The walls of Matey's were thick with brightly colored pictures of grinning, or snarly-looking pirates, but – as Twyla murmured to Oliver in a jokey voice – the owners hadn't gone ridiculously overboard. There was a carnation in a vase on the table, not a candle that looked like a skull. She was right. The waitress who came up to their table by the window wasn't wearing a kerchief on her head or an eye patch. Brian would probably have been disappointed that she didn't have a fake parrot on her shoulder. Oliver thought she looked a nice, friendly sort of person. She had round rosy cheeks and shiny brown hair. He was also ninety-nine percent sure she was going to have a baby. But Grandpa had warned him that this was something risky to comment on. When he was around Oliver's age he'd asked a woman if she was hoping for a boy or a girl and been told, 'There is no impending happy event, thank you very much!' Grandpa said the memory still haunted him and he could never afterwards offer congratulations to a woman being wheeled into Delivery without fearing he was about to step on a landmine.

'Any minute now, is my guess,' Twyla said with a smile after the waitress left to fetch their drinks.

'It should freak me out, the way you do that.' He leaned forward, eyes wide with awe. 'Read my mind, I mean.'

'Just plain old-fashioned love sight, lamb baby. Don't you go thinking I've got spirit guides helping me out, the way they do Brian's Aunt Nellie. Not that I'm taking her down, you understand. She's a grand old lady.' Twyla looked as though she was going to add something to this, but the waitress had returned and was setting down their drinks. Coffee for Twyla and chocolate milk for Oliver. When they both ordered orange juice and French toast with bacon Oliver suddenly discovered he was so hungry he could eat a cavalry of horses. Grandpa used to say that. Last night's supper at Cully Mansion had been one lonely little pork chop, with only a teaspoon of peas for company. And breakfast had been a very small bowl of cereal.

'I'm sorry that Elizabeth's not feeling well.' Twyla stirred milk and sugar into her coffee. 'Headaches can bring you down real low.'

'She did look bad.' Despite his negative feelings toward his aunt, Oliver had felt sorry for her. Even the hardest heart would have noticed she looked gray and kept walking in circles as if she didn't know where she was, or what she was doing. 'She said she kept seeing these weird lights behind her eyes.'

'Sounds like migraine. They're spitefully cruel, Oliver.'

Oliver downed his chocolate milk as if it were a noggin of rum on a pirate ship. 'Gerard was real mean to Elizabeth when he came into breakfast. He said getting out the box of corn flakes had obviously been too much for her.'

'There's those that don't have patience, especially when they're full up with their own problems.' Twyla hadn't pressed him for information on how things were going at the Cully Mansion beyond asking if it was difficult to find his way around with it being such a big place. She'd always said that if there were things he wanted, or needed, to tell her he'd do so in his own good time.

'What problems does Gerard have, except for being stuck with me?' Oliver scowled. The five minutes grace period after church was definitely up. He'd already stopped striving to be a better person. As Brian's mother, Mandy Armitage, had said when she shut the car door on her foot and came out with a whole paragraph of bad words: 'We're not all cut out to be Mother Theresa.'

'He didn't look to be a man at peace with himself yesterday; there's surely something all tangled up inside him, was my thought. Grown-up worries. Happy people don't lash out for no reason.'

'I wasn't nice to him, was I? About his fly being unzipped, I mean. And I went off some in the car on the way there.'

'He and his wife were both surely bound to expect some resistance. They must have given some thought to a rocky start.' Twyla sipped her coffee.

'Maybe it's just his nature,' Oliver conceded. 'Being crabby, I mean. Brian's Aunt Nellie says some people are just born plain miserable. She says she's known plenty who'd have to take lessons to learn how to smile. Actually, I hope they are sick of me already.'

'I know it's hard, lamb baby, don't think I don't ache inside for you. But, if it's in any way possible, will you try and make this work?'

Oliver was tempted to say he didn't want to, that he wished that on his return to the Cully Mansion he would find his suitcases out on the front step; he stopped himself in time. Twyla hadn't added that it was Grandpa's peace of mind that mattered; she wouldn't, even if she thought Oliver was forgetting for the moment. He had to cut out the whining for her sake too. Looking into her loving eyes, it came to him with a sickening jolt that the situation had placed an invisible wall between them. Just as he could no longer pour out his entire heart to her, she couldn't question him about how things were going at the Cully Mansion without feeling she was acting against Gerard and Elizabeth and in doing so make matters even worse for Grandpa. Oliver had never felt this alone in his entire life. The temptation to be cowardly and selfish was almost overwhelming. Being noble didn't feel anything like as great as he'd imagined it would when watching the hero of *A Tale of Two Cities* standing bravely under the guillotine. If he was to get out of this dark tunnel he had to cling to hope – that Gerard and Elizabeth would come to their senses and admit it would be better all round for him to go and live with Twyla. Somehow he would have to find a way to persuade them, but not by rudeness or temper tantrums that would put him squarely in the wrong and upset Grandpa and Twyla. It would have to be something crafty that would make Gerard and Elizabeth look unreasonable. What this could be he had no idea, but something would come to him. 'Anyway,' he said, as if introducing a brighter note, 'if it hadn't been for Elizabeth's headache they might not have let me phone to ask if you could pick me up for church.'

'That opportunity made me happy.' Twyla patted his hand. 'Let's get hoping the poor woman took something to ease the pain and went for a lay down in a dark room.'

'The whole house is dark,' Oliver managed to speak casually. 'It's like the one in that old movie we watched with Grandpa. Remember? There was an old lady sitting in a room wearing a horrible old wedding dress and veil and when the young man started shouting at her and tore down the drapes there were these huge cobwebs everywhere and mice running all over the cake.'

'*Great Expectations*, the book by Charles Dickens.'

Oliver nodded, his mind returning to the guillotine. 'He's the getting much, if any, sleep at night. She would say she was used to that and had long ago worked out a routine of naps. With Mrs Garwood there she might be able to take them without one ear on the listen, but even so he mustn't be selfish. Just knowing she was close by was the biggest thing. His thoughts turned to Aunt Nellie and from her to Reverend Marjorie Ansteys' sermon about the two men on the train. And how the one who was out of work had never afterwards taken the time to seek out his old friend and thank him for the gift of the gold cuff links that he'd been able to sell so he could look good when he went for the job interview, even though getting the job had changed his whole life for the good. Oliver understood that Reverend Ansteys was pointing out how often people forget to thank God for answering their prayers. In this case He had worked through Aunt Nellie. It wasn't the big miracle Oliver had begged for – that Grandpa would get well – but it wasn't small either and maybe just the start of something even more wonderful. He would definitely go and thank Aunt Nellie.

'That man and lady in church next to us were rather inspiring, weren't they?' he said as Twyla came to a stop at a red light. 'You could just see how much they loved each other. I wonder if they'd been married a very long time?'

'I was just thinking about them. That's what I took them for at first glance – husband and wife, but then I noticed what looked like a family resemblance and wondered if they were brother and sister. Now it's come into my head . . .' Twyla's attention returned to the road when the light turned green.

Oliver gave her a couple of minutes. 'What were you saying?'

'It crossed my mind . . .' A car from the opposite lane swerved with nothing to spare in front of them. Twyla had to break so sharply that Oliver lurched forward. The seat belt did its job but the jolt momentarily took his breath away.

'You all right, lamb baby?'

Oliver nodded. They were turning into the Pleasant Meadows arking lot and in the excitement of seeing Grandpa he forgot all bout the man and lady in church. The nursing home was a one-ory cream-sided building with a brown roof. It might have been insurance office made to look friendly by the surrounding lawns d flowerbeds. The rhododendron bushes were already in deep nk flower and the forsythia was brightly splashed with yellow. remembered Grandpa saying they looked as though they had

one who wrote *A Tale of Two Cities*, isn't he? I can never decide which one I like best. They both had awesome endings. But I can't see anything inspiring in sitting in a rotting old wedding dress for years and years, can you? It's not like marching up to the guillotine and giving your life for a friend, is it?'

'Love sometimes asks more of us than we think we can bear. Poor Miss Haversham! That was her name, wasn't it? I guess Nellie Armitage is right: some people are born with misery bubbling up inside them. It doesn't stand thinking of, lamb baby. So let's concentrate on that French toast I see coming.'

This mundane prospect did not immediately grab Oliver's full attention. 'I think I do like *A Tale of Two Cities* best. I wonder if I'd be brave enough to stand thinking noble thoughts while waiting to have my head sliced off for Brian?' He ceased musing on this when his plate was put in front of him. The bacon was all crispy, just the way he liked it, and the French toast thick, puffy and golden. He waited for Twyla to use the syrup then poured on a rich amber puddle and watched it seep slowly over the brown crusted sides. 'I was coming down the hall last night, Gerard and Elizabeth were in the living room, and I heard him tell her that he thought it weird the way I used such big words for a boy of nine. He said it gave him the creeps. That sounds unreasonable, doesn't it?' Not to speak about *them* at all would have worried Twyla more than an occasional whine.

Her expression gave nothing away. 'Seems likely to me he's never spent much time around children, so doesn't understand they're all individuals. Don't you go fretting on his opinion, OK? Truth is you do have an exceptional vocabulary for a child your age, part I'd say is a natural gift and the rest your grandpa's influence, and that's something to celebrate. I hope nobody went making Mozart feel bad because he could play the piano better than grown-ups at the age of two.'

'Could he really?'

Twyla laughed. 'You get the point, lamb baby.'

Oliver didn't tell her what else he'd overheard of that conversation, remembering in time that this could seriously worry her. What Gerard had said was: 'The boy's too bright for his and our good, Elizabeth.' What had he meant by the last part? The one person Oliver would discuss this with, along with what he'd overheard in the car when pretending to be asleep, was Brian. The part about Oliver's being crazy and possibly getting worse. Together they would try to puzzle out why Gerard and Elizabeth seemed to prefer this idea to his being overly bright. Although maybe it didn't mean anything other than they were just plain weird and nothing they said amounted to anything more than noise. Brian's mother said Mrs Ellis down the road was one of those people.

The waitress appeared at their table, asked cheerfully if she could remove their empty plates and did so without any suggestion she was hurrying them to vacate. She headed for the swing door at the back of the restaurant and Oliver saw Twyla was smiling at him.

'I've got a piece of news I think you'll like.'

'What?' He reached across the table for her hand, hope beating like fledgling wings inside him. It couldn't be that Gerard and Elizabeth had changed their minds already? She would have told him that right off the bat, but it had to be something that would make things better.

'It has to do with Brian's Aunt Nellie. I said something about her spirit guides when we first sat down and I hope I didn't sound like I was talking down about them, making fun of her beliefs, I mean. That would be unkind and narrow-minded. Who's to say who has things right and who has them wrong? Like we're taught – God moves in mysterious ways, his wonders to perform. And these guides of Nellie's do seem, from the way she tells it, the down-to-earth sort.'

Oliver smiled to let her know he got the joke, but he was impatiently eager to hear what else was coming. 'What do they have to do with the piece of good news?'

'They told her to get in touch with me.'

'They did?' Oliver sat up straighter.

'She phoned me yesterday morning about the possibility of a job in Sea Glass, more of a carer than a nurse, but one she thought would ideally suit me and this lady who's in need of help. Nellie's known her for a long time and says she's as nice as they come. I'd be mainly handling the nighttimes so would have plenty of spare time to visit your grandpa and keep the house up till he decides what to do about it.'

Something in Oliver's throat prevented him from answering. It wasn't exactly a lump, more a bubble of happiness. The rainbow glow showed on his face.

'Well, lamb baby?'

'You mean you'd be here – right here?'

Twyla nodded. Oliver was sure she had bubble in her throat too. 'Nellie called back after going to see the lady and I'm to meet her at nine tomorrow morning to work out the details. She lives up the hill a pace from Nellie and was more than glad to hear I'd be free to come and help out.'

'Is she very sick?'

'It's her son that's not well. What you could call a tragedy.'

'A little boy?'

'Oh, no. He's in his late fifties and suffering from Alzheimer's. Terrible for him and his mother. There surely can't be many parents who have to face what nature would say is the wrong way round.'

'Is his father still alive?'

'Been gone some years. He and the mother were divorced and she married again, so her and the son having different last names. He's Charles Norris and she's Gwen Garwood. The second husband has passed away too and there's no other children to help out, so she's been battling on alone after bringing in carers that didn't work out because Mr Norris wouldn't accept them.'

'He'll accept you,' said Oliver with total confidence, 'and mother will come to love you. How could anyone help it? Is terribly old?'

'Late seventies. She would have had him when she was young.' 'I'll know more about them after the meeting tomo Twyla picked up the bill and stood up. The waitress had told they should pay at the counter.

'Theirs is such a sad story. It feels wrong in a way to happy for us.' Oliver got to his feet.

'It shouldn't, lamb baby. There's always times in life whe walks hand-in-hand with joy. That's part of the great r I've heard your grandpa say many a time. Let's go see h

They sat in companionable silence for most of the sh Pleasant Meadows. So much to think about. Oliver why Gerard and Elizabeth would try to stop him from every day if she could manage. Probably they woul have her drive him into Ferry Landing on weekday n school was out if that could be agreed with Mrs course, he wouldn't want Twyla tiring herself ou

been produced by an artist of the Impressionist period. Oliver hadn't known what that was and Grandpa had brought out a book with glossy pictures of famous paintings. Some by someone named Monet and another man whose name had sounded almost the same. Oliver had agreed about the forsythia. He asked Twyla as they got out of the car if they could bring Grandpa out in a wheelchair to look at these bushes.

'Sounds a great idea. We'll see if he's up to it.' She took his hand as they walked to the entrance. His heart was beating fast. There was nothing miserable or scary-looking about the outside of the building. But they had to make it look that way, didn't they? If it were anything like the Cully Mansion no one would allow their old and sick relatives to live there. It never occurred to Oliver that people might be guided by desperation or self-interest. What scared him was knowing that however cheerful-looking the inside of Pleasant Meadows might be, it couldn't get away from being the final stop between this world and the next. Some of the patients must feel panicky and hopeless. The sense of being imprisoned would reach down empty hallways and creep into every room, like mildew from a cellar. And Grandpa would breathe it in. He would pretend not to notice, but Oliver wasn't sure he could do a real good job of pretending. He'd never been able to fool Grandpa. He held on tighter to Twyla's strong brown hand as they went through the door into a short narrow vestibule with a big window on their left looking into an office lined with gray file cabinets where a man sat facing them at a computer. Ahead was another door with a brass bell alongside. A notice above read: *Ring and wait for buzzer.* Twyla pressed the bell, the man at the computer looked up, shifted a hand sideways on the long counter desk top and they heard the buzz.

When they went through the door the man came out from the office to greet them. He was thin on top, had a bristly moustache and was of a comfortable and somehow encouraging sort of build. Rather like that nice man at the Post Office who pretended to look fierce when someone came in with an armload of packages, then winked at Brian and Oliver. Brian collected stamps. He was sure the one he'd bought of Elvis would be worth millions one day. Oliver drew in a slightly relieved breath. The air smelled faintly of what the lady in the Victorian Parlor gift shop had told him was called potpourri. He didn't exactly like it, but supposed it had to be there. He had to admit to being reasonably impressed. Wide openings connected one space with another and there were lots of windows, bringing the outdoors in. Oliver glanced around him, taking in the seating area with its walls painted the pinkish red of the rhododendrons. Its window showed a glimpse of them. There were a number of homey-looking sofas and chairs along with coffee and lamp tables. Inside the fireplace was a large brass plant pot. The plant wasn't real but it was doing its very best to look like it could sprout new leaves any minute. On one of the sofas was a thin-faced old lady. Sitting next to her was a much younger man wearing a baseball cap. She reached out, took it off his head and put it on hers. Oliver saw the man smile; it was a gently amused smile.

'That looks good on you, Grandma.'

'I bought it this morning. There's a nice shop in my room.'

'That will be her roommate's closet,' said the man who had come out of the office to greet Twyla and Oliver; he dropped his voice low enough not to be overheard. There was a twinkle in his eyes. 'Many of the women all like to shop. Labeled clothing enables us to keep track of where items really belong and a sense of humor on the part of staff and visitors can do a lot to lift the general mood, as you'll know, Mrs Washburn. Even our most confused residents respond to atmosphere.'

'Very important,' Twyla agreed.

Oliver was sure they were right. The lady wearing the baseball cap did look very pleased with herself, in a straight-backed self-important sort of way. But, he reminded himself, Grandpa wasn't confused. Or only late in the evening when he was very tired.

'This is Mr Braddock who's in charge here, Oliver,' said Twyla.

'Hi, Mr Braddock.'

'Make it Kevin, or better yet, Kev.' He had a similar twinkle in his eye to the man behind the counter at the Post Office. 'I was the resident RN here before they shuffled me sideways.' Oliver liked that he didn't say 'moved me up.' That could have sounded braggy. He also thought Kev had mentioned he was an RN because he knew Twyla had been Grandpa's nurse, and so hoped that information would be reassuring. 'Good to meet you.' He shook Oliver's hand. 'I've been looking forward to doing so. I know just how important grandsons are. I've one of my own, just three months old.'

'I expect he's lots of fun even though he can't do much yet.' Oliver had always thought it must be kind of boring being a baby, but he didn't let this show. 'How is my Grandpa? I don't see him out here.' Oliver looked around again, this time focusing on taking in the dining room with soft green paint and white-topped round tables. There were eight people seated at them in light-colored wooden chairs, mostly women, and all looking like residents. A young woman in a smock with cats on it was passing out brownies. Grandpa wasn't at any of the tables. The large area opposite, with folding chairs lined up around the walls and a music center, was empty.

'Is Grandpa in his room?'

'He hasn't been out of it today.' Oliver could tell Mr Braddock hoped this didn't sound worrying. 'It's very common for residents to be extra tired for a few days following their arrival. It's a huge emotional adjustment, in addition to the physically taxing experience of being transported here.'

'I saw how much it had taken out of Frank when I came yesterday,' agreed Twyla. It was why she had suggested on the phone yesterday morning that Oliver wait until today to come. 'We were just talking about taking him outside in the wheelchair, but we'll size up whether it would be better just to sit with him, don't you think, Oliver?'

'Right.'

'Can someone help me?' A woman with a ragged face and shoulder-length hair wearing a long flannel nightgown and fuzzy slippers was coming down the hallway to their left. An aid in a pink smock went over to her.

'It's all right, Muriel. Let's sit down. I was just coming for you to do your nails. How would you like blue polish this time, like I'm wearing?'

'There's something wrong with me – am I going to get better? Where's my husband?' The distressed voice rose.

'We'll have a nice talk. Let's go and sit at your favorite table.' The aid led her into the dining room, where another resident could be heard complaining that there was a man under her bed.

'I've yelled at him to go away, but he won't. I know what he's after, filth, filth, filth. Men! They're all the same and he's worse because he's got two of them. He showed me – the disgusting pig – and I told him I'd cut them off, but I can't find my scissors; someone's taken them.'

'Try your brownie, Lucy,' said the aid with cats on her smock, 'they're really good. Made from scratch. I know how you feel about things out of a packet.'

Oliver looked at Twyla. The outer doorbell sounded and Kev said he'd let the person in and then go down with them to Frank's room if they would like him to do so.

'That's not necessary,' replied Twyla. 'We don't want to keep you. Whoever's coming in could want a word.'

'I expect it's Mrs Robbins with her visiting companion dog; she brings him regularly at this time on a Sunday. A lot of the residents really brighten up when Goldie comes in. He's trained to size up which ones to pet him. We have another dog and its owner on Wednesday.'

Kev turned toward the door and Twyla and Oliver started down the hallway to their left.

'A great idea that,' she said, 'especially as some of those in here won't often, or ever, have anyone come to see them. Out of sight, out of mind. I know that sort of neglect is hard to understand, but it's a sad fact of life, lamb baby. And it doesn't do to judge. It's not always that people don't care; they just can't take seeing loved ones so terribly changed. They convince themselves the person they've come to see won't even remember they were there.'

'But their family person would know at the time,' Oliver protested.

'Not perhaps who it was visiting, but that it was someone familiar who cared enough to talk and listen – yes, I think that has to get through.'

'What's Grandpa's roommate like?' Twyla had explained that Pleasant Meadows had been unable to provide Grandpa with a private room. There were only six of them, all presently occupied. The twenty other residents all had to share.

'I didn't see him when I was here on Friday or yesterday. He must have been out in the communal space, unless someone had taken him out for a while. I do know he doesn't have Alzheimer's, which Kev said is the case with two thirds of the residents. Except for your grandpa all those with Parkinson's have private rooms and it's a matter of waiting for one to become available for him.'

Which meant someone else's loved one would have to die. Oliver couldn't wish, let alone pray for that. They had reached a door on their right close to the end of the hallway. Tucked into a meal holder was a white card with the name Willie Watkins printed above and that of Frank Andrews below. Oliver felt like his smile was printed on his face. It was so important that Grandpa should believe he was only happy and excited to see him.

The room could have belonged in a motel. Oliver had only been in a motel once when he was seven and Grandpa had taken him for a weekend to Orchard Beach outside Portland, but he remembered the plain furniture, the metal-framed window, the door opening into the bathroom and, most strongly of all, the feeling that it had no stories to tell. Nothing was left, or would ever remain, of the people who had stayed in it over the years. In this room there were two single beds, with two mid-brown dressers across from them, and two chairs with wooden arms tucked into corners. There was no one in the bed closest to the hallway door; it was made up with a faded patchwork quilt and a frog-green pillow case. Grandpa was in the bed by the window. It was brightened by the new red comforter Twyla and Oliver had picked out together. They had been able to tell on entering that Grandpa was asleep. His face was turned toward them, his skin a whitish gray stretched over his now painfully prominent bones. For the first time Oliver saw the impact of death's reshaping hand, the shedding of the flesh, the stripping down to the skull. He recalled, with a clutch at his heart, Grandpa saying before they left for that trip to Orchard Beach, 'He who travels light travels fastest.' The thought crept into Oliver's mind that he could understand why some of the relatives couldn't bring themselves to visit their family member; it hurt too much. If you didn't see it might not be happening; easier to think that death had already come. Oliver was horrified at the possibility that for the slightest moment he might have been thinking of himself and Grandpa. He would never, ever stop coming here. However much Grandpa changed on the outside, he would still be the same inside; even if the time came when he could no longer talk he would still be there breathing out love. Frank Andrews' mouth slackened and a trickle of saliva slid down his chin. Reaching for a tissue on the bedside table Oliver wiped it away.

'I love you a trillion billion,' he whispered. 'You're the best grandpa there ever was in the entire universe, even if there are little green ones on Mars.' The last part was the sort of joke he and Grandpa would laugh at; it had never taken much to make them laugh.

Twyla was beckoning to him. She picked up one of the chairs and crossed with it to the bed. Oliver tiptoed forward with the other one. They sat without talking for about five minutes and then began a quiet conversation about nothing in particular – how nice the new red comforter looked, wondering if the other residents were enjoying the visiting dog, how kind Kev had sounded. Grandpa slept on. The light from the window showed up the bruises on his arms and hands. They were the result of the blood thinners he took, nothing to do with the Parkinson's. They were called something that sounded like a spice, one that Mandy Armitage, Brian's mother, put in her chili. Cumin, that was the name – of the spice, not the medicine. Oliver retrieved the name that floated toward him, first in big letters, then smaller ones that grew smudgy before disappearing into a mist. Somewhere inside it were himself and Grandpa walking hand in hand across a bridge. He couldn't see, but he knew. Along with this awareness came the certainty that his parents and Grandma Olive were waiting on the other side in place of rainbow clouds and that soon he, Oliver, must turn and walk back on his own toward Sea Glass.

His eyelids grew heavy. He hadn't slept well the past two nights at the Cully Mansion or, for that matter, the past week. In the middle of last night he'd shot up in bed with his heart hammering. For a moment he had wondered where he was. The furniture stared back at him as if wondering what he was doing there and wishing he would go away. Alien shadows slithered and stretched, but it was the ones that crouched unseen in corners that bothered him the most. The fear gripped him that they were thinking slyly how much fun it would be to pop up for the purpose of making him yell out. The tall one alongside the open-curtained window, with the broad seat beneath, could have come from the high dresser, but it had a person-like look to it. What if those thin poky bits weren't reflected tree branches, but transparent fingers itching to touch him? His breath had frozen at the thought that it could be the ghost of old Emily Cully and he'd huddled back under the musty-smelling covers, willing himself back to sleep. It was all right for Brian to say what fun it would be but what if the talk around Sea Glass wasn't just hopeful made-up stuff, and she really and truly did haunt the Cully Mansion? Brian didn't have to live, let alone sleep here.

Voices woke him and he sat up to find himself in the chair in

Grandpa's room at Pleasant Meadows. What he heard was Twyla and Grandpa talking, but they stopped now and looked toward him.

'Good snooze?' Grandpa asked quite clearly. There were times when his voice came out better than others. The skull-like look was gone and his face even had some normal color.

Oliver beamed back at him. 'Was I asleep long?'

'About an hour.' Twyla smiled at him. It was a relaxed smile. The lines that showed around her eyes when she was tired or particularly worried weren't there anymore.

'You should've woken me up.'

'Your grandpa wouldn't let me; you know how he can be when he gets deciding to be boss.'

'Right!' Oliver laughed. 'You're both scared piddle pants of me, aren't you?'

'None of that language!' Grandpa tried to pull a fierce face. 'I thought if I'd slept the day away you could have a catnap.' The words continued to come without obvious difficulty. 'Twyla's been telling me about this new job of hers. Sounds great. That mother and son will be blessed to have her.'

The three of them continued on this topic for a while. On hearing that Sonny Norris had taught music, Grandpa brought up the fact that Clare had learned to play by ear on a friend's piano, but had never asked for lessons and said afterwards that it had been only a passing interest. Whenever Oliver listened to Grandpa talking about Mom, it felt as though she was reaching out her hand for his. This time sense of contact was especially strong because he had so often wished he could take piano lessons, but was sure they cost a lot. Holding his mother's hand was something quite different from being touched by a ghost. Twyla brought the topic round to Grandma Olive's wonderful recipe for soda bread, but quickly cut off what she had been about to say next. The fidgety movements under the bedcovering told them Grandpa needed the bathroom quick. Instantly Oliver remembered the piddle-pants joke and could have kicked himself. Grandpa had been wearing those grown-up diapers for over a year now, but still fought against having an accident. Twyla was in the room one moment and gone the next. She now returned with an aid pushing a wheelchair. This one wore glasses and a tie-died smock.

'I'll get you to the bathroom, Mr Anderson,' she said kindly.

Oliver was glad she hadn't called Grandpa Frank. She didn't know him well enough yet, and when you have to be taken to the toilet you've the right to hang onto your pride with both hands. Twyla had explained about that, saying often worse than pain was the loss of dignity. She had called Grandpa Mr Anderson after she came to look after him. With her help the aid now got Grandpa into the wheelchair.

'I can manage from here,' she offered, 'if you've something else that needs doing. I was Mr Andrews' nurse.'

The young woman looked relived. 'Are you sure you wouldn't mind? Mrs Middleton – Lucy – has worked herself into a state over the man she thinks is under her bed; says he has a knife. When she gets like that she can lose control and it usually takes two of us to calm her down.'

'You go along.'

'Thanks.' The aid vanished into the hall and Twyla wheeled Grandpa into the bathroom, closing the door behind them.

The chairs had been pushed back and Oliver now returned them to their corners. He guessed Twyla would suggest they leave as soon as Grandpa was settled back into bed. Being lifted out and returned always took such a lot out of him. Oliver heard voices coming closer down the hall and he turned round to see a man and a woman come through the door. The man was the older of the two. He was quite short and had the brownish-yellow face of a shriveled-up gnome; he even pranced like one, but in an unsteady sort of way. He still had a lot of hair; it curled up around the pointy ears, adding height the rest of him lacked.

'Sit yourself down on your bed, Father, and stop acting the fool. You'll fall over yourself one of these days, bust yourself inside out and that'll be the end of you.' She gave him a glare and muttered, only half under her breath: 'And good riddance to bad rubbish.' Catching Oliver's eye, she shrugged.

'He'll be the death of me first. I'll have a mouthful to say to the man at the pearly gates when I get there. There won't be no shuttling me about being stuck for the past fifty-some years with Willie Watkins for a father.' She jerked a giant thumb toward the bed. She was an extremely large woman, up, down and around, with a rough-skinned face and thick, coarse hair with a lot of gray in it hanging in a bulky braid over her shoulder almost to her waist, which was – as Oliver had already noted – a very long way down. Unable to come up with anything to say he watched lips form the gravelly words. 'His brain's turned to mush and they tell me his liver's shot, but the old goat will see me out, just like he did my poor mother. Didn't live to see seventy, she didn't. I used to tell her to push him in front of a truck. Didn't have it in her. Too soft for her own good.'

The man cupped a hand around a pointy ear. 'What's that you saying, Robin?'

'Just saying what an old dear you are, Dad.' The woman rolled her eyes at Oliver. Robin! The name didn't fit at all! It was like calling the giant at the top of the beanstalk Petey! What she'd said was terrible. How could he want to laugh? 'So who're you, skulking around in here?' she demanded as if about to pull a baseball bat out of the enormous front pocket of her faded blue jean jumper.

'Oliver Cully, Frank Anderson's grandson. He's your father's new roommate.'

'Oh!' She pretended to look startled. The braid shook as if preceding a rattle of iron links. 'I took you for a doctor come round in a hurry without your white coat.' A broad grin accompanied the joke. 'Good thing for you I was mistaken. I don't like doctors. Talk over your head like they think you've got a brain the size of a flea. Didn't do my mother any good or my husband, neither. Some big shot told me Earl had cancer. Could see by my face I didn't buy it. Nobody in Earl's family ever had cancer. Said he'd show me the X-rays. Like that'd prove anything! He points a finger and I say, "Oh, yare! I see it, that place that looks no different to me from all the rest!"'

'Hold on!' The gnome on the bed held up a knobby finger. 'Did the boy say he's a Cully?'

'You stay out of my private conversations, Dad.'

'And you think on who you're talking to my girl, or I'll put you across my knee and paddle your behind. Wouldn't be hard to find in the dark, big as it is.' His small eyes, still bright against the yellowed skin, slid toward Oliver. 'I was in your house.'

'Shut your mouth and lay down.' His daughter shot him a furious look.

'I'm not telling no lies, Robin, girl.' A whine crept into the voice. 'I'd a right to be there. It was wickedly cold outside.'

'You lay off talking about the Cully Mansion.' The daughter's face had turned red as beet. She stood silent for several moments, then squared her massive shoulders and looked Oliver in the eyes. 'I used to clean three days a week for Miss Emily. She didn't pay well – tight as a tick, but she was good to me in her way. Never minded when I brought Dad in for a bowl of soup. That makes what he did all the worse, creeping in after the place was empty and holing up in the cellar until the police found him. The shame of it put me low for months. I could just imagine the talk – Robin Polly shouldn't have let the old drunk out of her sight.'

'Mr Watkins hiding there sounds OK to me.' Oliver wondered if Gerard and Elizabeth knew about this. If Brian had heard through Aunt Nellie he hadn't said anything.

The heavy braid swung over Robin Polly's enormous chest as she shook her head. Oliver was sure he heard a clank. 'I hear your aunt and uncle have moved into the Cully Mansion and you're staying there with them.'

'I saw bones floating in the soup,' her father chirped in from the bed.

'Yes,' she rasped, 'I was just talking about how you were glad of a bowl on the days I worked at Miss Emily's.' She raised her thick brows on looking at Oliver. 'Always two steps and a hop behind in every conversation. But I'm glad to say the old lady was very fond of my split pea and ham soup.' Before Oliver could ask if she thought Emily would rather hang around and haunt her old home than go up to heaven, Twyla came out of the bathroom with Grandpa in the wheelchair, and the aid with the glasses and tie-died smock rejoined them.

After a nod of greeting, Mrs Polly ordered her father to lie down and shut his eyes and mouth. With that she was gone and very quickly afterward Twyla kissed Grandpa on the forehead and promised to come back soon. Oliver, blocking tears, kissed his cheek. 'Love you forever, Grandpa,' and followed her down the hall. A male aid told them the security code numbers to press on the small black panel by the door that opened into the entryway.

Oliver told Twyla about the conversation that had taken place while she was in the bathroom, but only in a general sort of way. He left out the parts where Mrs Polly had spoken angrily to, or about, her father. To have done so would have sounded like tattling, and Twyla would have been the first to say telling on someone was wrong, unless there was a sound reason. Mrs Polly might already be sorry and wishing she could take all the nasty parts back.

Afterwards they talked about Grandpa and how much better he had looked and sounded when he woke up. By that time Twyla was drawing up alongside the Cully Mansion. She hadn't come in to get him when she picked him up because he had been watching for her at the long window next to the double front doors and had walked out to meet her. She said that perhaps it would be best if she just stayed to watch him go inside, in case Elizabeth still wasn't feeling well. 'I wouldn't want her to feel she had to come and talk to me.'

'Right. You'll let me know how you get on tomorrow about the job?'

'I'll call you, lamb baby,' she kissed his cheek, 'as soon as you've had time to get back from school.'

Oliver went down the paved path with weeds and grass sprouting through the cracks and up the wide steps, determined not to let his feet drag because Twyla was waiting in the car to see him inside. He pushed on the handle of the right-side door and turned to wave goodbye before plodding into the overwhelmingly large, darkly paneled foyer. Gerard had called it the hall. The ceiling was a long way up, almost lost in shadows thickened by cobwebs. There was a good deal of heavy furniture which Oliver hadn't yet sorted out in his mind beyond a few chairs, their fabric seats thick with dust. When he arrived on Saturday he'd been vaguely aware of oil portraits with greenish black backgrounds and hadn't taken a close look at them since. He hadn't wanted to discover that he resembled anyone in the group, however long ago they had lived. The only color in the hall came from the red, green and yellow floor tiles that formed a pattern somewhere between floral and geometric. Oliver hadn't sized it up that way; he'd merely thought it was ugly and couldn't have been washed in fifty years. His overall impression had been one of stepping into a creepy movie. One where skeletons fell out of closets, bats hung from the chandelier, and when you accidentally pressed the paneling at the wrong place it spun you around into a room from which there was no escape. The wide treads of the towering staircase should have been a friendly touch; instead they suggested the wisdom of going up them only in pairs.

Now the thought came that oppressive (he had looked that word up in the dictionary recently) as the hall was, it was somehow better than Grandpa's room at Pleasant Meadows. Creepy as the Cully Mansion might be, there was no getting away from the fact that it having been home to generations it had stories to tell if someone was prepared to open his heart and listen. Oliver wasn't sure that he wanted to be that person as he continued down the hall. The living room was every bit as hideous as he had described to Twyla. Most monstrous of all was the four-poster bed at the far end with its pillows and covers still in place. But what stood out for him was the empty dome-shaped birdcage hanging from a tarnished brass stand. Oliver didn't like caged birds; he couldn't imagine them being happy, and the thought of one escaping to swirl around the ceiling and darting back and forth in a frantic flutter of wings scared him to squeaking fear. The thought of them brushing his face or arms was beyond chilling. Suddenly the notion of Aunt Emily coming back as a ghost didn't seem nearly as bad compared to coming down in the night to a cobwebbed, feathered form swinging on that perch. He continued on speeded-up legs to the kitchen, where he found Gerard seated at the weary-looking old table with his head in his hands. He had made up his mind to ask if he could have a dog or, if not, a cat. But this wasn't the moment. He didn't like Gerard. That wasn't going to change, but neither did he like seeing anyone looking miserable. The eyes that met his on looking up were brimming with it. Oliver saw the half-filled bottle and empty glass at his uncle's elbow.

'Hi!' he said. 'Where's Elizabeth?'

'Still in bed with her headache.' Gerard tried to get to his feet and sank back down. 'I guess we should be thinking about something to eat. Or is it that late?' He appeared to search for a clock without finding one.

'I could make us some soup.'

Gerard rallied to help search cupboards and they found two cans of chicken noodle and a jar of peanut butter. Bread for sandwiches turned up behind a box of cereal on the counter. Had Oliver been getting supper with Grandpa or Twyla it would have been fun, but he kept worrying that Gerard, although not actually unsteady, would trip on the buckled vinyl floor, or collide with the refrigerator that had to be two hundred years old and came too far out in the room. The next search was for a saucepan.

Having said he wasn't hungry, Gerard took a bowl of soup and half a peanut sandwich up to Elizabeth. Oliver finished his meal and waited for his uncle, but he didn't return. After an hour he went to his bedroom on the second floor – a few doors down

from theirs. It was a continuation of everything he hated about
the house. Gloomy, even with lights on, and musty smelling. He
flopped down on the bed, which was a smaller version of Emily
Cully's in the living room. But at least he didn't have to look at
a birdcage. Might as well have a nap, was his thought.

He must have slept for hours because when he opened his eyes
and sat up there was moonlight coming in through the window.
On the bench beneath it were deep shadows that shifted as he
stared at them into the shape of a boy of about his own age. He
appeared to be reading a book. It was all rather fuzzy until suddenly
he looked up. Then Oliver could see the thick, sandy hair and the
rounded face so very much like his own. His eyes were friendly,
if mildly puzzled. This was startling, but not frightening as it had
been to think he saw Gerard standing over him with unseeing eyes.

'Who are you?'

'Oliver Cully.' It came out in a croak.

'Oh, a relative! That's good. I don't mind at all that you're here,
but you do know this is my room?'

'Is it?' This had to be a dream, but somehow it wasn't the scary
sort and was becoming increasingly less weird. Just interesting.
'Who are you?'

'Nathaniel Cully. But you can call me Nat; that's what my
brothers' do. Will you think me rude if I get back to my book?'
He smiled apologetically. 'I'm at an exciting part. With a name
like yours you should read it, but of course not everyone likes
Dickens. Until now my favorites were *A Tale of Two Cities* and
Great Expectations. Goodnight.'

'Yes, just a dream,' said Oliver out loud, before closing his eyes
and lying back down. The next morning he was still sure that's all
it had been until he saw the leather-bound book – *Oliver Twist*
– placed face down in the middle of a chapter on the window
seat.

Seven

Sarah had driven back to Bramble Cottage on the Saturday morning
after her overnight stay at the house on Ridge Farm Rise, with

the curious feeling that Gwen Garwood and Sonny Norris were already woven into the fabric of her life. She had the strong feeling they would continue to be so in ways that would reshape its pattern, adding a richness and dimension that had been lacking. It wasn't only sympathy for their situation and a wish to help as best she could that tugged at her. She was drawn to Gwen as if to a part of herself yet unexplored. One previously avoided because it would have meant climbing a flight of invisible stairs to a clouded place that demanded every ounce of strength from those who reached it. An odd concept for someone who'd never thought of herself as fey.

Rounding the corner into Wild Rose Way she wondered in what ways, other than taking Jumbo the bull mastiff for walks, she could be of help to Gwen. Perhaps grocery items to be fetched and library books picked up and returned; these thoughts were brought to a halt when she noticed that there was no longer a break in her fence. Clearly Sid Jennson had made good on his promise to repair it. What a special man! She parked her car in the garage and went next door, but there was no answer to her ring. Her thanks would have to wait, but words alone would be inadequate. She needed to do something to express her gratitude; the sunny feeling it gave her was enhanced by the welcoming feel of her kitchen. She hadn't intended to do much cooking, let alone baking, until she had finished painting the cupboards and walls. In the interim unpacking more than the coffee maker, toaster and a couple of pans was pointless, but taking a grocery store purchased bakery item next door as a thank you gift just wouldn't do under the circumstances. There was that chocolate raspberry flourless cake that she always received compliments on, with people asking for the recipe, and she had made so often that she knew the recipe by heart. Making it only required a bowl, a whisk, spatula and a spring form pan; no hauling out her food processor. Why not make a cake for Gwen and Sonny as well?

Sarah sat down and began making a shopping list – a long one. Ten minutes later she drove out onto Salt Marsh Road and around the common to spend a very pleasant half hour in Plover's Grocery. It coupled old-fashioned charm with broad aisles, spotless floors and sensible organization. The varnished wooden service counter with its brass trim looked as though it had been in place for a hundred years, but the shopping carts came in three sizes and colors – red, green and yellow. She lingered longer than strictly necessary in the fruit and vegetable section, charmed by the bundles of asparagus tied with lavender ribbons and the lemons nestled in nests of mint. In her search for hazelnuts she wandered down an aisle to a subtle waft of spices emanating from clear plastic-fronted bins. She had never done any cooking verging on the exotic, but on impulse poured two scoops of saffron rice into a plastic bag, weighed and labeled it and did the same with the hazelnuts. Her one concern about the cakes was that she wouldn't be able to find the particular brand of dark raspberry chocolate the recipe called for and would have to substitute. She need not have worried. There it was on a shelf around the corner. Plover's might be small, but as she continued with her purchases, filling up the red shopping cart, it became clear that she wouldn't be left regretting her supermarket in Evanston.

On wheeling up the shopping cart and beginning to unload she asked the woman at the check-out counter if there was a home goods center anywhere nearby.

'Not one of the big chain ones, but there's Brown's Hardware just round the corner.'

Once there she zeroed in on the paint charts and sample strips, and was instantly enchanted. This was like playing doll's house, but she mustn't be deflected from her first priority which was choosing the exact shade of white for the kitchen cabinets and custard yellow for the walls. The latter she found quickly and was hesitating as to the other when a stocky, middle-aged man in a green apron with a pencil behind one ear came out from an aisle stocked with cans to ask if he could be of assistance.

Sarah held up the yellow strip. 'I've decided on this for the walls and ceiling, with a satin finish, because it's for the kitchen.'

'Most of the flats wash well; there's been a big improvement over the last few years, but I'm with you on the satin for kitchen and bathrooms.'

'I've just moved into an older home and am going to be repainting everywhere. Definitely flat for the living areas and bedrooms, but I've always thought the kitchen can do with a little extra shine.' Sarah wasn't usually chatty when shopping, but the man reminded her a little bit of her father; even the name on his plastic orange tag was similar – Berney to Dad's Barney. Besides, she didn't want to make any avoidable mistakes. 'I rather like this white for the cabinets, but I don't know what the best type for them is.'

'I'd suggest deck paint. Can't beat it for durability and it looks great. What you're looking at now is a good honest white and that we can give you.'

'I won't be taking it now. Have to work out how much I'll need of both colors and then I'll come back Monday.'

'Call in your order and we'll deliver.'

Twenty minutes later, having decided on the deck paint and with a half-inch stack of color samples for the other rooms in her purse, Sarah was about to leave when, on impulse, she turned round and went into the floor covering section. She'd been toying with the idea of painting the kitchen's tired beige vinyl with the intention of replacing it down the line with porcelain tiles. Now another temporary option presented itself when she examined the selection of self-stick tiles. Her eyes went to a periwinkle blue which, if teamed with a white, would be perfect, and the installation had to be preferable time-wise to painting a checkerboard design.

Sarah asked the salesman who appeared in the aisle if the tiles could be delivered along with the paint she was planning to order.

'No problem. Do your measuring and we'll work out the number of boxes.'

Sarah drove back to Bramble Cottage cocooned in domestic contentment. Interwoven with thoughts that the sea-green paint color was likely to be just right in subtle contrast to the natural linen slip covers in the living room, and that the teal should really cozy-up the study, was the realization of how inviting she had found the interior of the house on Ridge Farm Rise. It was all very well to claim the primary thing was your home reflects your taste. Undeniable was the hope that guests would enjoy the ambience offered sufficiently to settle back and relax or mingle animatedly in a group setting. She had always thought she didn't care much for period furniture; had considered it stuffy and self-important, suggestive of a determined retreat into the past. That had not at all been her reaction to Gwen Garwood's décor. Perhaps this was partially because she had responded to the living room's muted color scheme, the dusky gray-green velvet sofa and drapes; the time-dimmed patterned carpet, accented by the mulberry silk lampshades. She had particularly and surprisingly liked the pieces of pewter. A memory came of hearing pewter described as a friendly metal. To that she now added the word honest. And that was Gwen. A short amount of time in her company left no doubt of her ingrained integrity. Impossible to imagine her ever having a disloyal or deceitful thought, let alone acting on it.

The hope of a friendship with Gwen that would grow to include Sonny followed Sarah into the kitchen. She had just finished putting the dairy items in the fridge when she was caught up short on remembering that her jewelry box was still in the car's glove compartment. She had forgotten about it until now. Yesterday she had been fully occupied with other matters and it certainly hadn't crossed her mind during this morning's shopping. In the past she had rarely, if ever, left the car unlocked, but Sea Glass oozed safety. Not bothering had been a welcome shift, a sheltered time warp. Now misgivings arose. In that box was the diamond and garnet ring that had belonged to a great-grandmother. Until one of the stones had fallen out, and luckily been found, Sarah had worn that ring almost constantly in recent years. If she'd gotten round to getting it fixed she'd be wearing it now. Yes, Nellie Armitage had assured her that the local crime rate was low, but she had also mentioned that the Cully Mansion had been broken into during the winter. What if some passerby had tried the car door and made the most of a golden opportunity? She drew in a breath before darting out to the garage.

A wave of relief flooded through her on opening the glove compartment to see the jewelry box in place. It wasn't large or elaborate, but well-made and of a warm honey maple. Her parents had bought it at a craft show at the mall and given it to her for her fourteenth or fifteenth birthday. It was one of life's small constants; always ready to hand on her dressing table, bringing back happy memories of childhood and adolescence. She had left it till the last moment to pack, and then decided there wasn't room in either of her suitcases. Back in the kitchen she lifted the lid. Wasted panic. There was the ring. Box in hand she ran upstairs to put it on the dressing table under the window. In her relief she didn't think about transferring the bracelet to a safer place.

Her mind instantly turned to making up the bed and hanging the sheer curtains. There was the screwdriver to be located, in addition to three or four other trips up and down the stairs, one of which included taking the silver-gray paint sample from her purse and holding it up against the wall. Perfect. She thought about using the same color in the bathroom, but decided that might look as though she was trying to fake an en suite, and returned to her idea of painting it and the half-bath downstairs the sea green she'd picked for the living room. By now it had to be well past one o'clock, and she prepared a tuna salad, spooned out half of it onto a bed of endive and bib lettuce, sliced off the end of the baguette, and settled down at the kitchen table with her paint color strips alongside. After clearing up she got busy on the cake for Sid Jennson. She had decided to make the one for Gwen Garwood tomorrow and take it over to her on Monday. The last thing she wanted was to create the impression she was going to be no sooner out the door of the house on Ridge Farm Rise than back ringing the bell. She had sensed an underlying reserve in Gwen that was part of her own nature. Having closed the door on the spring form pan, she was noting the time on her watch – exactly two o'clock – when her cell phone rang. As she reached for it on the counter top the thought went through her mind that it would be her sister-in-law Kristen or her brother Tim calling to see how she was settling in. Good! The cake didn't need to be checked for forty-five minutes. Time for a lengthy chat. Both Kristen and Tim were talkers and the two girls would insist on having their turn with Aunt Sarah, wanting to know how soon they could come and visit.

Her 'Hi' was an enthusiastic one.

'Sarah?' A man's voice, but not Tim's pleasant rumble.

'Yes?'

'It's me, Sarah. Harris.'

Her mind went instantly blank. She hadn't spoken to him in nearly two years. She stood there, her back to the cabinet, unable to bring his face into focus. It wasn't that she didn't want to; she tried and couldn't get beyond the dark blond hair and a wedge of nose. She knew it was a good nose, but she couldn't see it. 'What uncharacteristic bad grammar,' she heard herself say lightly. 'The man I knew would have said, "It's I, Harris." Don't tell me you're nervous?'

'Merely surprised that you didn't seem to have a clue who was speaking.' He laughed. 'Deserved it, I suppose.'

'It wasn't an intentional slap in the face.' Sarah had recovered sufficiently to wonder why on earth he was calling. It seemed a long time ago that she had never left a room without her cell, even though she had a house phone, in case he should choose that moment to make contact. Desperate to let her know that he regretted the divorce, that his new marriage was a dreadful mistake and pleading for her to take him back. Her father had told her in no uncertain terms to change both numbers, and after some mental bleating she had done so. Now she filled in the pause by reminding herself to arrange to have a house phone installed in the next few days if possible.

'I've been hoping you'd moved on emotionally.'

No, you haven't, she thought without rancor, you much prefer the idea of my pining away in my lonely bed. Any protestations would bounce off his ego. He'd had plenty of good points and for a long time she had taken his arrogance for admirable self-confidence. 'How is Lisa?' She might have been speaking of a mutual acquaintance. 'And your little girl? She must be beyond the toddler stage now.'

'Thanks for asking, Sarah,' his tone was now bracing, 'it means a lot. I really was optimistic when I found out about your move to Maine and that you have left *us* in the rear-view mirror. Boyfriend out there?'

'How did you get this number?' She could hear a woman's voice in the background, coupled by a child's wailing.

'I've been wanting to get in touch and yesterday decided to phone your Aunt Beth and see if she could help me out. She and I always got along well and she didn't strike me as the sort to align herself with the rest of your family against me.'

'No, she wouldn't do that.' Trust Beth to relish being the reasonable party. She'd be preening herself for days. Well, good for her. Why shouldn't she get a little fun out of life?

'I hope you aren't annoyed with her for giving me your number. Not classified, is it?' Another laugh. 'So many divorced people I know manage to be not only civilized but friendly. I'd like it to be that way with us, Sarah. And Lisa is all for it. Aren't you, darling?' An indistinguishable murmur, accompanied by another wail from the little girl. Amazing that she could hear it with sympathy free of heartache. 'Anyway, getting to the main point of this call . . .' He hesitated.

'Yes, Harris?' She was surprised by how easy it was to say his name without experiencing the smallest twist of pain. Her heart went out to Lisa. However much she might have supported this call it couldn't be entirely easy for her, especially considering her long, very close friendship with the ex. Under Lisa's sophistication there had always been hints of insecurity, the sort that could produce enormous guilt masked by brittle indifference. Hopefully she'd come to realize that no woman can break up another's marriage that is essentially sound. Sarah was suddenly tremendously glad Harris had phoned and aware that her voice had warmed. 'Tell me what's on your mind.'

'A favor if you're feeling generous,' another of those punctuation laughs, 'or you could call it fair play?'

Before she had time to digest this, the bell rang. 'Excuse me a minute, Harris, there's someone at the door. I'll just check who it is . . . walking there now. Oh!' she said, opening up to see a van in the driveway and a man on the step holding a cellophane wrapped offering that could only be flowers. 'It's a floral delivery – I have to go.'

'I can hang on.'

'Better not. I've a cake about to come out of the oven.'

'Sounds like you're celebrating.'

'Just the moving-in kind.'

'Call me back. The number will show on the ID, but don't make it too long as we're going over to Lisa's parents and won't be back till late.'

'Got you.' Might be tricky explaining to the in-laws why he was on the phone to his ex-wife. She pocketed the cell phone, apologized to the delivery man and a few moments later was back in the kitchen unwrapping the flowers. The card was signed, *With much appreciation from Gwen and Sonny.* She stood smiling at it. The heavenly scent of roses filled the room – twelve pale pink ones, interspaced with ferns and baby's breath. They had to be an old-fashioned variety; the newer ones didn't have nearly that much scent. She should have been surprised that Gwen had chosen that particular shade of pink that had always been her favorite, but somehow she wasn't; it only deepened the sense of connection she had felt that morning. If a phone directory had been left behind in the house she hadn't come across it. So she pressed 411, asked for a Garwood on Ridge Farm Rise, Sea Glass, Maine, got the number and moments later, at the third ring, Gwen picked up. They had a short but warmly conversational chat. Sarah's delight in the roses bubbled through, and Gwen expressed pleasure that they had been delivered so promptly.

'A very small token of gratitude for your incredible kindness.' She went on to say that when Sid Jennson had returned her car that morning he'd told her about repairing the fence, adding that he had then taken Sonny back to his house for several hours and that the visit had been very successful. Sonny had returned in excellent spirits. 'I really must think of something special to do for Mr Jennson and his wife. People here are very neighborly, but last night you and he took the word to a new level.'

'I'm sure he was as happy to be of help as I was. Your roses have brought a breath of life to the house, but a four-footed visitor would be very welcome. How would it be if I came and fetched Jumbo for an outing on Monday?'

They agreed on early afternoon. The call ended rather hastily when Sarah remembered the cake in the oven. She checked it, decided on another fifteen minutes and went in search of her wire cooling rack. Harris's call had slipped from her mind when she unwrapped the roses; now it drifted back in. She had only the vaguest curiosity as to what he had wanted to ask her, but she would phone him back as promised after she had taken her cake out of the oven and set it to cool on the rack. But when she did so there was no answer. Apparently he had not lingered in setting off with Lisa and the little girl to visit the in-laws. Never mind, he'd try again or she would.

The chocolate cake came out just right: moist but not soggy to the touch. An hour later she was dusting it with powdered sugar prior to wrapping it loosely in two layers of tin foil. Four o'clock. Sarah headed out into warm sunshine to go next door, having made up her mind not to go in if asked. That was where she was a little shy, or perhaps old fashioned: a man on his own – Nellie had said his wife was away for the weekend visiting the college daughter. Also a lot of people didn't appreciate impromptu visits that dragged them away from whatever they were doing. Nellie Armitage's showing up to camp in her living room for a lengthy chat, especially on moving-in day, would have driven even her easy-going mother, Louise Draycott, right up the wall.

Sid Jennson handled the situation perfectly when he opened his front door. He thanked her enthusiastically for the cake, made light of repairing her fence, invited her to step inside but didn't press her when she said she really needed to get back and continue her unpacking. Entirely true – there were her clothes to be hung in the closet. Also towels and other necessities to be stored in the bathroom.

'Seems never-ending, doesn't it?' He gave her a rueful smile and she thought again what a genuine man he seemed to be. 'I remember when we moved in here five years ago we wondered if we'd ever get organized. Seemed to go round in circles for bloomin' days. The wife and daughter claimed I was chiefly to blame with all my tools. You'd think to hear them go on that I'd moved in an entire hardware store.'

That led to Sarah mentioning her visit to Brown's that morning and how she needed to work out the amount of floor tiles and paint she would need.

'My Libby's a great hand with a paintbrush should you welcome any help. And I've one of those special ladders for doing staircase walls. She's not much of a one for heights and if you're the same I could take care of that job. Expecting her back Monday morning from visiting our daughter, Phoebe, at college and getting her ready for going to England to stay with family for a month. She'll want to have you over for dinner one night, will Libby. How'd you fancy roast beef and Yorkshire pudding?'

Sarah replied that she'd love to try the real thing and was just about to say goodbye when she heard a meow and a large ginger cat sauntered through the living room on which the door opened. For not the first time that day she thought of the frightened one she had been holding when Sonny Norris crashed the car through her fence. She had been out several times calling and looking for it without success. Sid Jennson didn't mention bringing Sonny here and providing Gwen with a break for a few hours. He wouldn't be one to hold his acts of kindness up to the light.

'What a lovely-looking cat,' she said.

'Thinks he owns the world. Spoiled rotten, just like the dog. A great one for animals, my Libby. Would rescue a lion from the zoo if they'd let her and have it sleep on its own pillow at the foot of the bed. Still, mustn't grumble,' his smile deepened, 'she sees me right. Have to play fair and not hog all this cake before she gets home.'

On returning to Bramble Cottage Sarah hoped to get a glimpse of the stray cat, but only saw a grey squirrel dart across the road and skim up a tree. Without much optimism she put a saucer of milk on the front step and another on the back patio. Her fear was that the cat had succumbed to some predator the previous night. That Libby Jennson was an animal person encouraged her to hope that they would get on well. She spent that evening pleasantly occupied with a dozen small tasks. She had only one small television and, other than watching the news, rarely had it on unless she was sitting down to knit. She made a note to get cable or an alternative installed.

Sunday morning passed to the accomplishment of removing the kitchen cabinet doors, baking the cake for Gwen and getting to work on the sample of a design for a child's sweater – ages two to six – with its first name worked on the front. She used Julia. Her niece at eleven would consider herself way too old for it but she would enjoy seeing it in the magazine. In the afternoon she took a long walk along the beach, in the opposite direction around the bay than she had taken yesterday. The sun was warm on her shoulders, encouraging her to gravitate to the water's edge. It came furling up without fuss or foam over her canvas shoes. There were a couple of sailboats at rest sufficiently far out to be no more than graceful silhouettes, their naked masts piercing the thin, silver-blue sky. She paused to draw them into herself. Did they dream of past voyages, or future ones? A plump white and gray gull eyed her beadily from a barnacle-encrusted grouping of rocks. What did she want most as she spread her own wings? She felt something touch her hand. The strong, firm grip of a child's hand in hers. The gull shot upward to join in a fierce flapping of its cronies, accompanied by quarrelsome squawks. The foolish moment was gone with dizzying abruptness.

It had been hours since lunch. And that had been a skimpy one because her mind hadn't been on eating. Turning back, she skirted the bigger islands of rock and pocketed several pieces of sea glass before reaching the steps up to her garden. She would have to find a little glass bowl to put them in, along with the one she had found yesterday. Could she now call herself a collector? Even something of a connoisseur? Amusement erased that odd moment on the beach.

While eating dinner, the niggling thought crept in that there was something she had made a mental note to take care of – something small yet important – but she couldn't get further than connecting it with talking to her father on the phone shortly after her arrival. It would come back to her, but it didn't that evening. It was only after phoning Brown's hardware at nine the following morning to reel off her list – including a last moment addition of a drop cloth – that she remembered the note she had promised her father would be written promptly to Aunt Beth. A thank you for the overnight stay in New Hampshire. Best to take care of that small courtesy immediately. Brown's had promised a delivery between eleven thirty and noon. She had stamps in her billfold and quickly located a Hallmark card. Aunt Beth didn't think much of those who didn't 'care enough to send the very best,' and filled up both sides without mentioning Harris's call. He hadn't phoned again, so perhaps what he'd wanted to ask Sarah wasn't all that important.

On opening the front door she saw that it was spattering rain – must have just started – and ducked out at a run to the mailbox at the foot of the drive. She pulled down the front, slipped in the card and was just about to close it again when she noticed another envelope further back. Mail for her already? How nice! Her heart sang as it had done so often during the last three days. No possibility occurred to her, but when she withdrew the letter she saw that it was addressed to Nan Fielding. It must have arrived after her death, but it would take studying the postmark to tell how long it had been there. That wasn't something to do with the rain coming down; if it wasn't smudged already it soon would be. She slipped the envelope in her jeans' pocket, closed the box and raised the red plastic flag to alert the deliverer that there was outgoing mail.

As she turned to hurry back inside, a woman wearing a light-weight pink jacket and a white cotton scarf wrapped around her neck came around the near side of the house next door. Her hair, with its blond highlights, was drawn back in a ponytail. At her heels was a small, fleecy dog of a yellowish white that suggested he wasn't bleached along with the scarf. Sarah had paid more attention to dog breeds over the last year or so and hazarded a guess this one was a mix. Half shiatsu, half poodle. Possibly. As it approached her in a short-legged charge it was clear from the *joy de vive* in his eyes that this was one compact bundle of mischief, who'd relish pulling the wool – or fur – over your eyes just for the fun of it at every given opportunity. He, or she, actually appeared to be laughing at her as he scooted to a halt.

'Hello, there!' The woman's greeting was an unmistakably cheery one. Also noticeably British. 'I'm Libby Jennson.' She could have been Sarah's age had Sid not mentioned the daughter in college. Rather lovely eyes, an unusual shade of golden gray, coupled with the proverbial English rose complexion. Also indicating her country of origin were the calf-high green rubber boots. Sarah was enchanted. She had always loved the word Wellies. Libby breezed on. 'You must be Sarah! I've really wanted to meet you! Especially after having three slices of that chocolate cake! Sid kept tapping my hand away and reminding me it was at least half his! I'd love the recipe! Don't tell me it's been in your family for three hundred years and is a fiercely guarded secret!' All said in large print with super-sized exclamation points, undampened by the rain.

Sarah laughed. She was to discover that Libby often had this effect upon her. 'Wish I could say it had been handed down, but I found it on the internet. I'll gladly print you up a copy. It was so good of your husband to fix my fence.'

'Don't give it a thought. Sid isn't happy if he isn't busy. I'm over the moon I didn't come home to find he'd torn out a wall like he did the last time I went away for the weekend. I said to our daughter Phoebe last night that I think I'd better set off for home now rather than wait for morning; I've a nasty feeling Dad will turn the garage into a disco room if I don't. At sixty-six you'd think he'd be slowing down. Fat chance! And to think of the flack I got for marrying a man twenty years older. He'll be the one pushing me in a wheelchair!'

Sarah responded with that old line about age being only a number.

'He's off now doing a hundred errands and there was me down on the beach with Sheridan, with not one industrious thought, just miles away in my head with the fairies. We'd be down there still if it hadn't started to rain.' Libby wiped a spatter from her face. 'Crikey! It looks ready to come down cats and dogs and I'm keeping you standing here. How about coming back to my house for a cup of coffee or tea?'

Sarah hesitated. She needed to wash the kitchen walls and scour out the interiors of the cabinets, but that shouldn't take much more than an hour and surely establishing friendly relations with her next-door neighbor was more important.

'I'd love to,' she said as several heavy drops plopped on her head to trickle down her neck.

'Let's make a dash for it then. Come on, Sheridan, you need drying off and tucking up under your blankie.'

The little dog did now resemble a wet mop, but considering he skittered in circles, risking getting stepped on as they headed for the Jennson's house, he gave no indication of readiness to plop down for a nap. Libby entered the house by a side door that opened to a mud room. Unhitching an orange towel from a row of hooks she told the mop to sit, which he did with the offended look of someone asked to submit to a strip-search. Maybe it was the color orange that got to him. There was no mistaking the frown. With a name like Sheridan he could be excused for having expanded ideas of his own importance.

To prove Sarah wrong about the nap he shot toward a cushion-lined basket the moment Libby opened the door into the kitchen after shedding the pink jacket and white scarf. It was a light, spacious room, with a lengthy farmhouse table at the far end surrounded by a mismatch of chairs painted in various colors, echoed by the Toulouse-Lautrec prints on the cream walls and the up-to-date Tiffany-style pendants suspended about the butcher block island. Libby excused herself to spread the blankie over Sheridan, who was giving a good impression of being asleep if he wasn't.

'Are you wet through?' she asked Sarah on straightening up. 'I can lend you a sweater; it would be wretched if you got pneumonia, especially after your narrow escape from that car.'

'I'm fine, thank you. Just a few damp spots.'

'So what will it be? Tea or coffee?'

'Tea, please.' Sarah had been looking at the wooden sign on the door to the mud room that read: *Second Chances Are Better Than First Ones.*

'You may find it stronger than you're used to, even if I don't let yours steep. I use British blend, you see. And I'm out of lemons. Sid and I still take ours with milk and he's been here twenty-five years to my ten. We met on one of his trips home, in a pub where I worked evenings as a barmaid.'

'I'd really like to try tea the proper English way.'

While Libby got busy putting on the kettle and getting out cups and saucers, Sarah wondered about Phoebe, the college-age daughter.

A faint snoring drifted their way from the basket. 'That's always the way with the little tyke. He's always worn out after a good run,' said Libby. 'You wouldn't think to look at him how fast he can go. Should be in the Olympics.'

Sarah thought about Jumbo's sedate indoor pace. Would he too go all out if released from his leash on the beach? She hoped the rain would clear by the afternoon so she could go and collect him.

'It's a great name, Sheridan. How did you come up with it?'

'From the TV series *Keeping up Appearances*. The one with Hyacinth Bucket – pronounced Bouquet. Sheridan's her son, who never appears on scene, but brings lots of laughs.'

'My mother won't miss it, even though she's watched every episode half a dozen times. I've been over when she has it on and it is funny, but I don't remember anything about the son.'

'Who could blame him for not visiting? The dreaded Hyacinth causes someone to fall off a bike when she mentions an invitation to one of her candlelight suppers with the Royal Doulton. Everyone wondering how her mild-mannered husband, Richard, stands it. I always get the biggest kick out of her,' Libby continued to enthuse as she poured steaming water into a brown earthenware teapot, 'when she's on the phone to Sheridan wanting to know how he's doing with needlepoint studies at the university. Thrilled to the core by his devotion to Mummy until he asks for seventy pounds for a pair of silk pajamas. Anyway, as soon as I saw my little guy – the one presently snoring his head off – I knew I was going to be every bit as batty and braggy about him.' Libby was now filling the teacups. 'Do you want to put in your own milk?'

'No, you do it, please.'

Libby reached for the pitcher. 'That's another of Sid's things.'

'Snoring?'

'Needlepoint. Mostly cushions. His mother taught him to sew when he was six; told him every man should know how. Along with being able to darn his own socks – not that anyone does that anymore. But she certainly did Sid a favor; he trained in upholstery and got in with a good firm before getting a job offer over here from an American on a buying trip in England on vacation. Sid stayed with that company till he retired. Now he does jobs part time. We usually head south for a couple of months in the winter and he's like a bear with a sore head, pining for his sewing machine.'

Libby handed over a cup and saucer. 'Would you like some lemon bread with that? Don't mind if I hang on to your wonderful cake?'

The alternative proved to be delicious when they took it along with their tea into a living room that opened off the end of the kitchen with the farmhouse table. They sat in bright yellow armchairs that went excellently with the black and cream toile sofa, a repeat of the wallpaper pattern. If Sid had done the uphol- stering he was a master. Sarah summed up the general vibe as mod-traditional. What fun! Against the staircase wall was a cabinet with broad cranberry and cream stripes. Its oversized black knobs added just the right amount of mischief chic without detracting from the silver tray and sparkling cut glass decanter and wine glasses, or jibing at the elegant walnut-framed mirror above. Sarah admired the cabinet.

'I painted it,' Libby admitted.

'I'm impressed. You really have a knack; I love this room and the kitchen.'

'Thanks. For all my grumbling it makes it nice that Sid takes a big interest. Did you look at a lot of houses before deciding on the one next door?'

'It was the first I was shown and a case of love at first sight. I had this instant feeling that we belonged together and refused to look at any others.'

Libby looked at her across the glass coffee table. 'Are you a bit that way?'

'What way?'

'Psychic?'

'Oh, no! Not a grain of anything like that.' Up through the voiced denial wriggled a worm of uncertainty that wouldn't have been there a couple of days ago. There was the suddenly remem- bered episode on the beach yesterday afternoon, which she had shoved from her mind as a waking dream, and the strong feeling of connection to Gwen Garwood. 'I'm like a lot of people in thinking houses have atmospheres. Probably something to do with ones we have related to in the past, without really remembering them. Anyway,' she added lamely, 'that's just my thinking. Do you believe in psychic phenomena?'

'Well, I'm not as strong on it as Nellie Armitage across the road with her spirit guides.'

'I've met her. Quite a character.'

'Showed up on your doorstep within two minutes of the movers taking off is my bet,' suggested Libby shrewdly. 'Not one to let the grass grow under her feet is Nellie. But you can't help liking her. Can't do enough for people she likes. She goes to a spiritualist church in Dobbs Mill, that's about four miles from here, towards Ferry Landing. I got interested when she got talking one day, soon after Sid and I moved in here, about circles outsiders are invited to attend. They're held in the evenings mid-week and I suppose you could call them séances, but without the lights being turned off and the holding of hands. You sit on folding chairs lined up around the walls like you're there for a book club meeting or what have you.'

'So you went to one?'

'I'd been to a fortune teller a couple of weeks before Sid showed up in my life.' Libby paused as the ginger cat, having come down the stairs, jumped on her lap. 'She told me I was about to meet an older man, we'd get married, go to live abroad and he'd adopt my little girl. Phoebe was ten at the time; I'd been divorced for five years and had no intention of getting into a serious relationship. We'd done just fine on our own.'

Sarah took this in, allowing for the fact that memories of what is actually said can be elastic. She hoped no hint of skepticism showed in her voice. 'Did anything happen for you at the circle?'

'I don't remember what was said until about halfway through when the medium – a very ordinary, middle-aged woman, the sort you see all the time pushing a cart round the supermarket – asked if anyone there had a grandmother named Margaret. There were about eight of us there and I put up my hand.'

Not an unusual name, thought Sarah, and if it hadn't struck gold there could have been a shift to Marjorie or Mary, drifting down to any name beginning with M; classic flim-flam. 'Was there a message?'

'That she loved me and hoped I wasn't ruining my hair having those bleached streaks put in; then she said she had to go because it was someone else's turn.'

'You must have been excited.'

'Not really.' Libby's golden gray eyes held a musing expression. 'You see, I'd been really hoping my Mum would come through. But then, when I thought about it afterwards, I realized it would've been unbelievable if she had. She was always one to stand back and let others push in front.' This was said with such complete seriousness that Sarah suppressed a smile. It was at that moment she knew how very much she was going to enjoy knowing Libby Jennson.

'That's all so interesting,' she said, 'but I think if I had the glimmer of a gift I'd have had a shiver of premonition before that car came through the fence.'

They went on to talk about the situation relating to Sonny Norris and his mother. Libby didn't know either of them, but said Sid had been extremely moved by the hand they had been dealt. She mentioned his having brought Sonny home with him for a few hours and that they both hoped they could do more without being overly intrusive. Sarah spoke of her plan to take their bull mastiff, Jumbo, out for walks, starting that afternoon if the rain would kindly let up.

Libby glanced toward the window. 'It looks like it's practically stopped already. How about another cup of tea and slice of lemon bread?'

'I'd love it, but I'd better get back.' Sarah explained about the Brown's Hardware delivery, looked at her watch, saw it was approaching ten thirty and got to her feet.

'Let me know if you'd like any help,' said Libby on opening the front door for her. 'I live for a paintbrush or roller in my hands; I'm as much of a nut about it as Sid is with his sewing and all the rest of his relentless activities.'

The rain had indeed become negligible. Just the odd drop, as if bored with the whole business. Sarah turned onto her own driveway with a smile on her face, which broadened to one of delighted relief when she saw what was on the step. It was a gray cat. Was it the bowl of milk, diluted now by rainwater, that had worked the charm? She moved forward with concentrated nonchalance, afraid to breathe as she reached to open the door. So far so good! The animal remained seated as if cemented in place. Then the amazing moment. When she stepped inside it followed as if this were an accepted pattern. In clear light it looked even more painfully emaciated than she remembered. She made no attempt to pick it up – best to let it get its bearings while she opened a can of tuna. It was the kind packed in water which would surely be better on an empty stomach than the oily kind. She also got out the milk. As soon as she set the two bowls down on the kitchen floor the cat crept up like a dusky shadow to hunch down and begin devouring the contents of both, interrupted only by the occasional flinch-eyed sideways glance. 'Dusky.' That's what she would name it, male or female – for its color and the time of day when she had first seen it. She'd ask Nellie and Libby if they knew of a lost cat and if that wasn't successful ask for their suggestions for attempting to track down the owner, but she didn't feel much optimism. Its almost skeletal frame suggested it had been attempting for fend for itself for some time. Meanwhile, she would need to scoot out as soon as Brown's had completed their delivery and pick up food and a litter box. Leaving it while she did this, and afterward taking Jumbo for his walk would, she hoped, provide a calm settling in period.

She stood with her back to the kitchen counter watching it, while confining her movements to a minimum and murmuring soothingly.

'Thanks for coming; I was worried about you. That's a big scary world out there; I hope you'll get to like being an inside cat. I'll get you some toys. This is really going to be fun.' Both bowls were empty and she would have loved to bend down and pick the sad little thing up, but after looking up at her for a moment it shifted away through the opening into the living room. She remained where she was; hands pressed to her hips, felt the stiffened quality of her right jean pocket and realized it was the letter. The one she had found in the mailbox addressed to Nan Fielding, that she had forgotten when Libby and Sheridan had come up to her in the rain.

She pulled it out and stared down at the handwriting on the white envelope, not business-size, written with a black ballpoint pen, angular strokes, which suggested to her a man, possibly in a hurry. Ridiculous! The initials EB in the top left hand corner above the return address gave nothing away. She was romanticizing a secret love interest between the writer and a lonely elderly woman. Or willing a devoted nephew on her. In another moment it would be the son Nan had left on the church steps with a note pinned to a blanket saying *Mommy loves you*. What did she think she was? A medium at one of the Dobbs Mill circles? Even more foolish was the powerful insistence, seeming to come at her from all corners, that what she held in her hands was somehow vital to her own future. Medium nothing! She had to be off with the fairies, as Libby had described herself when down on the beach. Translation – let loose in Never Never Land. All that was required was that she write *deceased* and put the letter back in the mailbox. But she knew she couldn't bring herself to do that for purely compassionate reasons. She couldn't chance that it had been sent by someone requesting a donation to a once-attended poetry club or even a former neighbor. Already the letter she would write and enclose with the envelope was forming rapidly in her head, as if propelled by something outside herself.

> *Dear EB,*
>
>   *I moved into Bramble Cottage over the weekend and found your letter in the mailbox this morning. I am sorry to say that Nan Fielding died, peacefully as I understand it, sometime in March; I'm uncertain of the date. You may already know this, but if not I hope this isn't very upsetting for you. My sympathy if this is a personal loss. The garden promises to be lovely which seems to me to say a lot about her.*
>
>   *Sincerely,*
>   *Sarah Draycott*

Eight

Within five minutes of sitting down with Twyla Washburn on that Monday morning, Gwen could have kissed Nellie Armitage's spirit guides for suggesting this woman to be the ideal person to help care for Sonny. He was still upstairs in his bedroom, having not appeared at the head of the stairs when the doorbell rang. They were seated in the book room. Twyla was on the sofa and Gwen in her preferred armchair with Jumbo lying alongside it. The coffee, prepared in readiness, had been poured. A plate of oatmeal raisin cookies was placed within easy reach of both women. The room wore its antiquity well. Very comfortable in there. Even cozy, against the blurred windows, with the table lamps lighted under their mulberry silk shades. The sound of the rain at the windows had a softly musical quality as if on the brink of coming up with a melody. On welcoming Twyla into the house she had instantly recognized her as the woman seated, with the endearing-looking sandy-haired boy, in the same church pew as Sonny and herself. She and Twyla had exclaimed at the coincidence on shaking hands. The strength and kindness of the remembered face, framed by the becomingly cropped gray hair, seemed to settle upon the room like a healing touch. The steady eyes, several shades darker than the smooth brown skin, and the rich, warm voice, both calmed and brightened the moment.

Gwen heard the amusement in her own voice as she described the two previous helpers to whom Sonny had so strongly objected. 'I wondered with the first one if he'd pull some schoolboy stunt, such as putting a frog in her bed or food coloring in her shampoo. They both treated him like a child which he naturally resented. Oh, dear!' Her expression sobered. 'I sound as if I'm trying to warn you off.'

'Not at all. You're saying what needs to be said upfront: that your son is due the respect owed to a grown man. I surely believe that can be provided while managing situations that could get out of hand. The loss of self, the sensation of being swallowed up in a fog of confusion has to be terrifying at times. It's understandable that it should bring on angry, even violent outbursts. Very painful and disturbing for you as his mother.' Twyla directed a look at Gwen that included both sympathy and encouragement. 'If you decide you want me to come here, I'll do all I can to make sure you get a proper night's rest and some breaks during the day. It's so important that you don't wear yourself out if you're to keep up a reserve of strength. I'm sure your doctor would say you should do something that makes you happy three times a day, Mrs Garwood.'

'Do please make it Gwen. And if you don't mind I'll call you Twyla, but whatever makes you feel the most comfortable. Of course I want you to come. I'm convinced you're just what Sonny and I need. Bless Nellie Armitage! She explained that you have personal reasons for wishing to be in Sea Glass, relating to your patient Frank Andrews' grandson. Would that be the boy with you in church yesterday?'

'That's him.' Twyla's tall, bony frame instantly seemed to fill out like a down pillow. 'I call him my lamb baby, because that's what I saw first time I laid eyes on him. God surely broke the mold when he made Oliver Cully. And Frank and his wife Olive, before she died, more than did their part bringing him up the way his parents would've wanted.'

'The news of the plane crash that took them and the other grandparents shook-up the community.' Gwen motioned sadly with her hands. 'In itself it was a terrible thing, and then there was the Cully name and all the excited chatter when Clare Andrews married into the family. I met her once when she was an adolescent – I'll tell you about that sometime. From what I saw and have since she was lovely inside and out.'

'There was an estrangement between Max Cully, Oliver's father, and his family when he married Clare. Did you know about that?'

Gwen nodded. 'Through the grapevine and in particular Nellie Armitage. She said when she came to see me about the possibility of your coming here that Oliver has very recently gone to live with his father's brother and wife at the old Cully Mansion. She stressed that until now they've been virtual strangers and you'd like to be close by while he settles in – to be right on hand if he should need you urgently.' Gwen set down her coffee cup. 'I'm afraid I'm putting that badly . . . as if implying something negative against the uncle and aunt.' She'd very nearly used the word sinister. It had to be the forbidding aspect of the Victorian house, too long abandoned, that suggested macabre possibilities. So foolish! The result of reading too many gothic novels of the sort satirized by Jane Austen in *Northanger Abbey*. Twyla sat silent, as if caught up in her own thoughts and Gwen continued positively. 'Nellie explained how close you and Oliver have become since you started taking care of his grandfather. A bond I could see for myself in church. However kind Mr and Mrs Cully may be, it has to be a wrenching experience for Oliver being removed from everyone and everything he loves. Anguishing, I can only imagine, for Mr Andrews. Nellie could not speak highly enough of him and the entire family, including the son-in-law.'

'Frank is one remarkable, rare man.' Twyla's eyes remained reflective. 'Never a thought for himself when it became clear he'd have to go in a nursing home. His life since his wife died has been all about Oliver. Not an ounce of love spared from morning to night. Those two surely took my heart from the first day.' She stared into her empty cup before slowly putting it down. 'I didn't marry until my mid-forties so no children of my own. My husband and I made a very happy life for ourselves until his death. Big families on both sides – plenty of nieces and nephews to help out and enjoy. All grown now. But how I feel about Oliver is different; he's more bone of my bone than any of them, much as I'm real fond of them all. I can't wrap the words around it . . .'

'You've explained it beautifully,' said Gwen gently, 'and if being on the spot here with Sonny and me can benefit you and Oliver, it will be a blessing that makes me extra happy. Evenings and nights are when I'll be glad of your help, but whatever the time I want you to feel free to go to him at a moment's notice.'

'I'm hoping Mr and Mrs Cully will let me drive him to his school in Ferry Landing and fetch him back in the afternoons. There's only a few weeks left till the end of the school year. I'm going to call them; what I'm hoping is that they'll agree to me going over to talk to them about it.' Twyla added as if thinking a thought out loud, 'Come fall they plan to take him back with them to New York.'

'How is Oliver dealing with that prospect?' Gwen's heart ached for the boy.

'It upset him real bad. But yesterday, when we went out to eat before going on to see Frank, I could tell he no longer felt he could open up to me completely, couldn't confide anything that's gotten him upset because of setting me worrying, and having to ask me not to tell his Grandpa. There's an old head on those young shoulders.' The tenderness was visible in Twyla's eyes and around her mouth.

'Do they have to return to New York because their careers are there?'

'Frank mentioned that Gerald Cully works from home as a day trader on the stock market, but his wife does a lot of volunteer work supporting the arts. If they could only stay on here while Frank is alive.'

'Perhaps they'll decide to do that.'

'I'm praying on it. It's more than good of you to listen to all this, Mrs Garwood – Gwen,' she corrected herself, smiling. 'Now how about the arrangements for me starting working here? Would this evening be too soon?'

'That would be perfect.'

'I'll be going to see Frank later this morning and there's hope-fully that visit to the Cullys. If they agree to me getting Oliver from school I could take him back to the house while I pack my case and take care of a few jobs so that everything's left straight. How'd it be if I got back here around five?'

'I'll have a meal ready.' Gwen suddenly realized there had been something they hadn't discussed – the matter of Twyla's salary. Twyla responded with an amount that struck her as extremely modest, and refused to accept more when Gwen insisted.

'What I'll be doing here doesn't require an RN.'

'But it's so reassuring that you are one.'

'I started out way back as an aid; that's where most of what used to be considered nursing is learned and that's most of what your son is going to need from me, same as Frank.'

'Sonny has these raging verbal outbursts . . .' Gwen's voice trailed away. She had heard his bedroom door open. Footsteps making their way down the stairs, with a heavy, half-hearted tread.

'Every patient has emotional needs that need to be met.' Twyla got to her feet and turned to face the man with the uncombed hair and morning stubble entering the book room. He was wearing dark trousers from what was obviously part of a suit, but still had on his pajama jacket with the button askew. 'Good morning, Mr Norris. I've just been talking with your mother about me coming to help out here. She seems to think we'll all get on fine together. I'm sure hoping you'll come to feel the same.'

Sonny looked past her to Gwen, who had also risen from her chair. Jumbo had tensed, his eyes steadily aware, protective devotion apparent in every line of his velvety body. 'What about Lilly?'

Lilly Hatter had been coming for years on Wednesdays to help with the housework. A very pleasant, though never chatty, hard-working woman. As his condition declined Sonny had increasingly ignored her, although mercifully without belligerence. 'She'll still come; but, dear, it will be different with Twyla, she'll . . .'

'Be like Mrs Broom?'

'In a way,' Gwen felt a tiny surge of hope, 'but she'll be spending her nights here, because she wants to live close to the house where the little boy she loves very much lives. The big red Victorian down from the common on Salt Marsh Road.'

'The old Cully Mansion,' he said surprisingly while inching into the room, finally looking directly at Twyla. 'Mrs Broom loved me very much. She used to say that I was her best pal.'

'Mrs Broom,' explained Gwen, 'was our housekeeper and dear

friend in Boston. She was with us from shortly after Sonny was born until several years after he left for college and I moved to Maine. I did my best, but nothing would persuade her to transport so far north. But we continued to visit her often, didn't we, my dear?' Her optimism increased. Sonny's bemused gaze continued to linger on Twyla's face.

'She had brown eyes like yours. Kind eyes.'

'She sounds one fine woman; I hope you'll tell me more about her?'

He shifted restlessly. 'I can't always remember everything. It's like someone locked in my head is trying to shut her out.' He turned back to Gwen. 'Are the other two coming back?'

'Which two, dear?'

'You know! Don't pretend you don't!' His voice escalated. 'The young woman who looks like Aunt Rowena and the man who took me back to his house. I liked them. I should be able to have people I like here. You've got that dog,' he pivoted to Twyla, 'tell her it's not fair. She spends more time with it than it does with me.' Fortunately, in one of those verbal sidesteps of his, tugging irritably at his pajama jacket, he then said, 'I can't find my clothes – that blue sweater or the gray one. I can't stand to have things moved – you know that, Mom. I shouldn't have to tell you over and over again.'

'Would you like me to help you look, Mr Norris?' offered Twyla. 'I'd enjoy seeing your room, if you'll show it to me. This is one good-sized house and I can see myself getting lost in it without someone putting me straight on the layout.'

Gwen held her breath. This presented an all-important moment.

'If you like.' Sonny's response was one of indifference, but compared to hostility that was cause for profound relief. His connecting Twyla with his memories of Mrs Broom might have vanished temporarily or permanently, but it had to be hoped it had seeded a willingness to give her presence a try.

The two of them remained upstairs for about ten minutes. When they came back down Sonny was wearing the blue sweater that was the last Christmas present from his wife Beatrice. He might not remember that, while still knowing it meant something special. For once in the longest time his eyes had regained, if only for a moment, their former bright blue. Suddenly a memory emerged, as vividly as if her mind had just painted a picture in oils, of the boy he had been, seated on the kitchen table, contentedly swinging his legs as he chatted with Mrs Broom and herself. A rosy half-eaten apple in his hand. The sun coming in through the broad window above the sink created a draped, golden chiffon background, as artistically arranged as if twitched in place by an unseen hand. Such memories of the three of them together were almost always golden. This one faded, leaving Gwen torn between the urge to smile or weep. Oh, that smile of his! The one that had sadly so rarely emerged in the presence of his father.

Sensing that Twyla needed to leave to handle all that needed doing before her return in the late afternoon, she planted her feet firmly back in the present. Sonny had headed without a word into the kitchen, and Jumbo came out of the book room to join her as she said goodbye for the moment and opened the front door. She sensed that Twyla was satisfied with what transpired between her and Sonny, but she felt it important to refrain from asking about it. As much as possible she must stand aside and allow their relationship to progress at its own pace. As she headed into the kitchen to encourage him to eat a breakfast, she told herself firmly that she must not be overly hopeful; even so it was hard not to feel uplifted. Plain sailing it wouldn't be, certainly not at first, but she put her faith in the ability of the woman recommended by Nellie Armitage's spirit guides to cope. There was the added factor that Sonny had seen in her eyes a connection to Mrs Broom. He had remarked on their being the same color, but so many people have brown eyes. There must have been something internal and comfortingly familiar shining through that had seemed to reach him, as it had for herself. In outward appearance the two women could not otherwise have been less alike. Twyla tall and spare, Mrs Broom well-padded, full-bosomed as if born to wear a floral apron and her wealth of graying hair in an enormous bun at the nape of her neck.

Gwen began stirring scrambled eggs in a pan over a low heat in the way that good woman had taught her as a young, undo-mesticated bride. She was still smilingly convinced that she wouldn't yet have achieved the level of boiling water, if not for that patient tutelage. Sonny elbowed around the kitchen with a knife and fork he had lifted from the table. She had mixed feelings about telling him about Sarah Draycott's anticipated visit this afternoon. Until he had mentioned her and Sid Jennson half an hour ago it would have been reasonable to assume he had forgotten them. So much slipped in, to have life only in the moment, and then be lost unless quickly reinforced. But as with Twyla he had connected Sarah with someone loved in the past. And in her case it had definitely been the physical resemblance – to Rowena – that struck the chord. And if this had given him a possessive feeling toward her he might resent her coming not to see him, but to take Jumbo for a walk – there might be eruptions. As it turned out, not all that surprising, he'd gone to take his nap when Sarah arrived at one o'clock as promised, bringing the cake with her.

'Oh, my dear! You shouldn't have, but I have to admit I'm delighted you did. Flourless chocolate is one of my ultimate favorites. Do you have time to stay for a moment before taking my boy on what for him will be such a welcome treat? I'd like to tell you about an unbelievably blessed result of what happened with Sonny, the car and you.'

'Of course.' Sarah, still wearing the worn jeans and elderly sweater, was only too glad to be back in the friendly old house with Gwen.

'Do you mind sitting here in the kitchen?'

'Not in the least.'

'I've a fresh pot of coffee ready, and it would be time-wasting to traipse into the book room with cups. That's if you would like one?'

'I'm a coffee fiend.'

When they were seated at the table Gwen explained that Twyla had been providentially guided to Sonny and herself by Nellie Armitage. 'We had such a good visit. My dear, it seems like a miracle. I really think he will accept and even warm to her as he so quickly did to you. His playing the piano for the first time in months while you were here speaks volumes.'

'I responded to him too,' said Sarah warmly, 'in a way that went beyond feeling sad for him. I'd like to spend more time with him, if I wouldn't be a nuisance, getting underfoot.'

'You could never be anything but welcome.' Maybe it was because the morning rain had cleared that Gwen suddenly felt that summer was on the lark's wing. Her mother had told her she'd thought of naming her 'Lark' because she was born at 6 a.m., but that her usually amenable father had put his foot down. Summer – always her best-loved season – when the garden came fully to life, re-delivering all that had been banished by winter and only half reborn in spring. Summer that she would always associate with John coming down the path toward her as she bent with the sun on her shoulders tending the rose. Summer offering the eternal consolation of the soil when hands, heart and soul would have been otherwise empty. Gwen drew a sobering breath. So easy for her, as a creature of life's revolving experience, to believe there was no being trapped permanently in darkest winter. But how very different for a child . . . Gwen's expression saddened and her coffee splattered over the side of her cup.

'Is anything the matter?' asked Sarah.

'I was thinking how often one's own good fortune comes as a result of someone else's misfortune. In this case Twyla's former patient, who is now in need of nursing-home care and can no longer raise his young grandson Oliver.'

Sarah's face was open to her concern. 'Nellie told me what was happening with that when she came to see me, and how the boy is related on his father's side to the members of the Cully family.' Sarah smiled impishly. 'She didn't put it in quite those Gothic terms, but her description of the interior of Cully Mansion sounded pretty grim.'

'I've never been inside myself,' Gwen mopped her saucer with a paper napkin, 'and Nellie may be given to exaggeration in deference to dramatic impact. But I'm prepared to take what she says about the Cully Mansion as fact. Those windows have such a sly, watchful look. My dear, I don't consider myself easily spooked, but I can't imagine willingly spending a day, let alone a night, in that place. There must have been many happy times there in the distant past but, from all I hear of Emily Cully, she felt cheated in life by lameness resulting from polio as a child.' Gwen smiled wryly. 'So melodramatic to suggest that sort of bitter resentment can so permeate a house that it blots out every vestige of joy that went before. It makes me sound – to my own ears – like a very foolish old woman.'

'I don't think what you're saying is silly.' Sarah shifted her coffee cup aside to lean toward her. 'I believe all houses have a story to tell – some you can't wait to read and some you'd just as soon not put a finger on, because you know they'll scare you up the wall.'

'Exactly my feeling. And now the Cully aunt and uncle have taken that nine-year-old boy to live with them there. They may be the most wonderful people in the world, but knowing almost nothing of them, other than the uncle was Oliver's father's brother – indeed only sibling, has to invite concern. They don't know the boy, hadn't ever seen him until a few days ago. How likely is it they can successfully support him through what has to be an extremely difficult transition?'

Sarah visibly searched for something encouraging to say. 'Maybe they'll seek outside support – a therapist specializing in childhood trauma. And, most important of all, Twyla will be right here, on their doorstep almost, to prevent Oliver feeling cut off from his past. And she'll take him to see his grandfather as often as possible, won't she?'

'That's the idea. I was even hoping that once Sonny starts to enjoy Twyla's presence, I could suggest to her that she bring Oliver here sometimes. Now I have this doubt that everything will work out as originally hoped with her having easy access to him.'

'You're not convinced the Cullys will be accommodating?'

'I was, until Twyla phoned some five or ten minutes before you arrived to let me know she should be back here earlier than planned, because she'd just called and spoken to Elizabeth Cully, asking if she could fetch Oliver from his school in Ferry Landing, and was told arrangements had already been made with a neighbor to take Oliver in each morning and bring him home in the afternoons.'

'I see.'

'Apparently this woman has two sons a little older than Oliver who attend a private school a little further out than Ferry Landing, so it's absolutely no trouble for her. It all sounds very reasonable, but wouldn't it have been appropriate, or at least considerate, to have talked this over with Twyla before making the decision? She'd made it clear to the Cullys that she was willing to do the ferrying. And that was what Oliver wanted. It struck me as insensitive at the time, but now – and here comes more melodrama on my part – after talking my thoughts through with you, I'm wondering if this may be an ominous predictor of what's to come.'

'I've watched those movies on late-night TV. Is this the first of a number of doors that will gradually close one by one, shutting Oliver away from Twyla and even his grandfather?' Sarah sounded embarrassed by what she was saying. 'But why? Why would they do that?'

Gwen sighed. 'Possibly a well-meaning, if misguided attempt on

the part of two people who know little or nothing about children
to center Oliver in his new environment. Any other reason is
unfathomable. As is why anyone would name their sons Emjagger
and Rolling Stone.'

'What?' Sarah stared across the table as if unable to believe she'd
heard correctly.

'Sorry, my dear!' Gwen smiled ruefully. 'That was an abrupt shift
into reverse. Those are the names of the neighbor's two boys, the
ones who'll be in the car with Oliver on the drive to and from
school. When Twyla spoke of them I instantly thought, those poor
kids! They'll either be bullied unmercifully or defensively turn into
bullies themselves. Why their parents didn't think beyond a desire to
be cool is beyond me.' She told Sarah about her mother's whim to
name her Lark and her father's flat refusal.

'But I think Lark's a lovely name,' Sarah's hazel eyes lit up,
'although I think you were meant to be Gwen. There's a huge
difference between the unusual and the weird. I hope those parents
are still mad about the Rolling Stones, or they could now want
to shoot themselves. But the boys could go by abbreviations.
Actually, the name Emjagger wouldn't be so bad – it's the brother's
one coupled with it that does the real damage.'

'I would like to think they get to go by Jag and Stone at school,
but apparently such is not the case at home, or Twyla wouldn't
have given the names the full treatment as presented to her by Mrs
Cully. She's so obviously not a spiteful person.'

'There were two brothers in my neighborhood when I was in
grad school,' volunteered Sarah, 'called Captain and Lieutenant.
Their father regretted not going in the armed forces and they got
stuck with his regret. No shortening to Cap or Lew for them.'

'It might be funny on stage or film. But in life the damage is
done the moment the birth certificates are processed. After that it
may not make too much difference how much abbreviating is done.
In a place as small as Sea Glass word doesn't leak out, it floods.'
Gwen paused. 'It's so good of you, Sarah, to let me talk. I hadn't
realized how much I'd missed sitting down with a friend and
voicing how I feel about things. But I've been dreadfully selfish;
there's no excuse for my taking the helm of the conversation,
especially when you've interrupted your day on Jumbo's and my
behalf. Do tell me how things have been going settling into your
new home.'

Sarah told Gwen about the cat she had taken in that morning and how she had already been out to fetch supplies for it. She asked for the name of Gwen's vet and said she would phone him before five that evening. Then, after a momentary hesitation, she went on to mention a letter addressed to Nan Fielding she had found in the mailbox that morning and that she had decided to enclose it in a letter to the sender at the return address.

'Quite right, my dear. Very thoughtful. To receive the original one back marked deceased could be a jolt. As you say there's no knowing how close the relationship between Ms Fielding and this person with the initials EB may have been. I will be very interested to know if you hear back.'

Shortly afterwards Sarah left with Jumbo. They were gone a little over an hour and on their return both seemed to have enjoyed what had turned from a walk into a jog after the first ten minutes. By that time Sonny was downstairs and showed definite signs of being pleased to see Sarah again, even agreeing to play the piano for her, before suddenly turning restless. Which was possibly just as well, because Gwen didn't think it fair to delay her unduly.

Twyla arrived ten minutes after Sarah left, and Sonny came wandering up to her. 'Oh, you came back too. My friend, the one who looks like my aunt Rowena, was here but she had to go home or her father would have been angry. He shouts. She told me that.'

Gwen refrained from shaking her head as her eyes met Twyla's and received the most understanding of smiles in return before Twyla turned to focus fully on Sonny.

Two suitcases were set down at the foot of the stairs. 'Sounds to me you've found something special there, you and this friend.' The rich voice was like warm honey – nourishing to the mind and body. 'We go through life sometimes thinking we've met all the people we're ever likely to be friends with, and then comes along this new person and it seems like we've known them all along. There comes that sort of understanding that turns into trust. I sure do hope, Mr Norris, it can be like that with you and me.'

There was something so strongly reminiscent of Mrs Broom in the cadence and putting together of the words Sonny was beginning the process of blending the two women together. That was evident to Gwen in the bewildered tone of his voice.

'Why are you calling me Mr Norris instead of Sonny?'

No, it would be foolish and unhelpful to expect smooth sailing, but Gwen felt a calm assurance that the introduction of Sarah and Sid Jennson into their lives – that had shrunk to just her and Sonny – had paved the way for Twyla's arrival. She went to bed that night, knowing it was safe for her to sleep deeply for the first time in months. It was her hope that she wouldn't dream at all, have eight hours in which even her subconscious went blank. But it wasn't to be. Again she found herself wandering, as she had done on so many previous nights, in a shadowy maze where iron-barred doors presented themselves at every turn. Behind one of them was a child trapped in desperation, silently waiting to be rescued, becoming less substantial with each terrifying second of her fruitless search, because all the doors opened into the place she was already in. There was one significant difference in that night's dream. Added to the sense of frantic hopelessness was a heart-hammering confusion. Who was she looking for? Sonny or Oliver Cully?

She awoke at 3 a.m. with a dull pain in her chest as she struggled to breath. A panic attack, she told herself. Best to clear her mind and lie completely still until it passed, then turn on the bedside light and read a soothing chapter of *Barchester Towers*. This she did and a half hour later, the physical effects of the nightmare gone, drowsiness claimed her. The next time she woke, at a little after six, she felt well rested and free from any indication that she wasn't in excellent health for a woman of seventy-eight. What became crystal in daylight was that Twyla was as much alone in her worries over Oliver as she herself had been with Sonny until yesterday. Twyla couldn't burden the grandfather with her fear that she might find herself with limited access to Oliver, let alone reveal such concerns to the boy. Two women, she thought, with the same maternal instinct; we can help each other. The 'how' of her contribution was the question. An answer would come when it was ready. She had no doubt that in the meantime her relationship with Twyla would strengthen so that they could confide increasingly in each other.

That day and several others slipped by into the establishment of a mostly peaceful routine. Sonny had surprisingly few outbursts and those were directed against herself, never Twyla. Mostly these had to do with his belief that he played second fiddle to Jumbo. He was initially angry that Sarah took the dog for a walk most mornings, and occasionally in the afternoons.

'You make her do it,' was his accusation. 'You make her feel sorry for you because I'm a burden to you.'

But this minor cloud gradually dissipated in his enjoyment of seeing Sarah.

'You like her, don't you?' he would say to Twyla, as if this were vitally important to him.

'She's one special young woman, Sonny. It couldn't be plainer she has a big place in her heart for you.'

It gladdened Gwen that the two women she was becoming increasingly fond of had taken to each other immediately. Sometimes on an afternoon the three of them would sit, usually around the kitchen table, getting to know more about one another in a leisurely, conversational way. During one of these sessions Twyla talked about having spent most of her life, until coming to Maine, in Louisiana, mentioning that a great-grandmother had been Creole, which naturally led to an enthusiastic discussion of that type of cooking. Sarah had learned from Libby Jennson that there was a neighborhood potluck group that met once a month, with each member taking a turn hosting, and that a gumbo or shrimp Creole would be a fun dish to serve.

Twyla's manner of speech was of a much more relaxed form than had been present during her initial meeting, technically the interview, with Gwen. The change had been there when she had talked to Sonny on returning with her suitcases and had increasingly extended to herself and Sarah. But it was always hearing that soothing voice flowing over Sonny like balm that brought the deepest comfort.

'Now don't you go fretting that someone made off with your socks. Those creatures have a way of thinking of places to hide themselves. Nothing more mischievous than socks. But you and me are more than a match for them; by now, after hiding under the bed, they've likely popped back in the drawer. And if they haven't we will hunt them down to the last one.'

It was so very much what Mrs Broom would have said if Gwen couldn't find something. When two weeks of Twyla's presence became three, Sonny's frame of mind had so improved that he sometimes spent half an hour or more at a time playing the piano, with one or the other – sometimes both – of the women sitting listening to him. Gwen had told Twyla that Clare Andrews, Oliver's mother, had come to talk to her about taking lessons, and of her deep regret that she hadn't suggested the girl come and practice on the instrument at which Sonny now sat. The imprint of that memory — the sweet, open face framed by the red-gold hair — became more vivid with Gwen's every recurring thought of Oliver. Twyla had taken him on several occasions to see his grandfather and to Sunday church, which she and Sonny had not attended because he'd been apathetic about doing so. Elizabeth and Gerald had put up no opposition to these requests, but they had never encouraged her to linger beyond what was polite when she returned him to the house. It was Sonny who had started urging Twyla to bring 'her boy.' Gwen read in Twyla's eyes that she welcomed doing this, but doubted the Cullys would agree to it. Indeed, she sensed the suggestion had been posed and refused. Perhaps they had genuine concerns about Oliver being around a man with Alzheimer's. One had to be understanding on that point, even while thinking such fears out of touch with life today. And yet there had to be a way to support Twyla in an attempt to reach these people. An idea was forming . . . when she had talked about Clare's visit as a teenager, Twyla had responded that Oliver had recently said he would like to learn to play the piano.

Gwen's own world was much less constricted than it had been. She and Twyla had ceased to think which of them should be doing what for Sonny at a given time. Whatever worked on a particular day or night is how it went. This understanding had made it unnecessary for Gwen to write to the garden club offering her resignation as president. A few informal gatherings, over coffee at someone's house, tended to be planned or crop up, but the only firm date on the calendar was the monthly meeting. It was thinking about the one coming up the following week that suddenly suggested to Gwen a means for her to make contact with Elizabeth and Gerard Cully and hopefully bring the conversation around to Twyla and Oliver. Embarking on the plan required phoning Madge Baldwin, one of whose responsibilities was special events. Saying anything to Twyla ahead of time might raise her hopes only to dash them. Then if Gwen got the go-ahead, the final decision would be Twyla's.

Madge always tended to make it difficult to get to the point. If someone had called to say they'd noticed her house was on fire she would have interrupted to say how bad the flu was this year, although not quite as dire as predicted. In a way, thought Gwen, this was part of her charm. Now Madge rattled on for what seemed like five minutes about how relieved she was that Sonny's carer was proving to be such a godsend, because this showed the car accident was meant to be – the intervention of a higher power, which made her feel so much better, because for several days afterward she had been worrying herself sick about having been the one who gave Sonny the keys. As she had said to her husband, knowing she was a piece of the grand plan . . . This continued until she paused to draw breath, allowing Gwen to quickly insert her idea of a garden club project that she would – with Madge's approval – like to present to the membership at next Thursday's meeting. The response was not only enthusiastic but short-winded, enabling Gwen to get off the phone smartly when she heard Twyla come in through the backdoor, having been gone for an hour or so doing errands. An appreciative OK being given, along with the required phone number, Gwen dialed and spoke to a surprised Elizabeth Cully. After a momentary hesitation, she agreed to see her at the Cully Mansion the following day at two in the afternoon.

Now Twyla expressed her mounting concerns. 'On the day Oliver's aunt and uncle came to collect him, they – or I should say Elizabeth – made all the right noises about the importance of him and I staying in close touch, but it sure hasn't worked out that way. Other than taking him to church and on to see his grandpa on Sundays, there's always some excuse for us not getting together, and never one mention of me being invited over to the house. Did something change or did they always intend it that way? That's what I've been asking myself.'

When the time came to set off in the car for the appointment Gwen did so with some trepidation. So much counted on her not risking antagonizing the Cullys before hopefully working her way round to the real purpose of her visit: attempting to encourage them to allow Twyla more time with Oliver. It was Elizabeth Cully who admitted her into the oppressive hall and then into the truly ghastly living room with the gargantuan four-poster bed at the end where the windows overlooked the rear of the house. Or would have done so had they not been shrouded in disintegrating gauze curtains framed by presumably once red velvet panels. Of Gerard Cully there was no sign, but there could conceivably have been a half dozen people hiding out under the bed or among the conglomeration of massive Victorian furniture. This period always conveyed to Gwen both self-importance and a patriarchal dominance of the lesser female mind. Before sitting down, at Elizabeth's invitation, on a decrepit sofa of some moldy green fabric, Gwen had counted four towering display cabinets. The overflow crowded every flat surface to the point of obsessive compulsion. Tarnished Indian brass bells, snuff boxes, blackened silver nutcrackers, grape scissors, little carved boxes and a myriad of other knickknacks jostled each other for breathing space. Let the womenfolk fritter their time away obsessing over trivia.

Such a mindset was on view in the oil portrait of a ferociously bewhiskered old man; its heavily layered, blackish olive background seemed entirely a product of his personality, making the artist superfluous. Those eyes surveyed the room as if it remained, and always would, his personal kingdom. Nathaniel Cully? Gwen didn't think so. She had heard stories of the devoted doctor making his rounds in his horse and buggy, or setting out in a rowboat during a storm to rescue a group of strangers. Perhaps one of his two brothers or, even more likely from the manner of dress, his father.

Elizabeth Cully half-heartedly offered coffee or tea and, accepting the polite refusal without suggesting a cold drink as an alternative, she sat down on the equally ancient sofa facing the one on which Gwen was perched in careful avoidance of poking springs. For some moments she had felt herself shrinking in size like poor Alice in Wonderland. How very small and powerless must Oliver feel in this dreadful room!

'It's good of you to come, Mrs Garwood,' she said as if reciting the beginning of a prepared speech. 'I hope you won't take it that my husband doesn't appreciate your garden club's interest in us if he doesn't join us?'

'Not at all.'

'The fact that he works from home inclines people to think that he can stop what he's doing at the drop of a hat, but he'd never have gotten where he has – trading in the financial market – with that attitude.' Elizabeth's hand moved restively from her long skirt, made from some loosely woven material in a deep rust color, to the neckline of the matching top.

'That's absolutely fine. You and your husband can discuss at leisure my suggestions for how the garden club might best help in the restoration of your grounds. As I said on the phone, we consider ourselves mutual beneficiaries in projects of this type. They are splendid opportunities for honing skills and gaining knowledge. If you find yourselves willing to participate I will put the matter before the full membership next Thursday. I'm optimistic it will meet with enthusiastic support, given the Cully history and Sea Glass's good fortune in having members of the family back in residence.' Gwen wondered if she had sounded obsequious. If so, had Elizabeth taken it as her due?

'We hadn't planned to focus on landscaping this summer.' She waved a dismissive hand. 'As is obvious, from spending five minutes in this room, we are overwhelmed by what needs to be done inside. I've only this week found a woman to come in and make an attempt at cleaning. And I don't think she would have stepped in the door if she hadn't worked for Emily Cully and has some loyalty to her memory. She's a Mrs Polly, and she told me that Emily had addressed her only by her last name. Confusing because there was a dreadful old parrot called Polly.' Elizabeth's eyes went to the naked birdcage on its pole near the four-poster bed. 'Every time the old lady shouted at it Mrs Polly jumped.' She shrugged expressively. 'This is one of her days with me, so she's around the house somewhere mopping floors. Not that I expect them to look any better for it.'

'I've met her; she has a very pretty front garden. English cottage style, lots of sweetly old-fashioned varieties . . .'

'Really? It's hard to imagine her handling a flower without crushing the life out of it. She's so huge, isn't she? Like a giantess in a Grimm Brothers' fairytale.'

Jabs at people's looks bothered Gwen. She hoped for Robin Polly's sake she wasn't within hearing range; from what she'd heard the woman hadn't had an easy life dealing with her father's drinking problem. 'Let's hope you're happy with her work and she enjoys being back here.'

'Yes.' She restively shifted her position, turning toward the marble fireplace that resembled a graveyard monument. Above it hung a painting of cows that appeared in desperate need of milking. 'Udderly ghastly, isn't it?' She frowned, drawing a hand through her tangled mane with its obvious natural care. Even though the light that penetrated the front window was of a murky quality the dark roots visibly needed a touch-up. Was it a matter, Gwen wondered, of not having yet found a hairdresser in Sea Glass, or was she never one to obsess about her appearance? 'I'm sorry, that was a gross way of putting it, but I'm one of those unfortunate people who suffer physical pain in the presence of amateur daubings. I'm sure being surrounded by such horrors is the reason I've had more wretched migraines in one month than I did in six before coming here.'

'Our surroundings do have an impact.' Gwen's sympathy was genuine. Perhaps the Cullys' inability to understand a child's emotional needs stemmed from their having found themselves sunk in a quagmire since moving into the house. Gwen always tried to see the other side. She smiled kindly at Elizabeth while wondering how soon she could bring Twyla and Oliver into the conversation.

'I was brought up with a passion for fine art. My parents had a very fine collection of post-Impressionist works; we moved in those circles . . .' Elizabeth paused and shrugged, 'so you can imagine the toll this place is taking on me and my husband. Nothing would have induced us to move here, if only temporarily, but for our wish to take on the responsibility of his nephew. He asked us for a dog or a cat and we hated saying no, but there's no way we can deal with an animal wandering around having accidents God knows where.'

Again, Gwen could sympathize with her point of view. This was the moment to bring up her relationship with Twyla, but she found herself side-stepping it. 'Have you taken him to see the scrimshaws left to the historical society by Emily Cully?'

The response to this was a darting look of such antagonism that it not only startled Gwen but brought back a vivid memory of Rowena's eyes suddenly blazing with rage upon her on the day after their father's funeral. They were alone in the living room of the family home in Concord, Charles already returned to Boston where Sonny had remained with Mrs Broom, John also gone and their mother upstairs resting. Nothing had been said in the past few days about the upcoming wedding, and it was when Gwen asked her sister if she and John had talked about when they would feel ready to go forward. At that moment the torrent was unleashed. Hadn't Gwen noticed that Rowena was not wearing the engagement ring? Or had she been too delighted by the absence to profess interest, let alone sympathy? Didn't she want to hear the gory details? Well, too damn bad! The ring had been returned weeks ago. Reason? It had been blatantly obvious after that family weekend in Boston that the prospective groom had taken one look at the younger sister and fallen hook, line and sinker. Chalk up success number two to dear, sweet Gwen. First Charles, now John. But she needn't crow so hard this time because he'd been very much a case of second best. Why had Rowena sent John to break the news of their father's death? Because someone had to do it, and their mother couldn't be left alone.

'I'm not interested in folk art.' At the sound of Elizabeth Cully's voice Gwen groped her way back to the present.

'I'm sorry . . . ?'

'Scrimshaws.' No hint of lingering antagonism in those eyes. Had it indeed been there in the first place or just imagined?

'Oh, yes. Not everyone's cup of tea.'

'But Gerard and I should take Oliver to see them. This is the last day of school and we'd do anything to take himself out of himself. We've just been treading water where he's concerned, but it's so difficult. We're not used to children, and he's full of resentment at being forced, as he sees it, to live with us. There's this woman, Twyla Washburn, who was his grandfather's nurse that he would run off to in a minute if he could. And maybe we've made a mistake in trying to create a distance between them to make it less hard on him when we take him back with us to New York in the fall.' Elizabeth was again plucking at her skirt. 'I don't know why I'm bothering you with this.'

Because you know who I am and have a strong suspicion why I'm really here, thought Gwen, and if you have any sense you'll get as much free work out of the garden club as you can.

'I have been feeling a considerable interest in your nephew,' she began. And from then on the words flowed easily, steered toward her one meeting with Clare Andrews. 'Which is why I was touched when Twyla mentioned the other day that Oliver had said he would like to take piano lessons. It is my son who is the professional teacher and I believe on his good days could still be helpful, but I have played since I was a very young child and can certainly get Oliver off to a good start, if you would let him come to our house for a couple of hours once, or better yet, twice a week.'

Gwen had the sinking feeling that the answer would be a resounding 'No!' But at that moment Robin Polly entered the room and immediate further discussion of the matter was prevented. She was one of a very few people who could stand in the vicinity of that towering furniture and not look physically diminished. Her graying brown braid hung over her shoulder like a rope to be climbed. She sent a smile and a greeting Gwen's way.

'I'm off for home, Ms Cully.'

'OK.'

'Done what I could getting that rust out of Miss Emily's bathtub, but still looks like a donkey peed in it every day of its life. And speaking of the old lady, I noticed this morning and forgot to mention the little silver clock that used to be on the table next to her bed.' She jerked a thumb toward the four-poster at the far end of the room.

'What about it?'

'Not there. And when I see something's not in its usual place I make a point of saying so; that way there can't be no suggesting I helped it on its way. I'm not saying you'd take that line, Mrs Cully, but I've a right to protect my good name. And I certainly don't want it said my father, Willie, tucked it in his pocket when he was hiding out here in the house last January, because whatever else he is, he ain't no thief, let alone him not being able to get up from the cellar with the door locked.'

'I have no idea what clock you're talking about.' A fiery flush descended from Elizabeth's face to her neck. 'Who could pick out one object in all this morass of stuff?'

'A little silver one with a poem written on it . . . like something from a sailor to his wife or girl, about not counting the hours till he come home from the sea.'

Elizabeth was on her feet. Very much the lady of the house, but for the poking at her hair. 'It'll either turn up or it won't. No need for you to worry about it, Mrs Polly. I don't care about it one way or the other and neither will my husband. Perhaps,' she shoved back a tangle of hair, 'Oliver took it up to his room.'

'That's different, ain't it? He'll be thinking he's every right to it. Can't question that now.' The smile she turned on the room before she left Gwen wondering what it intimated. Elizabeth's expression when she spoke was equally hard to read.

'I'm not sure about the upheaval of landscaping this year, that I'll have to discuss with Gerard, but I do think it would be a good idea for Oliver to come to you for piano lessons, if he does want them. Please pass on to Twyla Washburn that his happiness is all we really care about. If she's gotten the wrong idea about that we're sorry.'

Mission accomplished. Gwen should have left the Cully Mansion feeling relieved and content, but as she drove home the last of what Elizabeth had to say lingered disturbingly.

'He's been through a lot in his nine years and we worry about his mental health. Gerard got up in the middle of the night a couple of weeks ago – following a Sunday I'd spent in bed with one of my worst migraines ever – and when he was passing Oliver's open bedroom door he saw him bolt upright in bed. He was talking – having a conversation – with someone who wasn't there.'

Nine

Oliver came down the dark oak staircase at a little after eight a.m. wearing shorts and a green T-shirt with a black Labrador on the front. Earlier in the week he'd hoped it would remind Elizabeth and Gerard how mean they were about not letting him have a dog. This morning it was a shirt he liked. He was feeling a little more kindly toward his aunt and uncle since they had told him he could go to the house where Twyla was living and have piano lessons with Mrs Garwood. Yesterday he'd gone for his very first one and it had been great. After five minutes he'd been able to find middle C with his eyes closed and was imagining himself on a stage playing for an audience of thousands with all the ladies and some of the men crying. Mrs Garwood made it seem easy and fun. He liked her blue eyes and pretty silver hair. When she left to let him to practice for a little on his own, while she went into the kitchen to make up a pitcher of lemonade, her son had come in and sat in a chair listening. He'd been mostly quiet, but once he said, 'Nice.' And then: 'Good job.'

Twyla had previously told Oliver that Mrs Garwood and Sonny Norris were the lady and man they had sat next to in church on that first Sunday in Sea Glass. What had made him feel especially good was seeing how much Twyla enjoyed helping with Sonny and what good friends she and Mrs Garwood had become. And

then there was Jumbo. Oliver had never seen, or even heard of, a
bull mastiff before. They had taken to each other right away, and
Mrs Garwood had said there was another new friend named Sarah
– *really Sonny's friend*, she had stressed – who came most days to
take Jumbo out for a walk and perhaps, if it was agreeable with
Oliver's aunt and uncle, he could go with them sometimes. When
Oliver got to the bottom of the stairs Mrs Polly was in the hall.
She didn't usually come on a Saturday unless she'd left something
behind from when she worked the last time. In this case it must
have been her instant coffee because she had the jar in her hand.
Oliver had adjusted his negative opinion of Mrs Polly since his
initial meeting with her at Pleasant Meadows. After seeing her
there again in her father's presence he had decided that she and
Willie enjoyed rattling each other's cages, as she called it, and that
she was in her way fond of him.

'Someone to see you, Mr Pal.' That's what she called him. The
Mr because she joked that he was her employer and the *Pal* because
she said that's what he was, a real pal in a place she'd always told
Miss Emily belonged back in the Dark Ages.

'Thank you, Mrs Poll.' Oliver inclined his head formally, which
always made her grin. 'Is it Twyla?' His mood soared. Maybe
Elizabeth was done with her excuses – that some other time would
always be better.

'A kid. Said he's a friend, but can't believe nothin' nobody tells
you these days. Could be a very short gangster on the lam. Wouldn't
hurt to look around for something to hit him over the head with
if he comes at you. I'd give you this jar of coffee to pitch, but I've
none at home and self comes first. He's in the living room, but
don't ask me to go back in there with you. For all my size I'm
Queen of Cowards.'

'Right!' Oliver now wished he'd stayed upstairs. 'I bet it's
Emjagger or Rolling Stone. And I do need a weapon. They're
worse bullies than any at my school . . . old school in Ferry
Landing. I hoped I was done with them now I don't need to ride
to and from Ferry Landing with them, but their mother and
Elizabeth had made up their minds we are going to be best friends.
I could puke!'

Mrs Polly shook her head, sending her heavy braid swinging.
'I know them brats of Satan. Caught them chucking stones at my
cat once and went after them at a gallop, yelling that I'd tear their

heads off with my bare hands and boil them in a pot for supper. Never heard such a caterwauling. You could've heard 'em a mile off. Almost slipped twice, I did, on the puddles of tears they left behind. Folks can say what they like about my Willie, but he weren't born evil. No, Mr Pal, the kid that's waiting to see you is younger than either of them two, and wears glasses.'

'Brian!' Oliver exclaimed joyfully. 'This is the first time he's been here. He's my true best friend.' He threw his arms around Mrs Polly's middle. All the rest was too far up. Now that he was no longer stiff with fear he could relish the image of her charging after Emjagger and Stone like a figure of vengeance blown up out of all human proportion. She stood patting his head, before prodding him toward the living room.

'Don't stand wasting time with the Ogress.'

He couldn't walk away from that. 'You're not . . .'

Mrs Polly chuckled deeply. 'I've been called far worse. Have to face facts in life. And when that's said, Mr Pal, it does to know it's never about the nice ones. But you won't go catching me whimpering or dripping tears. There's not too many is fool enough to step twice on someone my size, even though I don't have all my teeth.' She gave another pleased roar. 'Used to ask my husband for a new set for Christmas, but nothing doing. That man was so cheap if I'd said I wanted a brooch he'd have stuck a tick on my blouse and tell me I looked like a film star.'

'I'd buy you some new teeth, any kind you like, if I had the money.'

'One of these days I'm just might hold you to that.' Mrs Polly shot him a look that puzzled him. It was like she was trying to tell him something with what Grandpa would call a wink and a nod. 'A pity some grown folks don't realize having a bundle and wanting more ain't the way to happiness. Now off you go. Your gangster friend has his head stuck out the doorway and looks ready to shoot me if I don't disappear fast. It won't be long before you have your aunt and uncle on your hands. Had a round with her in the ring the other day and don't take smarts to guess who come off the winner? That look in her eyes when I said my piece put a smile on my ugly face that'll last through summer.'

'You're not ugly! Now we're friends, Mrs Poll, I get happier just looking at you.'

'Go!' The finger in the back was firmer this time.

'Just one more thing: when I was up in the attic the other day I found boxes and boxes of paperback books . . .'

'Romances! And you couldn't picture Miss Emily reading them, right? Well, she did, lapped them up like a cat at a saucer of milk and wouldn't have them given away or thrown out in case she wanted to reread them. So every so often I'd do a round up and take them up there.'

'Thanks. That makes her seem a more comfortable sort of person. I brought a few down with me to look through.' Oliver departed on a prod between his shoulder blades.

'So what was all that about gangsters and guns?' Brian asked when Oliver joined him in the living room. 'Was that woman trying to get you to join her gang?'

'She isn't *that* woman. And she was just joking about the gangsters and stuff. She's Mrs Polly. I told you about her. When I met her for the first time in Grandpa's room at Pleasant Meadows, I wasn't sure I'd like her. But I do; she's the only real nice thing about having to live here.'

Brian looked doubtful. 'You didn't say she looks like she'd cook people for dinner and pour on lots of ketchup.'

'Only ones like Emjagger and Rolling Stone.'

'You're not still stuck with them, Ollie?' Brian's eyes narrowed behind his ever-lopsided glasses. 'I thought it was goodbye to those creeps now school's out.'

'They live next door.'

'Guess I blocked that out.'

'Not me. My skin's still bruised from Rolling Stone pinching my arm in the car.'

'Why didn't you get back at him by calling him by his full name – put in the Rolling part? If that's what his parents want, and with his Mom driving, what could he do but suck it up?'

'They'd make me pay big time when there's no one but Emjagger around. Besides he's got asthma, has to keep an inhaler with him, and much as I can't stick him I'd be scared to send him into an attack. Twyla says in bad cases people can die from them. Elizabeth's been talking about them taking me out kayaking.'

'So she can stand on the shore and watch them drown you?' Brian waggled his fingers around his face to indicate her ghoulish delight.

It was tempting to laugh nastily at this; especially as Oliver was sure Elizabeth and Gerard were still up in their bedroom and no one could come down the uncarpeted stairs unheard. They never got up early, even on weekdays. But his conscience pricked him. He had been allowed the piano lessons, if not a dog or cat, and he supposed it was a start. More than that really, because on those days he would be in the same house as Twyla for at least a couple of hours. Until now his time with her had been restricted to church on Sundays and the visits twice a week to see Grandpa. He turned this over in his mind. 'I don't get Elizabeth and Gerard. Even when they're trying to be nice it's like there's something behind it. But why would they want me drowned or some other kind of dead, when they could just let me go live with Twyla?' He shrugged.

'I wouldn't have hung around wondering. Is your uncle still creeping into your bedroom at dead of night?'

'Sometimes, but I've kind of gotten used to that. I realized the second time that he was sleepwalking. He just stands there looking down at me and then goes away. I've tried asking what he wants, but he doesn't answer.'

'Creepy! Maybe this house had gotten inside his head. I already get the feeling something wicked is creeping up on us, getting ready to pounce and watch us squirm.' Brian gave an exaggerated shiver as he looked around. 'Talk about horror movies! Who's that spooky old guy?' He pointed at the dark oil portrait on the wall across from the tombstone fireplace.

'Elizabeth and Gerard didn't know, but Mrs Poll told me. She knows a lot from being here working for Miss Emily. He's the one who built the house. Father of Nathaniel Cully and his two whaler brothers. His wife was so scared of him she used to hide in the attics. I went up the back staircase the other day and looked round. There was loads more old furniture but not what I was looking for. I had the idea there might be a painting of Nathaniel Cully as a boy, or some really old photos, but no luck. I'd already asked Gerard and Elizabeth if they'd come across any. Both said they hadn't and couldn't be bothered looking for needles in a haystack. Guess I'll have to try the historical society next.'

'But I thought you decided you only thought you were awake when you saw and talked to Nathaniel; that it was really just the end part of a dream. Remember, I was the one who told you that he had to be a ghost, or how do you explain that book you found

in the morning? You said Gerard and Elizabeth acted like they
truly didn't know anything about it.'

'I guess I didn't want to believe he was really there. But he did
seem so real. If only there was some way to at least prove my
bedroom was his as a kid.' Oliver shrugged. 'You're still the only
person I told. Saying you see and hear things no one else does
makes you sound whacko. And Gerard and Elizabeth already seem
to think I'm weird enough to be dragged off to a psychiatrist.'

'Lots of people go to them,' countered the worldly-wise Brian.
'My Mom's friend went and it just had to do with thinking she'd
never learn how to text on her phone as fast as everyone else.
Besides,' he drew out his trump card, 'Aunt Nellie and the people
at that church of hers think having contact with the spirit world
is perfectly normal. By the way, that's why I walked over here. I
stayed over last night with her and don't have to go home until
this afternoon. She wants me to bring you back over so we can
hang out.'

'Cool!'

It was Brian's first visit to the Cully Mansion. Oliver hadn't
suggested his coming over because he'd been afraid the answer
would be no, forcing him to look deeper into the half-formed
fears that swirled murkily beneath the surface of his relationship
with Gerard and Elizabeth. Theirs wasn't clear to him. He'd never
heard them arguing. They just seemed to move around each
other, when they weren't sitting staring into space. He'd been
told not to interrupt his uncle when he was in one of the back
rooms working, but when he'd pass the door he always heard a
television, or it could be a radio, going. What Oliver tried to do
was think about them as little as possible. It seemed a long time
ago that he'd planned to make them so sick of having him around
that they'd be glad to let Twyla come and take him, but he'd
quickly grasped that wasn't going to work. When he'd tried acting
up they'd said it looked like he'd been allowed to get out of hand
since Grandpa was ill and they hoped Twyla wouldn't continue
to be a negative influence. He had been left struggling to come
to terms with the realization that there wasn't going to be a
miracle resulting in Grandpa's recovery. This house did not allow
desperate hopes to survive. Or maybe love had more to do with
it. Each time Oliver went to Pleasant Meadows he became more
aware that for Grandpa staying alive was an exhausting effort.

Tired to the bone. They both knew he was ready to go home, not to the one they'd shared in Ferry Landing, but to his long forever home where Grandma Olive and Mom and Dad and all the other people he'd loved would be waiting for him. It was so clear the only thing keeping him here was the worry of leaving Oliver behind in the wrong hands. And for whatever reason Elizabeth and Gerard weren't going to give him up. He would have to talk positively about the piano lessons and any other opportunities that offered temporary escapes into happiness.

'I'll go find Elizabeth and Gerard and tell them you're here and that I'm walking back with you to Aunt Nellie's.' He stepped into the hall.

'You think they'll say yes?'

'I'm not going to ask them if it's OK, I'll just tell me that's what we're doing. It's not like they can make out you're a bad influence. Your name's not been in the paper for robbing banks.'

'I see them as jailers; but Aunt Nellie says that with school out could be they won't be so keen to have you underfoot all day.'

'Right.' Oliver was about to head up the stairs, not all that keen on knocking on Elizabeth and Gerard's bedroom door, although he couldn't imagine them in there kissing, when he saw them coming down. No need to have worried. They said it was fine for him to go off with his friend. Elizabeth smiled quite brightly at Brian, and Gerard remarked that it looked like it was going to be one of the first really hot days, so it was good to make the most of it.

'We're going out ourselves this morning, Oliver, and when you get back we should have a surprise for you,' said Elizabeth, 'so we'd like you back here by twelve thirty or one.'

Could it possibly be they'd changed their minds about getting him a dog or a cat?' Oliver told himself not to get his hopes up, but there was nothing else he'd asked for. He went out the front door with Brian into bright sunshine under clear blue skies. Lupines, blue, pink and corn-colored, sprang tall along the edges of Salt Marsh Road. His aunt and uncle had not asked if he'd had breakfast. Neither of them seemed much interested in food. Dinner was usually something bought frozen, although there was always a salad and fruit.

He and Brian said goodbye to Elizabeth and set off. 'It wasn't like his name was in the book,' Oliver said, as they turned onto Wild Rose Way. Brian stopped to look at him.

'Whose wasn't?'

'Nathaniel Cully's. So even though it was an old leather book there's no way to say it belonged to him.'

'But you can't pretend it wasn't weird that it was *Oliver Twist*. Have you started reading it?'

'No. It just seemed too . . . well, you know. The next time I saw Grandpa I asked him if he liked it and he said he did, that it had some of Dickens' best characters – some named Fagin and the Artful Dodger, but he hadn't been sure about talking to me about it, or having us watch the movie because Oliver's mother died when he was born and it might make me too sad.'

Brian's eyes widened behind the glasses. 'You should look through all the pages; maybe Nathaniel wrote something on one of them, and that would prove it was him.'

'I did and there wasn't. Tucked in at the back, between the last few pages, there were two folded sheets of paper with boats drawn on them in ink, mostly sloops and frigates. I wondered if one of the brothers did them. Remember they're the ones that did the scrimshaws that were left to the historical society. But it could have been anybody, even Miss Emily.'

'You didn't tell me about the drawings.'

'Like I said, I've been telling myself it was just a dream. I asked Mrs Poll if she knew whether my bedroom was Nathaniel's when he was a boy, but she didn't know.'

'Well, he said it was and I believe it,' Brian replied firmly. 'I think he'll come back because he wants to help you somehow.'

'Right.' Oliver wasn't looking at him. His eyes were on the small white house with the steep green room and picket fence. For some reason – nothing in particular, just a friendly look – it brought stingingly to mind his old home that would sometime soon have to be sold so the money could be used to pay for Pleasant Meadows.

'Why don't you talk to Aunt Nellie about seeing Nathaniel?'

It was a sensible suggestion. She of all people wouldn't think he was nuts, but did he want to share the boy he'd seen and spoken to with anyone but Brian? Dream or no dream, Nathaniel was the one thing in recent weeks that Oliver could think of as his very own. With Brian it was different; talking to him was like thinking out loud.

'Not this time.'

When they reached Aunt Nellie's cottage, she welcomed them

into her overcrowded interior. There was too much of everything, from furniture to her collections of pickle crocks, patchwork quilts and colored bottles. But unlike the Cully Mansion it all made for a cozy muddle that made you feel right at home before you even worked your way through to the kitchen where three places were set at the table for breakfast. This turned out to be toaster waffles, but with real maple syrup, tall glasses of milk and what she called a fruit compote.

'Can't remember who gave me the recipe, but it's good. Least I think so. If you don't then leave it. No points gained under my roof for being members of the clean plates club.' Nellie set her cane aside and sat down with the same enthusiasm that she did pretty much everything else. I heard from your Twyla, Oliver, that you're starting piano lessons with Mrs Garwood. A real nice woman and seems happier about her son these days. Says she's never seen such a change since Twyla came. By the way, I appreciated your note thanking me for making the suggestion. Of course it was my spirit guides who put the idea in my head.'

Oliver pretended not to notice when Brian gave him a pointed look. He told Nellie that he'd started his piano lessons yesterday afternoon and that he really liked Mrs Garwood and her son. 'Twyla likes being there a lot.'

'Those two women were born good. Some of us have to work real hard at getting there and others just can't be bothered putting shoulders to the wheel. They're not what you can call bad; just want the easiest path to what suits them.' For emphasis Nellie reached for her stick and pounded on the floor. 'My old mother used to say you can learn yourself out of some habits – telling lies, making free with other people's things, a lousy temper – but selfishness is different because you just can't fathom there's any side but your own. Take Willie Watkins. Saw himself entitled to live off his daughter while drinking himself into the grave, if not fast enough to my mind. All that business of him holing up in the Cully Mansion last winter and worrying her half to death with his absence.'

Oliver nodded. 'She's put up with a lot and keeps right on going.'

'Not a word out of your aunt and uncle about Willie being found in the cellar? Why, that's what brought her up to Sea Glass for the first time ever – to check out that he hadn't robbed the place and talk the situation over with the police. Maybe it points to them,' she said as if begrudgingly giving the devils their due, 'that they kept that from you for Robin Polly's sake. All the talk couldn't have been easy on her, but on the upside it did end with his being taken into Pleasant Meadows.'

'He's Grandpa's roommate there.'

'Is he now? And I hear Robin Polly's back working at the mansion after all her years with Emily Cully. Wonder what's behind that? Her idea of restoring what she'd see as her tarnished good name after what Willie pulled, or because no one else would break their backs digging through all that rubble? How'd you like her, Oliver?'

'She's great.'

Nellie nodded. 'Her size could put some folks off hiring her. Hard to boss around a woman that can look down her nose at you from the clouds. Emily told me straight out that's how she got her on the cheap. And maybe she's felt obliged to cut her rate even lower for your aunt and uncle, if she thinks she owes them.' The dark eyes, well-padded face with its mesh of cobwebby lines turned thoughtful. 'Dora Jones who comes in to clean for me one morning a week is off to spend a month in California with her daughter. So maybe I'll talk to Robin Polly about filling in for her. Well,' she got nimbly to her feet, 'no point in sitting here wasting the day. You boys go off and amuse yourselves while I talk this over with my spirit guides. If I ignore them for more than a day or two they get uppity and threaten to go where they're appreciated.'

When they'd finished doing the dishes, over Aunt Nellie's protests, Brian asked her if it would be OK if they went off on their bikes for an hour or so.

'Suits me, so long as you ride safe.'

'What bikes?' Oliver followed him out the door.

'Yours and mine. Dad brought them over in the back of the truck last night. You can take yours home if you want to, or leave it here in Aunt Nellie's garage. Whatever. How 'bout we ride over the historical society to see if they have pictures of Nathaniel Cully as a boy?'

'Right. Tell your Dad thanks for bringing over the bikes,' Oliver said as he and Brian pedaled back to Salt Marsh Road. The water shimmered a deep blue and there were quite a number of sail boats drifting sleepily under the sun's gold haze. Oliver found himself thinking of the drawings tucked at the back of *Oliver Twist*. They had been really good. If only he could know if Nathaniel, or someone else, had done them.

'I expect that's why Gerard and Elizabeth keep the door from the hall to the cellar locked,' he spoke the thought out loud as he and Brian glided down an incline.

'What?'

'Because of Willie Watkins hiding out there last winter and wanting to be sure no one else could get in them and up the stairs. When I couldn't find a picture of Nathaniel as a boy in the attic I thought I'd go search the cellar, and when I asked them at dinner the other night that I'd like to check them out to make sure there's nothing scary down there so I wouldn't be nervous at night, Elizabeth said she didn't have a clue where the key was and didn't care because nothing would make her go down there – the rest of the house was bad enough. And she wouldn't want me doing so either because there could be a well or something equally dangerous.'

'Well,' replied Brian as they moved closer to the side of the road when seeing a car coming toward them, 'I suppose that makes sense.'

'Yes, but there was something about the way she said it, sort of a panicky look in her eyes. And right away she started talking about something else, saying what a shame it was that Gerard had twisted his knee last year and been told by his doctor to give up golf for a while, which meant he couldn't join the club here.'

'What about the outside door?'

'Also locked. I thought at first it could just be stuck, but I pushed and pushed. No go. I'm going to ask Mrs Poll if she knows where Miss Emily kept that key, the one to the hall door. Could be there was more than one. If I don't have any luck at the historical society finding out what Nathaniel looked like as a kid I'm going to get down there somehow.'

'Cool! But obviously it can't be when your aunt and uncle are around. You'll have to sneak down in the middle of the night and make sure you don't fall in the well.'

'There isn't one. I asked Mrs Poll and she said she knows there isn't one because she went in with the police to persuade Willie to come out peacefully. I was just about to mention the key when Gerard showed up.'

Brian's eyes glinted with excitement behind his glasses. 'Count me in on your midnight adventure or I'll never speak to you again.'

'First I have to get the key.' They had reached Narrow Street and stood straddling their bikes outside the Sea Glass Historical Society.

Brian's focus was still on the key to the cellar. 'Bet your Mrs Poll knows. She looks like she has magical powers. I was afraid when she let me into the hall that she'd turn me into a toad if I didn't smile right. When she comes through you'll have to get Gerard and Elizabeth to let me come for a sleepover. It'll be like being pirates boarding a vessel for plunder. Captain B. Curdle and Walker Plank again strike terror in the hearts of honest seamen bringing back treasure for King and Country!'

They leaned their bikes against the side of the building and went inside. Seated behind an old-fashioned desk sat an equally old-fashioned lady who greeted them in a friendly if somewhat nervous manner, as if children were something she had read about but not previously encountered.

'Oliver Cully! How very exciting. I must shake your hand and your friend's too!' Unfortunately her answer to Oliver's question was disappointing. 'I'm afraid we don't have any paintings or photos of Nathaniel Cully, or his two brothers for that matter, when they were young boys. Those we have show them later in life; although never all three of them together after Nathaniel's marriage to Amelie Courtney. You will know of course that she was a great beauty, from one of the most important Baltimore families?' At Oliver's shake of the head she continued rapidly as if reciting from a brochure. 'Amelie met the Cullys while vacationing here one summer and all three of the young men fell desperately in love with her. But it was Nathaniel, the middle son, who she accepted. One gathers this came as quite a shock to the family, he being the prosaic family doctor and the other two far more dashing and sought after by belles of the ball. The younger one never married and the oldest remained a bachelor until late in life, producing no children. Sadly, according to Miss Emily Cully, it was one of those rifts that never healed, the bitterness being all on the part of the disappointed brothers. Such a pity. The three of them were all so close as children.'

The volunteer now offered to show them the portrait of Amelie Cully, gifted to the society by Miss Emily. 'If you will follow me upstairs to the room which also houses the scrimshaws I think you will agree with me that she was indeed very lovely. Nathaniel commissioned its painting shortly after their marriage. How very proud you must be,' she did all her talking to Oliver, 'of your illustrious family tree.'

'You're giving him a big head,' Brian warned.

'Oh, I'm sure not,' the volunteer tittered awkwardly. 'Much too nice a boy, if he's anything like his father.' Oliver was too startled to speak and she proceeded on. 'Once, years ago, Miss Emily very kindly invited me to one her evening soirees – in appreciation of my work here – and she told me, or I should say the group I was standing in, that she was enjoying a very pleasant correspondence with a distant cousin's young son. I remember her saying his name was Max, because mine is Maxine.' Before there could be more the doorbell pinged downstairs and she departed to attend whoever had stepped inside.

The portrait of Amelie Courtney Cully hung above a cast iron-fronted fireplace. She was beautiful in her long green velvet gown with her corn-colored hair curled over one shoulder, but more importantly she looked lovable with her kind, amused eyes and gently curving mouth. Not at all the sort of girl to enjoy breaking guys' hearts. Oliver felt sure she had done everything she could to put things right with Nathaniel's brothers, which had probably only made things worse. Angry people, he thought, want . . . need other people to behave badly. Probably Gerard and Elizabeth preferred it when he was difficult. He followed Brian over to the glass cases displaying the scrimshaws, but unfortunately he couldn't concentrate because he was thinking of his father alive, young – maybe in high school or college, writing letters to Miss Emily that made her happy.

'Imagine climbing the rigging of one of those vessels in gale force winds,' mused Brian as they came down the stairs. 'Better than any ride at the fair, I'd say.'

'Because you seriously could die? I don't think so.'

'Forgot you've a problem with heights.'

An uneasy memory crept in on Oliver of mentioning this weakness in the car with Emjagger and Stone when their mother mentioned that she had grown up in Colorado and asked if he liked skiing or snowboarding. He caught the slyly considering looks the brothers instantly exchanged. But what could they do about this discovery except gloat?

He and Brian collected their bikes and pedaled around the green onto Salt Marsh Road. Neither let their eyes drift to the Cully Mansion. The visit to the historical society museum had been a bust as far as finding out what Nathaniel Cully looked like as a boy. Oliver felt bad not telling Twyla about him, but remained worried she would think his appearance on the window seat resulted from the stress of living at the Cully Mansion.

Aunt Nellie made sandwiches for them on their return and afterward they went down to the shore and skipped stones. Brian was the better of the two at this. One of his popped up eight times, like it was having great fun itself. They couldn't remember if this was a record or not. By that time it was a quarter to one and Oliver decided he'd better head back to Gerard and Elizabeth. After some thought he left his bike in Aunt Nellie's garage. He wouldn't put it past Emjagger and Stone to make off with it if he took it back with him. Brian agreed that this was too big a risk and they parted after an exchange of friendly punches.

Oliver had forgotten Elizabeth's suggestion that there might be a surprise waiting for him. The hope that it might be a dog or cat had quickly dwindled. What met his eyes wasn't pleasant: Emjagger and Stone were with her in the drawing room. To him they were fiendishly, horribly alike, except that Emjagger, the older by ten months – twelve to Stone's eleven – was an inch or so taller. Other than that they could have been identical twins. Thin, greasy-haired, narrow-eyed and horribly pleased with themselves.

'Look who's come round to see you,' she said as if fully expecting him to dance with delight. 'They're off for ice cream and their mother's given them the money to treat you. Aren't you lucky to have found such nice friends so quickly?'

Fortunately Oliver didn't have to answer. 'We just love Oliver, Mrs Cully!' Emjagger bared his ferrety teeth in a smile. 'Don't we, Stone?'

'Too true!' The equally dreadful brother gazed dreamily into Oliver's eyes. 'This summer will be the best ever. The three of us will do everything, absolutely everything together. We won't let him have a lonely or dull moment. Every time he sets foot out of doors we'll be waiting for him, with some great scheme we've thought up for the day. That's the idea, isn't it, Emjag?'

Oliver wondered numbly how Elizabeth gave no sign of hearing the threat behind the words. Playing for time, he reminded her of the promised surprise.

'Oh, yes. Mustn't forget that.' She pushed back her always untidy, thickly curling hair. 'Take a look around the room and see if you spot anything different.'

Staring up and down the room, Oliver shook his head. But after turning back to her he saw that she was smiling, really quite pleasantly in the direction of the four-poster bed with the birdcage that had once been home to Miss Emily's parrot Polly, hanging from its pole alongside it. He felt suddenly cold, as he had half feared what might happen in the church at Dobbs Mill. That cage was now covered with a cloth. He thought he'd told Gerard and Elizabeth that he hated the idea of caged birds, but maybe he hadn't.

'Come and take a look!' She was still smiling, almost like a real aunt who was genuinely fond of him. 'We were sorry to disappoint you about a dog or cat and one can't do more than look at goldfish.' He trailed miserably down the room after her, with Emjagger and Stone prowling in his wake. 'So here's what we came up with!' A shudder passed through him, all too visible to Emjagger and Stone, as she tweaked off the cloth. A blue and yellow parakeet was perched on the swing, apparently unfazed by the sudden light. Not that the room was ever really bright. 'Of course we'll expect you to take responsibility for filling the trays with seed and water, and doing the cleaning out. As Gerard said when we went into the shop, "If a child wants a pet they can't expect others to look after it."'

'It's beautiful.' Oliver stared bleakly at the beady eyes and sharply curved beak. 'And I am grateful, Elizabeth.'

'You don't sound it.' Her smile vanished as if wiped off with a washcloth.

He heard a giggle escape one of the brothers. 'It's just that I have a phobia about indoor birds.'

'Oh, not another one!' Rolling Stone oozed sympathy. 'As if it isn't bad enough for you being terrified of heights. Maybe you should get him help, Mrs Cully – sounds like he's badly scarred from something in his childhood. It could be anything from his parents dying in that plane crash or being spoiled to death by his sick old grandfather and that black woman, and then her deciding she couldn't be bothered looking after them any longer. No offence, Oliver. We're only thinking of you, aren't we, EmJag?'

Choking down tears, he rounded on them. 'You're haters! Racist ones!'

'Now you've hurt our feelings,' responded Emjagger mournfully, 'but because *we've* been well brought-up we won't go back on our offer to take you out for ice cream. There's this place called Cones on the other kind of the common. You really should try their butter pecan, Mrs Cully.' The smirk was back full force. 'We'll bring some back for you.'

'That's very kind, but I stay away from anything frozen for fear of aggravating my headaches.'

'And being made upset can't help, I'm sure.' Stone sounded ready to spurt tears.

'You're wonderfully understanding, and so is your brother.' Elizabeth turned to Oliver, jerking at the sleeves of her flowing flax shirt. 'This parakeet isn't going back. You're petulant because you didn't get exactly what you want. And Gerard and I aren't giving into that behavior. You have been spoilt. That's why we haven't welcomed Twyla Washburn here – so she can't keep it up – and why we haven't encouraged too many outings with her, but we've decided to relax on those. That should have been apparent when we agreed to the piano lessons at the house where she works, even though there's that impaired man under the same roof.'

A realization came cold and clear to Oliver. *Mrs Garwood's coming here made you worry that people could start talking if you and Gerard don't loosen up on the reigns, that they could start wondering just why you want to keep me mostly to yourselves.* The remnants of his gratitude for the piano lessons vanished.

Elizabeth appeared to get her anger under control. Her voice when she continued was almost conversational. 'I know we've come late into your life, Oliver, and it's understandable that you harbor resentment for that, although there are always two sides to a story. The point is we've now brought you to live with us and, whatever you may think, we have your best interests at heart. It's important to us that you be responsible and respectful. So before you and the boys leave I'm going to fetch Gerard out of his office so you can thank him – and it must be nicely – for picking out this bird for you. While I'm gone why don't you think of a name for it?'

When she left the room the brothers sat down on one of the

sofas with their hands piously folded on their laps. 'Just think,' crooned Emjagger, 'when it gets really tame you can take it up to bed with and fall asleep with it perched on your head and you can wake up in the morning with sweet little poop in your hair. I know! How about naming it "'Shit"?'

'No worse than yours.'

Both boys started to get up and then sank back down. Their meek expressions would have turned Oliver's blood cold at any other moment. They'd make him pay for that crack when they got him outside, but what did that matter? They'd arrived with no intention of going easy on him. Hell waited out in the bright sunshine. He went into the hall, barely registering when they didn't follow. All he could think about with any clarity was that however hard he tried, he was never going to warm to the parakeet. And he'd end up feeling more and more wretched about that because everything deserved to be truly loved. It wasn't fair to it to be stuck with him. Maybe if he prayed real hard . . . He was halfway down the hall without realizing he'd taken a step. The door to Gerard's office was half open and Elizabeth's voice carried to him even though it was low pitched. It was the vibrating anger that jolted it to audibility.

'Just stay put. You positively reek. It has to have been one after the other since we got back. Spare me the tired old excuses. I've had them up to here. I don't care if you think the devil himself is after you for the part you played in what seems like a lifetime ago. You're my nightmare. You got us into this mess and you won't be helping to dig us out, but at least try not to make it any harder. The kid's not stupid. He may not have been brought up around booze, but he's got a sense of smell. Let him get one whiff and word will go straight to her and then on to the grandfather. The only saving grace is that this binging is relatively new, so if checked up on no one we know will say you're an out-of-control drunk. And then there's the beauty that all kids exaggerate, especially when they think it will work for them. Count yourself lucky this time. I'll get him out of the house with those boys from next door and you can go take a long cold shower while I make a gallon of strong coffee.'

Oliver, who had already been backing up, speed-turned and slid the rest of the way back to the drawing room. He was standing several feet from the opening, wondering what Gerard had done

that haunted him, when Elizabeth came in. Behind them Emjagger
and Stone stood up in perfect little gentleman fashion.

'Gerard's right in the middle of something crucial; he'll see you
when you get back, Oliver. So off the three of you go and have
fun.'

She opened the front door, waited barely till they were down
the steps and closed it. The clear blue sky and glowing sunshine
struck him as sinisterly unreal, like some smirking trick of nature.
That Emjagger and Stone weren't smirking didn't help. They eyed
him with a solemn innocence that was even more frightening,
before each taking one of his arms and marching across the road
to the common. Their grips didn't hurt, but he knew if he struggled to get away the pressure would instantly increase, leaving
bruises that would last a week. And even if he did manage to break
away they'd run him down in seconds. Perhaps it would have been
different if he'd brought the bike back from Aunt Nellie's and had
left it alongside the house. Why hadn't he refused to come with
them? The answer came with wretched hopelessness. If they didn't
have their fun with him now, they'd think up something even
juicier for next time. Better to get whatever it was over with now
than live in dread for what was inevitably in store. Besides, after
what he'd overheard of Elizabeth going on at Gerard she would
have pushed Oliver out the door if he'd so much as opened his
mouth in protest.

Emjagger and Stone drew him to a standstill in the middle of
the common where the statue of Nathaniel Cully rose toweringly
from its pedestal. A few feet in front was the wooden bench with
its oval brass marker providing the name of the donor. A few
people passed up and down the curved, surrounding paths, but
there was nobody coming or going on the grass. Oliver could have
been alone on a desert island with a couple of cannibals. He
couldn't think what was coming but found himself hoping under
thudding heartbeats that the granite figure would suddenly come
to life and swoop him to safety. Brian had been so sure that the
boy Nathaniel was real and had showed up to show that he wanted
to help Oliver. The sculpted face did look kind, but not a shadow
brushed across it; no suggestion of movement.

'You must feel so proud of being descended from him,' said
Emjagger.

'The great Cully name.' Stone poured awe into his voice. 'We're so impressed we'd like to take a photo of the two of you together and hang it on our bedroom wall. You wouldn't mind that, would you, us all being new best friends and all.'

That sounded harmless, so there had to be more. 'OK, I'll stand here and you can take it.'

Stone had pulled a disposable camera out of his pocket. 'Real big of him, isn't it, Jag? But we can't let him stand down here looking like a chipmunk. No, Oliver, we're going to get you up on that pedestal. It's wide enough to stand on; that way it can be a real family picture.'

What could he do? Scream and yell for help? There wasn't anybody close enough whose attention he could attract in a normal voice and then what could he say that wouldn't make him sound a fool? Oliver's vision blurred. Emjagger and Stone had gotten him onto the bench and were now hefting him onto the pedestal. It was about six feet high but might as well have been sixty. His hands reached back to clutch at the statue. He was going to faint or be sick. He couldn't open his mouth to plead to be let down.

'Couldn't ask for a better picture,' caroled Stone. 'The town's big hero and the even bigger coward.'

'Smile and say *cheese* for the camera!' That was Emjagger. He was spluttering with uncontrollable laughter. The sound seemed to go on and on, before being abruptly cut short by an angrily raised voice.

'Hey, you two! What game are you playing with this boy?' Prying his eyes open Oliver saw a man coming fast across the grass from one direction and a woman doing the same from the other. It was the man who had yelled out. Emjagger and Stone stood as if locked in place as Oliver was. He jabbed a finger their direction. 'Don't you budge one inch, or I'll file a report with descriptions of you both that won't allow for wriggle room.' Emjagger and Stone shrank together, merging into one trembling, open-mouthed entity. The woman was now standing on the bench, reaching up to take a steadying hold on Oliver's ankles. Now that help was here tears slid down his cheeks.

'It's going to be all right.' She smiled up at him. 'We'll get you down.'

'Even if I could get up the courage to jump,' a sob broke through, 'the bench is right there and if I'd landed on the back rail I could have gotten all twisted up and broken a bone.'

'Maybe more than one. Not worth chancing.'

'They knew I'm afraid of heights.'

'Naturally.' It was the man speaking now. He signaled to the woman and took her place on the bench when she got down. 'Bullies can sniff out fear a mile off. It's what makes them tick.'

Oliver found himself being lifted down by the strongest arms he'd ever had around him. Safely back on ground level, he saw the woman open her purse and the next thing he felt was a tissue in his hand. He really didn't need it because he'd wiped some of the tears away with his arm after prying his fingers away from Nathaniel's statue, and the rest had dried on his face, but for something flimsy it felt hugely comforting. He saw her properly for the first time and decided that she was very pretty with her short dark hair, hazel eyes and clear, pale skin. Best of all, her smile was lovely and filled with concern.

'Better?' She asked it as if it were really important to her to know he was OK. He had the feeling she wanted to put her arms round him. Strangers couldn't do that, but somehow she didn't seem the least bit a stranger.

'Much. Thank you.' His smile trembled, then steadied.

'Good! You conducted yourself like a champ,' said the man. 'I share your thing about heights and at your age I'd have been screaming bloody murder. We'll hope these loathsome bullies are no longer feeling quite so pleased with themselves.' He was tall and lean; for some reason fitting Oliver's idea of how a schoolteacher should look, even though he'd never had one who resembled him. Maybe it was the relaxed way he stood while seeming to size up the situation with measured calm, as if it was one of dozens he dealt with in a day. He took an elongated moment before angling toward Emjagger and Stone who had not budged an inch, let alone attempted to bolt.

'I was deadly serious about considering filing a report. Being a member of the Boston police force I won't have any difficulty getting the local boys to hear me out. Whether I go ahead will depend on you. I'll be giving my new friend here . . .' He paused, tilting his brown head expectantly.

'Oliver – Oliver Cully.'

The man inclined his head, as if acknowledging a useful piece of information presented by a valued colleague during a murder investigation. 'Right then, you scurrilous pair, I'll be giving Ollie, as I'll presume to call him – since I've the feeling we're going to be such good chums – my card with my cell phone number and work extension. I want him to call day or night if you so much as flicker your eyelashes at him. Are we entirely clear on what the repercussions will be if I have to leave my bed or even my desk?' At no point had he raised his voice. He might have been stating when he was expecting homework turned in. And somehow that did not lessen, but magnified the steel behind the words.

The brothers opened their mouths but no sound came out. All they could manage were jittery head jerks that looked liable to snap their necks.

'Then get out of our sight before I regret not marching you to jail right now.'

'Thank you, sir,' quivered Emjagger.

'Sorry, sir,' bleated Stone.

They slithered sideways a yard or so, before zigzagging, as if unable to get their legs in sync, back across the common. Oliver should have savored the sound of one, or both of them, wailing like four-year-olds, but they no longer mattered. He'd never felt so completely protected since the last time he'd sat on Grandpa's knee.

'Are you really from the police?'

A surprisingly boyish grin twitched at the man's mouth, mobilizing the thin scholarly face. 'No, but I am from Boston. How'd I do?'

'Superb!'

'You had me racking my brains trying to remember if I'd run a red light in the last month,' confessed the dark-haired lady with a widening of that lovely smile.

'I didn't go at it exactly cold; I used to write modern police procedurals before switching to ones featuring a mid-nineteenth-century sleuth.'

'You're an author!' Oliver's instant hero worship increased a hundred fold. 'Wow! No wonder you used that word *scurrilous*! I like it almost as much as *ventriloquism*! I'll have to add it to my word collection! My grandpa and I think of them like stamps, only we stick them in our heads instead of an album.'

'Great! Something in common beyond our mutual fear of heights.'

'That was really true.'

'I only lie – gray ones at that – to people I despise. I'm in possession of your name – that it should be Oliver is interesting.

I'll explain why in a moment, but I haven't given you mine. It's Evan Bryant.' His amused gaze shifted to the third member of their little group.

'Sarah Draycott,' she said. 'And although I hadn't yet met Oliver, I've heard great things about him from a new friend, Twyla Washburn, who loves him very much.'

'She's told me about you, too.' Oliver was about pour out his knowing of her – how kind she'd been to Mrs Garwood, coming to see her and the son and taking their dog for walks. But he cut himself off on realizing Mr Bryant was staring at her as if she were the Statue of Liberty come to life in front of him.

'You're Sarah Draycott?'

'Yes . . . Why?'

'I'm EB.'

'Oh!' Her expression was equally startled.

'I've been away from home on a book tour and only got back yesterday to find your letter waiting for me. You must have thought me incredibly rude and unappreciative.' He tilted his head to include Oliver in this exchange. 'A month or so back I wrote to a friend of mine named Nan Fielding who used to live in the house Ms Draycott has moved into. I'd no idea she'd died around that same time and that my letter was left languishing in the mailbox until Ms Draycott found it and most kindly wrote to explain. I had a book signing in Portland and decided I couldn't miss the opportunity of coming here to personally say thank you, rather than trying to get in touch by phone.'

'It was such a small thing.'

'Not to me.'

Oliver looked from one face to the other, and liked both.

'Was Nan Fielding a very dear friend?'

'She was my senior year high school English teacher. When my first book came out she sent a letter through my publisher and we've corresponded reasonably frequently ever since. I'd no idea she was ill.'

'I think it was very sudden. I'm so sorry – the news must have come as a shock.' Her hazel eyes remained locked with his gray ones. There was no one else on the common, but Oliver was sure they wouldn't have noticed if there'd been hundreds. They both looked startled by the coincidence of their meeting.

'There were two Evans in that class, myself and Evan Richards, so rather than her addressing us by our full names, he became ER and I was EB. That's how she wrote to me in her first letter. I liked that; it made for a special link.'

'I didn't know if you were a man or woman.'

'I'd decided to stop for lunch before showing up unannounced on your doorstep, when I saw what was going on with Oliver in front of that statue.'

Sarah Draycott wrenched her eyes from his to look at it. 'That's Nathaniel Cully. One of your ancestors, right, Oliver?'

'Some sort of distant cousin.'

Evan Bryant followed her gaze as if not wanting to miss a single glimpse of her profile. 'Emanates strength and kindness; I'd be honored to claim relationship with him and interested to know what made him a town hero.' He paused as if drawing himself together. When he continued a full share of his attention returned to Oliver. 'How about we go celebrate the three of us meeting up? Is there a coffee shop or ice-cream place close by?'

'That's where Emjagger and Stone were taking me – for ice cream.'

'Does that thoroughly put you off the idea?'

'Just the reverse,' replied Oliver staunchly. 'They've lost out big time.'

'I hope they never again get so much as a lick of a cone,' said Sarah, eyes radiating mischievous malice. 'Were you going to Cones?'

'Yes. My friend Brian says they have the best ever hot fudge sundaes.' He turned, embarrassed, afraid that sounded greedy. 'But I'd be happy with a small cone.'

'We're doing this in style.' Mr Bryant, without shifting position, looked as though he had reached out to touch Sarah. 'I've my cell; should you call your parents to ask if it's all right for you to go with us?'

'They're dead.' It was always painful to say this. 'And I can't live with my grandpa anymore because he had to go into a nursing home. Twyla took care of him until he got too bad. We both loved her from the start.'

Sarah explained for him. 'Oliver recently moved in with his father's brother and wife – Gerard and Elizabeth Cully. The house is that big red Victorian.' She pointed across the road.

Mr Bryant assessed it at a glance.

'I'd just as soon not call them.' Oliver hoped they wouldn't feel obliged to insist. 'Gerard's not having one of his best days and when he's . . . like that . . . Elizabeth sometimes gets one of her headaches and goes to bed.'

'I'm sure it'll be all right.' Sarah placed a hand on his shoulder though obviously speaking to Mr Bryant. 'It's not as though we're leaving the immediate area. Cones is straight ahead between the grocery store and the flower shop.'

It took no more than a minute or two to reach its door; almost equally quickly the three of them were seated at a small, round white-topped table. In front of each was a tall glass dish full of vanilla ice cream, deluged in fudge sauce, hugely piped with cream and topped with chopped nuts. No maraschino cherries. That they had all decided against them gave Oliver a wonderfully comfortable feeling. It suggested an already established bond. He told himself this was silly; the result of gratitude for their having rescued him from a bad situation, but the feeling wouldn't be banished. Sarah and Evan weren't just being kind. They liked having him with them. He was as convinced of that as he was that Brian had been right – Cones did have the very best hot fudge sundaes.

Amazing how the conversation flowed as if the three of them had sat around a table together for years. Afterward he couldn't remember what got the ball rolling. Somewhere in the middle they'd asked him to call them by their first names.

He heard himself talking about Emjagger and Stone with the indifference of referring to characters in a book that wasn't worth finishing, explaining that the latter's full name was Rolling Stone. Evan had promised to let him have his latest in his series and Oliver couldn't wait to read it, especially as he'd described the period as Dickensian. Sarah had flushed when admitting she only knew of Agatha Christie when it came to mysteries.

'Twyla says maybe their names may have turned them into bullies.'

'Don't think of making fun of us; we're real tough dudes?' Evan laid down his spoon alongside the empty sundae. 'It's an explanation but not an excuse. My guess is this has nothing to do with what they think of you as a person. They want to bring you down a peg or two because of that statue out there making a visible point that the name Cully means something around here.'

'I think that's right.' Sarah leaned forward. 'What matters is that they don't start up again after they get over their fright. I don't like the idea of them living next door. Ten miles away would be too close.'

Oliver felt a need to reassure her; to offer the tenderness he'd so often received from Grandpa and Twyla. 'I don't think they'll pull anything else.'

'Neither do I, but just in case they so much as breathe on you the wrong way, let me give you this as promised.' Evan reached into his jeans' pocket, pulled out a small black leather case and handed Oliver a business card. He'd never seen one before. 'My home and cell numbers are both on there, along with my street and email addresses. Here, take two, that way you can keep one on you and put the other away for safekeeping. Don't worry about calling too early or late. I meant what I said about day or night.'

'Thanks, Evan!'

'That makes me feel better,' said Sarah. 'Why don't you give me those, Oliver, and I'll write my numbers on the back. I just got a home phone and I always take my cell with me even if it's just to go into the yard.'

Evan handed her a pen. 'Always best to have at least two contacts.'

Oliver nodded. 'With Twyla taking care of Sonny Norris she mightn't be able to leave him if Mrs Garwood wasn't home.'

'You will tell your aunt and uncle what happened?'

'I don't think I can. They've gotten neighborly with the parents and I can't see them risking messing that up; besides Elizabeth acts like she thinks I'm lucky Emjagger and Stone want to be friends with me. She'd say it was nice they wanted to take a photo of me on the statue and they couldn't have realized they'd scare me. But I promise I'll tell Twyla tomorrow when she takes me to church and to see Grandpa.'

Evan drew out another couple of cards and handed them to Sarah. 'One for you to have on hand. And may I have your info on the back of the other one?'

'Of course.'

'Good!' Oliver heard a lot in that one word. Evan glanced at his watch. 'I hate to cut out but I have to be heading back to Boston if I'm going to be able to make my dinner engagement with a woman who considers unpunctuality one of the deadly sins.'

'Having to wait around can be so annoying.' Sarah's face didn't give anything away, but Oliver sensed her disappointment.

They got to their feet and moved to the door. Once outside

Evan continued casually, 'On this occasion I can't shave off a minute. It's her seventieth birthday and we've got reservations at her favorite restaurant. She also happens to be my favorite aunt.'

'That's fortunate. My Aunt Beth is a pain.'

'Do either of you have plans for next weekend? If not, I could come back Friday or Saturday and take you out to celebrate the pleasure of meeting you.'

'I'm free either day.' Her voice was every bit as casual as his had been. 'What about you, Oliver?'

'Are you sure I wouldn't be in the way?'

'Of course not.'

'A lady in the era I write about,' said Evan gravely, 'would never consider setting foot out of doors in a man's company without a chaperone.'

'And quite right too,' laughed Sarah.

They were nearing the road when Oliver asked Evan the titles of some of his books.

'The first in the series was *Twist*, the second *Dodge*. It got a little tougher after that. They're based on Dickens' *Oliver Twist*, which makes meeting you not only a pleasure, but an intriguing coincidence. Oliver Twist and the Artful Dodger cross paths as adults and pair up as champions of the downtrodden.'

Oliver felt the ground shift under his feet. Coincidence was right! 'Someone just gave me a copy of *Oliver Twist*. Grandpa is really big on Dickens, but he'd never read that one to me. Wow! How cool is this!'

Sarah and Evan waited outside until Oliver let himself into the house, where he found Elizabeth and Gerard seated on the facing sofas. No sign of continued friction lingering from her anger on finding her husband drunk. She was leafing through a glossy art magazine. His eyes were closed, presumably listening to the classical music drifting around them from an unseen source.

'So.' Elizabeth raised her eyes in Oliver's direction as he hesitated in the doorway. 'Did you have a fun afternoon?'

'Great, thank you.'

'And have you come up with a name for the newest member of the household?'

Oliver didn't have a clue what she was talking about until she swiveled round to take in the birdcage. He'd forgotten all about the parakeet. 'Feathers.' The name just popped out.

'Fits.' Gerard had cracked open his eyes. 'Are we getting close to dinner?'

As a meal it didn't count for much of one. A couple of mouthfuls of some sort of casserole, but at least husband and wife seemed back to normal with each other, and there was no mention of Emjagger and Stone to disrupt Oliver's thoughts of Sarah and Evan and the prospect of being with them again next weekend. If Gerard and Elizabeth didn't like it, too bad.

When he went up to his room that night he was going to take *Oliver Twist* into bed with him, but instead he picked up one of the paperback romance novels he'd found in the attic. Hearing from the volunteer at the historical society museum that Miss Emily had exchanged letters with his father made her a much more friendly reality. He leafed through that book and a couple of others before taking up another that opened up close to the middle, for the reason that there was a letter tucked into that space. Oliver's heart thudded, hoping that it was from his Dad until seeing in the left-hand corner of the envelope the name and address of a law firm. Inside was a single page with the same letterhead above, dated December 1998 and containing only a few typed lines: *Dear Emily, I think you are wise not to change your estate plan. To single out one brother over the other for preferential treatment might cause a family rift reminiscent of the estrangement between your grandfather and his brothers. I am always at your disposal, my dear friend. Yours most sincerely, Arthur Rappaport.*

That letter had been written four years before Oliver was born. He returned it to the envelope, which he replaced in the book. He lay trying to figure it out. What was an estate plan? Was it the same as . . . ?' A yawn took over his face. The happiness and excitement of the afternoon had made him incredibly drowsy. He would just close his eyes for a moment. Weird thing, time. This time he wasn't sure that he'd been asleep when he opened them to see the young Nathaniel Cully again – with legs stretched out – on the window seat.

'So you've met them,' he said. 'I could have told you everything was going to work out in the way that's best for everyone.'

'Right!' Oliver barely blinked, before snuggling down and re-closing his eyes. 'Goodnight, Nat. Talk to you later, I hope. I'll try to love Feathers.'

'Sleep well, friend. And ask Mrs Polly about the key to the cellar.'

Ten

It was a perfect morning in early July, with just enough breeze to edge the deep blue silk of the bay with ripples of lacey foam, when Sarah came down her wooden garden steps to the beach. She stood taking additional pleasure in the hillocks of seaweed-covered rocks, thinking that those at a distance resembled a miniature mountain range, and that the splatters of greenish brown could have been the tangled tresses of mermaids washed in face down by the tide. Turning, she saw Libby Jennson on the beach. They often met down there on what they thought of as their beach at around eight thirty. Usually Libby had her little dog Sheridan with her, but not today. She explained his absence.

'He's at the groomer's. Want to walk or sit?' Her hair, with its blond highlights, hung around her shoulders until she drew a ruched black fabric band from around her wrist and converted to a ponytail.

'Sit, if it's OK with you. I'm going to collect Jumbo at ten and take him for a run.' They perched on Libby's steps, which were wider than Sarah's. A moment passed with them both eyeing the scattering of sailboats set at intervals on the blue canvas as if by a master artist's hand. The sun was warm on their backs. The perfume of red and white sea roses drifted on the air. Sarah loved it so much she wished she could bottle it to carry with her at all times. Maybe it was the feeling of utter relaxation that eased Libby, who couldn't be called nosy, into asking her next question.

'So, are you falling for him?'

'Impossible not to and Oliver's crazy about him too. So strong and gentle.'

'Can't think of a better combination.'

'And so obedient. At first I worried some about letting him off the leash in case he took off, but . . .'

'Hold on a minute,' Libby interrupted, 'who are we talking about?'

Sarah returned the wide-eyed look. 'Jumbo.'

'You may be, but I wasn't. I'm dog crazy as you know, but . . .

push me off this step if you like – I deserve it – your frequent weekend visitor is who I meant.'

'Evan. Of course. He *has* been down three times in the last month since we met.' Sarah didn't resent the question. Over the past couple of months she'd grown to like Libby more and more; she'd been generous with her help painting the walls and trim and had made those sessions fun. They had gradually come to exchange more confidences with each other. You could both laugh and talk in depth with Libby. 'In your place *I'd* be wondering if romance was in the wind and would need to be gagged not to ask. But no, it's not like that. Purely, no pun intended, a friendship that revolves around our growing affection for Oliver. That doesn't mean I don't find him attractive; I imagine lots of women would and maybe under different circumstances, who knows? What's wonderful is how much the three of us enjoy being together, and the aunt and uncle haven't put any obstacles in the way of letting Oliver spend most of his time over here on Evan's weekends or come over a lot on other days.'

'Are those two bullies still leaving him alone?'

'So far so good. And his aunt has stopped pushing a friendship.'

Libby shook her head. 'What an odd pair, that Mr and Mrs Cully! I'd like to know what motivated them to take Oliver in. He's wonderful, but have they noticed? Sid says it's simple, that – as his only relatives – there'd have been talk if they hadn't, but I'm with Nellie who considers the situation to be very murky.'

'The spirit guides haven't pushed aside the veil to step forward with answers?' There was no bite to the question. Sarah had grown fond of Nellie Armitage; it would have been impossible to not have done given her intervention with Twyla on behalf of Gwen and Sonny and her obvious affection for Oliver.

Libby laughed. 'Could be they only speak out after Nellie's tipped them her opinion. I'm never sure how much of a fraud she is, but – as I pointed out to Sid – whatever Sea Glass locals said on the subject wouldn't have been an issue for them if they'd stayed in New York instead of appearing on the scene and shutting themselves off in that mausoleum. Every time I walk past I think Halloween Horror House.' She returned her gaze to the sailboats.

'Twyla's amazed the Cullys didn't nix Oliver's visits here for fear of her trotting down. She's the one they tried their best to close the door against. As it is, if she, Gwen and Sonny don't come to us for an hour or so during Evan time, as Oliver and I call it, we go to them. By the way,' Sarah turned her head to smile at Libby, 'Gwen's so grateful to Sid for his kindness to Sonny, taking him out for rides and treating him as if they're two regular guys who enjoy spending time together.'

'Sonny seems to prefer it that way – without me cutting in.' Libby sat with her arms wound round her knees.

'I hope he knows how grateful I am that he painted the staircase walls.'

'He does, but doesn't understand why you should be. That's the main reason I married Sid – he's nice. That sounds dull, but I'd learned from life with my first husband that great sex and drowning in each other's eyes isn't half enough. It can even end up tasting like stale bread. But the man who brings you up a cup of tea in bed, and rarely leaves the dinner table without telling you how lucky he is to have a wife who can make shepherd's pie or whatever taste gourmet, gets to be more of a turn-on every day.'

'Sounds anything but dull to me.'

'You've got it right, Sarah. Having a platonic male friend you can be completely yourself with isn't to be sneezed at. What time are you expecting Evan today?'

'Around noon. He plans on staying until Sunday afternoon or evening.'

'What does he say about the Wealthy Poor House, B&B?' The place had gotten its name from a Mr Poor marrying a Miss Wealthy at the tail-end of the nineteenth century.

'Can't say enough about the comfort and welcome from the owners. They serve such a bountiful breakfast he ends up having two. One there and one here, though mostly mine doesn't stretch to more than muffins, fruit and coffee. Oliver and I are boggled that he stays so trim. Being tall has to help, but even so he should by rights have gained ten pounds in the last month.'

'Is it still on for you to bring him and Oliver to Potluck?' It was the Jennson's turn this month to host, and Libby had already told Sarah that they would be providing a main dish of spiral ham and au gratin potatoes.

'They're both really looking forward to it. We're all set to make fudge-topped brownies this afternoon. The super-good news is that Oliver gets to sleep over both nights. I did tell you I got a double bed – a queen would have been too big for the spare room.'

'Yes. Do you need a loan of sheets and pillows?

'All set, thanks. Evan asked if it would be all right to bring his aunt this weekend, the one he took out to dinner on her birthday, and we were really looking forward to meeting her, but she'd forgotten she had to be at a wedding.'

'Well, I can't wait to meet him.' Several people came striding along the water's edge. Libby unwrapped her knees to stretch both arms above her head, in demonstration, perhaps, should they glance sideways, that those who sit aren't necessarily incapable of getting a workout. As it happened Libby was anything but an exercise sluggard. She did badminton once a week and aerobics twice, and never missed taking Sheridan on a good walk. For all his mini-size he was no slouch either. What she didn't do was run, which Sarah loved to do, especially on the days she had Jumbo alongside. 'What about Evan's parents? Any mention of a get-together with them? Don't they live in Boston?'

'They did, but both are gone now. His mother died four years ago and his father a few months later.'

'You said he's forty, so that probably put them in their late fifties at the time. That's horribly young these days. Sid's already had his sixtieth.' Libby turned her head to look up at her house. 'I hope Sid's not stuffing his face right this minute with a full English breakfast, including the fried bread. The only thing that might put him off what he calls good old-fashioned grub is if enough people told him it's now called health food. Perhaps tomorrow evening at the potluck you could casually mention that fresh fruit and green veggies are now considered the forbidden foods. And toss in yogurt and cottage cheese while you're at it.'

'And have him decide I'm not the sort of woman he wants living next door? I don't think so! Anyway, no need to panic. Evan's father was in his eighties and mother her late seventies when they died. They'd been married for over twenty years before he showed up.'

Libby visibly relaxed. 'Any brothers or sisters?'

'No. He was the late-life surprise. And he said he couldn't have asked for more wonderful parents. Now he only has his aunt – his mother's younger sister – as a close relative. But fortunately they're very close. She sounds delightfully eccentric and I would like to meet her.'

'I hear a "but" coming.'

'There isn't one.' Sarah hesitated and the words wandered out, 'Except that I wouldn't want her to get up any false hopes about Evan and me if she's hoping he'll marry again. Because, even if our friendship did deepen into something more, I don't see it working out long term. We've talked briefly about our divorces. I told him that in the end there wasn't enough left between us to stop Harris from falling in love with someone else and he said he and his wife had come to realize they wanted different things out of life. He wanted a family – at least one child – and she didn't.'

'Hadn't they discussed that along the way?'

'People change their minds and she had. It was the same with Harris. He was for, then against, then for again with Lisa. Evan's wife said they'd reached an impasse. So what's the point of dragging on a marriage with him unhappy and her feeling guilty? As in my situation, there wasn't enough love remaining to keep the marriage intact.'

'Did you tell him that it was the reverse in your situation? That you continued wanting a child when Harris didn't?'

'Why get into that? I couldn't produce a baby in the three years we tried. None of the fertility treatments worked.' Sarah got up off the steps. 'The last resort would have been in vitro and by then Harris had gone off the idea.'

Libby also stood up. Uncertainty as to what to say showed in her eyes. 'But it's still out there as an option.'

'Doesn't always work.'

'OK. Let's say your friendship shifts into higher gear – what about adoption?'

'I've thought about looking into that on my own. Lots of single women who want children are doing it. But Evan may be someone who's set on his own flesh and blood. I know Sid looks on Phoebe every bit as much his daughter as yours, but not every man can make that leap.'

'But look how he's taken to Oliver. You've told me those two have so much in common they might be twin souls. It could be the same with a child he brought up.'

'Being a father involves more than being a friend. Besides, Oliver's one of a kind. He's already stolen our hearts and he's not available.' Sarah looked at her watch. 'The aunt and uncle will be taking him back with them to Manhattan for the start of the school year. That thought is enough to deal with on its own without throwing in unlikely complications.'

'I shouldn't have butted in,' Libby apologized.

'You didn't.' Sarah smiled at her. 'What's the point of having a friend you can only skim the surface with? When do you have to pick up Sheridan from the groomer's?'

'What time is it?'

Sarah checked her watch. 'Nine thirty.'

'Whoops! I'd better be making tracks. He didn't really need to go in, but I want him looking spiffy for the potluck. I thought about going full hog with white tie and tails, but as everyone else will come casual he'd feel a fool and that's when he turns his most uppity and chases the cat. Your little Dusk has come on well. I was telling Sid the other night how's she's filled out.' Libby waved before mounting a couple of steps, and then turned back. 'Last thing.' This was typical of their partings – one of them always remembered that last thing. 'I did tell you I invited Gwen and Twyla, leaving them to decide who would stay with Sonny? Yesterday afternoon Gwen called back and said it was pretty much decided it would be her coming and would it work for her to bring Twyla's shrimp Creole and rice.'

'I've had it and it's fabulous; one of Oliver's favorites.'

Now they really were on the move, Libby up her steps, Sarah heading toward hers. The kayaks and dory she had noticed on her first morning down on the beach were still tucked under overhanging shrubbery. She had never discovered who owned them or seen any sign of them having been moved. Evan thought it very unlikely they had belonged to Nan Fielding. She had never mentioned boating of any sort in her letters. That had come up after his saying he'd sailed in college and would like to take it up again. Sarah had said she'd been thinking about taking lessons, but when asked his opinion Oliver had been less sure, admitting to being afraid of deep water even though he loved to swim – so long as his toes could touch the bottom.

She'd reached the top of the steps and was crossing the lawn, re-picturing his face at that moment – so open and trusting. She felt such a rush of tenderness and love for Oliver, and it scared her. It was one thing to have grown fond of him – who wouldn't? – he was a delight. But to have this strength of feeling for him was the way to heartbreak. And she hadn't been completely honest with Libby about Evan.

She more than liked him and would have needed to be unconscious not to know he was physically attracted to her too. But she'd given no indication of wanting to move things beyond a kiss on the cheek when he left to return home at the end of the previous weekends. And he'd done nothing to maneuver for more. If not for Oliver she would have taken the chance of mentioning she might never be able to have children and seeing what happened. But knowing how devastated she would be when Oliver's aunt and uncle took him with them to New York, she couldn't risk losing Evan as a friend when she was going to need him most. She knew him so well already. He was decent, kind and considerate. If he decided there was no future for them as a couple – but sensed that was what she wanted – he would get out of the picture for her sake. And the thought of his not being there when her life was empty of Oliver was unbearable.

She liked Libby – liked her a lot – but the person who would understand every nuance of what she was feeling was Gwen. Talking to her was often like thinking out loud. But how could you tell a woman, who was watching her son disappear behind a fog of forgetfulness and would at sometime lose him completely in death, that you were anguished at the prospect of being separated from a child who had never been yours? What she could do was seek to draw strength with Gwen from her example of courage, the serenity that seemed to bathe the air around her. It also wouldn't be fair to dump any of this on her mother who, along with her father, were delighted that she had settled so happily in Maine. But she must not let any of this cloud her anticipation of Oliver and Evan's arrivals. Once she was with them all this would fade into the background; there would be no room for anything but happiness.

Sarah went in by the kitchen's sliding doors. It now looked exactly the way she had wanted it, with the white cabinets and custard-yellow walls. The periwinkle and white-tiled floor left no regret that she'd gone for vinyl tiles rather than the real thing. The butcher block counter glowed from its recent oiling. In the center of the round kitchen table was a small bowl containing her growing collection of sea glass. On the stove was a baking tray of cinnamon rolls she'd made at six a.m. Gwen had given her the recipe from one she had gotten years ago from her housekeeper in Boston. It had required not only raisins soaked in heated orange juice and vanilla, but using fresh yeast, which Sarah had found rather intimidating. But the delicious aroma was well worth the effort. She followed Dusk who shifted off a kitchen chair to wander into the living room. She was also pleased with muted aqua walls offset by the trim, white fireplace and bookcases on either side. Her beige slipcovers had come into their own. As in the kitchen with the kettle, she had included a pop of tomato red, in this case a cushion on the sofa and ginger jar on the table under the front window. The same shade showed up amongst other vibrant colors on the unframed abstract canvas above the fireplace. She scooped Dusk up from one of the armchairs and rested her chin on the furry head.

'Have to make the most of this togetherness,' she murmured. 'Once the guys get here I'll be out in the cold. Do you have to stick in my face that you prefer male company?' It was true. Every time Evan or Oliver sat down Dusk was on his lap. When they were together on the sofa Dusk spread herself between them. If she could have doubled in size she would have done; but to be fair both made it clear they couldn't get enough of her. Oliver had explained that he'd wanted a cat almost as much as a dog, the optimum being both. And Evan had a cat at his condo named Fagin. Sarah had listened meekly while together they filled her in on who that character was in *Oliver Twist*. The book was on the coffee table waiting for them to read the final chapters. Only two more, they had told her with regret. The pattern had been Oliver reading stretches on his own, and Evan then joining him to continue out loud. Those were among Sarah's most treasured moments when the three of them were together. Oliver had said he was sure his grandpa hadn't introduced him to the book because the fictional Oliver's mother had died when he was born and he didn't have a father. It might have made him feel too sad. Instead he felt more blessed than ever. Imagine growing up in a workhouse and having to face up to the wrath of the beadle when asking for more porridge? Even having to live with Gerard and Elizabeth wasn't that bad. His grandpa had smiled when he'd explained that to him.

Sarah returned Dusk to the armchair and looked up at the painting above the fireplace. Nellie Armitage had observed on seeing it that her usual opinion of abstracts was that a child of six could have done them, but this one she actually liked. Not wishing to burst her bubble at having arrived as an art connoisseur, Sarah didn't let on that this one was the work of a six-year-old. Julia, on one of her visits, had kept herself occupied daubing away with acrylic paints on a spare canvas brought out from a cupboard. When Sarah repeated the Nellie anecdote to Oliver he had asked for more stories about Julia which had led to her showing him the sample sweater she had knitted her niece's name into. Instantly she'd seen the longing look in his eyes and been surprised. She'd assumed he'd believe himself too old for one but quickly told him she'd be glad to make one for him. She needed a name for the boys' sample and could use his, then make a second one. But that hadn't been Oliver's hope. He'd asked if it would take too much time to knit a throw blanket with 'Grandpa' on it. She'd replied that it was a brilliant idea and she should have thought of it herself. In future when it came to working on children's patterns she would, if he didn't mind, use him as a consultant. The finished throw in a deep blue – Oliver's choice – lay folded in a plastic bag on the pine dining room table so Dusk didn't add fiber. What she hadn't told him was that between work projects she was knitting a charcoal gray one with another name knitted into it. It was a color she had noticed that Twyla wore frequently.

Dusk got off the chair and angled around her feet. A signal that her feed bowl might need replenishing. She lived in obvious fear of finding it empty. Sarah had just completed this task and was putting away the plastic container of cat food – Libby had advised her never to leave it in the box because that could attract mice – when she heard the front door open and Oliver's voice.

'Sarah?'

'In the kitchen.'

'I went up to see Twyla and Gwen said I could bring Jumbo down to save you a trip. Do you want me to wipe off his paws?'

'Has he been in a ditch?' Unlikely. Jumbo trod the straight path unless off the leash and encouraged to ramble. But Oliver, who had become devoted with him, enjoyed being involved in taking care of him, from feeding to taking him outside when he needed to go. There were also brushings – unnecessary – but extremely pleasing to both. Sarah, not wanting to look as though she felt a need assess the paw situation, didn't go into the narrow foyer.

'No, he's not muddy or anything.' Boy and dog appeared in the doorway. 'What's that delicious smell?'

'Cinnamon rolls.'

'Sarah, you're amazing!'

She bent to pat Jumbo, who'd been looking up at her as if in full agreement. 'Well, I have to say I'm feeling rather pleased with myself. Not having made them before, I was all prepared before taking them out the oven to find they needed to go in the trash container, which would have meant driving to Plover's Grocery for replacements. Would you like one now?'

'Yes, but I'd rather wait till Evan gets here so it won't look like we started without him. Do you remember he said last week,' Oliver was removing Jumbo's leash, 'that he could live on cinnamon rolls?'

'You're right, he did. His metabolism must beat world records.' Dusk wandered out from under the kitchen table and eyed the dog with complete indifference before stepping around him to reach a framed opening in the cellar door – kindness of Sid Jennson – that provided access to the litter box. When she'd gone through, Oliver hung the leash on the hook next to the door.

'I left my backpack in the hall, till I take it upstairs to my bedroom.' It came out so naturally that Sarah could feel herself tearing up. 'I also brought my quilt from my old one; Twyla fetched it for me. That's partly why I went up to see her before coming here.' He turned toward her, anxiety in his eyes, as if it had suddenly struck him that he might be crossing a line.

'Ever since I got the bed I've been thinking of it as your room too. We'll go up in a minute, but first I'd like to show you something I think you'll be as pleased with as I am with my cinnamon rolls.'

His eyes had their glow back. 'A surprise?'

'Well, not exactly.' She led the way into the dining room and handed him the clear plastic bagged package.

He stared down, then up. 'The throw? You've finished Grandpa's throw?'

'Take a look and tell me what you think, business consultant?'

He took it out of its wrapping and held it up, studying it with awe. 'It's beautiful! I can't believe anyone can knit like that. Thank you. Thank you. Are you going to make up any more for the magazine?'

'Not with "Grandpa." I think this should be a one-off, don't you?'

'It would make it super-super special, wouldn't it?' He refolded it, put it back in its wrapping and reverently returned it to the table.

'That was my thinking.'

He stood absolute still as if unable to move, before turning and throwing his arms around her. 'Oh, Sarah, I do love you. I guess I knew I was going to when I met you and Evan, and ever since it's been like the three of us were meant to find each other.' His head stayed against her shoulder. 'Someone told me he knew it was going to happen.'

'Oliver, I love you too.' She pressed her lips to his sandy hair. 'And Evan?'

'Yes, in a different way.' It was the only answer, but she realized when he stepped back, wiped his eyes with the heels of his hands and beamed at her, that he might have misconstrued her meaning. But he shifted them onto safer ground.

'Brian thinks you're both cool.'

'That's good to hear.' She'd guessed that the foreseeing someone was this great friend, the great nephew of Nellie Armitage who always seemed delighted to have him visit. Brian had shown up at Bramble Cottage a couple of times when Oliver was there and Sarah had taken to him in a big way.

'Shall we go upstairs with the backpack so I can show off how I've got things set up for you?'

'Yes, but can I ask you something first?'

She laughed, though wondering if what was coming would be another awkward moment. 'Like I'm going to say no!'

'Twyla said I should ask you and it's even more important now. Will you come with us to see Grandpa after church tomorrow?'

'I'd love to.' She was the one now giving the hug.

'Great! You can give him the throw.'

'I want to see you do that.'

'Twyla would like Evan to come too.'

'I'm sure he will. We've both heard him say it would be a pleasure and a privilege to meet the man who taught you to love books, and just words in themselves. When I'm around the pair of you I feel in serious need of a return to third grade.' It was the wrong thing to have said; Oliver's face clouded.

'You don't. Remember Evan saying he couldn't decipher a knitting pattern to save his life, let alone invent one. Have you felt left out when we've been reading *Oliver Twist* together?'

'Not a bit, I love being around at those times. What the two of you have done is inspire me. Yesterday I took out several mysteries from the library.' She didn't add that three were Evan's. She had started one last night and been captivated as she rather hoped she would be. They were on her bedside table. To tell or not tell him was the question. She wouldn't want to sound as if she were trying to win points. What if she slipped from enthusiastic into gushing? She continued quickly, 'I'd be happy to go to church first. Before heading out to visit your grandpa, if that's OK with you and Twyla.'

'I hoped you'd say that.' He stretched up to kiss her cheek. The inclination to press her hand to it was strong. 'I'll ask Evan when he gets here. Twyla says you shouldn't assume someone wouldn't mind going, like they ought to believe in it.'

'A wise as well as a truly good person. The first time I met her I understood fully why you think the world of her.'

They had wandered back into the kitchen when the doorbell went. 'Can I get that, Sarah? I bet that's Evan.' Oliver could have been a lamp radiating light.

'Maybe too soon.' She looked at the clock; it was minutes off eleven. 'He said most likely around noon, but could be earlier if he got clear of the city faster than usual. Perhaps it's Brian?'

'No, he's visiting Aunt Nellie this weekend.'

'You'd better hurry before whoever it is thinks we're out and takes off.'

Oliver practically skidded to the door with the benefit of wood flooring, Jumbo in his wake. If there'd been a mirror handy she would have been tempted to look into it and tweak her short curls into better shape. There wasn't and the thought was a silly one. She'd decided against putting on lipstick after her shower. What an idiot! As if he'd have taken that limited amount of makeup as encouragement. Anyway, it would have worn off by now. She heard the familiar voice blending with Oliver's excited exclamations and plugged in the coffeepot, turned the oven on at 200 degrees and popped the tray of cinnamon rolls back in. She was straightening back up when they came through the doorway.

'See, I was right!' proclaimed Oliver, and Jumbo's nod appeared to be one of agreement.

'He really should be doing the weather forecasts.' Sarah divided her smile between the two of them. 'Our local expert isn't really . . . expert. Hi, Evan!' She sounded exactly right. Pleased without suggesting she hoped he'd kiss her.

He did. On the cheek as Oliver had done some minutes ago, but without the vigor. 'Hi, Sarah. Not too early, I hope?'

'We'd been wondering what was keeping you.' She'd relaxed sufficiently to add, as she might have to her brother Tim: 'You're looking remarkably handsome this morning.' Jumbo was certainly looking up at him with approval. 'Is that a new outfit? Or have you done something new to your hair?'

'She's teasing,' Oliver laughed happily, 'we both remember you wearing those same jeans and black T-shirt last weekend.'

'Yes, but she's right about the hair. I got it cut yesterday.'

'Well, there you are! I didn't get my nickname Eagle Eyes for nothing.'

Evan looked at her in a way that could have made her heart turn over if she hadn't got her armor on. Even so she tightened the metal straps in the nick of time. 'Talking about that rose-colored outfit you're wearing . . .'

'It's a dress,' said Oliver solemnly.

'No, it's not.' Evan eyed him sternly. 'Don't take me for a complete fashion Neanderthal. It's a skirt and top.'

'Just testing!'

'Well, cut it out! You're always trying to make yourself the favorite!'

'Boys! Boys! Do I have to put you both in time out?' Sarah was back in the groove. 'Thank you, Evan, for a charming compliment. But let's all turn our attention to less worldly matters. Oliver, ask him about church tomorrow before you forget.'

'Right. Here goes.' He explained about Twyla suggesting the visit to Grandpa after church on Sunday.

'I'd be delighted; you know how much I've been hoping to meet him.'

'Sarah and I were sure you would say that, but the thing is, she'd like you to go to church with us, but we don't want you to feel you must.'

Jumbo sat looking as interested as anyone else. 'Hmm.' Evan

rested his back against the refrigerator, his grey eyes half closed in concentration. 'That needs mulling over. What brand of church are we talking about?'

'Episcopalian.'

'Ah! I think I've heard of them, yet still find myself hesitating? Aren't they the ones that still keep up the otherwise obsolete tradition of human sacrifice?'

'Oh!' A smile spread over Oliver's face. 'You were kidding.'

'I wouldn't go that far. Perhaps I was thinking of the Methodists.'

'Really, Evan,' scolded Sarah. 'You really should go into time out. Do we take it you are coming with us?'

'Of course.' He peeled himself away from the refrigerator. 'I'd come even if I thought all religion was bunk. Which I don't. The inside of a church sees me fairly frequently.'

'Any particular one?'

'Episcopal.'

Oliver doubled up laughing. When he got himself vertical again his voice had a hint of a hiccup. 'Grandpa says when I was little – about three – I used to say Episcopagan.'

'Now that's amusing,' said Sarah.

Evan's mouth twitched. 'Why does he get points for repartee and I don't? I bet I called it the same thing at that age, which explains what put human sacrifice in my head.'

'You had your one good moment when you complimented me on my skirt and top. It's been all downhill since then.'

'She does look nice, doesn't she? When Brian saw her first he said she was tight.'

'Really? He thought she'd been at the bottle?'

'No, silly! That's she's terrific-looking. It's Gerard who drinks. I think it's worrying about that that gives Elizabeth her headache.' A silence that spoke. Oliver's face flushed. 'I shouldn't have said that.'

Sarah avoided Evan's eyes. 'You can say anything, Oliver; it won't go any further. Now take this man away while I brood over his not mentioning the wonderful aroma of cinnamon rolls in the air. The ones I began making from scratch at dawn. After that there was nothing much he could do to please me. See that guilty expression on his face?'

Evan *was* eyeing her, looking apologetic. 'I did notice, but in the round of greetings it slipped away.'

'Excuses!'

'How I could have guessed the from-scratch part?' He appealed to Oliver. 'I thought women who did that had gone the way of the dinosaur.'

Sarah folded her arms. 'No point in sucking up. Help my loyal friend here get his backpack and quilt upstairs to his bedroom. While you're there give him the masculine perspective on how to perk it up. What kind of pictures should go on the walls, that sort of thing?'

'Pictures? When I was his age I went for posters!'

'Right!' Oliver beamed at him. 'I have a *Pirates of the Caribbean* one that Brian gave me. I'll bring it next time.'

'There! Being female I'd never have thought of posters.'

Evan quirked an eyebrow. 'Do you buy this befuddled woman act, Mr Cully?'

Oliver appeared to delve deep into the question, but it was clear when he answered that he'd sidetracked. 'That's a pretty good word.'

'Befuddled? I thought so yesterday when it crossed my mind. This competition of ours is wearing me to skin and bone. I'll need at least six of those delicious-smelling cinnamon rolls to survive.'

'Much too late,' said Sarah.

'What do you both think of altruism?' Oliver inquired. 'That's almost as much of a tongue twister as ventriloquism.'

'Not bad,' mused Evan. 'How did you come up with it?'

'Mrs Polly said it had nothing to do with Elizabeth and Gerard taking me to live with them.'

'Did she sound befuddled?'

'Good comeback! No, she said she'd always had eyes in the back of her head and it didn't do to take her for a fool.'

'How about narcissism?' Evan had not looked at Sarah during the exchange. 'I think that's more of a tongue twister, if that's the requirement, than altruism.'

Oliver conceded that it might be. They departed, still going back and forth, leaving Sarah to her thoughts as she laid the table and took a bowl of fruit from the refrigerator. Dusk meandered from living room to kitchen and back. What was the real situation with the Cullys? Why had they taken Oliver? A sense of duty? To spite his grandfather because his daughter's marriage to Gerard's brother had ended in his death and those of their parents? That seemed far-fetched, but if Gerard was an alcoholic his thinking might be . . . befuddled. But was he? If Oliver's home had been teetotal he could possibly have misconstrued. No, that wouldn't wash. Twyla enjoyed a glass of wine and Oliver had mentioned that his grandpa had liked an occasional beer. What did Evan make of it all?

Footsteps on the stairs preceded a return to the kitchen. The cinnamon rolls and fruit bowl were on the table, along with a glass of milk for Oliver.

'Coffee, Evan?'

'Yes, please.' He stood and admired. 'Couldn't get those at my Frenchified bakery. They look every bit as impressive as they smell.'

'Thank you.'

'I still feel it's too late – that I've badly let the male side down' – this in an aside to Oliver. 'Maybe I should button my lips until I can think of a way to make amends, but how can I do that and drink and eat?' He took the mug she handed him with a smile that would have melted the most unsusceptible female.

'Still take it black?'

'Mine isn't a fickle heart.' His voice was teasing, but the look in his eyes wasn't. Sarah poured her own coffee and the three of them sat down. Jumbo lay angled toward the French windows, contemplating nature. She hoped he wasn't pining for Gwen. Oliver passed her the milk. Evan's enjoyment of his cinnamon roll was obviously genuine, although he didn't eat the six cinnamon rolls as he'd said he would. He stopped at one as Sarah did, but Oliver was reaching for his third before withdrawing his hand.

'I'm being greedy, aren't I?'

'Absolutely not.' Sarah put a roll on his plate. 'We're all entitled to a splurge. It's not as though you don't enjoy variety. You've helped put a dent in the fruit bowl and I've seen how you enjoy protein – especially chicken and fish – along with salad and green vegetables. That's something that can't be said for most kids.'

'Elizabeth and Gerard aren't into food. They seem to eat less than Feathers and don't get I can't too.' It was his first reference to the parakeet in several visits and Sarah, knowing it was a sore point, never brought it up. 'Elizabeth got irritated once and said the small portions were to help me lose weight.'

'Why on earth should you?' There was more than irritation in Evan's voice. 'You're fine just as you are. I see no virtue in attempting to emulate the skeletal looks of those two bullies if that's what she's after.' He picked up his coffee mug. 'Still staying clear, I hope.'

'Yes, thanks to you. But I still never go out without one of your cards in my pocket.' Oliver patted his shorts pocket. 'I asked Twyla after some other kids got on at me about being fat, knowing she'd be honest, and she said I wasn't – that I just had a sturdy build.'

'She was on the mark.'

Sarah, pouring more coffee, agreed. He was clearly relieved, but she saw there was still a question in his eyes. She sat down. 'What is it, Oliver?'

He began twisting his paper napkin. 'There's something I've been wanting to ask you both, but I'm afraid you'll think I'm weird.'

'I don't believe so,' said Evan, 'but give it a chance and see.'

'Do you think,' Oliver's eyes went from one to the other, 'that I could look like Nathaniel Cully?'

Sarah was about to say that wasn't a weird question, but realized in time that more had to lie behind it. 'I don't see why not; family resemblances travel from one generation to another, maybe skipping some and then picking up again. My brother, who's into genealogy, told me that. He said he'd found a photo of my maternal great-grandmother and I look more like her than either of my parents.'

Evan leaned forward, elbows at home on the table. 'Nathaniel's statue shows a strong physique – what my Aunt Alice, who's a complete romantic, would call a fine figure of a man. And I think it quite likely you've inherited his bone structure.'

'I mean,' the napkin was now a paper corkscrew, 'could I really, really look like him when he was a boy, maybe a couple of years older than I am now? Even to his having a round face like me and the same colored hair? You see . . . the weird part is I've seen him twice on the window seat in my bedroom at the Cully Mansion. He told me the first time that it used to be his. He was holding a book and said he was surprised I hadn't read it. And it was on the window seat the next morning. *Oliver Twist*, the same one we've been reading. I know it wasn't there when I went to bed.'

Sarah was aware of Jumbo resettling his position by the window. Evan leaned back in his chair, head cupped in his hands. 'Yes, I think it entirely possible you could look that much alike. You'll have searched for confirmation one way or another. No luck, or inconclusive?'

Oliver shook his head. 'There are no portraits of him at any age in the house. There's one of his father looking fierce. I bet he didn't think any of his three sons important enough to be painted. And the photos of Nat at the historical society – Brian and I went there – are all of him as a grown-up. Most of them when he was old. One moment I thought I saw a resemblance and then I didn't. And I haven't done any better at the house, though I've kept on looking, even after Mrs Polly told me Miss Emily said she'd had all family photos put on a bonfire because looking at them made her feel lonely.'

'A few could have escaped; I'd go on with the search.'

'There's still the cellar, but I've promised Brian I'll wait until I can get Elizabeth and Gerard to agree to him staying overnight, and so far there's always an excuse. And it has to be at night.' Oliver didn't elaborate and Evan didn't press him. 'It's kept locked, but when I asked Mrs Poll if there was a spare key she showed me where it was.'

'What's the big question?'

'Do you think my imagination's gone haywire, or that I could have seen his ghost? Do either of you believe they really exist?'

'Someone left the copy of *Oliver Twist* on that window seat,' Sarah pointed out.

'Elizabeth and Gerard said they didn't.'

'Hmm.' Evan continued to relax in his chair, as if they were merely talking hypothetically. 'Could be that for some reason they'd rigged the previous night's appearance electronically and left the book to seal the deal.'

'But he and I had a conversation. How could they fix what I'd say to blend with Nathaniel's end? I don't like them – I can't pretend I do – but why would they?'

'I can think of several reasons. I not only write mysteries but, having read the best and sometimes the worst, I tend to the opinion that Gothic villainies work better in fiction than in life. If your aunt's and uncle's intent is to play havoc with your mind, I think they'd have put their devotion to you on public display, which – from what I've gleaned – they haven't. I'd say they're a couple with problems and leave it at that for the moment.' Evan turned to Sarah. 'Would you like to go first in answering the main question? How do you stand on a belief in ghosts?'

She'd been sitting thinking, knowing she had to be honest with Oliver. To lie would be a betrayal of his trust. Luckily, her answer wasn't a negative one. 'At one time I'd have said I was skeptical, verging on I didn't; but since coming to Sea Glass I've been edging toward the possibility. Nellie Armitage I can take with a pinch of salt. I'm never sure if she really believes in her spirit guides or came up with them to provide herself with a persona. But if it's the first option I don't think she's nuts. And Libby Jennson next door says she's up to the idea of contact with those beyond the grave, enough to go to a séance – or circle – at Nellie's church and was disappointed when it was her grandmother, not Mom, who came through.'

'Sounds quite wholesome described that way,' interposed Evan.

'Still my turn,' said Sarah with a mock frown. 'Nellie and especially Libby, who are so down to earth, may have cracked the door open for me, but you can't base your opinions on other people – there's more. When I came to Sea Glass, for what was to be no more than a weekend visit, I had this strong feeling that this was the place that had been waiting for me always and it became even more powerful when the real estate agent showed me this house. I knew absolutely it was where I belonged. Oh, I know people have vibes, occasionally experience déjà vu and that all houses have atmospheres. And I kept telling me that's all it was. But first came the sense of immediate connection with Gwen, that she was one of the reasons I'd been meant to come here. And then . . .' This wasn't going to be easy to say in front of Evan, but she couldn't see not doing so for Oliver's sake.

'Go on, Sarah. You've made me feel so better big time already.'

'It was when I found Evan's letter to Ms Fielding in the mailbox,' she couldn't look at him, 'I think I felt her presence urging me to write to the EB on the return address corner, that it was,' she searched her mind – not being as good as the other two at finding the perfect word, 'crucially important to do so.'

'Interesting!' said Evan, sounding as if he meant every syllable. Unfortunately it was a word open to interpretation. Never mind. This was all about Oliver. She was about to mention the sensation she had experienced of a child walking beside her along the beach but changed her mind. How could she lay the possibility on Oliver that the child might have been him? It could sound as if she believed she had some emotional claim on him, which she didn't. Even if Elizabeth and Gerard Cully decided to give him up, it would be Twyla he'd want to be with. 'Your turn, Evan.'

'Right.' Oliver picked up a cinnamon roll. 'Even if you're convinced this ghost and other spirit stuff is garbage you have to tell it like it is.'

'OK, here goes. Even if I thought it was I wouldn't think you or Sarah nuts. Thousands – millions, probably – believe in ghosts. I heard on TV recently that statistics of those who do, gathered from a survey of the United States' population, was surprisingly high. I don't remember the percentage. That said, leaving Sarah out of it,' he smiled at her, 'I still think you may have projected the entity of Nat Cully. His looking like you, if a little older, would make for a safe connection. And being thrust into an alien environment you need a friend. It's quite common for younger kids to have imaginary ones. I wouldn't think enlightened parents wig out about that. What induces a five-year-old to create a Fred or Harry has been delayed in your case.'

'Right.' Oliver had finished the cinnamon roll, which seemed to Sarah to be a very good sign.

'What I absolutely don't believe is that you're seriously disturbed. If you were you wouldn't have conjured up a perfectly nice boy sitting reading a book. You're not being tortured by the dark visions and voices that urge their sufferers, often on the grounds that it's God's will to hurt – even kill themselves – or others. Now, time for me to own up to my own suspected brush with the unseen, which as in your cases could have been entirely my imagination. In my line of work I can't disclaim having a vivid one, can I? But I can't remember experiencing any similar before.' Evan got up to refill his coffee cup, continuing with his back turned. 'Count me in, Sarah, on that business of the letter to Nan Fielding.'

Neither she nor Oliver interrupted. It wasn't the moment. But he continued as if one of them had spoken. 'No, I didn't feel any special prompting to write it. We'd corresponded by snail mail over the years after getting back in touch. She hadn't a computer and didn't like talking on the phone. Only had one for emergencies. During the time she taught at my high school a man broke into her house and brutally attacked her.'

Sarah and Oliver both exclaimed in distress.

'The talk pointed to some guy who'd been pursuing her big time; she called a halt and he was waiting when she came in one night. Looking back I can see she was good-looking, somewhat in Gwen's style. The experience sent her into a withdrawal from which she never recovered. Life, personality, can make some of us more vulnerable than others. There were always lags in our correspondence, so I thought nothing of it when she didn't get back to me in a couple of months, certainly no unsettling premonition that she'd died or even might be ill.' He was still turned away, for some unknown reason realigning the coffeepot. Sarah had never seen any signs of obsessive compulsion before. If anything he was inclined to be untidy, which – instead of checking off as an unwelcome trait – she had put in the endearing column. 'What "happened,"' he put it in quotes, 'was when I returned from the book tour and found your letter waiting among a bunch of mainly junk mail. The moment I picked it up I had this feeling that it was a life-changing moment. Regrets to the prosecution, it came before I'd even glanced at the writing or return address. Afterwards, I didn't bother trying to find your phone number; I knew I had to come down to Sea Glass the next day. Let's not even bother throwing in the three of us showing up at the same time on the common at a crisis moment. No arguments if they're coming. That has to go into the chance category.'

'Wow!' said Oliver. 'This is getting way cool.'

'What has to be put into evidence in defense of imagination is that in returning from my travels late in the evening I was tired to the extent of being in something of a fog.' Evan finally returned to the table with his mug. Sarah had the feeling he'd have preferred to restrict his glance to Oliver, making clear he believed the opportunity to become a healthy male influence in the life of a boy, who already lacked a father and was likely to soon lose his beloved grandpa, was the foreshadowed life-changing moment. And for her it had to be the only one that mattered.

'I don't believe it was imagination,' she said after picking up and putting down her own coffee. It had been drained some considerable minutes before. 'I think Nan Fielding may have longed to be able to embrace life again and transferred that wish to us. Continuing to forge relationships matters.'

'I most certainly hope so.' He smiled at Oliver, whose eyes brimmed with tears; Sarah felt a catch in her throat which wasn't about to go away. 'We've already agreed in one of our companionable male moments that we need each other and that we need you too.' There was no mistaking the intent in his voice or the look he gave her. A knock-out blow to an already battered imagination.

She was both heady with joy and blissfully peaceful. She returned his gaze with the same evident honesty.

'I need both of you. You're my two top guys.' More wasn't required but she wanted to hear herself say it loud – removing the final barrier to her willingness to trust since the night at the restaurant when Harris had told her about Lisa. That could have happened to someone else. She was now worlds away from her life with him. That had already been clear to her when it crossed her mind the other day that she wasn't the least curious why he hadn't phoned back after not getting to the question he'd wanted to ask. 'I love you both too, more than can be put in words.'

The light in Evan's eyes, that had already been there, increased to a flame. She was fully aware of the effort it took for him to respond lightly. 'Well, that's a relief. I knew where Oliver stood with you, but I wasn't so sure about me. I'm the one who spills things and drops crumbs.'

Oliver wasn't fooled. 'You two!' He leaned back and raised his eyes to the ceiling. His smile could have reached it. 'It's not like I didn't know this was coming. I bet if I weren't here you'd fall into each other's arms,' his face suddenly sobered, 'wouldn't you?'

'No we wouldn't,' said Sarah firmly. 'I need a list of his other failings first. Untidy is OK, but a tendency to rob banks wouldn't be.'

'Nitpicky.' Evan shook his head. 'I only do it when I'm bored. What I'd like to know, my young friend, is what books you've been reading besides *Oliver Twist*? Dickens was a romantic but I don't remember any of his love duos falling into each other's arms. I may be wrong, but certainly not Agnes in *David Copperfield*. There was a woman fully occupied – "ever looking upwards."' It was the right approach. It didn't increase his embarrassment; he visibly shed the last thread.

'She sounds a dull bulb,' mused Sarah.

'Tedious,' agreed Evan. 'Otherwise the book's a great read. But let's not allow you-know-who to wiggle out of my question. You've been at the Harlequins, haven't you? Who's your source, pal? It wouldn't have been at your grandpa's.'

'Wow! You're amazing!'

'Not so much. I saw one sticking out the pocket of your backpack.'

'Cheat!' accused Sarah. 'Even Jumbo looks shocked.'

Unabashed, Oliver laughed. 'You know I finished the ones of yours. We talked about that and how great I thought they were . . .'

'Wiggling!'

'They were Miss Emily's. I found boxes of them in the attic. Mrs Poll told me she had them sent every month. And they aren't all Harlequins. There are other sorts, but similar. Mrs Poll said she was addicted.'

'Drunk on love! That's a line that crops up.'

'Mrs Poll said they were only the modest ones, so there was no harm in giving me them.' He straightened his back and stuck out his chin in mischievous defiance. 'You don't have to talk like you're all that and a bag of chips, like Twyla would say, just because you don't read them.'

'He obviously does, or has,' said Sarah.

Oliver rewarded her with a grin. 'Well, I'm not afraid to say the ones I've read so far have been pretty good. I pick out the suspense ones, so I can't say about the others. The one I brought with me is about this dazzlingly beautiful bank teller with eyes the color of emeralds who's afraid she's falling for the man she suspects recently robbed it.'

'Very funny! Back to my foibles, are we?'

'Seriously!'

'And I'll bet with those eyes,' Evan looked deep into Sarah's, 'she turns out to be the sort to kiss on the first heist.' The attention of both was wrenched free by Oliver's next words.

'I found a letter to Miss Emily from her lawyer tucked inside one of the books.' He quoted as accurately as he could what had been written. 'I think the two brothers mentioned may have been my Dad and Gerard. Is an estate plan the same as a will?'

'Similar, but wrapped up in more details,' said Evan. To Sarah's surprise he dropped the subject. 'Let's get back to your Mrs Poll. Had she kept it a secret from your aunt and uncle that there was a spare key to the cellar door?'

Oliver nodded. 'But I don't want you to think she's sneaky. There's a good reason. Her father is Willie Watkins. He's now Grandpa's roommate at Pleasant Meadows. He's there because his mind's damaged from being a drunk. Last January he got into that cellar and holed up there for a while.'

'Nellie Armitage mentioned that,' said Sarah.

'And the thing is, when Mrs Poll found the key in an old

teapot in one of the display cabinets years ago, she took it home with her in case she ever came round to find the front door locked and was afraid Miss Emily had been taken ill or had even died and she'd have to get in through the cellar. It opens the outside cellar door and the one at the top of the cellar stairs. The only time the old lady walked anywhere beyond the living room and bathroom, she'd had polio you know, was to unlock and remove the bolt from that door on Mrs Poll's days. Now here's the reason she didn't spill the beans to Gerard and Elizabeth . . . she was sure they'd hint like mad that she'd given it to Willie to get him off her hands. And she didn't. She said she'd never had to get in that way and on thinking about it realized it may have been left unlocked forever – to save Miss Emily having to let the boiler people and such into the cellar without giving them the key from the hook in the kitchen.'

'Got you.' Evan leaned back in his chair.

'But if Gerard and Elizabeth thought they had a hold on Mrs Poll, she knew they'd try to weasel her to working for them for even less money, and she wasn't going to give them the satisfaction, although she'd pull something out of her sleeve if they tried. She laughed when she said that, and she'd only gone back to work at the house so she could size up the situation. And I didn't have to worry she'd abandon ship.'

'Cheers, for Mrs Poll.' Evan raised his coffee cup. 'I think you should make contact, Sarah, and find out if she thinks Mr and Mrs Cully have the capacity, mental or high tech, to rig up ghost scenes. Who knows, she may have tripped over a stray wire, noticed edgily twitching little green lights, or spotted a suspicious gadget.'

'I'll be on it. Promise.' She looked at the microwave clock. Noon on the nose. 'Sorry to break things up, but I think we have to get patient Jumbo out on his walk, before thinking about lunch.'

Oliver started guiltily up from his chair. 'We've been neglecting him terribly, haven't we?' He hurried over to where Jumbo was still lying angled toward the French window and laid his face to the brindled fur. 'We love you, dude, you have to be the very best dog in the world.'

Sarah had returned the fruit bowl to the refrigerator and was covering the remaining cinnamon rolls with plastic wrap while Evan cleared the rest of the table. 'I always thought I wanted a small dog but he's convinced me it has to be a bull mastiff. Gwen is going to check with Jumbo's breeder and see if there are any puppies available to choose.'

'Can I please, please go with you to choose one?'

'We'll insist on that, won't we, Evan?'

'I'd toast to that if I hadn't put my coffee mug in the sink.'

'And how about letting him pick the name? You can select the food and drink bowls.'

'Thanks a bunch! I see how I rate and it'll be all downhill from here on.'

'Oh, no! Don't tell me you have tantrums in addition to robbing banks!'

Oliver, who'd been standing still with delight, threw his arms around each of them in turn. 'This is one of the very best days of my entire life.' He unhooked Jumbo's leash and put it on the table. 'Sorry, but I have to go upstairs to the bathroom. Coming, Jumbo?'

'There's the one in the hall,' Sarah reminded him.'

'We know that!' He raised his sandy eyebrows and spread his hands, palms upward. 'We're just trying to give you time to kiss and stuff,' they heard him say to Jumbo as they went up the stairs. 'Don't feel too bad, I've neglected Dusk too. I think she'll like having a puppy, don't you, now you've taught her to behave around dogs.'

Sarah didn't fall into Evan's arms. He held them out and she walked into them on solid ground, but then it did shift beneath her. Their kiss was unlike any she had experienced before, desire and love so entwined that they were one and the same. The only thing imperfect was that they both felt compelled to end it too soon. She stood, still encircled by his arms, her head against his shoulder. A tremulous laugh escaped her.

'What do you think Oliver meant by "and stuff?"'

'Not what I obviously have in mind. In the kind of romance novels he's been reading – possibly from twenty years ago – the tortured hero always has himself masterfully under control. Presumably when he says "he must be off to his study" he's really heading fast for an ice-cold shower.'

'Does the heroine get to be tortured too?'

'Never! Unseemly. She drifts around chapter after chapter, unaware of her True Feeling, telling herself she detests Him, while vaguely hearing violins playing.'

'Then I'm a very unseemly woman.'

'The trouble is,' he kissed her hair, 'having thrown such flights of fancy into the mix, you may think I'm quoting when I say: Oh, God! I love you, Sarah. And that I've never felt this way about anyone else. But it's the plain and simple truth.'

'I know because it's the same for me.' She pressed her hand against his cheek. 'And we do have to continue being outwardly seemingly, don't we?'

'It's called observing the proprieties, and yes, we must while Oliver is with us. We could tell ourselves he wouldn't know if we slept together tonight and I left before he's up, but he might. Though that's not the primary issue. It would be deceptive and we can't ever be that way with him.'

'I know.'

'The only way I see to end the torture is for us to get married right away. Some proposal! But will you, Sarah?' His voice was for the first time uncertain. 'Or say you'll at least think about it?'

'I don't need to. It's the perfect proposal. And the answer, of course, is "yes."' She took a step back to look into his eyes. 'I wish it could be this afternoon.'

He drew her back and kissed her again. 'I fell in love with you when we met. And if that's equally like a romance novel, it's because most clichés are around because they are truths that have been sanded and buffed over time to say it like it is.'

'It was the same for me; only – like the heroines we've been talking about – I tried to pretend it was just an attraction. Partly because it seemed too perfect, but mainly because,' she again stepped back to meet his eyes, 'I may not be able to give you a child and I know that was a factor in ending your marriage. Harris and I tried for several years and I couldn't get pregnant. The only thing we didn't get to was in vitro, because by then he'd gone off the idea. He'd never been prepared to consider adoption.'

He reached for her. 'I'm open to either, if that's what you'd want. But we already have a child, whether or not it ever becomes possible to have him with us permanently. We mustn't raise our hopes too high in that direction, but I've sufficient faith in the existence of Nat Cully, or Oliver's projection of him, to have a feeling that it's all going to work out. What we have to do, darling, in addition to you talking to his Mrs Polly – or Poll as he calls her – is maneuver a meeting with his aunt and uncle.'

'I've phoned to invite them to come with him any time they

like. But they haven't taken up the offer, or suggested my going there. Evan,' she lowered her voice to an urgent whisper, 'we haven't talked about that letter Oliver found in the paperback. It has me wondering. People who make estate plans want every "I" dotted and "T" crossed so nothing goes wrong. And yet it seems Max Cully who, Oliver has told me, corresponded with Emily, ended up getting cut out of her estate. It doesn't add up, especially when it sounds as though she wanted to favor him. But come to think of it I'm only going on what Nellie told me.'

Evan kissed her again. 'We'll talk more about this later.'

'Ready?' Oliver called down from the stairs. 'Missing us yet?'

They got in a lengthy walk before returning Jumbo to Gwen, saying they wouldn't come in as they needed to get back to lunch, and they had already decided against going to a restaurant. Eating 'at home' was much preferred, especially when Sarah had said she had crab cakes in the refrigerator, which Evan and Oliver both liked, along with a green salad. Though both could wait till later, even tomorrow. Gwen, understanding as always, didn't press them to linger, but did ask them if they'd like to come back for dinner around six. Jumbo, still at her side, woofed encouragement. This invitation was appreciatively accepted, and they started back down Ridge Farm Rise on their return to Bramble Cottage. There was no sidewalk, so they were able to walk abreast with Oliver in the middle. They discussed whether or not to cook frozen French fries to go with the crab cakes, and had all voted in favor of both, when Oliver said there was something he hadn't mentioned about Nat Cully.

'Go ahead,' encouraged Evan, 'it was the sort of conversation, with so much talk going back and forth, that some things are bound to get left out.'

'That just how it was,' agreed Sarah.

'This could make you think he wasn't real. Remember me telling you he said that bedroom used to be his? Well, if it seems more likely it was one of his brother's that *would* make it look like the whole thing was in my mind.'

'Why do you think it may have been either of theirs?' Evan kept up his easy stride.

'Because folded at the back of that copy of *Oliver Twist* were several sketches of ships – frigates, sloops and schooners, that sort of thing – or would they be called boats . . . I'm not really up on that sort of things. It's Brian who is. But it was the brothers, not Nat, who were the artists. They're the ones who did the scrimshaws that are in the historical museum. Brian and I saw them when we went to look for pictures of Nat. They were super great. I don't know how anyone could keep their hand that steady.'

'He could have put the drawings in that book because he liked having them with him, because he was proud of their talents,' suggested Sarah.

Evan agreed.

'That's what I thought at first. Until the morning after his second visit. The one when he told me he'd known I was going to meet you both and everything was going to work out. It was that same evening, you see. You'd given me those two business cards and I'd put them on top of the dresser before getting into bed. But when I got up the next day I put one in my shorts' pocket and remembered what you'd said about putting the other away for safe keeping. I decided to put it in the third drawer down as that was the only one that I could tuck the card under and be sure of not having to search around for it. But I couldn't get it open. It was stuck. As the top two were so stuffed with stuff something had to be wedged at the back. I got out the first and I'd been right. The problem was pairs of socks. I turned it over to shake everything onto the bed. And on the back of the drawer were more of those great drawings. It was the same with the next drawer – and all the way down.'

'Evidence, inconclusive,' said Evan as they crossed into Wild Rose Way. 'If two brothers were accomplished artists, why not the third? He became a doctor, not a whaler as they did. All we can tell from that is they were led, out of necessity or desire, to lives on the open seas, which enabled them to fulfil their outstanding gifts. If he was equally passionate about not boarding a vessel, he may have entered medicine because that's where his heart really was, or as a second choice. From your description of their father, I can't see him agreeing cheerfully to let any of his sons sit at home crayoning.'

'Right!'

'If,' Sarah was opening the front door, 'he did have an artistic bent and kept it up as a hobby as an adult he might have left something signed around the place that could be compared by an expert, along with what you already have, with his brothers' works. But, as Miss Emily discarded photos because looking at them made her feel lonely, other mementoes may have gone the way of bonfire.'

That Oliver felt much better was obvious in his question upon their entering the foyer. 'Did they have crayons in those days? I have the folded up drawings in my backpack. Want to look at them after lunch?'

'Absolutely,' said Evan. 'This minute, but better to wait so we've time to linger over them without interruption from pangs of hunger.'

'I suppose,' she tilted her head to kiss him, 'that's a hint I should get busy.'

'I'm glad,' Oliver blew out a breath of relief, 'that you've stopped thinking you have to wait for me to disappear to do that.'

'Then just to make you happy.' Evan pulled her close for an encore.

'Definite progress.' Oliver shifted breakfast dishes from the sink to the dishwasher. 'It's more than fine with me if you lie on the sofa and lay your head on his lap this afternoon while we're finishing *Oliver Twist*.'

'What a sport! No wonder we can't get enough of you.' Sarah un-entwined her hands from around Evan's neck and turned on the oven for the French fries and crab cakes. 'Who wants to toss the salad?' She got out the French vinaigrette dressing she'd made up the previous evening. 'And who wants to lay the table? There's lemonade and iced tea to drink. Or milk if you'd rather, Oliver. There's wine, Evan – red out and white in the refrigerator. If you'd like a glass I'll join you.' They agreed on the Chablis.

Twenty minutes later they were back around the table, each in his or her established seat. Sarah remembered with a wave of unhappiness that's how it had always been with her family. Her parents, along with Kristen and Tim, would be surprised by her upcoming news. Maybe a little concerned by the suddenness of it all; she'd only mentioned Evan in passing – as with Oliver, no point leaving them thinking she was jumping blindly into whirlpools. But, once she explained, they'd be happy about Evan and supportive of their relationship with Oliver. There would never be an issue of either of them picking at meals she produced. Evan might be thin, but apparently not from starving himself half to death. After the last of the crab cakes and a second helping of French fries had disappeared from his plate, he gave a smile that made her dream of further expanding her cooking repertoire – which had been extremely limited since her arrival in Maine.

'That was delicious, but I don't think Oliver and I will leave you to slog it alone in the kitchen. We'll take our turns. He's likely to be of the most help at first; I've already gleaned he's a wizard at peeling potatoes and no mean hand at making tuna salad. But I have learned how to put a simple, tasty meal on the table – courtesy of *The I Hate to Cook Book* by Peg Bracken, given to me by Aunt Alice. It's her long-time mainstay, published back in the sixties, and – as she kindly informed me – idiot proof. My favorite of the recipes is Jetty Spaghetti. Time for Oliver to fetch down those drawings?'

'Absolutely.'

They listened to the fleet scamper up the stairs.

'You were the art major, Sarah. Your opinion will be the one that counts.'

'All we can judge them on is the belief they were drawn by Nat, at around eleven years old – or younger. If they show talent that would indicate he shared at least to some degree his brothers' gifts, but we can't make that assumption. What would tend in his favor is if they really aren't all that good.'

Evan had just cleared the table when Oliver came through the doorway and laid the thin sheaf of paper into the middle of it. 'Did you hear anything of what Sarah was just saying?'

'No, my mind was full of what you'd both think of these.'

While Evan briefly filled him in, Sarah shifted the yellowing sheets toward her. There were three. The voices of the other two faded out. As Oliver had said, the subject was sailing vessels, of which she knew nowhere near enough to even guess at the pen and ink accuracy. But she did know enough about art to be impressed by the skill of the dexterous delicacy of the artist's hand. Amazing, given their miniature size, that they all possessed that sense of movement – the heave to the wind and the roil of the few threads of sea in the first two, and the serene glide in the halcyon calm of the third.

'Incredible.' She finger-tipped them back to the center. 'If done by the boy you saw on the window seat in your bedroom, Oliver, he was one talented kid.' Before the conversation could progress, her cell phone rang.

'You go answer it,' said Evan, 'I'll stay here and look these over with Oliver; I know enough about the key details to make a stab at their accuracy.'

'Shouldn't be long.'

On hearing Harris's voice in her ear she was doubly certain of that. He didn't ask if this was a bad time, just continued on as if he'd been speaking to her three minutes ago, rather than a number of months. But when she heard why he hadn't gotten back to her after saying he need to talk to her again soon about what he'd curtailed from asking, she understood completely why doing so had faded fast into the background. The day after he'd rung her, his daughter had fallen off a swing at his in-law's home and fractured her skull. Naturally, he and Lisa had been panic-stricken until convinced she was going to fully recover. 'It left us shaken up for weeks,' he finished.

'Oh, Harris, what a dreadful scare for all three of you. How's she coming along?'

'Fine, thank you. But it was all way too much for Lisa to have to go through. She'd just found out she was pregnant again. What more needs to be said?'

'On my part, congratulations. And I mean that wholeheartedly.'

'I can hear it in your voice.' A pause. 'I get the feeling things must be going well with you.'

'It was the right decision to move here.'

'Good. The thought of you pining on bothered me.'

'That's kind, but you shouldn't have. I think we both know we stuck it out too long.' She was eager to get back to the kitchen to hear what Evan had to say about the accuracy of the renditions.

'We had our good times.'

'And I'm grateful for those, but tell me what it is you've been wanting to ask me.'

'Here goes! And don't go losing your cool. It's about that antique diamond and garnet ring my mother gave you. I'm sure she said she wanted you to keep it after the divorce, but Lisa and I wonder if, now the waters have calmed, you'd be willing to let us have it.'

'That wasn't a gift from your mother.' Her ear was cued to Evan and Oliver's laughter. Something had amused them. Possibly Dusk landing in one of their laps. She had a habit of that and had just wandered into the kitchen. 'It was my great-grandmother's.'

'That can't be true. Lisa says it was obviously valuable, and we know your family members were never loaded. Get over the spite, Sarah. For us it's the sentimental value. We want it to give to Adele when she's older. The baby on the way is a boy.'

'Lovely. But I'm busy, Harris. Check with your mother about the ring, and when you do please give her my love, I was always very fond of her. On second thought, I'll write to her myself.'

'Oh, there's no need for that!' Sarah couldn't remember hearing Harris splutter before.

'Isn't there? This seems to me to be the perfect time.' She hung up the phone. Threading its way throughout the phone call had been the thought that she would go to Portland and show the drawings to her friend, the one whose wedding had been the source of Sarah's coming to Maine. Anne taught high school art and should, therefore, have a pretty good idea of what a boy of, say, eleven, could produce.

Eleven

Gwen stopped at the top of the stairs with Jumbo at her side at four thirty on that Saturday afternoon to listen to the joy of fragments of Bach, Mendelssohn and Liszt mingled into each other drifting up from the piano. Sonny could no longer play cohesively; but that he was continuing to play at all, after having stopped until the evening that Sarah had come into their lives, was cause for celebration. And Oliver's lessons with Gwen had been further encouragement. Sonny was increasingly at his most peaceful when that dear boy was with them, a happy reminder no doubt of the many young students he had taught over the years and cared for deeply regardless of their musical promise. But also because there was something so incredibly heartwarming about Oliver's blend of innocence and the maturity that enabled him to empathize beyond his years. Best of all, perhaps, was that he had a rollicking sense of humor that brought laugher back to a house that had lacked it for much too long. He was showing definite ability at the piano, coupled with enthusiasm. Good in itself as well as having the bonus of his being able to tell his aunt and uncle he needed, and wanted, to practice often. Legitimate. But it also provided frequent opportunity for his spending time with beloved Twyla.

What interested Gwen was that the Cullys had been prepared from the start to allow him to spend plenty of time with Sarah, either on her own or with Evan. Elizabeth had phoned to say that she and her husband had appreciated the garden club's generous offer of volunteering to landscape the grounds of the Cully Mansion, but weren't prepared for the upheaval this summer. What upheaval? The members wouldn't be digging and planting in the living room. The only indoor intrusion would be the occasional request to use the bathroom or a pitcher refilled with iced water. She'd gleaned from Oliver that the only people, other than Robin Polly, who'd gained more than one-time admittance inside the Cully Mansion were those two boys with the weird names whom he disliked so much. And that had sprung from their mother's convenient offer to drive Oliver in to school and back.

To Oliver's relief that relationship had dwindled away, suggesting that the Cullys had never been sociable, which somehow Gwen didn't believe. Or did they have some other reasons for being bound and determined to keep as many people as possible from getting an inside look at their lives? Twyla being foremost in mind, and now perhaps Sarah, whose invitations to accompany Oliver on some of his visits had not only been refused with one excuse or another, but unreciprocated. Ah, but it seemed they had just been outmaneuvered by Evan, on the basis of the location of the potluck being changed that morning to Bramble Cottage. Poor Sid Jennson had been up most of the night in the throes of one of those wretched stomach bugs. Libby hadn't thought it right to go ahead with hosting when she might also be coming down with it, so she'd called Sarah at eight to ask if she mind pitching in. The other members of the group had either already taken their turn or were on the calendar to do so. The potluck started at six, but Gwen had dressed early and had asked to come ahead of the others for a chat.

Such a shame for the Jennsons. Anyone who had suffered one of those hideous bouts knew how they make you pray for instant death. And they were one of the nicest couples; Sid had continued to be incredibly kind to Sonny, taking him out for drives and sometimes lunch. But there is that cliché of an ill wind. Evan had seized the straw along with the day and phoned the Cullys to issue an invitation now the switch had been made. They must have found it impossible on the spur of the moment to reasonably refuse. So right for Sarah! As she was for him! It had been clear from the first time of seeing them together that they were made for each other and that they had both fallen hard for Oliver.

After a day's gardening Gwen had gone upstairs to shower and change into a narrow blue and white striped shirtwaist. Innumerable washings had vanquished the material's original stiffness, making for a cottony softness, light as air. Welcome on a hot evening. Libby had told her on calling with the invitation that the dress code was casual. In some places that could have meant coming in shorts or merely downplaying the diamonds, but not so here in Sea Glass, where overdone at such an event would be a man buttoning his sports shirt to the neck or a woman wearing perfume.

The music had ceased, but Sonny was still seated, head bent at the piano. Jumbo had followed her into the room. He did not retreat from Sonny, who no longer displayed hostility toward him, but indifference. The result, she was sure, of Jumbo being gone for part of each day with Sarah. She went in and bent to kiss her son's cheek. Her heart brimmed with love for who he was now and the boy and man he had been. So many moments still to be gathered for holding later in her hand like pieces of sea glass. Birthdays, Christmases, and other celebratory occasions had a way of fading one into the other, while the trove of tiny treasures remained to be recalled with thankfulness, even if sometimes viewed through tears. Thank God for those whose lives had been interwoven with theirs – Sonny's and hers – this summer. Her gratitude for this blessing had occasionally brought in its wake the thought that it might be a final benediction, but not this time.

'I love you, Sonny.'

'Love you, Mom.' He turned his head before resuming what appeared to be a blank stare, but might mean he was peering into his own shifting memories, one overlapping the other at random, perhaps making it impossible to hold onto any treasured ones – even his wife Beatrice's face – for more than a few seconds without some reinforcement.

'I'm going out shortly, but only for a few hours. Twyla has set aside enough shrimp Creole for the two of you. But she'll make you anything you like. Pancakes, if that's what you want.'

'Do they have meat in them?'

'They can, if that's your wish.'

'How does Mrs Broom make them?'

'To your special instructions.' She again kissed his cheek.

'I don't know.' He stirred restlessly. 'Did you say you're going out?'

'Yes, dear.'

'Is he going with you?'

'Who, dear? Jumbo?'

'Father.'

She stroked his hair, her sadness for Charles surfacing. He and Sonny could have had a close relationship with each other after the divorce if he'd put in the time and love earlier. Or perhaps made an attempt to mend fences later. Sonny had not been one otherwise to bear grudges. 'He won't be here, dear.'

'Then that's all right. She'll read me a story. Twyla. I didn't know that was her name.' He got up and sat in one of the armchairs, closing his eyes, one hand moving up and down in response to the music he was hearing.

Gwen went into the kitchen to see Twyla stowing the containers of shrimp Creole in a large wicker basket. She was never one to rush at the last minute. 'Is he OK about you going?' The warm brown eyes met hers.

'I think so, but remember – don't hesitate to call if you feel I'm needed back here.'

'You breathe easy and enjoy your outing – you surely don't treat yourself often enough to going off and playing on your own some.'

'I could if I wanted to,' Gwen smiled at her, 'but being able to continue with the garden club and return to playing for the choral group is all the community activity I need. As for the personal stuff – being able to take walks again alone with Jumbo and go down to see Sarah, either with him or without, is bounty enough. And let's not forget my going in for a physical at your urging. I still have an appointment coming up for a treadmill test, but my doctor seemed reasonably confident, from what I described, that the episodes I've been having are panic attacks, not my heart. For the main part my happiness is here in the house and garden, either when it's just the three of us or when our visitors come, especially Oliver – for your sake and because he's such a joy.'

'That's my lamb baby.' Twyla spread a red and white checked cloth over the wicker basket. As with Mrs Broom she was one for the extra homely touch. 'I surely can't thank you enough, Gwen, for making that possible by coming up with that garden club plan as a way to get past the barricades, then working your way round to the piano lessons. He's coming on real good, isn't he?'

'His mother would be so pleased with his quick progress. I'm sure she and his father are cheering us on, along with Sarah and Evan, for trying to find out as much as we can about all that goes on at the Cully Mansion. Nellie Armitage told me it was Nathaniel's father who imposed that grandiose name upon it, which should surprise no one who's sat in that living room under the surveillance of his austere patriarchal portrait.'

Twyla moved the basket to the edge of the counter near the garage door. 'That Nellie is some woman to have in your corner. She slipped word to me that to hopefully find out from Mrs Polly about what goes on at that house was the reason why she asked if Mrs Polly could come in once a week to clean. Said she's never cared a hill of beans what her place looks like, but with Oliver being best friends with her Brian she's gotten real fond of him and has been fretting about how things are going with him. Even more so when I'd told her Oliver doesn't feel he can talk to me about problems for fear I'd worry myself sick, especially since I couldn't bring it up to Frank in his continuing failing state.'

'What a difficult position for him and you.'

'It sure is a comfort now he has Sarah and Evan to turn to.'

'Talk about turning up at the right moment.' Gwen let Jumbo out to the fenced area in the back. She had wondered in recent days if Twyla might be a little wistful as well as thankful at this turn of events. Either this thought showed on her face, or the woman she had come to admire as well as like profoundly was a mind reader.

'Don't you go worrying that I'm feeling a little displaced, Gwen. It your kind nature to see things from every angle, but even if Oliver could bring his worries to me same as always, what he's going to need after Frank is gone is what he's lacked for as long as he can remember – parents of the right age. Mine was always something of a concern, even before the Cullys stepped in. And I don't need Nellie's spirit guides to tell me that Sarah and Evan will end up married and my lamb baby couldn't be better off than with them. And then my relationship would be how it should, as his one living grandmother.'

Gwen let Jumbo back in. 'You are a remarkable woman, Twyla – no wonder Oliver loves you so much. I was foolish. It's so obvious nothing can ever diminish the bond between you. As for Sarah and Evan, I'm not only convinced there'll be a wedding, but that they'd also be thrilled – honored – to take guardianship and if possible adopt him. But that can only be wishful thinking. I imagine this would require court approval.'

Twyla glanced at the wall clock, which showed it was close to five. Gwen would need to leave shortly to be in time to get to Bramble Cottage ahead of the other guests. 'Nellie said it took time gaining Mrs Polly's confidence sufficiently for her to open up about Gerard and Elizabeth Cully. Said she's not readily the gossiping sort.'

'That's usually the opening line with most gossip, but I tend to believe it in her case. Robin Polly may have had to withstand enough talk going the rounds about what her father's gotten up to over the years, and how she's to blame for not keeping him under lock and key, to put her off gossip for life. But, let's say the Cullys have been holding it over her head that her neglect as to his whereabouts contributed to his holing up in their cellar as a means to get her to work on the cheap, and she's found other reasons to dislike them, then she may well have decided to make an exception to her closed-mouth rule.'

It was Twyla's turn to smile. 'You sure have a way of getting the pieces in the right places. That is pretty much what I got from Nellie. Mrs Polly told her she agreed to go back and work at the Cully Mansion out of curiosity after Elizabeth got in touch with her. And when it came to paying her, the amount wasn't as promised, for the reasons you just said. There was even talk about civil charges for aiding and abetting. All nonsense, but Mrs Polly said Elizabeth must have figured she was too dumb to realize that.'

'Wrong there, from the sound of it. I'll hazard that she's sharp as a tack,' said Gwen.

'She took her time opening up to Nellie, but sounds like it didn't take her long to suss out at least one thing at that house: said she knew more than enough about boozers to know Gerard Cully is into the bottle the best part of the day and it isn't likely to be that way only when she's there. Her guess is he doesn't do a lick of work from one week to the next. When she's peeked in on him in his home office he's had the radio going and been slumped in an armchair with a glass in his hand or asleep at his desk. Usually I'd feel bad repeating that. We've all more than enough shortcomings of our own to be casting stones. And I don't need to be a nurse to know alcoholism is a disease and mighty cruel to be stuck with. But this is about Oliver.'

'Gerard may well be an alcoholic, which I agree wholeheartedly is something we should all be grateful to be spared, but if he's a mellow drunk, not one to go off into violent rages, I doubt that would be sufficient for a court to take custody of Oliver away from him. It could be he doesn't need to work, but likes to make a pretense of it and his drinking has escalated from having too much time on his hands; though somehow I got the impression from that meeting with Elizabeth that they're not as loaded with funds as was thought. It might have been because the roots of her hair could have done with a touch-up, but I don't think that necessarily means anything. She struck me as very much the arty type, perhaps not overly inclined to focus on her appearance; although what she wore did show a personalized sense of style. What put the idea that there might be some financial issues in my head were her fidgeting hands when telling me that getting the landscaping done for free was no inducement. To be objective, she did quite a bit of poking her hair and smoothing her skirt throughout, but it struck me that time as fluttery to the point of agitation. And now we know she wangled matters to get Robin Polly to work on the cheap.'

'There's one more thing Nellie passed along, and then you really need to be going, Gwen.'

'What's that?'

Twyla sighed. 'I surely dislike this smearing people and it's not your way either. This time it was about the parents of those boys – with the strange names – that Oliver didn't take to from the start. Like you know, he's not one to look for reasons, so I've right along had the feeling they must have gone on making his life miserable and that that's one of the things he's been keeping from me. But back to their mother and father; according to Mrs Polly they've a reputation at their local bar for regularly knocking it back to the point of someone intervening and dragging them off home. She said it's her guess that's why they were allowed in, even welcomed by the Cullys.'

'Maybe Elizabeth hoped Gerard would agree to confine his

drinking to a glass or two on those visits. If he does have a serious problem, sufficient to keep him from working, that alone would be enough to give her those severe headaches. And there could be other problems that we don't have a clue about.' Gwen stroked Jumbo's head and told him soothingly she wouldn't be gone too long. She was about to pick up the wicker basket, having decided it was best not to say another goodbye to Sonny, but Twyla got to it first.

'I'll get it onto the front passenger seat. It's sufficiently weighted not to slide. You'll have your turn at the other end.'

'Thank you.' They went out into the garage. 'I already feel like the wicked stepmother leaving Cinderella at home.'

'We agreed that if I went the Cullys could think the whole thing was a setup to thrust me on them and leave quick as they could. And it's been made plain they're set on avoiding me like the plague.' Twyla paused while getting the basket onto the seat. 'Seems it's Mrs Polly's thinking that has much to do with me being a nurse as my closeness to Oliver. She said there are some who have it stuck in their heads that those with any medical knowledge have ways on zeroing in on what's the least bit off, especially when it comes to the mental.'

'We came up with that possibility ourselves. And to be fair, Robin Polly's viewpoint is also slanted. Nevertheless, a second opinion is always something,' Gwen responded, adding while getting into the car a reminder that Twyla mustn't hesitate to call if Sonny's behavior required her presence.

Once out of the garage she pressed the automatic door return. Even driving at well below the speed limit to ensure the basket stayed put, she arrived at Bramble Cottage within a couple of minutes, making it five thirty as aimed for. She wasn't concerned about being hemmed in on the drive and had thought it likely that almost everyone else would come on foot. Even if they didn't, the potluck rule was arrive at six, depart at eight – with no shilly-shallying to delay the hosts from getting on with the clearing up – unless invited ahead to stay on. Libby had made all of that clear to Sarah. And Gwen did anticipate staying on an extra half hour or so. If she had to make an early getaway she could walk if it meant asking too many people to move their cars.

She was about to put the basket down on the step when Sarah opened the door, saving her from having to do so. They had gotten into the habit of letting themselves into each other's houses when expected without ringing the bell first. Both knew they were welcome to come in a hurry if need be, but were punctilious about never dropping in unannounced. Sarah took the basket from her before she stepped inside.

'I was watching for you because I knew you'd have the Creole and rice to carry. It's so good of Twyla to make them. I knew she wouldn't say no, but do you think she's disappointed?'

'No.' Gwen smiled into the hazel eyes. 'For starters, she believes I should get out and mix more socially. She had already insisted, against all my arguments, that I be the one to come. When we got the good news that Oliver's aunt and uncle would be here I knew she was right in saying that if she were present, they'd likely think they'd been tricked into having her foisted upon them.' She glanced into the den, noticing the teal wall paint new this week and thinking how well it worked with white bookcases and trim. Sarah was wearing culottes and a top in a similar shade of deep turquoise that suited her very well. Her only jewelry was a pair of gold hoop earrings. Such a pretty girl, as well as so dear. They went into the kitchen.

'Elizabeth did casually ask Evan when he phoned this morning, before agreeing to come, whether Twyla was included in the invitation.' Sarah took the two aluminum-covered casserole dishes out of the basket and set them down by the stove.

'Twyla suggests warming those in a 275-degree oven for fifteen minutes, but if you don't have the room you could use the microwave, although she thinks that tends to toughen the shrimp.'

'There'll be plenty of room in the oven and I have to warm up the au gratin potatoes anyway. Libby had made up a big dish of them yesterday, but she was squeamish about passing them along on the off chance she was fermenting her work with this bug Sid went down with in the night. But Oliver had already told us that he's a wiz at potato peeling.' Sarah gave Gwen a sparkling look. 'And he wasn't exaggerating. Evan thought, as I did, that there'd be bits left on and too much potato taken off. But we agreed when he was done that he could be national – if not world – champion for speed and dexterity.'

Gwen laughed joyfully. She often had similar moments with Sarah, especially in this house. There was something that invoked happiness about Bramble Cottage, especially now much of the redecorating Sarah had wanted to accomplish had been completed. 'What about the spiral ham you mentioned the Jennsons were going to serve when the three of you were over for dinner last night?'

'Libby didn't have any reservations about that because it was still in the original wrapper. But she told me before Evan went over to collect it that he should let himself in and she'd stay clear while he got it out of the refrigerator. Such a shame,' again that sparkling look, 'because she's been dying to meet him.'

'And well worth the waiting. How is poor Sid doing today?'

'Feels like a dishrag, but – according to Libby – no longer honking up.'

'Good. Let's hope she lucks out and doesn't come down with whatever it is. Now, where are the two hosts?'

'Evan's giving a final wipe round of the upstairs' bathroom – he's already given the half bath down here a second go – and Oliver is in my bedroom explaining to Dusk why she has to be shut in there for the next few hours. She's been very good about adjusting to life as an indoor cat and has never made any attempt get outside; I think she's not at all keen to re-explore that world. But we've never had all the coming and going that'll go on this evening.'

'Has it been a great rush getting things ready?'

'No problem at all. Libby called all the neighbors except you to notify them of the change. Oliver made the potatoes this morning, and I made the brownies this afternoon.' Sarah indicated the large plastic-wrapped platter on the counter. 'I'd intended that he and I would do that yesterday but the three of us did so much talking before he and Evan sat down to finish *Oliver Twist* and then decide what to read next. They've settled on *Alice in Wonderland* and *Through the Looking-Glass.* Oliver had been read to by his grandpa, but wanted to start back from the beginning. And of course we weren't going to allow making brownies to keep us from having dinner at your house.'

'I'm glad you didn't.'

'It was a wonderful evening.' Sarah kissed Gwen's cheek. 'As for what else needed doing it was next to nothing, especially as it's customary to use paper plates, coffee cups and plastic cutlery.'

'Sensible.'

'Libby says we'll be inundated with appetizers and salads, side dishes and very likely more desserts. It's mostly been a matter of getting in plenty of ice, preparing lemonade and iced tea, getting in some soft drinks, red and white wine, and beer. That's the rule of drinks offered and everyone sticks to it.'

'Again, very sensible.' Gwen took in the rows of glasses and couple of openers and corkscrews, along with the red wine, close to the sink. The stacks of paper plates and their accoutrements were at the other end of the butcher block counter, all of similar custard yellow to the kitchen walls. The sort of detail that would come naturally to Sarah, as did the spray of flowers in an old milk bottle on the kitchen table and other arrangements glimpsed in the dining room. A woman with a career and a home touch. Gwen's mind drew a rosy picture. 'How many do you expect?'

'When Libby phoned back to give me an updated count she said about twenty, besides us and the Cullys. Dinner is announced at seven. I bought a captain's bell at Grandma's Attic last week. Oliver's thrilled at being the one to clang it.' Sarah's smile radiated. 'And I am feeling relaxed. When it came to bringing the house up to par, I did the kitchen and bathrooms while Evan did the shopping and Oliver helped him with any needed vacuuming and dusting, in addition to collecting a dozen folding chairs from the Jennson's garage and setting up some in the living room and others out on the patio. A good thing the patio furniture I'd ordered arrived late yesterday afternoon. If I hadn't suddenly decided to obsess and asked Evan to go round the bathrooms again with a magnifying glass and a damp cloth, he'd be sitting in the living room with his feet up. But I expect he's doing that up in the bedroom with Oliver and Dusk. That'll be why he hasn't come back down.'

'Or because he wanted to give us a little one-on-one time. There's no mistaking that he's a very kind and thoughtful man and given that he managed to get Elizabeth and Gerard Cully to come this evening, one who must exercise impressive powers of persuasion when the cause merits it. I think it a wise decision, my dear, to have had him be the one to make that call.'

'Oliver's emotional and physical security means so much to him and there was,' Sarah grinned impishly at Gwen, 'the fact that he's a writer. One I've come to realize,' this said with a decided touch of pride, 'is really quite well known. Oliver had already told them that fact and I'd the feeling from what you sized-up about Elizabeth that she'd be the sort to be readily impressed by someone in the creative field. Also, she would be concerned that those of like minds around here would be inclined to listen and take seriously any negative comments Evan might make, if given provocation, about the aunt and uncle with custody of the young heir to the Cully legend.'

Gwen's admiring response was cut short by Evan coming in and giving her a one-armed hug, as had become his usual greeting. Immediately behind came Oliver to provide the full-throttle treatment. Here, she was thinking, is – or should rightfully be – a loving little family, when the doorbell rang.

'Someone's early,' Sarah glanced at her watch, 'it's only ten to six.'

'Bet it's Aunt Nellie,' predicted Oliver. 'Brian says she's always first to arrive anywhere; can't stand not to be in from the start.' He followed Evan out to the foyer.

'My dear, you're more than ready. All organized and the house looks great. You've done such a wonderful job making it welcoming and comfortable. I love the new wall color in the den.'

Sarah visibly relaxed. 'Thank you, and I'm so glad you encouraged me to do the foyer and staircase wall – which Sid kindly painted – and the upper hallway white. I'm all for rooms in different colors, hopefully complementary ones, but not the rainbow effect. We still need more in the den than the two leather recliners my parents gave me, but I'm hesitant to buy furniture because . . . if Oliver were staying in the area I'd put a piano in there.'

It was Nellie's voice coming to them in full sway, so as yet no budging of feet. 'He does have a talent and desire that should be accommodated. And he has other gifts, ones of intellect, conscience and compassion that could lead to his teaching or entering the medical profession as did Nathaniel Cully. However,' Gwen was now the one to kiss Sarah's cheek, 'I have a strong intuition Oliver will follow in Evan's footsteps and become a writer.'

Sarah smiled through a shine of tears and kept her voice low, although Nellie was still holding strong by the front door. 'I knew you realized last evening that Evan and I had told each other how we feel about each other.'

'My dear, you were both walking on air, and Oliver along with you.'

'But we can't allow ourselves to dream beyond getting married, because even if the Cullys were to become reasonable, there's Twyla, whom we'd never do anything to hurt.'

'No difficulty there – she's told me what she believes is best for Oliver. As for the rest – that intuition I just spoke of tells me everything is going to work out as it should.'

'Dear Gwen! Someone else said that to Oliver . . . now here come the guys and Nellie.'

That lady entered with a typical flourish of her stick that always seemed more of a conductor's baton than a necessary mobility aid. She had a long brown paper-wrapped something tucked under her free arm, but did not hand it over, instead spreading a beaming smile before rattling on. 'Sorry to have kept these fine fellows hog-tied, but I was telling them how my two spirit guides showed up around noon. It's been that long since they've put in an appearance I'd gotten to thinking they'd ditched me for someone living in a warmer climate.' She made it sound as if the negligent pair had bought bus tickets to Arizona or Florida. 'Our summers are a joke. My spirit guides came to urge me to attend the peace rally that always gathers at the corner of Main and Narrow Street on Saturday afternoons.'

'Were there a good number of supporters there?' asked Sarah.

'Usual dozen or so, but now's the prize part.' Nellie chortled. 'A man stuck his head out a car window and yelled straight at me: "Get a job!" Like I'm a sluggard for giving up looking at ninety.' Her glee was so infectious they all joined in her laughter, with Oliver doubling over with mirth. 'Of course, *he* wasn't from here. Hereabouts, whatever their politics, folks are live and let live.'

'What was your response, if any?' Evan was patently charmed, despite probably having already heard most of this.

'The one that gets right up the snouts of people who think demonstrators are for hell in a hurry: "God bless you, sir."' Nellie handed Sarah the brown paper object. 'French bread, it's always my contribution.'

'Wonderful. Libby told me or I'd have had to buy some.'

'But this time I forgot the butter.'

'No problem, I've already put a couple of sticks out to soften.'

The doorbell rang again. It seemed to do so constantly for the next ten minutes bringing a stream of people bearing bowls of salads and fruit, plates of appetizers, casserole dishes . . . the list went on. Gwen helped to get the main course items, if they didn't need to be re-warmed, onto the dining-room table, while Oliver – exuding cheer – put the nibbles on the one in the kitchen. Evan continued to let newcomers in.

'That's the one thing we didn't think of – leaving a note taped on the outside of the door telling people to just walk in,' said Sarah to Gwen amidst the growing buzz of voices as they stood checking to make sure there were sufficient serving utensils. The majority of participants had brought their own.

So far Elizabeth and Gerard had not showed. Some of the appetizers had been taken out to the patio and others to the coffee table in the living room that to Gwen had become a blur of hands holding drinks and faces that were unfamiliar to her. The age range seemed to be between the thirties and eighties. Everyone she had spoken with had been pleasant; the difficulty lay in trying to retain their names. She knew Carolyn Hepplewhite, who was president of Friends of the Sea Glass library, and was pleased to hear her telling Sarah that she had several boxes of Nan Fielding's books and had that morning come across a hardcover copy of Evan Bryant's book signed personally to Nan. It was such a pleasure to have been introduced to him a moment ago and did Sarah think he'd like it returned? Gwen missed the rest because Maurice Fisher, whom she had long known from the choral society, took the opportunity to ask about Sonny. He then went on to discuss how some natural remedy was doing wonders for his arthritis. He was a dear man married to a woman – only visible as a silhouette from across the room – who if beside him would have contradicted every second word he said if up to her usual form. Gwen also knew Celeste Rogers and Diane Thorn, a couple who were both in the garden club and devoted to their two Pekinese. They also inquired very kindly after Sonny, and then Gwen had moved away after Nellie tugged her elbow.

'Been trying to catch your eye. Need to talk to you.' Her voice drilled into Gwen's ear. 'Has to be quick as it needs to be before those two show up – if they ever do. That way!' She directed her stick at the doorway to the foyer and once out there darted into the den, saw that it was unoccupied and gusted a relieved sigh. 'Ideal! Here they can't catch us by surprise. If the doorbell rings and it's them we scoot.'

'I assume you're talking of the Cullys,' said Gwen mildly after checking her watch. 'Perhaps they don't consider six thirty late if Evan told them dinner would be served at seven.'

'The later the better, although if they don't come at all it'll be shame on them. I was going to see if I could get together with you and Twyla, but I know she takes Oliver to church and then on to see his grandpa. And I've been itching to spill the beans of what I got from Robin Polly this morning. Don't go taking offence that I'm asking you to hold your horses and let me steam ahead. The nub of the matter is the aunt and uncle don't have full ownership of the Cully Mansion. A half share is held in trust for Oliver until he's eighteen.'

'Oh!'

'Robin P got that info straight from Miss Emily. Seems the old girl confided in her. Who else did she have? Even better, Robin was one of the witnesses to the will, as was Miss Emily's longtime doctor – so there couldn't be any suggesting she wasn't in her right mind at the time. Wanted every "I" dotted and "T" crossed. The house and its contents, except for the scrimshaws, went into trust for Oliver's grandfather for his lifetime and then on the grandfather's death to his descendents. Max and Gerard!'

'But Max died. Will Oliver get anything?'

'Oh, my, yes. Oliver is a descendant of his grandfather and after Max died he and Gerard each became entitled to a half share, but Oliver can't get his until he's eighteen. I was right about Max's parents cutting him out of their will and assumed that went for the Cully property as well.'

'Interesting!' Gwen was still assimilating. Did Twyla know the relevant point of Miss Emily Cully's will, but had not felt free to pass on the information? Or had Frank Andrews kept it to himself? She thought the latter unlikely.

'And now to a nifty little update. Robin noticed that a small silver carriage clock was missing from the table beside Miss Emily's four-poster bed that's still weirdly in the living room and she mentioned the absence to Elizabeth.'

Gwen felt it incumbent to interrupt. 'I was there, on my visit about the garden club, when Robin brought up the clock. And Elizabeth's response seemed unreasonably heated.'

'Small wonder as it turns out.' Nell was practically prancing, if such a word could be applied to a ninety-year-old, without the aid of her stick. 'That got Robin's dander and suspicions up. Particularly as she felt strongly about that clock, said it had a verse engraved on the front and Miss Emily had told her Nathaniel gave it to his wife on their fortieth wedding anniversary. Devoted to each other, they were. And it hadn't taken long for Robin to get right fond of Oliver. Calls him Mr Pal. Making her grim determined – besides disliking his uncle and aunt, her in particular – to look out for his interests. So she takes to searching round to see what other items that might have gone missing and came up with a dozen or so; ones she could be sure about, that weren't where they'd been in the china and curio cabinets. So she does the rounds of places like Grandma's Attic, but no luck. Now we get to where I came in.' Nellie did another bounce. 'When she's spilling the goods this morning I thought of the shop in Dobbs Mill, right near the spiritualist church I go to. It seemed to me that if Elizabeth has been selling the stuff she'd be a fool to do so in Sea Glass.'

'Absolutely,' Gwen concurred. So far, as luck would have it, none of the other guests had strayed into the foyer.

'So I told Robin to hop in my car – hers is an old clunker and I can better afford the gas and I'd drive her out to Dobbs Mill. And – you've guessed it – bingo! The sign outside the place says *Fine Antiques*, which looked true of some of the stuff, but there's also a lot of what the owner called "collectibles" that I'd call junk. Said most of his trade is summer tourist-based, not the local. The church being the kind it is, along of providing readings and séances, draws people from away. Anyhow, it didn't take Robin long to spot not only the clock, but most of the other items. Good thing I always keep a few thousand in my checking account so I could buy back the lot. Came to a pretty penny. The man knew his stuff and in a way that's good, or else some of the things might have gone before we got there.'

'What a blessing.'

'I'm rushing, but one more thing. And it's real suggestive. Robin came up behind Elizabeth on her cell phone on Thursday in time to hear her ask the person at the other end if he, or she, would still be at the gallery in Boston next week, instead of the one in New York, because if so she'd come down for the day on Tuesday. That's when she got wind and turned round. Robin told me if looks could kill she'd a bin splattered like a fly to the wall.' Another jig. 'What you think of them apples?'

The doorbell rang.

Nellie dropped her voice to a whisper. 'That has to be them. I'll show you and Twyla the reclaimed treasure soon.'

Gwen was the one to open the door, recognizing Elizabeth of course but seeing her husband for the first time. He was a tallish man with thinning dark hair and hunched shoulders and arms pressed close to his sides, giving the look of a schoolboy who had been summoned due to an infraction at the principal's office. But for the posture he would have been quite good-looking. 'How good that you could come.' Despite her crowded thoughts, Gwen greeted them with her serene smile as they stepped inside. 'Sarah and Evan have told me how pleased they are at the opportunity to meet you both.'

'Nice to see you again, is it . . . Mrs Garfield?' Elizabeth was glancing around. If not for the box of chocolates in her hand, she could have been a potential house purchaser mentally taking measurements.

'Garwood. Not that it matters, my memory is now such,' Gwen accompanied this with a laugh, 'that *I* forget who I am on occasion.' Nellie had not exited the den, and a guest came out of the kitchen and opened the door to the half bathroom. Wafting toward them was the hum of conversation.

'Nice of you to take it that way. This is my husband, Gerard.'

He proffered a damp hand and introductions were exchanged. To Gwen he appeared in something of a haze, although she did not catch the whiff of alcohol. He could merely be shy or otherwise socially awkward – the latter could also be said of Elizabeth in her own way.

She was dressed very much as she had been on that other occasion – a long, loose skirt and matching top. But today her earrings – long, modernistic ones with hammered metal rounds, becomingly enhanced the Bohemian arty effect. Even to the extent of making the tangled hair appear artfully achieved rather than insufficiently combed, as indeed might be the case. The addition of lipstick made her look an attractive woman. 'I realize we're late arriving, but Gerard lost track of time at his computer.'

'I don't have one, too lazy to attempt getting the hang of them.' Gwen saw benefit in sounding verging on doddery. The less eyes and ears the Cullys felt upon them the better. Oliver came out from the kitchen at that moment and was greeted by his aunt and uncle in a casually affectionate manner – that couldn't be faulted. No one could expect them to meet him with faces wreathed in smiles and rapturous exclamations when he'd only been gone a couple of days.

'Hello,' said Oliver. 'Everyone's glad you could come. How's Feathers? Said anything yet? I haven't had any success so far.'

'Nothing when I've been around.' Elizabeth shrugged a peach linen shoulder, then looked at her husband.

'Still incommunicado when I've been around too.' Gerard's attempt at a joke, if that's what it was, suggested he might be weaving his way out of his befogged state, and Gwen, determined to be as objective as possible, gave him points. His personality couldn't be termed instantly objectionable; he was neither overtly full of himself nor disdainfully aloof, both of which she always found off-putting.

'I'd come looking for you, Gwen,' said Oliver, 'to let you know I'm about to ring the bell to announce dinner is ready.'

'Well, we wouldn't miss that for the world! Why don't you escort your aunt and uncle and introduce them to Sarah and Evan, while I help Nellie Armitage out from the den where she's been taking a short rest.'

During the half hour or so that followed Gwen caught only an occasional glimpse of Elizabeth and Gerard. There were the initial merges around the dining-room table, one group following another. And afterwards still a good deal of coming and going. She overheard a good many compliments of Twyla's shrimp Creole, amidst favorable comments on other items, including the sautéed fiddle-heads, for which, after fifteen years in Maine, Gwen had never acquired a taste. Those she did not attempt but everything she tasted was excellent. During and after the meal she engaged in several enjoyable conversations. Particularly with Anne Sullivan, a relation of Mr and Mrs Plover, who worked for them at their grocery store. While recounting the delights of her recent visit to New York, Gwen had noticed Elizabeth looking up at the abstract painting above the fireplace while talking to Sarah. Was she saying it looked to have been done by a child? True in regard to origin, given that Sarah's niece had painted it at a very young age. Gwen liked it.

It was now closing in on eight, and Elizabeth and Gerard had seemingly disappeared. Sarah and Evan thought they were either in the kitchen or out on the patio, and regretted they had not had more time for fruitful moments with them. Gwen's one observa-tion was that, at least from the little she had seen of husband and wife, they were both drinking diet soda. Not necessarily revealing in itself, had she not overheard Elizabeth say, with perhaps undue emphasis while gesturing with a can in her hand, that such was the beverage of choice with them.

Gwen was standing near the opening to the foyer while others now gravitated toward the kitchen to collect dishes and serving-ware preparatory to leaving, when she saw Oliver at the bottom of the stairs with Dusk in his arms. It seemed unlike him to have gone and collected her before all the guests apart from herself were gone. He was still standing on the step when she stood looking up at him.

'Anything the matter, dear?'

'I guess someone went into the bedroom by mistake and let her out. Gerard came up to me a few minutes ago and asked if I'd seen Elizabeth because it was time to leave and he hadn't seen her since she went off to the bathroom what seemed like ages ago, and he was getting worried because she'd said she'd had one of her headaches coming on.' Oliver stroked the cat while talking. 'So I went and knocked on the one down here, but nobody answered and when I turned the handle it was empty. I thought if Elizabeth had found that door locked, she might've gone upstairs. When I checked that bathroom there wasn't anyone using it either. That's when I saw Sarah's bedroom door was open and suddenly Dusk slipped by from the other end of the hallway. And here's where I caught up with her. I was about to take her back up and close her in for safety, when I started thinking about Elizabeth. Wondering if she'd returned before Gerard started wondering why she wasn't back, only he didn't realize because she was in another room from him.'

'Very likely, Oliver. But there's more, isn't there?'

He gazed at Gwen with something approaching fear in his eyes. 'When I looked in the bedroom to see if Dusk was still there, I noticed something.'

'Let's go into your bedroom and you can tell me, dear.' She was guiding him up to the hallway. Several people had already emerged into the foyer. She opened the door, and upon his entering with Dusk, closed it.

'Will it look rude if I don't go down to say goodbye?'

'To your aunt and uncle?'

'They're the ones I want to avoid; I'd feel uncomfortable right now.' Oliver put Dusk on the bed where she immediately curled up on the pillows, and sat down on it himself. Gwen joined him.

'Then don't feel guilty. No one else matters.' She placed a hand on his. 'I'm sure our absence will go unnoticed. Tell me, dear, what's troubling you?'

'You won't think I have a wickedly suspicious mind?' His lovably round face turned to her in appeal.

'Never.'

'OK, then.' He squeezed her hand before placing both his own palms down on his legs, fingers cupping his knees. 'When I saw the door to Sarah's bedroom gapped open her dressing-table lamp was on. And it hadn't been when Evan and I left Dusk in there. I noticed that at once, even though I was upset that she'd gotten out. Somehow I was so sure she had because I didn't think to look under the bed. There was something else about the dressing table.' Oliver's hands shifted as if prior to gripping them, and then re-flattened. 'Sarah's wooden jewelry box had been moved. It was still in the middle, but it had been pushed back against the mirror. I remembered exactly where it had been because Evan and I dusted that room this afternoon. He did the other furniture and I did the dressing table and he joked about it being a fair deal, because if I didn't put everything back in precisely the same place I could be in hot water. He said women tended to be very fussy about that area of personal space and that when he was a boy his mother wouldn't let him go within a yard of her dressing table, for fear that just by standing looking at it he'd send hairpins flying from their appointed dish.' A smile touched his mouth. 'I like talking to Evan. In lots of ways he's like Grandpa, especially when it comes to words. I wish there was time for them and Sarah to really get to know each other. Has Sarah shown you that amazing wrap blanket she knitted with *Grandpa* on it?'

'Not yet because you had to be the one to see it first. I'm so glad she and Evan are going with you and Twyla to visit him after church tomorrow.'

'Evan said he thinks she should teach both of us to knit. He says he read or heard somewhere that it's now manly and it could give me an extra leg up when I've grown up and meeting girls. I told him I'd like to get married someday, but she'd have to be kind.'

'Important.' Gwen understood that Oliver was reeling out the moment before going back to what was distressing him.

'I'd only want a wife that likes children. And let me have a dog and a cat. Sarah told me you've talked to Jumbo's breeder about a puppy for us . . . I mean for her and Evan. I love Jumbo and Dusk.' He stroked the sleeping cat. 'I suppose if my wife wanted a bird I'd have to deal with that, but I've really tried to get fond of Feathers and I can't, however long I stand talking to him. It's sad for him; he should be with someone who loves him, instead of just making sure his cage is cleaned, and he always has enough water and seed, and can reach that calcium thingy from his perch.'

'Perhaps it would make the talking part easier if you recited poems to him. I'm sure with your memory you know several by heart.'

'That's a good idea.' His smile flickered again. 'Evan says there's a great one called *The Walrus and the Carpenter* in *Through the Looking-Glass*. But for the time being I could recite one of Pooh's hums. They always make me feel happy and safe.' A pause, during which the little flame went out. 'About that jewelry box, Gwen.'

'Yes, dear.'

His hands were again on his legs, but the grip on his knees was tighter than before. 'I know what you have to be thinking, it's what I'd figure in your place – that Sarah went into her bedroom after Evan and I finished dusting, and moved it herself. But I don't see why she would have done. Those earrings she has on this evening were the ones she's been wearing all day. Same with her watch.'

'Perhaps she couldn't remember where she'd put either before taking her shower and did what we all do in frustrated moments – start searching any likely place, even while knowing we didn't put the item, or items, there. But that's not the issue, is it, Oliver? You think someone went into Sarah's bedroom, either by accident or out of curiosity, and in the course of poking around may have stolen something from that box. And your dreadful fear is that someone was Elizabeth.'

He nodded, unable to look at her.

'Do you know of anything in that box that was of special value to Sarah?'

Now he looked at her, tragedy written on his face. 'A ring that belonged to her great-grandmother. It had diamonds in it and some other stone. Yesterday afternoon Sarah got a phone call from her ex-husband. And afterward she told Evan and me what it was about. He'd thought his mother had given Sarah the ring and wanted it back. I guess it's quite valuable. She explained his mistake and I expect he felt a fool. She hasn't been wearing it because it needs fixing and she should get it into a jeweler instead of leaving it languishing in the . . .'

'Jewelry box on her dressing table,' Gwen finished for him. 'And will have felt safe doing so, home burglaries in Sea Glass being few and far between. I understand your panic Oliver; what we need to do is go tell Sarah so she can take a look and see whether or not the ring is missing.'

'If it is gone there'd have to be a police investigation. It would be terrible if it turned out Elizabeth was the one who stole it, but at least then Sarah would get it back. It would be even worse if it never turned up. The never knowing for sure whether it was my uncle's wife who did this to her.'

Gwen put her arm around him. 'What makes you think Elizabeth capable of having taken it?'

'I feel wicked,' Oliver squeezed his hands together, 'because maybe she wouldn't do anything like that in a million years, but what if she and Gerard are broke? I'd always thought they were loaded. I don't know about her people, but my grandparents on that side seem to have had lots of money and it all went to Gerard. Grandpa didn't tell me that; I overheard Brian's parents discussing it a while back. But for some time now I've been wondering if it's all gone.'

'Fortunes placed in the wrong hands can disappear almost over-night. The stock market hasn't been kind in several years.' Gwen was glad to see Dusk open her eyes and gravitate to his lap. 'I understand your uncle is a professional investor, but even they can sometimes get things badly wrong.'

'He's something called a day trader, and he's in the room he turned into an office most of every day. Only I think he's only been pretending to work since moving into that house.' Oliver stroked Dusk. 'I know Elizabeth's upset at how much he drinks and she has those bad headaches. Twyla knows about them and she says they can be worsened by stress.' The eyes now meeting Gwen's were shining with tears. 'I keep remembering Grandpa telling me that we shouldn't be too quick to condemn, because desperate circumstances can lead to desperate measures. And I suppose I can see why Elizabeth could've been tempted to steal that ring, but there's Sarah . . .' His voice trailed miserably away.

Gwen put her arms around him, knowing that the person he needed most at this moment was another. She was also recalling a beloved voice from the past – reassuring her as a daughter that a mother is the forever shoulder. She was also picturing a three-year-old Sonny standing in the open doorway as she was about to drive away on a short errand and how she had always kept the car windows open so she could respond to his 'Wave Mom, promise to keep waving.' The echo of that small voice had returned hauntingly through the years. She suddenly ached to hold that little boy in her arms again. She wished she could tell Oliver that his mother had never stopped waving . . . and what she and his father wanted most was for him was the love and security of two wonderful living parents. She disengaged him gently and got to her feet.

'It's the not knowing, dear, that can sometimes be the worst part. Why you don't stay here and continue keeping Dusk company while I go down and tell Sarah and Evan about the jewelry box being moved.'

'But that would be cowardly of me.'

'Not at all.'

'Are you sure? I don't want her to see me looking upset.'

'Good thinking.' She gave him an encouraging smile before going out the door. As it turned out she didn't have to go down the stairs because Sarah and Evan were coming up them.

'Everything OK?' they asked simultaneously.

She explained as succinctly as possible without lowering her voice; it wouldn't do for Oliver to think she felt compelled to whisper.

'Oh, that poor boy!' Sarah reached for Evan's hand. 'As if he hasn't been through enough already!'

'Why don't you two take a look. I'll go back and sit with him.'

They nodded and she returned to Oliver. Several minutes passed, during which she held his hand without speaking. Nothing can be more stress adding at tense moments than someone offering up platitudes and clichés. The brief but endless wait ended when Sarah and Evan came in. Both were smiling and Oliver was instantly on his feet. Relief flowed through Gwen on watching them gather him into a hug. It was Evan who spoke; she thought Sarah might well be too choked up to do so.

'Sarah's ring isn't gone.'

'It isn't?' There was no describing the joy in Oliver's voice. 'I was so scared.'

'Understandably.' Evan clasped his shoulder. 'The box had been moved. Human nature being what it is there are always those types who have to look in other people's medicine cabinets and otherwise nosy around.'

Gwen slipped out and returned to the living room, intent on collecting up any remnants of the potluck, but that had already been done. The same proved true of the kitchen and patio. Everything back to normal. She phoned Twyla to ask how Sonny was doing and, that news being reassuring, said she would stay on a little while longer. Sarah and Evan joined Gwen in the living room. She was seated in one of the linen-covered armchairs and they took the sofa.

'How is he?' she asked.

'Like a huge weight has been lifted,' said Evan, 'but worn out. Fell almost immediately asleep after we tucked him in and listened to him saying his prayers.'

'We have to do better at remembering to say grace before meals.' Sarah's face was troubled.

Gwen looked at them both. 'There's something the two of you are holding back. The ring really is safe, I trust?'

'Oh, yes.' Sarah bit down on her lip. 'But something else was taken. Some drawings Oliver had found in his bedroom at the Cully Mansion. I'm sorry, Gwen, that we can't be more explicit now – it's a matter of keeping Oliver's confidence . . .'

'I understand, my dear.'

'He gave them to us yesterday and I put them in the jewelry box; it was a convenient storing place and it looks like Elizabeth found them and was sufficiently motivated for some reason to risk taking them. Evan thinks she panicked.'

He returned her look. 'Guilty consciences have that effect.'

'It certainly looks as though she made a hurried departure because she dropped one sheet of paper. We found it on the floor by the bed; the side closest to the door. Of course we could be judging unfairly,' her eyes sought comfort from Evan, 'but, rightly or wrongly, Elizabeth does stand out as the likeliest person, given that Gerard, who does come off as amazingly self-absorbed, was concerned by what he believed to be her prolonged absence.'

'Sadly, I'm with you there.' Gwen sighed.

Evan reached for Sarah's hand. 'This is the possible scenario. Elizabeth, feeling the onset of her headaches, decided to look for a place to lie down for, say, five to ten minutes, and while lying on the bed saw the jewelry box and on getting up lifted the lid out of curiosity or . . . in hope of finding something worth taking. My Aunt Alice has a saying she says came down from her Scottish grandmother – a needy body is a greedy body. We are assuming some financial reverses on the Cullys' part. But right there on top, to drive out any possible larcenous thoughts, were those folded-up drawings.'

'Regrettably, I too wonder if she thought about helping herself to a piece of jewelry. With so many people in the house it would be difficult to point suspicion in one direction.' Gwen shook her head sadly. 'Before Elizabeth and Gerard arrived, Nellie talked to me in the den about what she learned this morning from Robin Polly about the likelihood of their being in financial straits.' Gwen relayed what had been imparted to her, ending with the discovery of missing items, including the silver clock that had first ignited Robin's suspicions, at the antique shop at Dobbs Mill. 'They're all at Nellie's house and she wants to show them to us.'

'I think that little clock would have a very special meaning for Oliver, considering its provenance being a gift from Nathaniel Cully to his wife on their fortieth anniversary.' Evan was still holding Sarah's hand. 'He's developed a strong interest in Nat, as he's come to think of him.' His eyes gleamed thoughtfully. 'I do think the one positive thing we can glean from this incident of the drawings is that if Elizabeth is the one responsible for such a stupid move, she would not appear capable of contriving an intricately malevolent plot.' He was looking at Gwen, but she was sure he was communicating privately with Sarah about something that had been worrying them both.

'Yes, there is that.' What Gwen thought of as the lovely face eased. 'It certainly wasn't smart of her to sell what she'd lifted from the Cully Mansion so close to Sea Glass.'

'And now we have it from Robin Polly,' Evan was still holding her hand, 'that's she's going to some gallery in Boston on Tuesday. Meaning she's either rethought the wisdom of disposing of stuff so close to her own backyard or what she has at her disposal is

significant enough to warrant taking it to someone who would
pay the full value of what's on offer.'

'I wonder if it could be that dour portrait of Nathaniel's father,'
suggested Gwen. 'She could always claim to have put it in the
attic. I can't imagine it was painted by someone famous, but I
suppose even great artists could have their off days.'

Sarah spread her hands. 'From your description he, or she, would
have had to be comatose at that time.'

'I'll talk to Aunt Alice and have her help make up a list of
galleries we can check on starting Wednesday. The trouble is,' Evan
paused, 'even with something – and if it's big, what then? – I'm
sure Oliver wouldn't want us to turn her into the authorities, or
rat her out to her husband, who may not be in the know. Whatever
else those two are, Gerard was Oliver's father's brother and only
sibling. And yet how do we, including Twyla of course, abandon
him to their supposed care?'

This was unanswerable. Gwen saw zero comfort in Sarah and
Evan saying optimistically, if tritely, that something might occur to
present a solution. She got to her feet. 'I'm going to leave and let
you talk some more on your own. I need to be getting home.
Sonny may still be up.'

They came with her out to her car, Evan carrying the picnic
basket with the cleaned dishes inside; before getting in she looked
up at the sky. Pink clouds. They always brought memories. Her
mind went to them on the short drive home. Sonny in the car
with her one late afternoon or evening; she pointing upward, and
his awed delight. Throughout his childhood they would always
smile in a moment of special closeness on seeing them. One day
when he was a young man, still in college, they were having lunch
together when he paused in the middle of a sentence and said, 'I
love you Mom.' She told him that was wonderful to hear, that
she loved him too. And he looked at her and said, 'I saw pink
clouds today.'

She entered the house through the garage and put the basket
down on the table. Twyla came in from the foyer and told her,
without delaying for questions, that it had been a good evening
and Sonny was in the book room. She found him seated on the
sofa and sat down beside him. He was staring straight ahead.

'I love you, Sonny.'

'I know. I love you too.' He leaned his gray head against her shoulder and they sat like that until he went up to bed. She followed him to the stairs, stood gathering herself together, then returned to the book room with Twyla and told her about the potluck and all that ensued.

'What should we do, Gwen?' The consternation was visible. 'Even if I were to take this to Frank, which would be so hard on him, I don't know what he could do at this stage, having handed over guardianship to them.'

'Wait a minute, dear.' Gwen sat thinking. 'Did he see a lawyer to take action through the courts?'

'No, definitely not. He'd wanted to have Oliver remain with me, but Gerard as his next of kin insisted on taking him.'

'Well, then, I don't know much about the law, but I'd think Frank could petition to have Oliver removed from their keeping to be with the person, or persons, of his choosing.'

'They might say he's non compos mentis?'

'Somehow, I don't see them putting up that kind of a fight, given what can be presented against them, with witnesses. Elizabeth should already be shaking in her boots. If Frank has been praying to secure a better future for Oliver, as must be the case, then this may not be as distressing to him as you fear. I imagine when it's explained to him the relief will be enormous.'

'You're right.' Twyla's face and body relaxed. 'Absolutely right. Thank you, Gwen. I'll set it up tomorrow, out of Oliver's hearing, of course, to have a doctor with me when I talk to Frank. And now that his health is down-hilling, that surely can't wait until we find out if Evan and his aunt's sleuthing is successful – what Elizabeth gets up to Tuesday in Boston. I'm also going to tell Frank. I'm certain he'll be able to rest easy if Oliver is with Sarah and Evan. The parents of his own choosing.'

They talked for a little while longer before going up to bed. The next morning Twyla left on her own for St Anne's where she would meet up with Oliver, Sarah and Evan. Gwen had two reasons for remaining at home. She didn't want anyone to feel she should be included in the visit to Frank Andrews after the service. And for some reason, possibly those memories of the past that had come to her yesterday evening, she felt a pressing need to spend time alone with Sonny, who had expressed no wish to go to church as he sometimes did. The thought caught up with her as she came downstairs that time was pressing at their backs.

A clock was ticking faster and faster, leaping from seconds to minutes, so out of control that it was bound to stop suddenly forever. Gwen pressed her hand to her heart, aware that Jumbo was looking up at her anxiously. She sat down in her chair by the fireplace in the book room. She hadn't had one of these panic attacks – which is what her doctor had been almost sure was all they were – in several weeks.

The few hours alone with Sonny were good ones. She talked to him about Beatrice – bringing forth smiles, if no verbal response – of childhood friends of his time in Boston and then of times spent with her parents and Rowena.

She had been thinking often of her sister recently – of the rage she had expressed toward her after their father's funeral. Rowena's firm distancing of herself in the following years, while maintaining devoted contact with their mother, who had never brought the matter up with Gwen, knowing that doing so would only add pain. That distance had only been breached once, by an incredible act of generosity on Rowena's part. Reconciliation. But, no . . . when Gwen phoned the number in France to express her over-whelming gratitude, she had merely said it was the right thing to have done. A plea that they could see each other was brushed aside. They each had their own lives and could remain fond of each other from different sides of the ocean. She also made it clear that in future she preferred letter contact to phone calls. Gwen saw no hope of the wall coming down. She wrote at first every couple of months, but Rowena only responded to the second or third letter, so gradually she spaced her own further apart and that seemed to work better, in that Rowena began replying after a month or so to individual letters. When John died she didn't make an attempt at another phone call to suggest a hope that her sister would come to his funeral. Rowena had already given to them more than could ever have been expected. That letter had received a prompt and kind response, but still no mention of a wish to see Gwen again. Acceptance had come over the years. And then had come Sonny's diagnosis. Should she, or should she not, let Rowena know about it? Didn't she have a right to be informed? Yes. But it would put her in such a difficult position if she still preferred to stay away. Here would be her sister in another crisis, compelling her out of decency and generosity to come to the rescue. So far Gwen had said nothing, keeping her letters as always light, but increasingly she was wondering if she had made the wrong decision.

'It's sad Grandpa died.' Sonny suddenly spoke for the first time.

'Yes, dear. He loved you very much.' Jumbo shifted closer to her chair. What peace he brought.

'What's Grandma doing?'

'Being her always lovely self.'

'Can we go and see her?'

'Sometime, dear.'

'I'd like that.' His smile was so broad it even seemed to include Jumbo.

After that he slipped back into vague-eyed silence. He barely touched the breakfast she'd prepared. She was contemplating a pork roast, although what she was really yearning for was fried chicken, which she hadn't eaten in years. Her thoughts were interrupted when Twyla returned. Sonny had moments previously gone up to his bedroom having wandered in to stare at the piano before turning away.

'How was Frank today?' she asked when she and Twyla were seated at the table drinking freshly-brewed coffee.

'Praise be, this was one of his good times. His speech was clearer than usual and it was obvious he took mightily to Sarah and Evan. You should have seen the way his eyes lighted up when she gave him that blanket she knitted. And, oh, you should've seen how Oliver looked when he tucked it around his shoulders. Then Frank asked Evan about his books and they got off talking about other ones they'd read. Well, Evan said the most of it, as was necessary, but you could tell right enough Frank was enjoying himself to the full. The three of them said their goodbyes and went out a little ahead of me. And he said, though it was a little hard to hear because his voice was failing some: "Those are two good young people. Good for our Oliver." And I said, "Loving, level and kind – along with being the right ages. I'll talk more about that tomorrow, so get you some good rest."'

'Did you manage a word with anyone about having a doctor with you?'

'I surely did. Slipped away while they were discussing *Alice in Wonderland* and how Oliver had loved it so much when Frank read it to him, and he and Evan were going to revisit it before going on the next one. Mr Braddock – he's the manager at Pleasant

Meadows – was in his office. Nice man. When I explained he said
he'd contact Frank's own GP, Doctor Marshall; the one he's had
from way back and was so good to him and Olive when Clare
and Max died. The hope is he can come at ten tomorrow morning
when Frank should be at his best.'

That afternoon Twyla received a call from Mr Braddock, saying
the time and day worked well for Dr Marshall. A few minutes
later, Nellie phoned Gwen saying she hoped both women could
come round to her house at nine thirty the next morning to look
over the items she had retrieved from the shop in Dobbs Mill. If
so, she would ask Sarah to join them. Later wouldn't work for her,
nor anytime today, because she would be attending lengthy church
meetings.

There would be no problem with Sonny. Sid Jennson had been
in touch earlier with the good news that he was back fit as a fiddle
from whatever bug had ailed him and, if possible, he'd like to pick
Sonny up at nine tomorrow and take him on a run to look at
light houses and then out to lunch if all went well.

Gwen asked for a moment to consult with Twyla. She explained
the timing of the invitation. 'That's no good for you, Twyla. And
you're the one who should be there. Shall I tell Nellie you'll go
on your own on Tuesday?'

'I'd rather you went ahead with it tomorrow, Gwen. I'm sure as
houses you and Sarah have a better eye for what's valuable and what
isn't than I do. And we're all eager to the jumping point to know
as much about Elizabeth's activities as possible. Could be she tried
to sell this man whatever it is she seems like to be taking up to
Boston, and he told her his wasn't the right kind of shop for it.'

And so it was agreed. The following morning proceeded
according to the arranged timetable. Sid Jennson collected Sonny
as promised. Twyla left in her car for Pleasant Meadows, and Gwen
headed down to Nellie's in hers with Jumbo in the back. She had
asked if it would be all right to bring Jumbo because she wanted
to take him for a walk along the beach afterward, hopefully with
Sarah.

Oliver had returned to the Cully Mansion the previous evening.
At the potluck Elizabeth had reminded him of his responsibilities
to Feathers. Poor little parakeet! He wasn't where he was meant
to be either. 'And that is one more thing to weigh Oliver down,'
Gwen said to Jumbo on getting him out of the car.

Gwen had never been in Nellie's house before, but once ushered inside it was very much what she had expected, having been told it was still much the same as when lived in by Nellie's elderly parents. They'd liked farmhouse plain, same as she did, not caring for furniture that talked down to her. The door opened directly into the living room and thence through a rounded archway into the dining room. There was a red brick fireplace, heavy-weave dark blue and cream check on rods at the windows, and beneath the coffee table a multicolored rag rug. Instead of a sofa there was a grouping of four comfortably shabby armchairs. Jumbo lay down beside one of them.

Sarah had arrived earlier and she said, standing in the archway, 'Isn't this an inviting house, Gwen?'

'It certainly is. I can understand why the spirit guys enjoy stopping by.'

'But Nellie just told me she's thinking of moving out to Ferry Landing,' Sarah said, 'to be close to her great-nephew, his wife and Brian.'

'They've been pushing for it,' said Nellie from behind Gwen, 'but I'm still mulling things over. If Frank Andrews should decide to sell his house that might be the clincher, it being just around the corner from them. Let's get started in there.' She pointed her stick toward the dining room. 'I've moved my stuff and set out Lizzie's loot on the bottom dresser shelf.'

Sarah, being nearest, reached it first and was holding a Meisen figurine when they joined her. 'The man asked for four hundred for this, but he let Nellie have it for three hundred and fifty. What do you think?' She handed it to her.

Gwen looked it over before returning it to the dresser shelf. 'Rather nice. A pretty piece and in good condition. I'd say that was fair, but I wonder how high his markup was.' She and Sarah looked over the other pieces. Mostly china, a couple more figurines, including one of Napoleon. And there was the teapot Nellie had mentioned. It was Minton and, Gwen thought, at least pre-World War Two. Probably the person most likely to pay the most would be someone wishing to increase or complete a set. But it would be a matter of him, or her, happening by, unless the shop owner was on eBay. What she found most personally delightful were four Georgian or Regency enameled snuff boxes. She thought it likely, not having looked at the itemized sales receipt, that they might have accounted for a sizeable portion of what Nellie, now hovering in the background, had paid out. There were also some silver pieces – a nutcracker, a pair of grape scissors and a miniature frame without its intended photo – sensible of Elizabeth to have removed it. And in addition to these, the small silver carriage clock Robin Polly had said was given to his wife of many years by Nathaniel Cully. Sarah passed it over.

'Read the verse, Gwen; I think you'll agree Oliver would love to have it.'

The engraving required her reading glasses; she drew them out of her skirt pocket. *Count not the hours as lost, when I am gone from thee, my love so deep transcends, the widest lonely sea.* She stood, remembering John and her parents, her eyes misting. 'I know Oliver would treasure this. Nathaniel and his wife were an elderly couple when he gave this to her. I have this sense, I don't know why – unless sentimentality – that his health was failing and that verse expressed his belief that the love for those left behind never dies and that he would always be there, some way, somehow, for her.'

'I go along with that!' proclaimed Nellie with a dangerously close wave of her stick. 'Mighty comforting notion for young Oliver, I'd think, losing both parents so young and now his grand-father failing bad. Then there's his interest in Nathaniel – came asking if I knew of any photos or pictures of him as a young boy to get a look at.'

'Yes,' agreed Sarah, 'living in that house, Oliver naturally wants to learn as much as he can about him. Do you want us to look at that receipt, Nellie?'

'Well, don't neither of you faint at the total. You'll see it's three thousand, seven hundred. And it's not like I can count on getting it back, seeing as no one asked me to stick my nose in. Still, worth every penny to my mind if it helps get Oliver away from that pair! I don't know if what she did here is a misdemeanor or a felony, if let's say Elizabeth's take home was two thousand, and half of that would be Oliver's share.'

'It's not like stealing a handkerchief, is it?' Gwen looked down at the receipt Sarah had just handed to her. As she had guessed, the snuff box had been the costliest of the items. 'Either way Oliver is going to hate it. He has the most susceptible heart. He's suffering enormous guilt because he can't sufficiently love that parakeet they gave him, so imagine how he'd feel with Elizabeth and Gerard being a thieving aunt and uncle.'

'You've got me there, good.' Nellie's still, rounded face deflated. 'But that poor child can't be left to their mercies.'

'And he will not be,' said Gwen, 'but by the appropriate person, Frank Andrews. Twyla has gone to talk to him now. Knowing Frank as she does, she is sure he will wish to handle the situation in the most restrained and productive way possible.' Gwen had informed Sarah and Evan on the phone yesterday evening, after Oliver had gone back to the Cullys, of what Twyla was going to say to Frank with the doctor present. The only part omitted concerned the suggestion Oliver should be placed in the care of – as Twyla had said – the couple he had evidently chosen for his parents.

Gwen and Sarah remained for coffee but did not linger because Nellie had to get to her church meeting. There was no rush for Gwen to get home in case Sonny wanted to come home early because Sid Jennson had said he'd nothing on that day and would be glad to stay with him until her return. Jumbo again in the back and Sarah now beside her, Gwen drove her car across the road to Bramble Cottage and parked in the drive. By what felt like an unspoken agreement, nothing was said about what had transpired at Nellie's, but it hovered – an impenetrable blend of rainbow and gray cloud as they left the car and strolled together on the beach with Jumbo. It was another gloriously warm day under a cloudless blue sky.

Sarah said as they neared the steps, 'Evan and I are going to get married in a couple of weeks. We don't want to wait because it's so important to us that Oliver be there and that Evan can be living here and not missing time with him.'

They had stopped walking. 'I'm so very pleased for you both.' Gwen placed a hand on Sarah's shoulder. 'You're two very special people and meant for each other.'

'It has to seem so quick. We only met four weeks ago but we just knew . . . right away, that something incredible was happening. I know that sounds ridiculous.'

'Not to me. It was exactly the same with John and me, but in our case it was initially an impossible situation. I was married to Sonny's father, Charles. And John had recently become engaged to my sister, Rowena. I only saw him one other time in the next five years, when he came one evening to break the news that my father had died.'

'Oh, Gwen! What a painful situation. Do you mind telling me what happened?'

'Not at all. I've been thinking back on it all so much lately. It was all so painfully tangled. On the day after the funeral Rowena's bottled-up resentment of me exploded. She had been under so much stress. She had been staying with our parents for several weeks. Our father had been depressed – afraid he was losing his memory. He was only in his fifties. They didn't talk about early onset Alzheimer's in those days, but a brain tumor had been ruled out. When Sonny was diagnosed I immediately thought he must have inherited the susceptibility, although the medical thinking is it doesn't skip the next generation and then genetically crop up in the following one. So it may just be one of those sad coincidences. My father took an overdose while my mother and Rowena were out one afternoon, so you can see why she was distraught.'

'What did she say to you?'

'That she'd ended her engagement to John because she had eyes and wasn't a fool. That she'd been in love with Charles before he set her aside to marry me. We'd both known him from childhood onwards because our parents and his were close friends. But he'd told her that after much soul-searching he'd decided Rowena was cut out to be the ideal mistress, not the suitable wife. That I was the sister much better suited for that role. And as money wasn't the issue – we'd both come in for a very nice inheritance one day – best to go for the woman he wouldn't need to worry might stray.'

'How cold-blooded! Had you wondered during your marriage if there was an attraction between them?'

'I should have seen it.' Gwen looked down at Jumbo, sitting patiently at her feet, and back to Sarah. 'But I didn't, until the day Rowena brought John to our home in Boston to introduce him as her fiancé. We'd already known she was coming with our parents for the weekend. John was the surprise. They arrived early and I was out in the garden. She sent him out to break the news to me . . . it was as though she knew what was going to happen. From lunch onwards Charles was in a thunderous mood that I don't believe had anything to do with me, except as a means of venting, because when we went up to our bedroom that evening he made no attempt to hide his raging jealousy over the engagement. He said Rowena was a fool and that if the marriage did come off it wouldn't last, because she'd soon lose interest in John – she wasn't meant for anything permanent.'

'Were you and Rowena able to patch things up after her outburst?'

'Only on the surface, and very little of that. She moved shortly afterward to France, where she still lives. Our mother visited her there frequently through the years until her death. And occasionally – more toward the end – Rowena came and stayed with her. I don't know what excuses she made for not seeing me, but knowing she would want to see Sonny I arranged with my mother for him to spend time with them.'

'You said you didn't see John for five years?'

'Yes, and that came about from an extraordinary generosity on Rowena's part when my life caved in. I'd suspected for some time that Charles was having affairs. Looking back, I think he may have started in the first few years of our marriage. But I told myself I had to think of Sonny, though that was wrong thinking – Charles had never shown him affection, and as a result he resented and disliked him. I'd gone with Sonny on the train, because he loved it, to stay with my mother for a couple of weeks as we always did in the summer. Charles was always too busy with work to accompany us, but after a few days I wasn't feeling well, suffering from nausea and a nagging pain in my side.'

'Appendicitis?'

'Yes, as it turned out, but my mother's doctor wasn't sure. I was feeling better the day I saw him, so he advised me to go and see my own. It didn't seem fair to curtail Sonny's time with his grandmother, so it was agreed he should stay on with her; there didn't seem to be any problem in my going back on the train alone as I was still feeling better. And I didn't phone Charles to tell him I was returning because he was supposed to be in Chicago.'

'Supposed?' Sarah touched her arm.

'I walked into the house, after taking a taxi from the station, and went immediately upstairs to lie down because the pain was starting up again. Charles was in the bed with a woman. You can picture the scene that ensued. She clutching at the sheets and going into hysterics, hurling vitriolic darts at me as the rotten wife who had only herself to blame. Charles red in the face, yelling at me to get out so he could pack and leave for good. Amazingly, I had felt sorry for him. All his talk about Rowena not being the type for marriage, and he was the one who should never have made a lifetime commitment. But afterward the shock began to sink in. I phoned my mother to say I was home, but nothing else except that I would see the doctor. I needed time to prepare myself for explaining calmly to Sonny that his father and I had come to the realization we didn't suit each other's needs sufficiently to make it seem right to stay together. I was foolish in not going to the doctor for three days, but I wanted to pretend there really wasn't anything wrong beyond an upset stomach – this wasn't the time for an operation. The result was that my dear housekeeper Mrs Broom had to call an ambulance, and I had to be rushed to the hospital. My appendix had ruptured and I was in danger of not making it. I'd wake to find my mother sitting at my bedside. She told me later that I'd said things in my semi-conscious state that alerted her to the fact that something had happened between Charles and me, so she'd asked Mrs Broom for the facts. She also conveyed this information to Rowena during one of her phone calls giving updates of my condition.'

'Did she come to see you?' Sarah's hand was still on her arm.

'No, she said she thought doing so would scare me. But when I was on the mend and sitting up in bed talking to my mother and Sonny, John walked into the room. Rowena had sent him. She'd called the friend who had introduced them to ask for his phone number.' Gwen inhaled the beauty of the day. 'We had an incredibly good life together until his death ten years ago.

'Thank God for second chances,' said Sarah. 'What became of Charles? Did he marry the other woman?'

'No. I heard from mutual acquaintances that he continued to play the field for years. I could feel sorry for him but for one final piece of information that someone made sure to pass along, and I pray to God Sonny never heard.' Gwen pressed a hand to her cheek and bit down on her lip before continuing. 'Charles would have been in his fifties or sixties at the time . . . when he was suspected of physically attacking a woman who'd told him to leave her alone or she'd take out a restraining order. If it's true, he got away with it because she refused to name the assailant.'

'Oh, Gwen!' It was all Sarah could say.

'There's that fear of retaliation – immediate or delayed.'

'I know. A friend of mine had a similar experience.'

They stood in the sunshine looking out at the purity of the ocean. Gwen reached for Sarah's hand. 'Now for something I've never told anyone, but of all people you should know. That woman lived in Boston. I remember her name. How could I forget it?'

Sarah knew what was coming. Evan's revelation of what he'd heard in high school had paved the way.

'She was Nan Fielding.'

Twelve

Oliver was paddling a yellow kayak into shore when he saw Sarah coming down her steps to the beach with Gwen behind her. They were understandably staring at him with startled faces. He remembered telling both of them he was nervous of being in boats because he wasn't keen on deep water. Even if he hadn't said that, he was sure they wouldn't think it sensible for him to have gone out on his own. Grandpa and Twyla wouldn't have agreed to it; neither would Mr and Mrs Armitage have let Brian, who was super good in his kayak. Oliver was dragging it by the bow cord further up the beach when Sarah and Gwen reached him.

'I know,' he looked apologetically up at them, 'but I had to do it. I was on an unavoidable mission, you see.'

'What sort of one?' Sarah's mouth twitched but the concern was still there, as it was on Gwen's face.

'I was coming along the beach to see you. Elizabeth and Gerard said I could when I'd seen to Feathers. And I did spend time talking to him. Halfway along, I slowed down because I saw *them* – Emjagger and Rolling Stone – ahead of me. I thought they'd keep going but they stopped to drag the dory out from under the overhang.' Oliver pointed slightly to his right at the top of the beach. 'I waited where I was till they had it in the water and pulled away. When I got to where they had been standing, I saw an inhaler on the ground. Rolling Stone has asthma. His mother told me he sometimes has really bad attacks, can't get a breath, and it could be life-threatening if he didn't have his inhaler with him. So I had to take one of the kayaks and follow them.'

'I do see,' Sarah said. 'But, oh, Oliver, you didn't even have a life jacket!'

'Neither did they. I hope whoever owns it won't mind that I took the kayak and a paddle. I know the boats never look like they've been budged, but that doesn't mean they've been abandoned forever, does it?'

'No, but I have wondered. No question you did what you had to do; it was very brave and amazingly generous considering those two boys have hardly been kindness itself to you.' Oliver appreciated Sarah's putting it that way, knowing he'd only told Twyla soon after meeting them that they were the bullying sort, but nothing of the incident involving Nat's statue. Gwen would also be in the dark about those frightening moments on the common before Sarah and Evan rescued him. 'I only wish there had been some life jackets lying around too.' Sarah hugged him. 'Don't Emjagger and Rolling Stone have boats of their own?'

'I'm not sure. But if they wanted to cross to the other side of the bay it would be a shorter cut from here than from where their house and the Cully Mansion are.'

'How far out did you have to go to catch up with them?' asked Gwen in a kind voice, sunlight shining her softly curling hair to polished silver.

'No great distance.' Oliver didn't let himself think how long it had seemed. 'And it would've been less if they hadn't picked up speed when they saw who it was coming after them. Maybe Stone suddenly realized he'd dropped his inhaler because they slowed down and stopped, and I handed it over to him.'

'What did he say?' said Sarah and Gwen together.

'Mumbled something. I couldn't get if it was "thank you."' Oliver grinned widely. 'But if looks could kill I'd have been dead on the spot. That put me in such a great mood I really enjoyed the paddling back part. Remember, Sarah, when Evan talked about how he was thinking he'd like to get a sail boat and I thought I'd be too scared to go out in it? Well, that's all changed now.'

'I'm glad. And I've a very good idea what he'll say when he hears about your rescue at sea. And that is you're a worthy descendent of Nathaniel Cully, and he'd be proud of you.'

'I'd like to think he would be. But you're forgetting a few things, Sarah. I don't suffer from sea sickness, and I didn't have to set off at night in a storm, and I'm not seventy years old.'

Sarah took the kayak's stern cord and helped him pull it back to its place with the others under the overhang. 'For you to become the boy you are, your parents and grandparents must have poured love into you from the day you were born, along with Twyla coming into your life to add her share.'

'There's no doubt of that,' said Gwen. 'Oliver, your mother and father have to be smiling at this minute. Your happiness will mean everything to them.'

'I know it does. And the same with Grandpa. I don't want him to still be worrying when he goes to join them and Grandma Olive.' His face screwed up with emotion. 'Oh, Sarah!' He stepped back from the kayaks. 'I'd give anything to be with you and Evan.'

'And I hope you know,' she drew him into an embrace, 'that's what we'd want.'

'Twyla agrees,' Gwen assured him. 'She's told me so.'

'She has?' Oliver raised a tear-streaked face. 'I'd hate to hurt her. I can't imagine my life without her. I'll always want her close – to see her all the time. She's not just my friend; she's my grandma, the one here on earth.'

'Remember,' Sarah looked into his eyes, 'that someone whom I believe,' she emphasized the word, 'cares for you deeply told you that everything is going to work out.'

Gwen didn't ask who she was talking about; she wouldn't. She never probed.

'Yes.' Oliver's face cleared. 'We can hold on to that. Can't we?' This was quickly followed by a look of dawning horror. 'I don't want anyone but you and Evan and perhaps Brian – he's not a snitch – to know about me taking that inhaler to Rolling Stone. I'd die if the story got splashed over the local paper because Nat's statue is on the common and people started to make a fuss of me. Besides, I couldn't do that to Emjagger and Rolling Stone, however much I don't like them.'

'You have our word,' promised Sarah, on a nod from Gwen, who then said she hoped they wouldn't mind but she thought she should be getting back in case Sonny had returned with Sid Jennson. She gladly left Jumbo, who hadn't gotten in his promised walk with them. Oliver offered to bring him back early afternoon if that was all right.

'I'd get to see Twyla and Sonny and could stay to do my piano practice.'

'That would be great, dear.' She handed him Jumbo's leash. 'I'll start you on a new piece if you feel ready, which I'm sure you will be, the way you're going.

Oliver and Sarah watched her head up the steps. 'I love her too,' he said when they started off along the beach. 'She's become family. Same with Sonny. I think this has been as good a summer as he could have had, don't you?'

'Absolutely, and Gwen will find a lasting comfort in that.' Sarah bent to pick up a piece of amber sea glass, buffered and smoothed to rounded edges. 'All those everyday moments to be held onto and treasured.' She passed it to Oliver and his eyes filled with understanding before returning it to her.

The pure blue sky remained without a strand of clouds; sunshine bathed them in warmth, and only a breath of silken breeze touched them. The water slipped foamless onto the pebbles and the gulls glided silently overhead. After a few minutes Oliver released Jumbo from the leash and they watched him exploring among the rocks.

'Don't those ones covered with long seaweed look like mermaids sleeping face down, Sarah?'

'Our minds do work alike.' The love in her eyes was more warming than the sun. 'I was thinking the same thing the other day when I was down here.'

They followed Jumbo as he emerged onto a stretch of pebbles keeping a leisurely pace. He only took off on a run when given the OK to do so, always returning instantly when summoned. He never went splashing into the water without permission.

'Gwen must have spent lots and lots of time training him. It was kind of her to say she'd help with the new puppy.'

'We're going to need every piece of advice and time she can give us. Wasn't it good news her telling us when we went to dinner at her house on Friday that the breeder she got Jumbo from will have a litter available in three weeks and that we can have first choice?'

'I can't wait; can you and Evan keep from jumping up and down?'

'We need glue on our feet.' They were approaching Lighthouse Point with a mile-long causeway leading out to it.

Three weeks and the new school year wouldn't have started, Oliver thought. Even if the worst came to the worst Gerard and

Elizabeth wouldn't have taken him back with them to New York by then. Unless they decided they needed extra time there for preparations. But Oliver refused to let that thought continue. He turned his face to Sarah's. 'Can I ask you something?'

'Of course you can.' She stopped walking. 'Anything in the world.'

'Could you love me like I was your real son?'

'Let's sit down on that big flat topped rock – the one that isn't covered with seaweed.' Sarah did so and Oliver joined her, his eyes full of expectancy. A couple of gulls, discreetly absent until now, hovered overhead uttering their hoarse throated caterwauling. She waited for them to flap off into the distance before continuing. 'I was down here on the beach soon after I moved to Sea Glass and the feeling came over me that a child was walking along beside me.' She put her arm around him. 'When you, Evan and I met on the common and there was such a power of connection, I was convinced that child had been you. That somehow your spirit and mine, in some inexplicable way, had come together because we were meant to find each other. I still like to believe that. Just as I'm sure that the intense pull to answer Evan's letter to Nan Fielding, and his same response on finding mine to him when he returned from his book tour, and then your need for our help when he and I turned up together, were events woven into place by benevolent forces beyond our full understanding. Skeptics might laugh themselves silly over our gullibility – the giving way to fantasy culminating in coincidence. They could be right. Maybe all the three of us are squirrelly. I can live very happily with that. You actually seeing and talking with Nat could mean you've an even bigger imagination than Evan and me. I lean toward Nat having shown up as your friend in need. One day you may feel differently about that. Right now I'm counting on his faith that all will go well for you.'

'Oh, thank you, Sarah, for not thinking I'm nuts. It's such a huge relief. I love you and Evan so much. And I could see yesterday Grandpa understood why.'

'He's a remarkable man. It was all there in his face, Oliver – his goodness, kindness and overwhelming devotion to you.' Her voice choked.

'Did you see his expression when I gave him the blanket you made for him with "Grandpa" on it?'

'I'll remember it always.' They got up and walked on a little further before summoning Jumbo to heel. 'Have you thought about what to call the puppy?'

'Evan and I want you to pick the name.'

'You do?' He stopped in his tracks. 'Super! We'll have to give Dusk lots of extra spoiling so she doesn't feel left out for a minute. I think we should get her some toys on the day we bring her baby brother or sister home.'

They talked cheerfully about all that would be needed – food and water bowls, baskets and training gates – until they mounted the wooden steps and crossed the garden with its shading trees and blooming flower bed, which brought Gwen back to mind because she had helped show Sarah what to plant and how to tend them. On several of those occasions Twyla had also been there. And Sonny, seated in a chair on the patio, his head tilted at times to the music of birdsong. Blooming among the roses and hydrangeas, and all the flowers' names Oliver hadn't yet learned, were the memories that he knew would remain linked with their scent forever.

Once in the house Oliver went looking for Dusk. Sarah got out her knitting and they sat companionably in the living room until she looked at her watch and said maybe it was time for lunch. She'd made up a batch of gazpacho the night before, but wasn't sure he'd like a cold soup.

'But I would.' He set about laying the table. 'Twyla makes it and Grandpa said Grandma Olive did too.' Demonstrating the truth of his enthusiasm he had two bowls followed by an egg salad sandwich. Beforehand Sarah asked him if he'd like to say grace, apologizing for neglecting this on other occasions when knowing it had always been a part of his childhood.

'I can always say it silently if you'd rather?'

'Not a chance. Evan will like it and I'm eager to get on board.' Sarah kissed the top of his head as she got up to refill his lemonade glass.

An hour later he left with Jumbo for his piano practice. He found Twyla looking particularly happy. 'Life seems to be coming up good, lamb baby.' She cradled him close when she came into the kitchen, where she and Gwen had been sitting having coffee. 'I went to see your grandpa this morning and he enjoyed yesterday's visit with Sarah and Evan, and he's hoping you and she can go see him early afternoon tomorrow. He's got something going on in the morning.'

Oliver was instantly anxious. 'With his doctor?'

'He'll be there. But no cause to fret; just a meeting. Happens routinely at places like Pleasant Meadows. Can't get away from red tape these days,' but while she said this she looked happy, so Oliver didn't think there could be anything new wrong with Grandpa. Sonny wandered into the kitchen, but afterward followed Oliver into the piano room and sat listening to him practice. He looked tired and fell asleep within moments. Oliver went through his small repertoire including *Chopsticks* and after about half an hour Gwen came in, produced a sheet from inside the bench and began working with him on *Michael Row the Boat Ashore*, which he'd told her he really, really liked. At the end of the session Gwen told him she was proud of him. And not to brag or anything, he was pleased with himself.

He stayed on for awhile when finished, talking and laughing with her and Twyla. The one disappointment was that Sonny didn't wake up, but Gwen explained he would be tired because of his outing with Sid Jennson, which was always an event, invigorating at the time but leaving him sleepy afterward. At four Oliver decided it was time to return to the Cully Mansion to spend his self-allotted time with Feathers. He didn't worry about Gerard and Elizabeth complaining that he'd been gone for too much of the day. That only happened when she was in a mood about something that made her lash out at him or sometimes Mrs Poll – for stupid stuff like her dropping a cup that was chipped anyway. And that morning when he'd left she'd been extra nice to him for some reason. Maybe she'd gotten Gerard to promise to stop drinking. As hoped, no tense atmosphere greeted his return. They were in the living room. Elizabeth had just come in from having her hair done. He'd have guessed so, even if she hadn't said. There were new light streaks in it and it was a little shorter.

'Looks nice,' Oliver told her.

Unfortunately Gerard got rid of her smile. 'What's all this in aid of, Liz?'

'My trip to Boston tomorrow.' Oliver had to admire her for not snapping, but perhaps that was because Gerard's voice wasn't slurred for once.

'I don't know why you have to go dodging down there.'

'I've told you. I'm meeting an old friend who's recently moved there.'

'Who?'

'Why the interrogation?' Was the calm about to end? 'Someone you've never met. We were in high school together.' Elizabeth was fidgeting with the shoulder of her blouse. 'Paula . . . Riviera.'

Couldn't she have done better than that? Oliver waited blank-faced for Gerard's reply, but he merely picked up a magazine and began turning its pages upon flopping into a scruffy chair. The evening meal was the usual sort: small portions of chicken, a few tufts of limp broccoli, and two or three baby carrots. Having had his offer to do the dishes accepted, Oliver did so in the ancient sink, put them away and went into the living room to talk to Feathers who gave him a couple of beady-eyed stares from his perch before closing his eyes. He wasn't an energetic bird at the best of times and now he seemed – Oliver groped for the word – lethargic, but it was evening. He told him to get some shut-eye and covered the cage with its sheet. On going up to his room he was hoping for a visit from Nat, but though he kept opening his eyes after getting into bed the window seat remained unoccupied.

When he came down stairs the next morning at eight Elizabeth had already left for the drive to Boston. Gerard made an effort to chat during breakfast about how the baseball season was going, somehow bringing climate change into it, which Oliver didn't get, and Gerard himself seemed unable to track. Was he wondering if Elizabeth's outing involved meeting a boyfriend? Gerard half-heartedly helped clear the table and said it was OK for Oliver to spend the day with his friends before disappearing into his office. Would a bottle and glass be produced from a drawer?

Oliver said a prayer this wouldn't happen. Whatever his lack of closeness to his uncle, there were times when he felt sorry for him and Elizabeth and the way they seemed to be in danger of destroying their marriage. He did the breakfast dishes and then went upstairs and laid on his bed for a while reading one of Miss Emily's books. This one was called *Intrigue in Interlaken*. The heroine, who had overheard two men talking in a train corridor about smuggling watches – the conversation had taken place in Finnish which she spoke fluently – was being relentlessly chased by a masked and goggled figure down a ski slope called a black diamond. It was quite exciting and he liked the girl because she had a boxer dog named Mozart and a cat called Chopin; but again his hope was that he'd look up to see Nat on the window seat. It didn't happen, even after he opened his eyes from a brief doze.

At ten thirty he set off for Sarah's. She told him that she'd just been on the phone with Evan and that he'd sent his love and was so proud of his setting aside his fears to take the inhaler out to Rolling Stone. She also asked if he'd like to call Brian and see if it would be all right with his parents if he came out to lunch with them in Ferry Landing before they went to see Grandpa at one.

'Cool!' Actually Oliver was a little worried that Brian might be feeling on the outs with him because he had yet to persuade Gerard and Elizabeth to a sleepover at the Cully Mansion, which would allow for a midnight exploration of the cellar. But there was no trace of crabbiness in Brian's voice when his mother put him on the phone. When they arrived to pick him up he was waiting at his open front door – with his glasses askew as if he hadn't wanted to waste a moment straightening them – and a smile the size of a crescent moon on his thin face. Good old Brian! Sarah took them to one of their favorite places to eat; it was similar in its good home-style food and friendly atmosphere to Matey's in Sea Glass. And they soon got to addressing each other by the pirate names Grandpa had given them along with their wooden swords.

'I'll have to remember to keep this straight when I tell Evan,' Sarah laughed. 'You, Brian, are Captain B. Curdle and Oliver is Walker Plank. That should set him quaking. I'm OK; I can fight you off with my knitting needles.'

During the meal they filled her in on other prime examples of their exploits over the years. Oliver brimmed with happiness that Sarah and Brian had taken to each other big time. Before leaving the restaurant plans had been outlined for activities during his visits to Bramble Cottage and Brian asked her if she'd teach him to knit along with Oliver – and Evan, when he was there. It was when they dropped Brian back at his house that he brought up the hoped-for overnight stay at the Cully Mansion.

'I'm going to make it happen soon, Bri. Promise.'

'What a nice kid. I can see why the two of you are such great friends,' said Sarah on the drive to Pleasant Meadows.

'He's like a brother. Although,' Oliver paused, 'that doesn't always mean as much as it should. Gerard could have stood by my Dad when he married Mom.'

'Perhaps he wanted to, but was afraid to stand up to his parents.'

'I'd rather think it was that, rather than liking the idea of being the only one to get their money.'

Sarah pulled into the parking area. 'I'm with you; I'd prefer to believe gain didn't come into it. If so what bitter irony if there wasn't anything like what was expected by way of an inheritance? There are people who talk and spend big without a thought for the future and it could be your paternal grandparents were in that category.'

Mr Braddock came out of his office to walk them down the hall to Grandpa's room and then tactfully retreated. Grandpa lay in his bed by the window with his eyes closed. Willie Watkins was seated on his bed jabbering to himself.

'Listen here, Robin Polly, you great tree trunk! No daughter to me, you ain't, sending the cops in to drag me out of the home I made for myself. What harm was I doing no one in that cellar? Done with you is what I am. You keep your rotten fangs off your poor old dad, or I'll be the one putting the law on you.' He turned his unshaven, bleary-eyed face to Sarah and Oliver. 'That's what I see when I take a look – fangs in that greasy slop.'

'Do you mean her soup, Mr Watkins?' Oliver asked as if this were a quite ordinary conversation.

'Greasy slop's what it was.' Willie turned away as if losing interest; either that or he was tired, because he flopped back on his blanket and pillow and several moments passed before he muttered anything else. 'Never rated Robin as a cook – too cheap to buy her old dad a steak. Stuck to her story I couldn't chew it.' Oliver wondered if seeing him would be a wakeup call for Gerard. His eyes closed as Grandpa's opened – followed by a smile.

'Dreaming you were here,' his tremulous hand shifted sideways, 'both of you. Chairs . . . bring cl-close . . . been wai . . . waiting.'

Oliver kissed his cheek and Sarah did the same before they drew two chairs up to the bed. 'Love you, Grandpa, always and forever.'

'Know. You've been ev-every thing . . . man could ask of . . . grandson and . . . more. Same as your moth . . . mother.' The devotion was visible in every worn, weary line of the immeasurably dear face. 'Couldn't rest,' his eyes went to Sarah, 'af-afraid . . . leaving him with . . . out those who'll love him like he des . . . erves.'

He went silent, re-gathering his strength. 'Twyla worried about her age, but says best thi . . . this way. Trust her judge . . . ment. Good woman. Gr-great friend. Certain you and . . . your gentleman friend . . . liked him, like you – kind faces, will do right by our boy.'

Sarah laid her hand over his blue-veined hand. 'We love him more than can be fully expressed.' Her voice broke. 'You have my solemn word Evan and I will let nothing stop us from being an ongoing presence – more if possible – in his life.'

'They're who I want to be with, Grandpa,' Oliver choked up, fighting back the tears. 'They know I'll want Twyla to be part of us.'

'Trust. God is g-good. Not true that busin . . . ess about blood thick . . . er than water.' The obviously tiring eyes returned to Sarah. 'Adop . . . ted Clare. Blessing till last for her mo . . . ther and me. Know she and Max smi . . . ling.' His eyelids flickered and closed.

Oliver sat with his hand in Sarah's. They stayed by the bed another half hour, not just in case Grandpa woke, but from the need to be near him. It was there for Sarah too, and Oliver was aware that the bond between them was being forged into one that was sacred. He knew, without any of the doubts that had come about whether or not Nat was real, that his Mom and Dad and Grandma Olive were in that room.

On the drive home neither he nor Sarah spoke about what had been said. Not only was it unnecessary, it would have taken away from what had been. He searched for the word and heard it in Grandpa's own voice – 'transcendent.' She did tell him when they neared Bramble Cottage that the next day she was going to meet up with her friend in Portland, the one whose wedding had first brought her to Maine, but would return by evening. The cell phone in her purse rang just as they entered the front door. It was Evan, and she talked to him while Oliver went in search of Dusk and found her snuggled down on the bed in his room. When he came downstairs with the cat in his arms, Sarah was in the kitchen and held out the phone to him.

'Hi, Oliver,' said Evan's voice in his ear, 'I've been hoping you and Sarah could come to Boston this weekend to take a look at my condo so you can decide together whether to keep it for weekends and vacations when I move to Sea Glass, but I agree with her that might be pushing things with your aunt and uncle.'

'Right.' Oliver would have loved to have gone, but saw the wisdom of not risking putting Gerard's and Elizabeth's backs up. 'We can do it another time, can't we?'

'Of course. It's a must. Another reason I was eager to get you down here is my Aunt Alice; she is chomping at the bit to meet you both. So, how's this for an alternative – I bring her with me when I come on Friday morning? Sarah's all for it, but I have to keep to the rules.' Evan's laugh made everything better than all right. 'It has to be a three-way decision.'

'I'm chomping too. From all you've told us about her she sounds super nice.'

'She likes to sail, so we could try renting a boat for the weekend and see how you take to it.'

'Cool!'

'There is one thing I should warn you about Aunt Alice.'

'What?'

'She spoiled me rotten as a kid and I've a nasty suspicion that half an hour in your presence will see her starting up her old tricks. Boys who read and love animals are a terrible weakness of hers. So beware!'

They continued talking for a little while before Oliver handed the phone back to Sarah. He tactfully went into the living room but even so he heard her say: 'Let's hope you and Aunt Alice get lucky at one of the galleries in the next few days. Maybe my going to Portland to show Anne that drawing is pointless, but I'm really interested in getting her opinion of it.' A pause. 'Thanks for believing we're making progress. I do feel Willie Watkins may have narrowed the search with his talk about fangs.' Oliver's curiosity bubbled to the boiling point, but he wouldn't have dreamed of asking Sarah what she and Evan had been discussing.

When he came back into the kitchen she asked him if he'd like to go to the five o'clock movie. There was a film on about a boy who befriended a stray dog that he'd mentioned he'd like to see, and afterward they could go for pizza, if getting back to the Cully Mansion around eight wouldn't be too late. Oliver said he was sure it would be OK, especially since Elizabeth had said she might not be back from Boston until mid-evening and Gerard had said he could be gone as long as he liked. Even so, Sarah rang his uncle's phone and, getting no answer, left a message on the answering machine.

The movie theater in Sea Glass was tiny. Walking into it Oliver and Sarah dubbed it the Elf Theatre. The film they were going to see was in the basement, making them feel like a pair of Hobbits, which got them laughing so much that Oliver spilled some of his popcorn. They both enjoyed the storyline. The dog who had been labeled savage became, through a boy's love, the hero who saved the town from evildoers. Entirely satisfactory, Oliver and Sarah agreed while eating pizza afterward. It had been for him a very special day, making the thought of returning to the Cully Mansion even more unwelcome than usual. Sarah walked him up to the front door and saw him inside after a final hug. As soon as it closed behind him he was inexplicably seized by a sense of dread; it darkened the already dim hall, cast shadows where they shouldn't have been. All this before Elizabeth appeared in the living-room doorway.

'So you again grace us with your presence! Well, I hope you've enjoyed your outing!' She hurled the words at him, eyes blazing, face so contorted he could have been looking at someone he'd never seen before. 'It's all about you, Oliver, isn't it? And how hard done by you feel unless surrounded by those prepared to pander to your every whim. More the fools they are to be taken in!'

'What have I done?' He was bewildered, his legs about to crumble under him. He grabbed hold of a piece of furniture.

'Done? Exactly nothing when it comes to showing an ounce of appreciation for Gerard's and my attempts to make you happy. It's been all about what we didn't do. Didn't get you a dog. Didn't get you a cat. Didn't, didn't, didn't!' Her hands were all over the place twitching, clutching, and slashing. He braced himself for her to come at him, but was too numb to shrink. 'And now you've got even, haven't you?'

'How?' The word squeezed itself out.

'By killing the bird we gave you.'

'Feathers?' The shadows in the hall thickened and began to swirl.

'I'm supposed to be grateful you bothered to name it. A nice homecoming for me after my day out to walk in to find it dead in its cage. I imagine that accounts for your timing. Why should I get to escape for even a short while from this mausoleum? Let's plan a surprise for her. You could count on Gerard not noticing. He's always on some other planet.'

'How am I supposed to have killed him?' There was a drumbeat in Oliver's ears.

'Squeezed the life out of it, I suppose. It's hard to imagine what sort of twisted mind could . . .' Only her voice now . . . she had faded . . . everything was going dark. Somewhere from a long way off came the pounding roar of what might be Gerard's voice.

'For God's sake, let him alone, Elizabeth.'

Oliver was spinning downward through the shadows into complete darkness.

What seemed like a long time later he woke to discover that he was in his room; a small lamp was on and someone was sitting beside him on the bed. He wished it could have been Nat, but it was Gerard.

'Back with us. Good.' He smoothed down his thinning dark hair. 'Glad I was in time to catch you before you hit the floor. So sorry about Elizabeth losing it like that. Of course she doesn't believe you killed that parakeet. It was probably just sickly from the start. What do these pet shops care what they palm off?' He paused and on receiving no answer continued. 'Something she won't talk about must have happened today to set her off. I could tell the moment she walked in the door that she was working herself up to lashing out. I got some of it first.'

'It doesn't matter.' Oliver felt nothing, not even the wish for him to go away. 'Horrible for her, finding Feathers like that.'

'Yes, well . . . that's very kind and understanding of you. Is there anything I can get you, or would you like to go back to sleep?'

'Sleep, please.'

Gerard stood looking down at him as if uncertain whether to make some physical gesture, before turning and going out the door. The clock on the bedside table with the lamp showed that only a half hour had passed since Oliver's return to the house. He closed his eyes and willed himself back to sleep, but the memory of Elizabeth's hate-filled words clamored inside his head. They sped up, faster and faster, vibrating so savagely he was sure he was going to faint again. Maybe he did. Suddenly Nat was on the window seat, but he didn't stay there; he came to stand at the foot of the bed. There was another difference from his previous visits. He appeared less substantial. Not quite, but almost, transparent. And older . . . quite a lot older . . . but still Nat.

'You can't see me clearly, Oliver,' he said, 'because of what you've just been through. Cruel, frightening and unjust. Gerard is lost in himself most of the time, but he was right in what he said to you just now. Feathers died because he wasn't strong.'

'I didn't love him like I should have,' Oliver answered drearily. 'Knowing that is even harder to take than Elizabeth saying I killed him. I feel so guilty. Trying to pretend would be a lie to try and make myself feel better.'

'I understand. You'd feel the worst kind of hypocrite. Often it is the people who have the least cause who reproach themselves most. But sometimes even the hardened have an awakening. Today Elizabeth saw herself for the first time in a long while for what she has become; that's what caused her to lose control – the desperate need to make someone else, anyone but her, the enemy. I've grown very fond of you since you came here.' Nat was fading until only his voice remained. 'Take heart you'll soon be where you belong with those who love you. Face the next and last hurdle; it will lead you where you need to go. You'll want to resist, but don't – the answer is there for you in *Through the Looking-Glass*. The time has come . . .'

'Will I see you again?'

The thinnest of echoes. 'Put a smile on Feather's beak.'

'What?'

There was no reply.

Oliver lay in bed without moving. The numbness he guessed was the result of shock had lifted sufficiently for him to wrestle wearily with what Nat had said about staying on a little longer at the Cully Mansion. Advice from a ghost who could come and go in the blink of an eye! Right! Oliver managed a tremulous smile. At the beginning, when Gerard and Elizabeth had brought him here, he'd been determined to make them dislike him so much they'd beg to get rid of him, but almost immediately he'd seen the distress this would cause Twyla whose focus had to be on Grandpa. So he had behaved, done his very best not to stir up any trouble. But now he had Sarah to go to, and after Elizabeth's frightening outburst how could she or Gerard create a stink? They wouldn't want the police involved. So all he had to do was wait till they went to bed and walk out. But Nat had told him to stay to face the next . . . and last hurdle. And he had to trust him in this, thought Oliver, feeling suddenly dreadfully tired. Not doing so would be telling himself that Nat wasn't real, that nothing depended on taking his advice – when here was the chance to find out. The decision whether or not to leave tonight mattered because tomorrow Sarah would be gone all day in Portland. Perhaps if he slept for an hour or two he'd wake to the right answer.

He pulled the covers up but a thread of thought snagged him back as he was about to drift off. Evan and his Aunt Alice were on a mission, like sleuths in the sort of books he wrote, searching galleries in Boston for something Sarah had said Willie Watkins had helped narrow down, something about teeth. Mrs Poll's teeth . . . Willie had talked about them . . . only he'd called them something else. Oliver couldn't reach the word – it was floating away from him. He was muddled . . . had to be . . . because why would anyone go looking for Mrs Poll's teeth?

He woke the next morning feeling anxious but accepting of Nat's advice to stay put for the moment. He clung to the know-ledge that Sarah would be back from Portland that evening. In the meantime he would see what the day brought. If there was trouble there wouldn't be any question that going to Twyla was right thing to do, but he hoped for her sake he wouldn't have to do that. He took his bath, a shower being far too modern an invention for the house, and got dressed in the first T-shirt and pair of shorts that came to hand. As always he removed Evan's card from the top of the dresser and put it in his pocket. His dread of going downstairs increased when he stood at the top and saw Elizabeth in the hall below. When he reached her she was still standing in the same place, rubbing her hands up and down her folded arms. She looked as if she hadn't gotten much, if any, sleep. There were dark shadows under her eyes, making her face look starkly pale.

'Hi,' he said in her general direction. He held his breath. Braced himself for whatever might be coming.

'I came up to your room last night but you were asleep.' Her voice was strained to a thin flat line. 'I wanted to tell you how sorry I was for everything I said to you. It was inexcusable. I'm not sure what came over me, except that I hate driving long distances and panic that the stress will bring on one of my head-aches.' She pressed a hand to her forehead.

So she was making an excuse. 'It doesn't matter.'

'Yes, it does. You must hate me.'

'I don't hate people.' Oliver wondered which of them looked more wooden.

'Gerard says you have every right.'

'I don't want to talk about this anymore.'

'But we must. I don't want you left with terrible memories about that bird's death. Please let me do something to help lessen the damage I've done.' There was now a look of desperate appeal in her eyes. 'I buried him in the garden this morning. Gerard was too squeamish to do it.'

He would be. Oliver felt a flicker of sympathy for her. Gerard would always leave the difficult or unpleasant for her to handle.

Elizabeth said quickly, 'But I thought if we were to have a little memorial service this evening, that might give you the chance to express your feelings about,' she was clearly searching for the name, 'about Feathers and what he meant to you – the hope perhaps that he's now flying free, or something of the sort. I'd like to think it may help put this unhappy episode, especially my part in it, behind you.'

Oliver stared at her, appalled. It would do the opposite – make the memory even worse. He was about to say he couldn't, wouldn't do it, when he remembered what Nat had said about a hurdle being faced – one that would lead him where he needed to go. And yes . . . a mention of Feathers. 'OK, Elizabeth, if you think it a good idea.'

She visibly relaxed. 'I've thought about who you'd want here. Twyla, of course . . .' This had to be important to her if she were prepared to make this concession, but Oliver was only too ready to let her off the hook. He wasn't going to put Twyla through watching his discomfort.

'Afternoons and evenings are her hours for looking after Sonny. And,' he added quickly, 'asking Gwen to come wouldn't be kind; she's such an animal lover she'd find such a service upsetting.'

'Yes, of course.' The relief showed. 'Sarah?'

'She'll be in Portland.'

'Disappointing.' Elizabeth twitched at her sleeves. 'That would seem to leave your friend Brian. You've been wanting him to spend a night, haven't you? What better time than this for the two of you to be together?'

The trapped feeling, one of being squeezed dry, vanished. Hope relit its candle. Here was an irresistible offering. Suddenly Oliver felt a surge of excitement; he was starting to get the riddle Nat had presented him with last night. The hurdle was the memorial service for Feathers and the place it would lead him to was the cellar, which he had promised only to visit with Brian. There was more to be unraveled; the reference to *Through the Looking-Glass* would at some point fit into place. His original interest in searching the cellar was to find a picture of Nat as a boy that would reassure him that his visitor's appearances in the bedroom had not been imaginary, but something insistent was telling him that there was something down there of far greater importance.

'Sorry, Elizabeth, I was thinking. It's great of you about Brian – fingers crossed that he can come.' Actually, there wasn't a shadow of doubt in Oliver's mind about this. Nat knew he would much prefer not to go down to the cellar at dead of night alone. 'Shall I phone Brian now?'

'Give me the number and I'll do it.' It made perfect sense for her talk to either Reggie or Mandy Armitage, but Oliver also felt sure she wasn't eager to hand over her cell phone and give him the opportunity to call others and spill the beans about her treatment of him yesterday. There was no house phone at the Cully Mansion. Saying she would be back in a moment, she left the hall, to return shortly with the news that Brian's father had said he would bring him over at seven that evening after he'd eaten.

So much for inviting him to dinner. But Elizabeth couldn't become someone else overnight, and Brian would have a much better meal at home. Mandy and Reggie were both good cooks. Actually, the timing was good. He and Brian could go up to the bedroom shortly after the service, without Elizabeth and Gerard feeling they had to sit and chat for too long, which Oliver was sure they would much rather not be stuck doing.

Elizabeth made a further gesture by having breakfast with him. Cereal and toast. Gerard came in halfway through. 'Looks like you two have made up,' he said, pouring himself black coffee. 'Onboard with her idea, Oliver? Not sure I go for it, but I'll sit in. Don't have to wear a suit, do I?' This was clearly an attempt at a joke.

Elizabeth closed her eyes, hands gripping the edge of the table. Oliver produced a smile, but doubted Gerard noticed. Having made his attempt at helping along a return to normal, he was all too eager to escape to his office. Elizabeth was also clearly ready to make a break for it. Saying she needed to take a walk to clear her head, she too left the kitchen. This wasn't unusual and this morning she did have reason to be distracted. Not only had the last half hour clearly not been easy on her, another concern might loom: the question of whether Gerard would stay sufficiently sober not to embarrass himself and her at the service.

After doing the breakfast dishes Oliver spent an hour cleaning the kitchen. If all of Mrs Poll's efforts couldn't get it to sparkle, he didn't expect much from his, but it gave him something to do. He would miss her, but he could always go and see her. The fear that he wouldn't get away from this house was gone. Sarah and Evan would make that happen. There was only this remaining day – and the start of the next – to be gotten through. And from seven onward he would have Brian at his side. He expected the time till then to drag, but it didn't. Back in his bedroom, he took down his two suitcases from the closet shelf and began emptying his dresser drawers, the ones with the drawings of ships on the backs, and neatly packed his clothes. He didn't take down the framed photographs of his parents, Grandpa and Grandma Olive, just in case Elizabeth or Gerard should come into the bedroom. This was unlikely, but he couldn't take the chance of their noticing the photos were gone and realize something was up. The suitcases went back on the closet shelf.

Oliver returned downstairs. Elizabeth was neither in the living room nor the kitchen, so either she was still out walking or had retreated to be alone, unless she was in the office with Gerard. Earlier he had thought it wouldn't be a good idea to go see Twyla today, but now he was feeling so much more hopeful that if the end was in sight he could go see her, Gwen and Sonny, without worrying about telling Elizabeth or Gerard. He left a note on the kitchen table saying where he was going and set off.

After a week of warm days and sunshine the weather had changed overnight. It was chilly under gray skies. The tall pines swayed and the other trees shivered in the sharp breeze. The patches of ocean he could see from the road showed waves scurrying along in the direction he was going, as if they too were eager to get somewhere else. Grandpa would have predicted a storm before nightfall. He should have worn a jacket, but Twyla or Gwen would lend him one if he took Jumbo for a walk, as he hoped to do.

He loved the house on Ridge Farm Rise almost as much as

Bramble Cottage. Gwen let him in, delighted as always to see him, and led the way to the book room where Twyla was seated on the sofa with Sonny, reading to him from a magazine. She got up at once and held out her arms.

'Come here, lamb baby, are you ever a sight for sore eyes!'

'Just what I was thinking,' said Gwen.

'Where have you been?' Sonny got to his feet as Twyla stopped hugging Oliver and stood up smiling. 'I've missed you.' The blue eyes were unexpectedly bright in contrast to the worn face and gray hair. 'I like you being here.' It was happily, not fretfully said and tears filled Oliver's eyes. If Sonny could at times work his way through the confusion that had become his life to show the kind and gentle man inside, anything was possible with sufficient trust and courage. Oliver went over and gave him the same kind of hug Twyla had given him.

'I love you, Sonny,' he said. 'You've taught me so much.'

'Wish could've had you in my life longer. Teach . . . yes, what I do. Teach you a new piece. Come to the piano. Never know – could be the last time.'

'It won't be. I promise I'll come back.'

'I may have moved away by then.'

Oliver didn't know what to say to this. Sonny knew he was disappearing into himself; that time was robbing him of those on the outside day by day until he would be entirely, utterly alone. Oliver saw the grief on Gwen's face and the sadness on Twyla's. He took Sonny's extended hand and went to sit with him at the piano. For nearly an hour music flowed through the house; lifting it, thought Oliver, toward heaven. The final piece was *The Swan.* When the last note ebbed away Sonny got up abruptly and, without a word, went to his room.

Gwen stood at the foot of the stairs, looking up, before turning to Oliver. 'Have I already told you it's by the French composer Camille Saint-Saens and that it's always had a special place in Sonny's heart and mine?'

He nodded, too moved to speak.

'So hauntingly beautiful. He played it at a students' piano recital when he was twelve. I remember how the hall rang with applause.'

'I'll never forget hearing him play it today.'

'Neither will I, dear. A sea glass moment,' Gwen touched his cheek, 'if ever there was one.'

They went into the kitchen where lunch was waiting. Twyla had made her special ham and asparagus casserole. The three of them sat talking for a while afterward about nothing important, just ordinary, cozy conversation. Then Oliver took Jumbo for a walk down to the beach and sat on the steps leading up to Bramble Cottage. It was growing colder, the waves darker and faster-paced, frothing with dingy gray foam. But the rain had held off and he had the jacket Twyla had lent him. Even if this hadn't been the case, Oliver wouldn't have budged. He needed to feel this closeness to Sarah and Evan. Each time he twisted round to look at the cottage he felt sure, as Sarah had told him she had done the moment she saw it, that it was waiting for him with open arms.

It had just started to rain in slow drips and drabs when he returned with Jumbo; by night it would be storming. Gwen and Twyla invited him to stay for dinner. They were having fried chicken which Gwen said she hadn't eaten in years but had been suddenly yearning for out of the blue. He said he wished he could but Brian was finally getting to come for a sleepover. And it wouldn't do not to get back till the last minute and spoil things with Elizabeth and Gerard. Also, given the weather Brian's parents might want to bring him in from Ferry Landing earlier than planned. So, at four thirty, Twyla drove him to the Cully Mansion, as always watching him mount the steps and go in the front door.

Typically, as opposed to yesterday evening, his return suggested he was entering an empty house. The overhead light was not on and only a couple of small table lamps fought back against the shadows. Then he heard Elizabeth's voice, overflowing at high pitch from Gerard's office. Any response was inaudible, but the source of the argument immediately became obvious.

'I begged you, begged you to stay sober for once. How does this look? I made this overture and now we've got this kid coming!' Silence, then: 'Oh, what does it matter? With luck we'll be out of here soon. I've taken the necessary steps to drag us up from the depths, while you've sunk further and further into the bog.'

'For God's sake, Elizabeth, you know why!' Gerard's voice finally broke through in tones of anguish.

'We've been through this way too many times. I'm done! If you insist on going through life believing you're a murderer, you're on your own from this point out!'

Only the certainty that the office door was about to open got

Oliver moving. He was halfway up the stairs when Elizabeth's voice caught up with him. 'Have you had a good day?' She didn't wait for an answer. 'Unfortunately Gerard is deluged with work, so it doesn't look as though he can make it for our little service at seven.'

'That's OK.' Oliver almost said it would be fine with him if she cancelled what for him still loomed as a hurdle, but then she might take that as an opportunity to put off Brian's visit, using the weather as an excuse. 'It doesn't matter how small it is, does it?'

'No, of course not. There has, however, been an increase in numbers.' The face below was veiled by the dim lighting. 'I got a call this afternoon from Emjagger's and Rolling Stone's mother, asking if it would be all right for them all, including her husband, to stop by this evening. When I told her about the memorial service she said both boys are such great animal lovers they'd really hate not being present, offering their support at what has to be a very sad time for you.'

'Right. I can picture their faces when she tells them of this golden opportunity . . . to do good, I mean. Is it all right if I go and read until Brian gets here?'

'Absolutely. I'll send him up when he gets here, if that's what you'd like.'

'Yes, please.' The moment Oliver got inside his room he flopped down on the bed without bothering to turn on the reading lamp. The shock of what he'd overheard was fading. Believing you're a murderer is one of those figure of speech things. If you really are one it's not the sort of thing you can be unsure about. Clearly Gerard felt horribly guilty about something – that would account for his drinking and sleepwalking – but at this moment Oliver had enough to think about without trying to work out the cause. Those two coming with their enmity rekindled, if it had ever faded, by his taking the inhaler out to Rolling Stone in the kayak! They'd think he'd done that to make them look even smaller, and now here was the opportunity to get even by sitting smirking as he fumbled not to look ridiculous when struggling for what to say about Feathers – or just as bad, sanctimonious. With so much else going on in his life this shouldn't matter, but it did; perhaps the case of one seemingly small thing stretching to become the final straw. He rolled over and squeezed his eyes shut. He didn't think he slept, but he must have done, because when he opened his eyes the bedside lamp was on and when he sat up there was a boy sitting on the window seat. It should have been Nat because his voice still lingered inside Oliver's head. *Remember, the time has come . . . the time has come . . .* His own question: *The time for what, Nat?* The repeated whispered answer: *Phone Evan . . . phone Evan . . . phone Evan.* Not Nat on the window seat looking at him with concern, but Brian.

'You OK, Ol? You must've been dead to the world, because I sure couldn't wake you, not without tossing something and giving you a black eye.'

'Fine. Well, not really – it was pretty bad about Feathers.'

'What happened?' One of the great things about Brian was that he didn't waste time starting off with useless stuff.

Oliver swung his legs over the side of the bed. 'Elizabeth met me in the hall when I got back from being with Sarah most of yesterday. She told me Feathers was dead and accused me of killing him while she'd been gone in Boston. I asked her how she thought I'd done it and she said by squeezing the life . . .' Oliver choked, unable to go on. When he prised his hands away from his face Brian had joined him.

'Hey, I'm here now and I'm getting you out of this creep house. We'll slip out and run to Sarah's.'

'She went to Portland for the day and may not be home.'

'Then we'll go to Aunt Nellie's.'

Oliver shook his head. 'Thanks, Bri. That's what I wanted to do last night, but then Nat came and talked me out of it. I'll tell you what he said and how this morning it began to fit together when Elizabeth apologized and suggested the memorial service.'

Brian listened with few interruptions, not bothering to readjust his glasses when a poke of the fingers sent them askew. At the conclusion he sat staring at Oliver as if needing more time to take it all in. 'Wow!' he said at last. 'There has to be an important reason for Nat wanting us to explore the cellar. And I don't think it can be to find a picture of him because by now he knows you're sure he's real. Talk about Walker Plank and Captain B. Curdle preparing for a midnight raid.' A flash of lightning briefly lit up the room in suitably eerie fashion. 'Where do you have the cellar key?'

Oliver patted the bed. 'Under the mattress, right about where we're sitting.'

'Awesome. What does stink is those two coming over.'

'I felt like throwing up when Elizabeth told me. And I think it was she who called their mother rather than the other way round. From what Mrs Poll says both parents like their drink, so they'd be a sort of cover for Gerard if he couldn't resist having a few, but she found him so far gone already he now has to be kept out of the way.'

'Got you! I know it's an illness, but Gerard could try getting help.'

'I wonder if Elizabeth's tried to persuade him, or pushed him to man up and do it on his own.' Oliver decided not to say anything about the snippet of conversation he overheard earlier. Brian would have made much of the scarily thrilling idea of Gerard's really being a murderer. And it was not one Oliver wanted to be talking about as the time drew near to descend to the basement.

'They're sure one messed-up couple, but not your problem, Ol. I wonder if he'll come sleepwalking in on us tonight. It would be something to see.'

'About that dream I just had, or the tail-end of it.' Oliver spoke over a rumble of thunder. 'Do you have your cell phone with you?'

'Natch!' Brian dug into his pants' pocket and handed it over. 'Want to call Evan, right? I'll leave you to it,' he said nobly, 'while I hunt for the bathroom.'

'Three doors down on the right; this side.'

Brian departed with his Captain B. Curdle swagger and Oliver took Evan's card from his pocket; originally it had been given to have on hand in case of trouble from Emjagger and Rolling Stone. That need had not arisen until now, so this was Oliver's first time phoning Evan from the Cully Mansion. He tried the cell phone number first and held his breath for two rings. Then the enormous relief of hearing the familiar voice answer with a 'Hello?'

'Evan, it's me, Oliver. I'm in my bedroom calling from Brian's phone. I had to talk to you. Nat told me I should.'

Evan was like Brian in that he didn't waste time asking such questions as *What's wrong?* Or, *How can I help?* He said simply: 'Tell me.'

'Feathers died, but there's more, a lot more. Nat told me to call you or, I should say, I woke from a dream still hearing his voice.'

'I'm listening. I've got all the time in the world. Keep going until you've got it all out.'

It was amazing how simple it was; Evan might have been right there in the room; his strength and comfort wrapped itself around Oliver. Things that he had forgotten from last night's visit from Nat slipped into place. 'You do see I have to go down to the cellar tonight with Brian after Gerard and Elizabeth go to bed? I know I'll always be sorry if I don't.'

'Yes. I'd feel the same in your place. Just make sure you take a flash light, a couple if possible, in case the lights go out in this storm that's heading your way, or because someone turns them off. And keep that cell phone with you. If anything causes the least anxiety make sure you dial nine-one-one.'

'Promise.'

'Now back to Feathers. From the sound of it Elizabeth's heading for a breakdown. I'm sorry the little bird died and know you are too. I've had my regrets about feeling I didn't love sufficiently, but I think you'll realize on looking back that you gave all you could, possibly even more than was required. So let's get down to this memorial service and your role in it. I think I know what Nat was getting at about *Through the Looking-Glass*. I have the lines following the one starting out *The time had come . . .* memorized and think we can make a small alteration that will put a smile on Feathers' beak, while we wipe the smirks off those two idiotically named boys' faces. Do you have a notepad and something to write with handy?'

'Right here.' Oliver reached toward the bedside table. 'Ready.'

When Brian returned to the bedroom his best friend was off the phone and looking much better.

'Big help?'

'The best, but that's Evan. After helping me out with the service for Feathers, he told me that he'd just spoken to Sarah and she'd agreed not to head home from Portland tonight if the weather gets too bad. I'm glad because I'd be worried too. Even good drivers have accidents when it gets ugly. He said he also hopes to get here in the morning. And he told me something else to keep me going till then. Twyla's found a lawyer to help protect Grandpa's rights in planning my future. Nothing was going to be said to me until it's settled, but he said,' Oliver's face brightened still further, 'he thought the time had come. Sorry, Bri, but you'll have to wait to find out why I'm no longer worried about *those two*, watching me turn to jelly when I speak about Feathers . . . Hey, it's six twenty. I'd just as soon not have to go downstairs a minute sooner than necessary, but I'm suddenly starving, which means searching the kitchen for something to eat.'

'No need for that, matey,' said Brian in his best Captain B. Curdle voice. 'I told Mom that if you don't want to half starve in this house you have to get your own food much of the time, so she sent along packets of sandwiches, peanut butter cookies and cartons of juice. All in my backpack on the window seat.' He looked toward it. 'Wish Nat would join us,' he added wistfully.

Mandy Armitage had indeed provided quite a feast. When they'd finished everything but crumbs, they disposed of the wrappings in the waste bin – the cartons were not yet empty – and got down to discussing how long to wait after Elizabeth and Gerard came up to bed before going down to the cellar. Oliver suggested an hour, but Brian wisely thought two would be safer. He'd taken two flashlights out of the backpack along with the food and now received the congratulations from Walker Plank on his forethought.

'Evan was right; it would be stupid to go down without them. I should have asked Mrs Poll where I could find some.' At that moment they heard the distant sound of the doorbell and both got off the bed. 'Guess the time has come, Bri.'

'You do keep saying that!' Brian attempted to flatten his dark hair, only to send it springing back up. 'But if you will have your little mysteries what can I do? Push you overboard?'

'If you mean down the stairs, I'd sooner you didn't.' Oliver gave him a poke of the finger. 'I'm not a good bouncer.' They headed downstairs with more cheer than is usually the case with people about to attend a memorial service. There was no one in the hall; the arrivals had to be in the living room. Oliver's optimism wavered as they went in. Elizabeth, it wouldn't have been Gerard, had lighted candles on the mantelpiece and tables. Perhaps this was to be prepared in case the lights went out in the storm, which was now hammering the windows, or to make the place look like a church. Their pale yellow gleam added more shadows to the gloom, making the room look unholy rather than the other way round. Emjagger and Rolling Stone were on one sofa without an inch between them, their parents on the other. All four fixed in place like people in one of those very old photographs. Whatever the mom and dad had in the glasses they were holding was of that same brownish-yellow shade. Elizabeth was standing in front of the fireplace. She alone saw Oliver and Brian come in. No other heads had turned in their direction.

'There you boys are,' she said brightly. Too brightly. The false cheer emphasized her color-stripped face and the haunted look in her eyes. 'Brian, you don't know our guests, do you?' She made the introductions, bringing only a nod from the dad, but the mom said in a thrilled sort of voice how nice it was to meet Brian and see Oliver again. Her enthusiasm did not cause her to shift position other than to lean further back on the sofa.

'Nice to meet you all.' Brian stepped forward into the distorting candlelight with Oliver alongside him.

'And yet the circumstances! So bitterly sad! As I said to Elizabeth when she phoned, our boys Emjagger and Rolling Stone were devastated by the sweet little birdie's death. They so adore animals. You see how it is with them now; they can't bring themselves to say anything. They truly had to force themselves to come, because it was the right thing to do. They both adore Oliver and wish they could see more of him, though being so understanding they accept that he has other friends.'

Oliver hadn't looked at Elizabeth when the phone call was mentioned – that she was the one who had made it. Had she noticed she'd been given away? He didn't think so; her face was increasingly blank, as if she had left the room leaving only her outline behind. 'Shall we get started?' he asked her.

'What? Oh, yes . . . yes, we should. So sorry,' she pressed a candlelight glossed hand to her forehead, 'I'm afraid I feel one of my wretched headaches coming on.' Her gaze shifted in what seemed like slow motion to the four people on the sofas. 'So, although I hate to seem inhospitable, we'd best keep this short.'

'It'll be from the shock, Mrs Cully.' Emjagger broke his grief stricken silence to simper consolingly. 'Finding Feathers dead and stiff and all in its cage.' He turned to his equally pasty-skinned, greasy-haired, ferret-eyed brother. 'We sobbed our eyes out when we heard, didn't we, bro?'

'Couldn't stop.' Rolling Stone sagged against him. 'Poor Oliver, we kept saying, he has to be heartbroken – we've pictured him so often snuggled up in bed with his feathery friend, stroking its soft little head, singing a goodnight lullaby.'

Brian started to say something but the father cut in. 'Don't be more stupid than you can help, boy. Elizabeth's right. Let's move matters along. Get me a refill.' He shoved his glass at his wife who, far from looking put out, got up eagerly, went to the table with the bottles and poured herself a sizeable splash too. The moment she was reseated Elizabeth beckoned to Oliver and when he stood with his back to the fireplace, dropped into a chair, fingers instantly plucking at its already snagged fabric arms.

The room and the faces turned to Oliver. He was back on the phone with Evan, feeling his calm strength, remembering the strength of those arms around him when lifting him down from Nat's statue, secure in the bond between them – the unfailing belief in a father for his son, the willingness to work through any problem brought to him, however big or small. What Oliver was about to say felt exactly right. It wouldn't be painfully false or miserably forced and that wouldn't be so without Evan's intervention.

'This is for Feathers, with an acknowledgement to Lewis Carroll and *Through the Looking-Glass,*' said Oliver. 'I hope it puts a smile on your beak.' He hadn't brought down the note pad; the lines were fixed in his head. His voice came out strong and clear. '"*The time has come," the Walrus said, "to talk of many things: Of shoes – and ships – and sealing-wax – Of cabbages – and kings. And why the sea is boiling hot – and whether birds like swings."*'

'Feathers had to like that. You nailed it, Ol!' Brian slid a glance at Emjagger and Rolling Stone, who weren't smirking. They sat slack-faced, then spoke as one. 'What's this looking-glass thing?'

'You'd know if you ever read anything,' snapped back their father.

'So clever not to make it morbid,' said their mother.

'I changed the last line.' Oliver was pointing this out when a cell phone rang. Elizabeth, who had been sitting in a trance, stood up and groped in her skirt pocket, said she had to take this and headed for the doorway. Her first words sifted back into the room. 'Hi, have you been trying to reach me for long? You were? I turned off my cell while I was lying down earlier and forgot to put it back on until half an hour ago.' Footsteps heading up the staircase and then what sounded like a moan. But that could be, probably was, the wind.

'Time for us to be heading out.' The father seized what Oliver was sure must seem to be a golden opportunity and hurried his wife and sons into the hall, and with goodbyes flung over their shoulders they exited the front door.

'Well, that's over!' said Brian.

'Yes.' Oliver couldn't entirely share his relief. He had looked up to see Elizabeth clinging, head bent, to the banister post before seeming to walk blindly toward her room. Should he go up and knock on the door? He was hesitating when Gerard came out of his office and said something indistinguishable before going past Oliver and Brian and onto the stairs. At least he didn't stagger. He might even have sobered up. A door opened and, after a weighted moment, closed.

'Seems like that call she got was bad news,' said Brian.

'Right. I hope it wasn't to tell her someone's ill or has died.'

'Doesn't have to be that bad. Maybe she went after a job she didn't get. You said she went up to Boston yesterday – that could've been for an interview. It wouldn't mean she'd have to work there. If it was with a big firm they'd probably have branches everywhere.'

Oliver thought this over. It made sense if Elizabeth and Gerard were in a financial mess and would explain her returning so on edge that she'd gone out of control over Feathers. But if they were that hard up, why not sell the Cully Mansion which they both hated? Entering his bedroom with Brian a couple of steps behind, he listened for sounds of an argument coming their way, but only the rattle of tree branches against his window disturbed the empty feel of the house. Instead of feeling wide awake, he had to smother a yawn and saw Brian's face stretch into one. But maybe that wasn't a bad thing when they lay down on the bed. If they nodded off while talking that would be OK. A nap would revive them, while trying to kill time until the moment came to explore the cellar could have the reverse effect. They managed to stay awake for nearly an hour. Brian was always the early to bed, early to rise type, and then they went out like a pair of lights.

Oliver started up in bed at the grasp of a hand on his shoulder and Brian's voice telling him to wake up. 'What is it? What's happened?'

'It's four in the morning. If my foot hadn't started to itch I might have slept right on till the time I usually get up, and I was starting to think I had to throw a pitcher of water over you. Too bad the storm's over; I bet it stopped hours ago. No violent rumbles of thunder or cracks of lightning to startle us awake.'

'OK, I'm up.' Oliver got off the bed as Brian was doing. They had lain down fully clothed, apart from their shoes which they now scrambled into. Oliver got the key out from under the mattress and asked Brian if he had the cell phone. All set, they tiptoed out of the bedroom, each holding a flashlight. Unnecessary to turn them on. The house was still illuminated above and below the stairs; seemingly neither Elizabeth nor Gerard had come out from their bedroom to switch off the lights. More strangely several candles, reduced to stubs, still burned in the living room. Oliver and Brian exchanged glances as they stood looking in, then without a word blew them all out. The scent of wax hung slyly unpleasant on the air. It followed them down the hall to the cellar door. What if the old, rusty iron key didn't turn? But it did so, with a grating sound that jarred the ears disproportionately to the night silence. Oliver returned it carefully to his pocket and reached for the light switch. A naked but high-wattage bulb flared overhead. The stone steps that he'd pictured as narrow and twisting, were – though a little uneven – wide and went straight down; the concrete walls weren't crumbling or moldy. The air smelled stale but there was only a faint odor of damp. Oliver closed the door behind him and they started down quickly, reaching the floor below. Again, he didn't see what he'd expected – a place crammed to the point of permitting only sideways movement by an accumulation of a hundred years of junk, including dressers, armoires, boxes and trunks, all to be searched through before dawn. The space they stood in had to match in size much of the floor above, but it was empty. Completely empty. Someone must have had everything cleared out. It was obvious Miss Emily had clung to her possessions, other than the family albums, surrounding her. But what would she care about a cellar, which due to her lameness, was off limits to her? And so had nothing to do with her home as she knew it. Why not let its junk go to the needy over the years?

'Is it a let-down, or a relief?' Brian was still whispering.

'Neither,' replied Oliver staunchly. 'There have to be other rooms off this one. Where's the boiler and the rest of the plumbing stuff, and the door to the outside?' He pointed to the far end. 'That dark stretch of wall! It has to be an opening.'

Brian adjusted his glasses and stuck out his neck. 'Hey, so it is! There's no light on in there, that's the trouble.' They both turned on their flashlights as they drew nearer, directing the beams into the rectangle of gloom, shifting them around in search of a light switch. Oliver found it, just inside, on his left. A narrow room with a couple of turnings flared into view. Here was the boiler and water tank and there the door to the outside. A mattress and couple of blankets that looked as though they'd been rescued from a dump occupied a corner. Willie Watkins' bed. Oliver was glad he hadn't had to sleep on the floor. He also felt a tingling down his spine. He was close . . . very close now to what Nat had told him he was being led toward – not the picture he had originally hoped to find but something else . . . something much more important.

'Come on,' whispered Brian, 'let's take a look round those corners.' They took the one to their left first; the overhead bulb showed a narrow area with a low ceiling. Again, empty. Whoever had done the clean sweep had been thorough. Now there was only one more place to look. They crossed to the right – their last hope of finding . . . anything. Brian no longer looked like Captain B. Curdle about to board the treasure ship. There were three items in this gangway space, 'All of them barrels.' Oliver must have said the words aloud without hearing them over his buzzing excitement. The captain corrected him.

'Kegs.'

'Whatever. Help me to get them open.' He was bending down. 'This one's top seems to be stuck.'

'Move over, Walker Plank, these wicked fingers grip like steel.' Brian wasn't idly boasting. He had that top and the second off in a second. Nothing inside either of them. 'Third time's the charm, matey!' And so it proved. This one was three-quarters filled with some kind of oil and beneath its surface could be glimpsed what looked like bones. Oliver reached into the slime and pulled one out. It was shaped like a tooth. It was . . . what had to be a whale's tooth. He shook off the excess while Brian dragged off his T-shirt.

'Wipe it off with this.' He stood, pale and shivery, looking as Oliver did so. 'Scrimshaw,' he breathed. 'Looks like a frigate to me.'

'And here's the signature: Nat. It's his work and there are all those others in there. I wonder why he hid them in oil?'

'Stored, more like. That's what the whalers did with them on ship. To keep them from drying out was the idea. Aunt told me about it.'

Oliver put the one he was holding back and wiped off his hands. His mind was working furiously. 'I know why Elizabeth went to Boston. Willie Watkins talked to me about seeing bones in greasy liquid at the Cully Mansion. Mrs Poll thought he meant those she'd put in the soup she used to make for Miss Emily. And yesterday, when Sarah and I visited Grandpa, Willie was on about them again – only he spoke about fangs, and we thought he was talking about Mrs Poll's teeth. It stuck with Sarah; she mentioned them to Evan on the phone. And get this! She said something about it being the tip-off to what he and his Aunt Alice were searching for at the galleries. Don't you see, Bri, something had already made them think that Elizabeth had gone to Boston to sell something that she shouldn't. If it was one or more of these scrimshaws, they were right. Everyone knew Miss Emily put it in her will that any in the house at her death would go to the Sea Glass Historical Society.'

'Wow! She could be in a lot of trouble. Wonder how she knew about them?'

'She came here last January after she and Gerard got the police report that Willie had broken in down here – in the cellar. She could've clued in from what they told her about Willie going on about bones. Supposedly, she knows a lot about art. Or maybe she looked in the barrels to see if he'd chucked rubbish in them.'

'Bet it was Willie's bones.'

'Agree. But I wonder what got Sarah and Evan thinking Elizabeth was up to something like this in the first place?'

'Let me know when you find out.'

'She was frightened and feeling guilty when she got back last night; that's why she made me her scapegoat over Feathers. But I wouldn't want her to go to prison or anything like that. I think Gerard may have driven her to it. Actually, I heard her say something about that . . .'

'Ol, we need to get out of here! What if she comes down and catches us!'

'Right. And you have to be freezing!'

'True. Toss me my T-shirt; a little oil won't hurt me. Where are the flashlights?'

'On the floor by my feet; I'll grab them and you turn off the lights as we make a dash for it.'

They made up the steps in no time flat, relocked the cellar

door and tiptoed along the staircase wall as if one squeak of a floorboard would bring disaster. Oliver glanced into the living room where the lights, along with those in the hall, were still on. Gerard was standing with his back to them near the fireplace. Both boys froze. He slowly turned and they saw he was holding a gun aimed in their direction. If that weren't frightening enough, his ghastly stare was terrifying – more so for Brian who hadn't faced it before.

'He's asleep,' Oliver whispered. 'Don't startle him. Let's back away and make a dash upstairs.'

Brian didn't look as though he could move, but as Oliver reached to grip his arm something appeared to switch on inside Gerard's head; he blinked a couple of times, swayed as if testing his balance, and stared down at the gun now dangling against his leg.

'I don't remember getting this out from my desk,' he said quite casually, 'but I've been thinking about ending it all for years now. Every time I went into my office I'd say this is the day, but I could never get up the guts. Any strength of mind I had went when that plane blew up with my parents, brother and sister-in-law on board. You see,' he looked off to the side of the room, 'I persuaded my father to use an outfit owned and operated by a pilot acquaintance of mine. I knew he had several near misses but I had money, gambling debts, which he agreed to forgive if he got the job, with the hope of further recommendations.'

Surprisingly this didn't deliver the emotional blow that it would once have done. The knowledge had been lurking on the outskirts of spoken range ever since Oliver had come to the Cully Mansion. It was the sort of thing Gerard would have done; he was weak and selfish, but not evil. Probably he had loved his brother very much at one time. Just as Nat was very likely loved by his brothers before they turned against him because he was the one who got to marry Amelie Courtney.

'Why don't you put the gun down, Gerard?' he said gently. 'I'm sure my mom and dad and your parents would want you to forgive yourself.'

'Great idea,' seconded Brian.

Gerard set it down on a bookcase and sank into a chair. His eyes closed and when he reopened them it was as though waking without recollection of what had gone before. 'Can't sleep either? Well, whatever your reasons they won't come close to mine in misery. No time like the present, Oliver, to tell you what's come to light.'

Brian sat on the stairs and Oliver walked up to the sofa. His heart lurched. He knew what was coming. 'Yes, Gerard?'

The lights showed the scalp beneath the thinning dark hair. 'I found out last night that Elizabeth has behaved stupidly . . . criminally. She stole some scrimshaws from this house yesterday and took them to an art dealer in Boston to sell for her. It appears the workmanship is superb, making them extremely valuable, but whether they are or not isn't the issue – Emily Cully left them to the Sea Glass Historical Society.'

Oliver couldn't bring himself to say that he and Brian had just discovered the rest of the scrimshaws and put together what was going on. 'Has this . . . this dealer sold them?'

'He had several buyers – collectors – in mind, but there hadn't been time for viewings. That may not help Elizabeth.' Gerard pressed his hands to the sides of his face, forcing the skin upward. His voice quavered. 'This afternoon a youngish man and an older woman came into his gallery, inquiring if a woman had brought in scrimshaws yesterday and left them with him. They described Elizabeth in detail. He told them any such transactions were a private matter between the client and himself. But naturally he was seriously alarmed.' Gerard was visibly trembling.

Of course. Evan and his Aunt Alice. It had to have been them, Oliver thought. He knew Evan would dislike having to take such action, but if he believed there was cause for suspicion he couldn't turn a blind eye to the historical society being robbed of Miss Emily's gift to them. And there was also the matter of getting him away from this house. Those had been the two goals – Evan's and Sarah's – not a desire to punish Elizabeth.

Gerard was talking again. 'As soon the man and woman left, the dealer tried to get Elizabeth on the phone but she'd turned hers off and he wasn't able to get hold of her till later. I found her up in the bedroom, completely hysterical; she poured out the whole story. Turned out the scrimshaws weren't the start – she'd been selling off other items from the house at local antique shops and was sure Robin Polly knew about it.'

'But that wouldn't be stealing! She can sell any of that stuff she likes. Everything here, except the scrimshaws, belongs to you and her.'

'You don't know because your grandfather didn't tell you. He told me he wanted to wait until you were older, so you wouldn't feel burdened. Emily Cully arranged for my father to have a lifetime trust in the house and contents. At his death it passed to Max and me. When he died you got his share, or will, when you're eighteen.'

So that was why they had brought him here. They were afraid of the talk there'd have been under these particular circumstances if they hadn't. Also they wouldn't want him going against what they wanted to do in nine years' time. Now he understood the conversation between the two of them after picking him up from Grandpa's. Elizabeth had said something about nine years and then there'd been that bit that made it sound as though he'd turn out to be crazy. Crazy people don't get to look after their own money. And yet he didn't think either of them really hated him. They were backed to the wall and he was an annoyance. Indifference, yes. Hatred, no. They might even have liked him if things had been going better for them.

Gerard got up and stood huddled in front of the fireplace. 'Burdened! That's grandfather's view of coming into money! To Elizabeth and me the burden is watching everything you have go out the window. We're down to the few last beans. Bad investments. I was a fool to think I knew what I was doing. And like any gambler the more I lost, the more I risked hoping to recover.'

'I think you should look on the bright side.'

'There isn't one.' His voice had weakened to a whine.

'Yes, there is. If that man and lady hadn't come in asking questions, the dealer could have sold the scrimshaws to people who'd make a fuss about giving them back. But if he returns them to Elizabeth and she hands them over to the historical society, I can't see a problem.'

'You're nine years old – what do you know about how these things work?' Gerard came to a standstill. He didn't sound angry, just terribly tired. 'This dealer could contact the police. She'd be arrested!'

'I bet he doesn't. Anyway, she could always say she hadn't realized she couldn't sell, didn't know – or had forgotten – that part of the will. Buck up, Gerard! It'll be OK.' Oliver paused. 'No hard feelings, but I don't want to stay here, and I'm sure you and Elizabeth don't want me with you either. I want to go and live with Sarah and Evan, with Twyla close by. That's how we all hoped it could be. And I'd like to leave as soon as Brian's dad or mom can drive over to pick us up.'

'I understand, Oliver.' What he sounded was self-pitying. 'Perhaps if I hadn't started drinking heavily a lot of things could be different. I failed Max and I've failed you, I don't expect you to believe it but when we said we insisted on taking guardianship of you it wasn't because it would have raised talk around here. We were desperate to cut expenses and it's now clear that Elizabeth saw a chance to recoup, but I did hope you and I could grow fond of each other.' Gerard stared into space. 'Being who am, I'm likely to shake off regrets soon enough. In that way I'm like my father. He could only ever think of himself.' A heaved sigh. 'How about a farewell handshake?'

This accomplished, Gerard sank back in the chair. Leaving the room, Oliver felt a surge of sympathy for Elizabeth. If she were really bad she'd have murdered Gerard. Maybe that's what she'd been wishing she could do when accusing Oliver of killing Feathers. Somehow this thought blotted out the incident sufficiently that he didn't think he'd be troubled by the memory.

He found his two suitcases at the bottom of the stairs and Brian, looking sleepy, sitting on top of his backpack. 'I came upstairs to get them when I heard you tell him you're leaving. I've phoned Dad and he should be here,' he looked at his watch, 'in about twenty minutes. He thought you might like him to leave you at Aunt Nellie's until Sarah gets home.'

'Thanks. What time is it?'

'Five forty.' Brian gave way to a yawn as he stood up. 'I'll take everything outside and wait on the steps, till you've said goodbye to Nat.'

'I don't think he'll be there.'

'Bet you he will.'

Brian was wrong this time; the window seat was empty, and there wasn't a figure standing at the foot of the bed. Oliver was OK with this; he wouldn't have wanted to leave Nat alone in this room or a house that had been allowed to die from the inside out.

'I'll always remember you, friend,' he said, 'and all your kindness and help. I'm glad your scrimshaws will go to the historical society. The people in this town still love you, like you're living just around the corner. Yes, I'll miss you, but I'm glad you've gone back home. Please say "hi" to Grandpa and Sonny when they get there.' The curtains stirred. A beam of sunlight streamed through the window to dance its way to Oliver's feet. Significant, because though it was no longer raining the sky remained gray and thunderous. 'Bye, Nat.'

He went downstairs and without looking back opened the front door, closed it softly behind him and joined Brian on the steps in the damp chill. A few minutes later Reggie Armitage pulled up in his pickup truck and within seconds of climbing inside Brian was fast asleep. His Dad wasn't one for questions or probing. He told Oliver that Aunt Nellie was up and expecting him, and if he wanted to get into bed she'd stay on the watch for Sarah's return.

As they turned onto Wild Rose Way, Sarah was opening her door from the inside. Reggie drew to a stop and told Oliver to forget his suitcases; he'd bring them into the house.

'Sure that's OK?'

'Get moving.' Oliver didn't need to be told twice. He raced into Sarah's open arms.

'I was just about to leave to come and get you when I saw the truck and recognized it.' She drew him closer and stroked his hair. 'Evan phoned after he talked to you and filled me in on what you were going through.'

Reggie, having put Oliver's suitcases in the foyer, said he'd be around providing another pair of eyes and feet and left. Oliver stepped back to look up at Sarah; he knew something was wrong. 'What's happened? Is it Grandpa?' He knew as soon as he asked that couldn't be it. What was Reggie talking about? And Twyla would have come for him whatever the hour of night if something happened to Grandpa.

She took Oliver's hand and walked him to the living room sofa. Sitting down beside him she put an arm around his shoulders. 'I'm so sorry to break this to you, sweetheart. It's about Gwen and Sonny, but it may turn out all right. We'll have to keep praying. It's waiting that's going to be so hard. I'll try to tell you as quickly as possible. About ten o'clock last night Gwen started having terrible pains in her upper abdomen, so severe that Twyla called an ambulance and the medics got her into it on a stretcher. The sound of the sirens must have frightened Sonny; perhaps he thought it was the police come to take him away. Twyla didn't lose sight of him during all the coming and going. But after the house was clear she went to phone Sid Jennson to ask if he could come over to stay with Sonny while she went to the hospital – she thought the stress of taking him with her would be too much. It must have been while she was talking to Sid that Sonny slipped out of the house. She went looking for him as soon as she hung up and searched the house, but he was gone. When she couldn't see him outside she got in the car and drove around for five to ten minutes. No sign of him.'

'Oh, Sarah!' Oliver was too stunned to cry.

'She was phoning the police when Sid arrived. He told her he'd wait for them and that she should go to the hospital to be with Gwen. At first they thought she was having a heart attack, and he said there was nothing at the moment Twyla could do about Sonny that he couldn't handle. She gave him my cell number. She knew I'd want to know immediately and I then called Evan. He got here a couple of hours after I did, and he's now helping search the woods that start at the top of Ridge Farm Rise. It's a large area, but the organizers know the terrain, and they're splitting people into small groups. Reggie Armitage is headed there now and of course Sid signed on. The problem last night was the storm. But they're confident they'll find him.'

'What about the roads?'

'The police are out. Twyla left a photo of Sonny for them. Oh, Oliver! All this on top of your last couple of days at that house! I should never have gone to Portland.'

'Of course you should. And that's all over, mostly because you tipped Evan off about the scrimshaws, and he and his aunt found where Elizabeth had taken them. Maybe the shock of being found out will end up being a good thing for her, help her think things through more clearly.' Sarah could tell from his face that there had been a climax of events at the Cully Mansion. 'Just like opening up about the plane crash may help Gerard, but I'll tell you about that too later. When I told Gerard I was leaving he said he understood and that he wouldn't make me come back. It's great, but even if it hadn't turned out this way, all that would matter is Gwen and Sonny. How is she doing?'

'They no longer think it's a heart attack. They're doing other tests and monitoring her carefully.'

'She doesn't know about Sonny?'

'Far too risky to tell her. Twyla says they're keeping her sedated, so she's sleeping a lot of the time.'

'But could she still die?'

'I don't know, Oliver. That will depend on what they find, I suppose.'

'Is there anyone who ought to be contacted?'

'Twyla phoned Rowena, Gwen's sister in France. Gwen was telling me just the other day that she's sad they are no longer close and afterwards she told Twyla she was going to write a letter; she was actually sitting at the secretary desk in the book room and had finished a couple of paragraphs when she began to feel ill. Twyla took Gwen's address book with her to the hospital last night and rang me just before you got here to give me Rowena's number in France. I rang and a man answered – fortunately he spoke English. He said he was a good friend, very sorry to get the news, but Rowena was resting after having fallen that morning and breaking her wrist, so he must hold off giving her the message.'

'Sarah! That's awful.' Oliver clung to her hand. 'What can we do to help?'

'Keep our strength up for when we're needed. You don't look like you've had much sleep. Could you try and lie down for a couple of hours? I'll wake you if there's any word. I'll come up and tuck you in. Libby Jennson's coming over shortly and we're going to make up sandwiches for the volunteers. There's bound to be a need until Sonny is found, so you can help with that later while I go and see Twyla at the hospital.'

They followed this plan. Oliver didn't think he could fall asleep, especially because rain was now clattering against the window to the accompaniment of booms of thunder. But he did so until noon, when he opened his eyes and sprang off the bed to race downstairs. He heard voices coming from the kitchen, Sarah's and Evan's. Something must have happened for Evan to leave the search party. And that it wasn't anything good showed on both their faces when he stood in the doorway.

'Bad news?'

Suddenly each of them was holding one of his hands. 'Sonny,' said Evan gently. Oliver noticed vaguely that he hadn't shaved and his jacket was soaked through; the unimportant little things you notice when your mind is backing up from what you don't want to hear. 'He was hit by a car as he came out from a thick growth of trees straight into its path. Unavoidable on the driver's part.'

'Is he dead?'

Sarah nodded, tears sliding in what seemed to Oliver to be slow motion down her face.

'On impact. Thank God it was that quick.' Evan now had his strong arms around both of them. 'And we just had an update on Elizabeth. Her car was behind the one that hit Sonny. It was she who dialed nine-one-one. Afterwards she sat beside Sonny on the ground, holding his hand until help arrived.'

'Gwen?'

'That's the good news. Heart attack completely ruled out. It was her gall bladder. Seemingly the symptoms can mimic each other. They think it was probably brought on by eating fried chicken for dinner. Twyla says fatty foods can bring on an attack. It'll mean an operation, a small one these days. Usually people go home within hours. Given her age they'll keep her in, but she should be all right.'

'When will they do it?'

'She's set for surgery in,' Evan looked at his watch, 'about an hour. We'll have lunch and go to the hospital.'

'I want to be there.' Oliver took the glass of orange juice Sarah handed him as he sat down on the chair Evan had pulled out for him at the kitchen table. After taking a sip, he looked up at them. 'I expect Elizabeth was running away because of what she had done and Gerard telling her she was going to prison.'

'There's no question of that, it was caught in time.' Evan drew out a chair for Sarah. 'The art dealer struck me and Aunt Alice as a decent type, even if he wasn't he wouldn't want to have his gallery involved in a scandal. He'll return the scrimshaws without delay and they'll go to the historical society.'

'There are more in a barrel in the cellar. Brian and I found them last night. There's so much to tell you both.' It was easier to think about Elizabeth than Sonny. He, as well as Sarah and Evan, had to stay strong for Gwen. 'Elizabeth could have driven away, but she didn't. She stopped to help. I hope she feels good about that.'

'She should,' said Sarah. 'It could prove to be an important turning point. I think it will.'

'So do I.' Evan was plugging in the coffee pot. He then set about getting lunch to the table, reheating the watercress soup Sarah had made that morning and preparing ham and cheese sandwiches. None of them could have eaten dessert, but there was fruit – apples, oranges and bananas – to choose from. Oliver ate without appetite and knew it was the same for Sarah and Evan.

Twyla phoned as they were getting up from the table to say Gwen would be going down shortly for surgery. They left for the hospital five minutes later in Evan's car. As they neared the entrance he said: 'I do hope Twyla isn't blaming herself for Sonny getting away from the house. It was one of those convergences of events. No fault on her part.'

'She's sensible enough to know that.' Sarah was in the back seat with Oliver, holding his hand. 'I'm worried that Gwen will be the one taking on guilt for keeping Sonny at home instead of putting him in a nursing home, but that would have killed him slowly.'

'He had happy times this summer,' said Oliver. 'I was there yesterday and Sonny played *The Swan*, one of his and Gwen's all-time favorites on the piano. Looking back,' his throat tightened, 'I think he was saying goodbye to her.'

'She'll have a lot to hold onto.' Sarah squeezed his hand.

They were directed by the woman at the desk in the lobby to a waiting room where they found Twyla seated alone. None of them said very much. Silence drew them more closely together than conversation. It seemed like a long time later, but it wasn't, when the surgeon came to let them know all had gone well. Gwen was in the Recovery Room and comfortable. A nurse appeared and said Twyla could now go in and sit with the patient. Evan fetched coffee from the canteen for himself and Sarah and milk for Oliver. When Twyla reappeared she looked relieved, though worn from the fatigue of a sleepless night.

'She's very groggy, goes in and out, mentioned Sonny in hazy snatches, but no awkward questions. I surely don't know how she'll take it when the time comes.'

Oliver hugged her tight, wanting to comfort her as she had him so many times. 'It will be all right, Twyla. The four of us are here for her.'

'I know, lamb baby, I know.' She raised her head. 'I told her you were all waiting to see her and the nurse said I could take you in.'

They turned down a corridor, to a right, then a left. Twyla opened a door. It was the usual hospital room with the square of window and a television on the wall. Gwen lay on her back on a gray metal bed, strung around with tubes. Her eyes were closed.

Twyla sat in the chair near the door as the other three stepped forward. Sarah and Evan stood behind Oliver so that it was his eyes Gwen looked into on rousing.

'I was dreaming about Sonny,' she whispered. 'He was lost . . . he's been lost for a long time now. I want him to be safe. Safe forever. He told me he saw pink clouds today.'

'He did, Gwen.' Oliver took her hand, his love pouring out to her. 'Sonny is safe at last. He's home.' Unnoticed, the door opened and a still dark-haired, elderly woman with her left wrist in a cast stepped into the room.

For Gwen all that was earthbound had receded. A look of utmost serenity touched her face. She was gazing upward. 'I'm waving, Sonny. I'll always be waving.'

Epilogue

Gwen woke after a long sleep to find Rowena seated by her hospital bed. Perhaps because her eyes blurred with tears what she saw was her beautiful sister unchanged by time.

'You came,' she whispered.

'Finally. Gwen . . . dear Gwennie! I've been such a willful fool. All these wasted years.'

'Finally is never too late. Not when it comes to sisters.' They sat and talked about Sonny as a child and a man, about John and then the late in life love who had come into Rowena's life, who had moved heaven and hell to get her from France to Maine in record time. Renewal . . . and so much else that had flourished over the past months.'

Sarah and Evan were married six weeks later at St Anne's Church. It was a simple wedding, with only those closest present. What mattered most was that Gwen was able to attend.

A couple of days later she walked with Sarah and Oliver along the beach below Bramble Cottage. She and Twyla would be leaving for France in the morning to visit Rowena and her gentleman friend for a few weeks. On their return Twyla was going to stay on with Gwen at the house on Ridge Farm Rise. They hoped to do some more traveling together in the future.

It was a cool morning; the sky was a clear, pale blue. Jumbo padded along with them; he would be staying at Bramble Cottage while Gwen and Twyla were away. Oliver had his new puppy on a leash. There was some toppling over and bursts of short rushes. He was another brindled bull mastiff, and Oliver had named him 'Pocket' because, as he'd said, compared to Jumbo he would fit into one.

Grandpa's lawyer had everything set up for Sarah and Evan to take guardianship of Oliver. As Gerard promised, he had made no difficulties about this. He and Elizabeth had returned to New York. Perhaps they were now ready to stare down their demons and start over. Oliver hoped so.

The Cully Mansion was to be sold because very little of the money left in trust for its upkeep remained available. The Sea Glass Historical Society had expressed a strong interest in buying it. Nat would like that, thought Oliver, picking up Pocket who was ready to be carried, just as he would like his scrimshaws finally being displayed along with those of his brothers. Such unity in death triumphed over a near lifetime of estrangement. There was only one thing Oliver wanted from the Cully Mansion: the dresser with Nat's drawings on the back of the drawers. He already had the little silver clock with the poem on it. The lawyer had said there was no problem about that. It was already in his bedroom. Nat's dresser would go in the book room because Oliver's bedroom furniture had been brought over from Ferry Landing. Grandpa had decided to sell the house, and Aunt Nellie was going to buy it. That made Brian and his parents happy and Bri wouldn't miss out on coming over to Sea Glass, because he'd already had several sleepovers at Bramble Cottage.

Oliver was thinking about Grandpa that morning, so many wonderfully happy memories. Sonny's death, and Gwen's courageous acceptance of it, had brought a sense of peace that would help Oliver when the time came to say goodbye to the man who had given him the very best start in life.

Sarah's thoughts were also of Frank Andrews and Sonny. Of the troubles and sorrows that are part of every life. Those that came without warning in the suddenness of a violent storm, while others slipped in on a slow, sad tide. But always for those who searched there could be recovered a treasure trove of memories washed in on the tide – reminders that even that which is broken can achieve renewed beauty. Fragments of what was once whole, but still priceless to the heart and never to be displaced by new beginnings.

Oliver and Gwen stood with Sarah on the shoreline. Soon they and the dogs would return by way of the wood steps and across the back lawn to the house, where Evan would interrupt his writing to join them in the kitchen. And Dusk would wander in to make sure she got her full share of Oliver's attention. Sarah had no need to voice these thoughts to the other two. They reached out for each other's hands and held on to this moment.

Shining up from beneath the incoming waves was another small treasure returned from the sea. Their eyes met in recognition that these gems, buffered by all kinds of weather, when gathered into a collection, would reflect for always the sunshine of a sea glass summer.